Eowyn LeMay Ivey works at an independent bookstore in Palmer, Alaska, where she lives with her husband and two daughters. *The Snow Child* is her debut novel.

THE SNOW CHILD

November, 1920. Jack and Mabel have staked everything on making a fresh start in a homestead 'at the world's edge' in the Alaskan wilderness. But as the days grow shorter, Jack is losing his battle to clear the land, and Mabel can no longer contain her grief for the baby she lost years before. The evening the first snow falls, their mood unaccountably changes. In a moment of tenderness, the two build a snowman — or rather a snow girl — together. Next morning, all trace of her has disappeared . . . yet there, in dawn's light, running through the spruce trees — Jack can't shake the notion that he glimpsed — a child? And how to explain the little but very human tracks Mabel finds at the edge of their property?

EOWYN IVEY

THE
SNOW CHILD

Complete and Unabridged

CHARNWOOD
Leicester

First published in Great Britain in 2012 by
Headline Review
An imprint of
Headline Publishing Group, London

First Charnwood Edition
published 2012
by arrangement with
Headline Publishing Group
An Hachette UK Company, London

British Library CIP Data

Ivey, Eowyn.
  The snow child.
  1. Alaska- -History- -*1867–1959* - -Fiction.
  2. Large type books.
  I. Title
  813.6–dc23

  ISBN 978–1–4448–1266–4

Published by
F. A. Thorpe (Publishing)
Anstey, Leicestershire

Set by Words & Graphics Ltd.
Anstey, Leicestershire
Printed and bound in Great Britain by
T. J. International Ltd., Padstow, Cornwall

This book is printed on acid-free paper

For my daughters, Grace and Aurora

Part I

'Wife, let us go into the yard behind and make a little snow girl; and perhaps she will come alive, and be a little daughter to us.'

'Husband,' says the old woman, 'there's no knowing what may be. Let us go into the yard and make a little snow girl.'

'The Little Daughter of the Snow'
by Arthur Ransome

1

Wolverine River, Alaska, 1920

Mabel had known there would be silence. That was the point, after all. No infants cooing or wailing. No neighbor children playfully hollering down the lane. No pad of small feet on wooden stairs worn smooth by generations, or clackety-clack of toys along the kitchen floor. All those sounds of her failure and regret would be left behind, and in their place there would be silence.

She had imagined that in the Alaska wilderness silence would be peaceful, like snow falling at night, air filled with promise but no sound, but that was not what she found. Instead, when she swept the plank floor, the broom bristles scritched like some sharp-toothed shrew nibbling at her heart. When she washed the dishes, plates and bowls clattered as if they were breaking to pieces. The only sound not of her making was a sudden 'caw, cawww' from outside. Mabel wrung dishwater from a rag and looked out the kitchen window in time to see a raven flapping its way from one leafless birch tree to another. No children chasing each other through autumn leaves, calling each other's names. Not even a solitary child on a swing.

3

There had been the one. A tiny thing, born still and silent. Ten years past, but even now she found herself returning to the birth to touch Jack's arm, stop him, reach out. She should have. She should have cupped the baby's head in the palm of her hand and snipped a few of its tiny hairs to keep in a locket at her throat. She should have looked into its small face and known if it was a boy or a girl, and then stood beside Jack as he buried it in the Pennsylvania winter ground. She should have marked its grave. She should have allowed herself that grief.

It was a child, after all, although it looked more like a fairy changeling. Pinched face, tiny jaw, ears that came to narrow points; that much she had seen and wept over because she knew she could have loved it still.

Mabel was too long at the window. The raven had since flown away above the treetops. The sun had slipped behind a mountain, and the light had fallen flat. The branches were bare, the grass yellowed gray. Not a single snowflake. It was as if everything fine and glittering had been ground from the world and swept away as dust.

November was here, and it frightened her because she knew what it brought — cold upon the valley like a coming death, glacial wind through the cracks between the cabin logs. But most of all, darkness. Darkness so complete even

4

the pale-lit hours would be choked.

She entered last winter blind, not knowing what to expect in this new, hard land. Now she knew. By December, the sun would rise just before noon and skirt the mountaintops for a few hours of twilight before sinking again. Mabel would move in and out of sleep as she sat in a chair beside the woodstove. She would not pick up any of her favorite books; the pages would be lifeless. She would not draw; what would there be to capture in her sketchbook? Dull skies, shadowy corners. It would become harder and harder to leave the warm bed each morning. She would stumble about in a walking sleep, scrape together meals and drape wet laundry around the cabin. Jack would struggle to keep the animals alive. The days would run together, winter's stranglehold tightening.

All her life she had believed in something more, in the mystery that shape-shifted at the edge of her senses. It was the flutter of moth wings on glass and the promise of river nymphs in the dappled creek beds. It was the smell of oak trees on the summer evening she fell in love, and the way dawn threw itself across the cow pond and turned the water to light.

Mabel could not remember the last time she caught such a flicker.

She gathered Jack's work shirts and sat down to mend. She tried not to look out the window. If only it would snow. Maybe that white would soften the bleak lines. Perhaps it could catch some bit of light and mirror it back into her eyes.

But all afternoon the clouds remained high

and thin, the wind ripped dead leaves from the tree branches, and daylight guttered like a candle. Mabel thought of the terrible cold that would trap her alone in the cabin, and her breathing turned shallow and rapid. She stood to pace the floor. She silently repeated to herself, 'I cannot do this. I cannot do this.'

There were guns in the house, and she had thought of them before. The hunting rifle beside the bookshelf, the shotgun over the doorway, and a revolver that Jack kept in the top drawer of the bureau. She had never fired them, but that wasn't what kept her. It was the violence and unseemly gore of such an act, and the blame that would inevitably come in its wake. People would say she was weak in mind or spirit, or Jack was a poor husband. And what of Jack? What shame and anger would he harbor?

The river, though — that was something different. Not a soul to blame, not even her own. It would be an unfortunate misstep. People would say, if only she had known the ice wouldn't hold her. If only she'd known its dangers.

Afternoon descended into dusk, and Mabel left the window to light an oil lamp on the table, as if she was going to prepare dinner and wait for Jack's return, as if this day would end like any other, but in her mind she was already following the trail through the woods to the Wolverine River. The lamp burned as she laced her leather boots, put her winter coat on over her housedress, and

6

stepped outside. Her hands and head were bare to the wind.

As she strode through the naked trees, she was both exhilarated and numb, chilled by the clarity of her purpose. She did not think of what she left behind, but only of this moment in a sort of black-and-white precision. The hard clunk of her boot soles on the frozen ground. The icy breeze in her hair. Her expansive breaths. She was strangely powerful and sure.

She emerged from the forest and stood on the bank of the frozen river. It was calm except for the occasional gust of wind that ruffled her skirt against her wool stockings and swirled silt across the ice. Farther upstream, the glacier-fed valley stretched half a mile wide with gravel bars, driftwood, and braided shallow channels, but here the river ran narrow and deep. Mabel could see the shale cliff on the far side that fell off into black ice. Below, the water would be well over her head.

The cliff became her destination, though she expected to drown before she reached it. The ice was only an inch or two thick, and even in the depths of winter no one would dare to cross at this treacherous point.

At first her boots caught on boulders, frozen in the sandy shore, but then she staggered down the steep bank and crossed a small rivulet where the ice was thin and brittle. She broke through every other step to hit dry sand beneath. Then she crossed a barren patch of gravel and hiked up her skirt to climb over a driftwood log, faded by the elements.

When she reached the river's main channel, where water still coursed down the valley, the ice was no longer brittle and white but instead black and pliant, as if it had only solidified the night before. She slid her boot soles onto the surface and nearly laughed at her own absurdity — to be careful not to slip even as she prayed to fall through.

She was several feet from safe ground when she allowed herself to stop and peer down between her boots. It was like walking on glass. She could see granite rocks beneath the moving, dark turquoise water. A yellow leaf floated by, and she imagined herself swept alongside it and briefly looking up through the remarkably clear ice. Before the water filled her lungs, would she be able to see the sky?

Here and there, bubbles as large as her hand were frozen in white circles, and in other places large cracks ran through. She wondered if the ice was weaker at those points, and if she should seek them out or avoid them. She set her shoulders, faced straight ahead, and walked without looking down.

When she crossed the heart of the channel, the cliff face was almost within arm's length, the water was a muffled roar, and the ice gave slightly beneath her. Against her will, she glanced down, and what she saw terrified her. No bubbles. No cracks. Only bottomless black, as if the night sky were under her boots. She shifted her weight to take another step toward the cliff, and there was a crack, a deep, resonant pop like a massive Champagne bottle being uncorked.

8

Mabel spread her feet wide and her knees trembled. She waited for the ice to give way, for her body to plunge into the river. Then there was another thud, a *whoompf*, and she was certain the ice slumped beneath her boots, but in millimeters, nearly imperceptible except for the awful sound.

She waited and breathed, and the water didn't come. The ice bore her. She slid her feet slowly, first one, then the other, again and again, a slow shuffle until she stood where ice met cliff. Never had she imagined she would be here, on the far side of the river. She put her bare palms to the cold shale, then the entire length of her body, until her forehead was pressed to it and she could smell the stone, ancient and damp.

Its cold began to seep into her, so she lowered her arms to her sides, turned from the cliff face, and began the journey back the way she had come. Her heart thudded in her throat. Her legs were unsteady. She wondered if now, as she made her way home, she would break through to her death.

As she neared solid ground, she wanted to run to it, but the ice was too slick beneath her boots, so she slid as if ice-skating and then stumbled up the bank. She gasped and coughed and nearly laughed, as if it had all been a lark, a mad dare. Then she bent with her hands on her thighs and tried to steady herself.

When she slowly straightened, the land was vast before her. The sun was setting down the river, casting a cold pink hue along the white-capped mountains that framed both sides of the valley. Upriver, the willow shrubs and gravel bars, the spruce forests and low-lying poplar stands, swelled to the mountains in a steely blue. No fields or fences, homes or roads; not a single living soul as far as she could see in any direction. Only wilderness.

It was beautiful, Mabel knew, but it was a beauty that ripped you open and scoured you clean so that you were left helpless and exposed, if you lived at all. She turned her back to the river and walked home.

The lantern was still burning; the kitchen window glowed as she approached the cabin, and when she opened the door and stepped inside, warmth and flickering light overcame her. Everything was unfamiliar and golden. She had not expected to return here.

It seemed she was gone hours, but it was not yet six in the evening and Jack hadn't come in. She took off her coat and went to the woodstove, letting the heat sink painfully into her hands and feet. Once she could open and close her fingers, she took out pots and pans, marveling that she was fulfilling such a mundane task. She added wood to the stove, cooked dinner, and then sat straight-backed at the rough-hewn table with her hands folded in her lap. A few minutes later, Jack came through the door, stomped his boots and dusted straw from his wool coat.

Certain he would somehow know what she had survived, she watched and waited. He rinsed his hands in the basin, sat across from her and lowered his head.

'Bless this food, Lord,' he mumbled. 'Amen.'

She set a potato on each of their plates beside boiled carrots and red beans. Neither of them spoke. There was only the scraping of knives and forks against plates. She tried to eat, but could not force herself. Words lay like granite boulders in her lap and when at last she spoke, each one was heavy and burdensome and all she could manage.

'I went to the river today,' she said.

He did not lift his head. She waited for him to ask why she would do such a thing. Maybe then she could tell him.

Jack jabbed at the carrots with his fork, then swabbed the beans with a slice of bread. He gave no indication he had heard her.

'It's frozen all the way across to the cliffs,' she said in a near whisper. Her eyes down, her breath shallow, she waited, but there was only Jack's chewing, his fork at his plate.

Mabel looked up and saw his windburned hands and frayed cuffs, the crow's feet that spread at the corners of his down-turned eyes. She couldn't remember the last time she had touched that skin, and the thought ached like loneliness in her chest. Then she spotted a few strands of silver in his reddish-brown beard. When had they appeared? So he, too, was graying. Each of them fading away without the other's notice.

She pushed food here and there with her fork. She glanced at the lantern hanging from the

11

ceiling and saw shards of light stream from it. She was crying. For a moment she sat and let the tears run down either side of her nose until they were at the corners of her mouth. Jack continued to eat, his head down. She stood and took her plate of food to the small kitchen counter. Turned away, she wiped her face with her apron.

'That ice isn't solid yet,' Jack said from the table. 'Best to stay off of it.'

Mabel swallowed, cleared her throat.

'Yes. Of course,' she said.

She busied herself at the counter until her eyes were clear, then returned to the table and spooned more carrots onto Jack's plate.

'How is the new field?' she asked.

'It's coming.' He forked potato into his mouth, then wiped it with the back of his hand.

'I'll get the rest of the trees cut and skidded in the next few days,' he said. 'Then I'll burn some more of the stumps out.'

'Would you like me to come and help? I could tend the stump fires for you.'

'No. I'll manage.'

That night in bed, she had a heightened awareness of him, of the scent of straw and spruce boughs in his hair and beard, the weight of him on the creaky bed, the sound of his slow, tired breaths. He lay on his side, turned away from her. She reached out, thinking to touch his shoulder, but instead lowered her arm and lay in the darkness staring at his back.

'Do you think we'll make it through winter?' she asked.

He didn't answer. Perhaps he was asleep. She rolled away and faced the log wall.

When he spoke, Mabel wondered if it was grogginess or emotion that made his voice gravelly.

'We don't have much choice, do we?'

2

The morning was so cold that when Jack first stepped outside and harnessed the horse, his leather boots stayed stiff and his hands wouldn't work right. A north wind blew steadily off the river. He'd have liked to stay indoors, but he had already stacked Mabel's towel-wrapped pies in a crate to take to town. He slapped himself on the arms and stomped his feet to get the blood flowing. It was damned cold, and even long underwear beneath denim seemed a scant cotton sheet about his legs. It wasn't easy, leaving the comfort of the woodstove to face this alone. The sun threatened to come up on the other side of the river, but its light was weak and silvery, and not much comfort at all.

Jack climbed up into the open wagon and shook the reins. He did not look back over his shoulder, but he felt the cabin dwindle into the spruce trees behind him.

As the trail passed through a field, the horse seemed to trip on its own feet, and then it tossed its head. Jack slowed the wagon to a stop and scanned the field and distant trees, but saw nothing.

Goddamned horse. He'd wanted a nice mellow draft, something slow and strong. But horses were scarcer than hen's teeth up here, and he didn't have much to choose from — a sway-backed old mare that looked to be on her last legs and this one, young and barely broken, better suited to prancing around a ring than working for a living. Jack was afraid it would be the death of him.

Just the other day he'd been skidding logs out of the new field when the horse spooked at a branch and knocked Jack to the ground. He barely missed being crushed by the log as the horse charged ahead. His forearms and shins were still tore up, and his back pained him every morning.

And there lay the real problem. Not the nervous horse, but the tired old man. The truth squirmed in the pit of his stomach like a thing done wrong. This was too much work for a man of his age. He wasn't making headway, even working every day as long and hard as he could. After a long summer and snowless autumn, he was still nowhere near done clearing enough land to earn a living. He got a pitiful little potato harvest off one small field this year, and it scarcely did more than buy flour for the winter. He figured he had enough money left from selling his share in the farm Back East to last them one more year, but only if Mabel kept selling pies in town.

That wasn't right either, Mabel scrubbing her own rough-cut floors and selling baked goods on the side. How different her life could have been. The daughter of a literature professor, a family of privilege, she could have studied her books and art and spent her afternoons consorting with other fine women. Servants and china teacups and petit fours baked by someone else.

As he rode through the end of a half-cleared field, the horse jerked again, tossed its head and snorted. Jack pulled back on the reins. He squinted and studied the fallen trees around him and beyond them the standing birches, spruce, and cottonwoods. The woods were silent, not even the twitter of a bird. The horse stamped a hoof on the hard ground and then was still. Jack tried to quiet his breathing so he could see and hear.

Something was watching him.

It was a foolish thought. Who would be out here? He wondered not for the first time if wild animals could give that feeling. Dumb beasts, like cows and chickens, could stare at a man's back all day and not give a prickle on his neck. But maybe woodland creatures were different. He tried to picture a bear shuffling through the forest, pacing back and forth and eyeing him and the horse. Didn't seem likely, getting this close to winter. They should be looking to den up.

His eyes caught now and then on a stump or a shadowy spot among the trees. Shrug it off, old man, he told himself. You'll drive yourself crazy looking for something that's not there.

He went to shake the reins, but then peered one last time over his shoulder and saw it — a flash of movement, a smudge of brownish red. The horse snorted. Jack turned slowly in the wagon seat.

A red fox darted among the fallen trees. It disappeared for a minute but popped up again,

17

closer to the forest, running with its fluffy tail held low to the ground. It stopped and turned its head. For a moment its eyes locked with Jack's, and there, in its narrowing golden irises, he saw the savagery of the place. Like he was staring wilderness itself straight in the eye.

He faced forward in the wagon, shook the reins, and let the horse gather to a trot, both of them eager to put the fox behind them. For the next hour, he rode hunched and cold as the wagon bumped along through miles of untouched forest. As he neared town, the horse picked up its pace, and Jack had to slow it to keep the crate from spilling out of the wagon.

Back home, Alpine wouldn't have been called a town at all. It was nothing more than a few dusty, false-fronted buildings perched between the train tracks and the Wolverine River. Nearby, several homesteaders had stripped the land clear of trees before abandoning it. Some went off to pan gold or work for the railroad, but most had hightailed it home with no plans of ever returning to Alaska.

Jack carried the crate of pies up the steps to the hotel restaurant where the owner's wife opened the door for him. Well into her sixties, Betty wore her hair short and mannish and ran the place like a one-woman show. Her husband, Roy, worked for the territorial government and was rarely about.

'Good morning, Betty,' Jack said.

'It's ugly as far as I can see.' She slammed the door behind them. 'Colder than hell, and no sign of snow. Never seen anything like it. Got some of Mabel's pies?'

'Yes, ma'am.' He set them on the counter and unwrapped them from the towels.

'That woman sure can bake,' she said. 'Everybody's always asking after them pies.'

'Glad to hear it.'

She counted a few bills from the till and put them on the counter beside the crate.

'So I know I'm risking losing a few customers, Jack, but I'm afraid we won't be needing any more after today. My sister's come to live with us, and Roy says she's got to earn her keep by doing the baking.'

He picked up the bills and put them in his coat pocket as if he hadn't heard what she'd said. Then it registered.

'No more pies? You sure?'

'Sorry, Jack. I know it's poor timing, with winter coming on but . . . ' Her voice trailed off, and she seemed uncharacteristically embarrassed.

'We could cut the price, if that would help,' he said. 'We need every penny we can get.'

'I am sorry. Can I get you a cup of coffee and some breakfast?'

'Coffee would be fine.' He chose a table by a small window that looked out over the river.

'It's on the house,' she said as she set the cup in front of him.

He never stayed when he brought the pies into town, but this morning he wasn't eager to get back to the homestead. What would he tell Mabel? That they had to pack up and go home with their tails between their legs? Give up, like all those before him? He stirred some sugar into the coffee and stared out the window. A man with scuffed leather boots and the dust-beaten air of a mountain camp walked along the river's edge. He wore a bedroll on his backpack, led a shaggy husky by a rope tether and in his other hand carried a hunting rifle. Past him Jack could see a white haze shrouding the peaks. It was snowing in the mountains. Soon it would snow here in the valley, too.

'You know, they're looking for help up at the mine.' Betty slid a plate of bacon and eggs in front of him. 'You probably wouldn't want to make it your profession, but it might get you all through a tight spot.'

'The coal mine up north?'

'Yep. Pay's not bad, and they'll be at it as long as they can keep the tracks clear. They feed you and bunk you, and send you home with a little extra money in your pocket. Just something to think about.'

'Thanks. And thanks for this.' He gestured toward the plate.

'Sure thing.'

A godforsaken job, coal mining. Farmers were born to work in the light and air, not in tunnels through rock. Back home, he'd seen the men return from the mines with their faces black with coal dust and coughing up dirty blood. Even if he had the will and strength, it would mean leaving Mabel alone at the homestead for days, maybe weeks, at a time.

Cash money is what they needed, though. Just a month or two might be enough to pull them through next harvest. He could stand most anything for a month or two. He ate the last bite of bacon and was ready to head out when George Benson came noisily through the restaurant door.

'Betty, Betty, Betty. What have you got for me today? Any of those pies?'

'They're fresh off the homestead, George. Have a seat and I'll bring a slice over.'

George turned toward the tables and spotted Jack.

'Hello there, neighbor! I'll tell you what — your wife bakes a mean apple pie.' He threw his coat over the back of a chair and patted his round belly. 'Mind if I join you?'

'Not at all.'

George lived about ten miles the other side of town with his wife and three boys. Jack had met him a few times at the general store and here at the restaurant. He seemed a good-natured sort and always spoke as if they were confirmed friends. He and George were about the same age.

'How's it coming out at your place?' George asked as he sat across from him.

'It's coming.'

'You got any help out there?'

'Nope. Just working away on it myself. Got one or two good fields cleared. Always more to do. You know how it goes.'

'We should swap a few days here and there

21

— me and my boys come over to your place with our draft horses, and then you lend a hand our way.'

'That's a generous offer.'

'We could help you get some work done,' George continued, 'and your wife could come over and get some girl time with Esther, talk about baking or sewing or whatever it is they talk about. She gets tired of all us men. She'd be thrilled to have you all over.'

Jack didn't say yes or no.

'Your kids all grown and gone?' George asked.

Jack hadn't seen that coming. He and Mabel were that old, weren't they, that their children could be grown and having families of their own. He wondered if he looked the way he felt, like someone had stuck out a foot and tripped him.

'Nope. Never had any.'

'What's that? Never had any, you say?'

'Nope.'

He watched George. If you said you didn't have children it sounded like a choice, and what kind of craziness would that be? If you said you couldn't, the conversation turned awkward while they contemplated your manliness or your wife's health. Jack waited and swallowed.

'That's one way to go, I suppose.' George shook his head with a chuckle. 'Heck of a lot more quiet around your place, I'll bet. Sometimes those boys of mine like to drive me to drink. Hassling about this or that, dragging out of bed in the morning like the pox was on them. Getting a good day's work out of the youngest one is about as easy as wrestling a hog.'

Jack laughed and eased, drank some of his coffee. 'I had a brother like that. It was almost easier to just let him sleep.'

'Yep, that's how some of them are, at least until they've got a place of their own and see what it's all about.'

Betty came to the table with a cup and slice of pie for George.

'I was just telling Jack they're looking for help up at the mine,' she said as she poured hot coffee. 'You know, to get them through the winter.'

George raised his eyebrows, then frowned, but didn't speak until Betty had gone back into the kitchen.

'You aren't, are you?'

'Something to consider.'

'Christ. You lost your ever-loving mind? You and I — we're no spring chickens, and those hell holes are for young men, if anybody at all.'

Jack nodded, uncomfortable with the conversation.

'I know it's none of my damned business, but you seem like a good fellow,' George went on. 'You know why they're looking for men?'

'Nope.'

'They've had trouble keeping crews on since the fires a few years back. Fourteen, dead as doornails. Some burned up so bad you couldn't tell 'em apart. A half dozen they never found at all. I'm telling you, Jack, it's not worth the pennies they'd pay you.'

'I hear you. I do, but . . . well, I'm backed up against a wall. I'm just not sure how to work it out.'

'You need to make it through until harvest? You got seed money for the spring?'

Jack gave a wry smile. 'As long as we don't eat between now and then.'

'You've got carrots and potatoes sacked away, haven't you?'

'Sure.'

'You get yourself a moose yet?'

Jack shook his head. 'Never been much of a hunter.'

'Well, see here — that's all you need to do. Hang some meat in the barn, and you and the wife will be set 'till spring. It won't be cake and caviar, but you won't starve.'

Jack looked into his empty coffee mug.

'That's how it goes for a lot of us,' George said. 'Those first years are lean. I'm telling you, you might get sick of moose and potatoes, but you'll keep your neck safe.'

'True enough.'

As if it were all settled, George finished off his piece of pie in a few huge bites, wiped his mouth with the napkin, and stood. He reached a hand down to Jack.

'Better get going. Esther will accuse me of pissing the day away if I don't get on home.' His handshake was steady and friendly. 'Don't forget what I said, though. And when it comes to getting those fields cleared, we'd be glad to come over and help you out. Can make the day go faster to have company.'

Jack nodded. 'I appreciate that.'

He sat alone at the table. Maybe it was a mistake isolating themselves the way they had, Mabel without a single woman friend to talk with. George's wife could be a godsend, especially if he went north to work at the mine and Mabel was left alone at the homestead.

She would say otherwise. Hadn't they left all that behind to start a new life with just the two of them? I need peace and quiet, she'd told him more than once. She had withered and shrunk in on herself, and it began when they lost that baby. She said she couldn't bear to attend another family gathering with all the silly banter and gossip. But Jack remembered more. He remembered the pregnant women smiling as they stroked their bellies, and the newborn infants wailing as they were passed among the relatives. He remembered the little girl who had tugged at Mabel's skirts and called her 'Mama', mistaking her for another woman, and Mabel looking as if she had been backhanded. He remembered, too, that he had failed her, had gone on talking with a group of men and pretended he hadn't seen.

The Bensons' oldest son was about to be married and soon enough there would be a baby toddling about the house. He thought of Mabel, that small, sad smile and the wince at the inside corners of her eyes that should have made tears but never did.

He nodded at Betty as he picked up the empty crate and walked out to the wagon.

3

The leaden sky seemed to hold its breath. December grew near, and still there was no snow in the valley. For several days, the thermometers held at twenty-five below zero. When Mabel went out to feed the chickens, she was stunned by the cold. It cut through her skin and ached in her hip bones and knuckles. She watched a few dry snowflakes fall, but it was only a dusting, and the river wind swept it against exposed rocks and stumps in small, dirty drifts. It was difficult to discern the scant snow from the fine glacial silt, blown in gusts from the riverbed, that coated everything.

Jack said people in town were relieved the snow hadn't come — the train tracks were clear and the mine was running. But others worried the deep freeze would mean a late spring and a late start on planting.

The days diminished. Light lasted just six hours, and it was a feeble light. Mabel organized her hours into patterns — wash, mend, cook, wash, mend, cook — and tried not to imagine floating beneath the ice like a yellow leaf.

Baking day was a small gift, a reason to look forward. When it came, she rose early and was taking out the bin of flour and can of lard when she felt Jack's hand on her shoulder.

'No need,' he said.

'Why not?'

'Betty told me to hold off on the pies.'

'This week?'

'For good. She's got her sister baking for her.'

'Oh,' Mabel said. She put the flour back on the shelf, and was surprised at the strength of her disappointment. The pies had been her only real contribution to the household, a task she took some pride in. And there was the money.

'Will we have enough, Jack, without it?'

'I'll work it out. Don't worry yourself about it.'

Mabel now recalled waking to find his side of the bed empty. He had been at the kitchen table in wavering candlelight, papers spread in front of him. She had gone back to sleep, not thinking of it at the time. But this morning, he looked so old and tired. He walked with a slight stoop, and as he climbed out of bed he had groaned and held the small of his back. When Mabel asked if he was all right, he mumbled something about the horse but said he was fine. She had started to fuss about him, but he waved her off. Leave it be, he said. Just leave it be.

Mabel brought him leftover biscuits and a hard-boiled egg for breakfast.

'George Benson and his boys are coming over later today to help me skid logs,' he said as he peeled the egg. He didn't seem to notice her stare.

'George Benson?' she asked. 'And who is George Benson?'

'Hmm? What?'

'I've never met the man.'

28

'I know I've mentioned him before.' He took a bite of egg, and with a half-full mouth said, 'You know, he and Esther live just downriver from town.'

'No. I did not know.'

'They'll be here in a few hours. Don't worry about lunch — we'll work on through. But figure three extra plates for dinner.'

'I thought . . . Didn't we agree . . . Why are they coming here?'

Jack was quiet, and then he got up from the table and picked up his leather boots from beside the door. He sat back in the chair, pulled them onto his feet and laced them in quick, jabbing motions.

'What am I supposed to say, Mabel? I need the help.' He kept his head down and tugged the laces tight. 'It's just that simple.' He grabbed his coat from the hook, buttoning as he stepped outside, as if he couldn't wait to get out the door.

George Benson and two of his sons arrived an hour or so later. The older boy looked to be eighteen or twenty, the younger not much older than thirteen or fourteen. Mabel watched through the window as they met Jack at the barn. They shook hands all around, Jack nodding and grinning. The men gathered tools and headed toward the field, leading the team of draft horses the Bensons had brought. They never came to the cabin. She waited for Jack to

29

look for her in the window, to give a wave as he sometimes did in the mornings, but he didn't.

Evening came, and Mabel lit the lamps and cooked a dinner for them. When the men came in from working, she would try to be gracious, but not overly friendly. She didn't want to encourage this. Jack might need help this particular day, but they were not in need of friends or neighbors. Otherwise, why had they come here? They could have stayed home, where there were people enough for anyone. No, the point had been to find some solace on their own. Hadn't Jack understood that?

When the men returned, they didn't give Mabel two blinks. They weren't rude. George Benson and his boys nodded politely and said thank you and ma'am and please pass the potatoes, but without ever really looking at her, and mostly they talked loudly to one another about work horses and the weather and the crops. They joked about broken tools and the whole blasted idea of 'homesteading' in this godforsaken place and George slapped his knee and asked pardon for his swear words and Jack laughed out loud and the two boys stuffed their mouths full. All the while Mabel stayed by the kitchen counter, just outside of the light of the oil lamp.

They were going to be partners, she and Jack. This was going to be their new life together. Now he sat laughing with strangers when he hadn't smiled at her in years.

❋

Later, after dinner, George dragged his tired boys to their feet and told them it was time to head home.

'Your mother will be wondering where the devil we went to,' he said. He nodded at Mabel. 'Much thanks for the great meal. You know, I told Jack here that you two ought to come over our way sometime. Esther sure would like to meet you. Most of the homesteaders around here are grubby old bachelors. She could stand to have some female companionship.'

She should thank them for coming to help and say she'd be over any day now to meet his wife, but she said nothing. She could see herself through their eyes — an uptight, Back-East woman. She didn't like what she saw.

After George and his boys left, she heated water on the woodstove and washed the plates, finding some satisfaction in the clatter, but her anger was deflated when she saw that Jack had long since fallen asleep in his chair. She was left with her own ineffective bustle and noise.

Covering her hands with her apron, she picked up the basin of dirty dishwater, pushed open the latch on the door with an elbow, and stepped outside. She strode across the hard-packed yard and threw the water into a small ravine behind the cabin. Steam billowed around her and slowly dissipated. Overhead the stars glittered metallic and distant, and the night sky seemed cruel to her. She let the cold air fill her nostrils and chill her skin. Here by the cabin the air was calm, but she could hear the wind roar down the Wolverine River.

It was several days before Jack mentioned the Bensons again, but he broached the subject as if halfway into an ongoing conversation. 'George said we should come by about noon on Thanksgiving. I told him you'd make up one of your pies. He's missing them down at the hotel.'

Mabel didn't agree or protest or ask questions. She wondered how Jack could be sure she had even heard him.

As she flipped through her recipe box, trying to decide what to bake, she thought of Thanksgivings back in the Allegheny River valley, where Jack's aunts, uncles, cousins, grandparents and grandchildren, friends and neighbors, gathered at the family farm for the feast. Those days had been the worst for Mabel. Even as a child she was uneasy with crowds, but as she got older she found the bantering and prying even more excruciating. While the men walked the orchards to discuss business, she was trapped in the women's realm of births and deaths, neither of which she was comfortable turning into idle chat. And just below the surface of this prattle was the insinuation of her failure, whispered and then hushed as she entered and left rooms. Perhaps, the whispers went, Jack should have chosen a heartier woman, a woman who wasn't afraid of hard work and who had the hips for childbirth. Those highbrows might be able to discuss politics and great literature, but could they birth a child, for God's sake? Do you see the way she carries herself, like she couldn't turn her nose any higher? Back as straight as a stick. An oh-so-delicate constitution. Too proud to take in an orphan child.

Mabel would excuse herself to go out of doors for some fresh air, but that only attracted the attention of a nosy great-aunt or well-meaning sister-in-law who would advise her that if she were only more approachable, more friendly, then perhaps she would get on better with Jack's family.

Maybe it would be the same with the Bensons. Maybe they would presume her unfit to survive as a homesteader in Alaska or judge her barren and cold and a burden to Jack. Already a pit of resentment grew inside her. She thought of telling Jack she was too ill to go. But early Thanksgiving morning she rose, well before Jack, put more wood in the stove and began rolling out the dough. She would make a walnut pie with her mother's recipe, and also a dried-apple pie. Was it enough, two pies? She had watched the boys eat, swallowing great mouthfuls and cleaning plates effortlessly. Maybe she should make three. What if the crusts were tough or they didn't like walnuts or apples? She shouldn't care what the Bensons thought, and yet the pies were to represent her. She might be curt and ungrateful, but by God she could bake.

With the pies in the woodstove oven, Mabel chose a heavy cotton dress that she hoped would be appropriate. She heated the iron on the stovetop. She wanted to look presentable, but not like an overdressed outsider. Once she was ready and the pies were done, she gathered wool blankets and face wraps for her and Jack. It would be a long, cold ride in the open wagon.

After Jack had fed and watered the animals and harnessed the horse, Mabel sat beside him on the wagon seat, the still-warm pies wrapped in towels on her lap. She felt an unexpected shiver of excitement. Whatever happened at the Bensons', it was good to be out of the cabin. She had not left the homestead for weeks. Jack, too, seemed more chipper. He clicked his tongue at the horse and, as they followed the trail off their property, he pointed out to Mabel where he had been clearing and told her of his ideas for the spring. He described how the horse had nearly killed him that day, and how it had spooked at a red fox.

Mabel threaded her arm into the crook of his.

'You've accomplished a great deal.'

'I couldn't have done it without the Bensons. Those work horses of theirs are something else. Puts this beast to shame.' He gave the reins a gentle shake.

'Have you met his wife?'

'Nope. Just George and his sons. George used to be a gold miner, when he was younger, but he met Esther and they decided to settle down and have a family.' Jack hesitated, cleared his throat. 'Anyways, he seems like a good man. He's sure been a help to us.'

'Yes. He has.'

When they arrived at the Bensons', someone came out of the barn hoisting a flapping, headless turkey. It was George, she thought at first, but this person was too short and had a thick gray braid hanging below a wool cap.

'Must be Esther,' Jack said.

'Do you think so?'

The woman raised her chin in greeting, then wrestled with the huge dying bird in her arms. Blood splattered about her feet.

'Go on up to the house,' she called out to them. 'The boys'll help you with the horse.'

In the cabin, Mabel sat alone at the cluttered kitchen table, while Jack disappeared outside with George and the younger son. With her hands in her lap, her back straight, she wondered where they would eat. The table was heaped with stacks of catalogs, rows of washed, empty jars, and bolts of fabric. The cabin smelled strongly of cabbage and sour wild cranberries. It wasn't much bigger than Jack and Mabel's, except it had a loft where she assumed the beds were. The cabin was catawampus in a dizzying way, with the floor dipping to one side and the corners not square. Rocks and bleached animal skulls and dried wildflowers lined the windowsills. Mabel didn't move, yet she pried just by allowing her eyes to wander.

She jumped when the door banged open.

'Blasted bird. You'd think it'd know enough to just give up the ghost. But no, it's got to raise hell when it doesn't even have a head left on its body.'

'Oh. Oh dear. Can I do something to help?'

The woman stomped past the table without removing her dirty boots and threw the turkey onto the crowded counter. A lard tin fell with a clatter to the floor. Esther kicked at it and turned to Mabel, who stood flustered and slightly frightened. Esther grinned, stretched out a bloodstained hand.

'Mabel? Isn't that it? Mabel?'

Mabel nodded and gave her hand over to Esther's vigorous shake.

'Esther. But I suppose you already figured that out. Good to have you out here finally.'

Under her wool coat, Esther wore a flower-print shirt and men's denim overalls. Her face was speckled with blood. She pulled off her wool hat and fuzzy strands of hair stood on end. She swung her braid over her back and began filling a large pot with water.

'You'd think with all these men around here I could find somebody to kill and pluck a turkey for me. But no such luck.'

'Are you sure there's nothing I can do?' Perhaps Esther would apologize for her appearance or for the disarray in the house. Maybe there was some explanation, some reason.

'No. No. Just relax and make yourself at home. You could fix us some tea, if you'd like, while I get this damned bird in the oven.'

'Oh. Yes. Thank you.'

'You know what our youngest went and did? Here we raise a couple of turkeys for no other reason than to cook on occasions such as these, and he goes out and shoots a dozen ptarmigan yesterday. Let's have these for Thanksgiving, he says. What do I need with a dozen dead ptarmigan on Thanksgiving? Why feed turkeys if you're going to eat ptarmigan?'

She looked at Mabel, as if expecting an answer.

36

'I . . . I haven't the faintest idea. I can't say I've ever eaten ptarmigan before.'

'Well, it's good enough. But Thanksgiving, it's turkey as far as I'm concerned.'

'I brought pies. For dessert. I set them on that chair. I wasn't sure where else to put them.'

'Perfect! I hadn't had a chance to even think about sweets. George tells me Betty's a fool to give up your pies. He raves about your baking. Not that he needs any of it. Have you seen the gut on that man?'

Again she looked at Mabel expectantly.

'Oh, I wouldn't — '

Esther's laugh was a loud, startling guffaw.

'I keep telling him he's single-handedly supporting that hotel restaurant, and it's starting to show,' she said.

It was as if Mabel had fallen through a hole into another world. It was nothing like her quiet, well-ordered world of darkness and light and sadness. This was an untidy place, but welcoming and full of laughter. George teased that the two women were 'talking a blue streak' rather than cooking the meal, and it was well into the evening before dinner was served, but no one seemed to mind. The turkey was dry on the outside and half raw on the inside. They all had to pick and choose their cuts. The mashed potatoes were creamy and perfect. The gravy was lumpy. Esther made no apologies. They ate with plates balanced on their laps. No one said a blessing, but George held up his glass and said, 'To neighbors. And to getting through another winter.' They all raised their glasses.

'And here's to eating ptarmigan next year,' Esther said, and everyone laughed.

After dinner and pie, the Bensons began to tell stories of their time on the homestead, of how the snow once piled so deep the horses could walk over the fence whenever they pleased, of weather so cold the dishwater turned to ice in the air when you tossed it out.

'I wouldn't live anywhere else in the world, though,' Esther said. 'What about you? You both come from farms down south?'

'No. Well, Jack's family owns a farm along the Allegheny River, in Pennsylvania.'

'What do they raise back there?' George asked.

'Apples and hay, mostly,' Jack said.

'What about you?' Esther turned to Mabel.

'I suppose I'm the black sheep. No one else in my family would think of living on a farm, or moving to Alaska. My father was a literature professor at the University of Pennsylvania.'

'And you left all that to come here? What in God's name were you thinking?' Esther shoved Mabel's arm playfully. 'He talked you into it, didn't he? That's how it often is. These men drag their poor women along, taking them to the Far North for adventure, when all they want is a hot bath and a housekeeper.'

'No. No. It's not like that.' All eyes were on her, even Jack's. She hesitated, but then went on. 'I wanted to come here. Jack did, too, but when we did, it was at my urging. I don't know why, precisely. I believe we were in need of a change. We needed to do things for ourselves. Does that make any sense? To break your own ground and know it's yours, free and clear. Nothing taken for granted. Alaska seemed like the place for a fresh start.'

Esther grinned. 'You didn't fare too badly with this one, did you, Jack? Don't let word get out. There aren't many like her.'

Though she didn't look up, Mabel knew Jack was watching her and that her cheeks were flushed. She so rarely spoke like this in mixed company. Maybe she had said too much.

Then, as the conversation began to turn around her, she wondered if she had told the truth. Was that why they had come north — to build a life? Or did fear drive her? Fear of the gray, not just in the strands of her hair and her wilting cheeks, but the gray that ran deeper, to the bone, so that she thought she might turn into a fine dust and simply sift away in the wind.

Mabel recalled the afternoon, less than two years ago. Sunny and brilliant. The smell of the orchard in the air. Jack was sitting on the porch swing of his parents' house, his eyes shaded from the sun. It was a family picnic, but they were alone for the moment. She had reached into her dress pocket and pulled out the folded handbill — 'June 1918. Alaska, Our Newest Homeland.'

They should go, she had said. Home? he asked.

No, she said, and held up the advertisement. North, she said.

The federal government was looking for farmers to homestead along the territory's new train route. The Alaska Railroad and a steamship company offered discounted rates for those brave enough to make the journey.

She had tried to keep her tone even, to not let desperation break her voice. Jack was wary of her newfound enthusiasm. They were both nearing fifty years old. It was true that as a young man he had dreamed of going to Alaska, of testing himself in a place so wild and grand, but wasn't it too late for all that?

Jack surely had such doubts, but he did not speak them. He sold his share in the land and business to his brothers. She packed the trunks with dishes and pans and as many books as they could hold. They traveled by train to the West Coast, then by steamship from Seattle to Seward, Alaska, and by train again to Alpine. Without warning or signs of civilization, the train would stop and a solitary man would disembark, shoulder his packs, and disappear into the spruce trees and creek valleys. She had reached out and put her hand on Jack's arm, but he stared out the train window, his expression unreadable.

She had imagined the two of them working in green fields framed by mountains as tall and snowy as the Swiss Alps. The air would be clean and cold, the sky vast and blue. Side by side, sweaty and tired, they would smile at each other the way they had as young lovers. It would be a hard life, but it would be theirs alone. Here at the world's edge, far from everything familiar and safe, they would build a new home in the wilderness and do it as partners, out from under the shadow of cultivated orchards and expectant generations.

But here they were, never together in the fields, speaking to each other less and less. The first summer he had her stay in town at the dingy hotel while he built the cabin and barn. Sitting on the edge of the narrow mattress that had certainly bedded more miners and trappers than Pennsylvania women, Mabel considered writing to her sister. She was alone. The ceaseless sun never gave her a moment's rest. Everything before her — the lace curtains at the window, the clapboard siding, her own aging hands — was leached of color. When she left her hotel room, she found only a single muddy, deeply rutted trail beside the railroad tracks. It began in trees and ended in trees. No sidewalks. No cafes or bookshops. Just Betty, wearing her men's shirts and work pants and issuing endless advice about how to jar sauerkraut and moose meat, how to take the itch out of mosquito bites with vinegar, how to ward off bears with a blow horn.

Mabel wanted to write to her sister but could not admit she had been wrong. Everyone had warned her the Territory of Alaska was for lost men and unsavory women, that there would be no place for her in the wilderness. She clutched the advertisement promising a new homeland and did not write any letters.

When at last Jack brought her to the homestead, she had wanted to believe. So this

41

was Alaska — raw, austere. A cabin of freshly peeled logs cut from the land, a patch of dirt and stumps for a yard, mountains that serrated the sky. Each day she asked, Can I come with you to the fields? but he said no, you should stay. He returned in the evenings bent at the back and wounded with bruises and insect bites. She cooked and cleaned, and cooked and cleaned, and found herself further consumed by the gray, until even her vision was muted and the world around her drained of color.

Mabel smoothed her hands across her lap, chasing the wrinkles in the fabric again and again, until her ears caught a few of the words around her. Something about the mine north of town.

'I'm telling you, Jack. Don't give it another thought,' George was saying. 'That's a quick way to leave this world.'

Mabel kept herself calm and seated.

'Did you say a coal mine?' she asked.

'I know times are tough, Mabel, but that's nothing to be ashamed of,' George said and winked at her. 'You just keep your man at home and hang in there. It'll all work out.'

When George and his sons began to talk about the many gruesome ways a man can be maimed and killed underground, Mabel turned to Jack and whispered fiercely, 'You were thinking of leaving me to work in the mine?'

'We'll talk of it later,' he said.

'All you folks have got to do is get a moose in your barn and save your money for spring,' George said.

Mabel frowned, not comprehending. 'A moose?' she asked. 'In our barn?'

Esther laughed.

'Not a live one, dear,' she said. 'Meat. Just to keep you fed. We've done it years past ourselves. You get mighty sick of mashed potatoes, fried potatoes, boiled meat, fried meat, but it'll get you through.'

'Pretty late in the year for moose,' the youngest boy mumbled from where he stood in the kitchen, his hands shoved in his pockets. 'He'd been better off getting one just before the rut.'

'They're still out there, Garrett,' George said. 'He'll just have to work a bit harder to find one.'

The boy shrugged doubtfully.

'Don't mind him,' Esther said, thumbing in the boy's direction. 'He thinks he's the next Daniel Boone.'

One of the older sons laughed and punched him in the arm. The younger boy clenched his fists and then shoved his older brother hard enough to cause him to bump into the kitchen table. A noisy scuffle commenced, and Mabel was alarmed, until she saw George and Esther taking no notice. Finally, when the ruckus became too much even for the Bensons, Esther hollered, 'That's enough, boys!' and they settled down again.

'Garrett might be too big for his britches, but I tell you, Jack, he is a hand with a rifle.' George

43

jutted his chin proudly toward the youngest boy. 'He shot his first moose when he was ten. He brings home more game than all the rest of us.'

Esther leaned toward Mabel and said, 'Including all those blessed ptarmigan.'

Mabel tried to smile, but her thoughts were unspooling. He was going to abandon her. Leave her alone in that small, dark cabin.

Now the men were all talking of hunting moose, and once again she had the unsettling sense that they had all conversed on this topic before and, once again, she was the ignorant stranger.

'You got to carry your rifle with you, even when you're just working in the fields,' she heard the youngest son tell Jack. 'Get up in the foothills. Most times, the snow'd already pushed 'em down to the river. But it's late in coming, so they're still up high, eating birch and aspen.'

The boy barely managed to conceal his disdain for Jack. 'Too bad you didn't shoot one in the fall,' he said. 'You're going to have to hunt hard. Moose only herd up during the rut. They're different then. Bulls go crazy through the woods. Knock their bloody antlers into the trees. Roll in their own piss. Bawl for cows.'

'I heard something, month or so back,' Jack said. 'I was out splitting wood, and something started grunting at me out of the woods. Then, 'Thwack. Thwack.' Like somebody else was chopping wood.'

'Bull moose. Calling to you, smacking his antlers against a tree. He wanted to fight you. He thought you were another bull.' The boy almost

44

smirked, as if Jack were far from the stature of a moose.

Esther saw Mabel's discomfort but misunderstood it.

'Don't worry, dear. You'll get used to moose meat. It can run a little to the tough, gamy side this time of year, but it'll keep you fed.'

Mabel gave a weak smile.

When it came time to leave, the Bensons tried to insist on Jack and Mabel staying the night, but Jack said they needed to get home to care for the animals, and Mabel said thank you but she slept better in her own bed.

'It's cold out there tonight,' Esther said as she helped Mabel into her coat.

'We'll be all right. Thank you, though.'

Esther tucked a jar inside Mabel's coat, buttoned it for her as if she were a child, and straightened the collar.

'Keep that sourdough starter warm on the way home or you'll kill it for sure. And remember what I said about adding a bit of flour now and then.'

Mabel hugged the cool jar against herself and thanked Esther again.

It was clear and windy. The moon lit the ruts of the trail and turned the land and trees to blues. As they rode away, Mabel looked back to the lighted windows of the Benson home, and then she pushed her face down into her scarf. Jack cleared his throat. Mabel expected him to say something about his plan to go to the mine. She was prepared to be righteous in her anger.

'They're quite the family, aren't they?' he said.

She didn't speak at first.

'Yes,' she said finally. 'They certainly are.'

'Esther took a liking to you. What all did you two talk about?'

'Oh . . . everything, I suppose.'

Mabel was quiet, then said, 'She asked why we never had children.'

'And?'

'She said we can have their boys anytime we want them.'

Jack chuckled, and Mabel smiled into her scarf despite herself.

4

The next evening, the snow fell with dusk. The first flakes clumped together as they twirled and fluttered to the ground. First just a few here and there, and then the air was filled with falling snow, caught in the light of the window in dreamy swirls. It brought to Mabel's mind how it was to be a little girl, kneeling on a sofa at the window to watch winter's first snowflakes filter through the streetlights.

When she returned to the kitchen window later, she saw Jack emerge from the woods and move through the snow. His hunt had been unsuccessful; she knew by his low head and shuffle.

She went back to preparing dinner. She opened the calico curtains over the kitchen shelves and took out two plates. She spread the tablecloth. She thought of the Bensons' cluttered cabin and smiled to herself. Esther in her men's overalls — how confidently she strode into the kitchen and flung the dead turkey onto the counter. Mabel had never met a woman like her. She did not quietly take her leave or feign helplessness or cloak her opinions in niceties.

Last night, George had told the story of how Esther shot a nine-foot grizzly bear in the yard several summers ago. She was home alone when she heard a loud thumping. When she looked outside, she saw a bear trying to break into the barn. The grizzly stood on his hind legs and slammed his massive paws again and again into the wooden door. Then he dropped to all fours, paced, and put his snout to the logs and snuffled. Mabel would have been terrified, but not Esther. She was spitting mad. No bear was going to get her cows. She calmly walked inside and got a rifle, stepped back into the yard and promptly shot the bear. Mabel could see her perfectly — Esther standing in the dirt, her feet slightly apart, her aim steady. Never one to hesitate or worry herself with decorum.

Mabel was at the window again. The snow fell faster and thicker. As she watched, Jack walked out of the barn carrying a lantern, and the snow eddied around him in the circle of light. He turned his head, as if he had sensed her eyes on him, and the two of them looked at each other across the distance, each in their pocket of light, snow like a falling veil between them. Mabel couldn't remember the last time they had so deliberately gazed at each other, and the moment was like the snow, slow and drifting.

When she first fell in love with Jack, she had dreamed she could fly, that on a warm, inky black night she had pushed off the grass with her bare feet to float among the leafy treetops and stars in her nightgown. The sensation had returned.

Through the window, the night air appeared

dense, each snowflake slowed in its long, tumbling fall through the black. It was the kind of snow that brought children running out their doors, made them turn their faces skyward, and spin in circles with their arms outstretched.

She stood spellbound in her apron, a washrag in her hand. Perhaps it was the recollection of that dream, or the hypnotic nature of the spinning snow. Maybe it was Esther in her overalls and flowered blouse, shooting bears and laughing out loud.

Mabel set down the rag and untied her apron. She slipped her feet into her boots, put on one of Jack's wool coats, and found a hat and some mittens.

Outside, the air was clean and cool against her face, and she could smell the wood smoke from the chimney. She let the snow float around her, and then Mabel did what she had as a child — turned her face to the sky and stuck out her tongue. The swirl overhead was dizzying and she began to spin slowly in place. The snowflakes landed on her cheeks and eyelids, wet her skin. Then she stopped and watched the snow settle on the arms of her coat. For a moment she studied the pattern of a single starry flake before it melted into the wool. Here, and then gone.

Around her feet the snow deepened. She kicked at it lightly, and it clumped, wet and heavy. Snowball snow. She clenched a fistful in her bare hand. The snow compacted and held the shape of her fingers. She pulled on her mittens and balled some snow together, patting and forming it.

She heard Jack's footsteps and looked up to see him coming toward the cabin. He squinted at her. She so rarely came outside, and never at night. His reaction spurred in her an unpredictable, childish desire. She patted the snowball a few more times, watched Jack and waited. As he neared, she threw it at him, and even as the snowball left her hand, she knew it was an outlandish thing to do and she wondered what would happen next. The snowball thumped into his leg, just above the top of his boot.

He stopped, looked at the circle of snow on his pant leg and then up at Mabel, a mix of irritation and confusion on his face, and then even as his brow stayed furrowed, a small smile appeared at the corner of his lips. He bent and carefully lodged the lantern in the snow beside him, then smacked his gloved hand across the pant leg, dusting away the snow. Mabel held her breath. He remained bent over, his hand down by his boots, and then, quicker than Mabel could react, he scooped up a handful of snow and tossed a perfectly formed snowball at her. It smacked her in the forehead. She stood motionless with her arms at her sides. Neither of them spoke. The snow fell around them, on the tops of their heads and their shoulders. Mabel wiped the wet snow from her forehead and saw Jack, his mouth open.

'I . . . that's not . . . I hadn't meant to — '

And she laughed. Melting snow dripped down her temples, snowflakes landed on her eyelashes. She laughed and laughed until she was doubled over, and then she grabbed another handful of snow and threw it at Jack, and he threw one back, and the snowballs lobbed through the air. Most of them fell at each other's feet, but sometimes they softly thumped into shoulders and chests. Laughing, they chased each other around the cabin, dodging behind the log corners and peeking out in time to see another snowball coming. The hem of Mabel's long skirt dragged in the snow. Jack chased her, a snowball in each hand. She tripped and fell and as he ran to her she flung loose snow at him, all the time laughing, and he gently tossed the snowballs down at her. Then he put his hands to his knees, bent at the back and breathing loudly.

'We're too old for this,' he said.

'Are we?'

He reached down and pulled Mabel to her feet until they stood chest to chest, panting and smiling and covered in snow. Mabel pressed her face into his damp collar and he wrapped his arms, thick with his wool coat, around her shoulders. They stood that way for a while, letting the snow fall down upon them.

Then Jack pulled away, brushed snow from his wet hair and reached for the lantern.

'Wait,' she said. 'Let's make a snowman.'

'What?'

'A snowman. It's perfect. Perfect snow for a snowman.'

He hesitated. He was tired. It was late. They were too old for such nonsense. There were a dozen reasons not to, Mabel knew, but instead he set the lantern back in the snow.

'All right,' he said. There was reluctance in the hang of his head, but he pulled off his leather work gloves. He took her cheek in his bare hand and with his thumb wiped melted snow from beneath her eye.

'All right.'

❄

The snow was perfect. It stuck in thick layers as they rolled it into balls along the ground. Mabel made the last, smallest one for the head, and Jack stacked them one atop the other. The figure barely stood above his waist.

'It's kind of small,' he said.

She stepped back and inspected it from a distance.

'It's just fine,' she said.

They patted snow into the cracks between the snowballs, smoothed the edges. He walked away from the light of the lantern and cabin window, into a stand of trees. He came back with two birch branches, and he stuck one into each side of their creation. Now it had arms.

'A girl. Let's make it a little girl,' she said.

'All right.'

She knelt and began shaping the bottom into a skirt that spread out from the snow girl. She slid her hands upward, shaving away the snow and narrowing the outline until it looked like a little child. When she stood up, she saw Jack at work with a pocketknife.

'There,' he said. He stepped back. Sculpted in the white snow were perfect, lovely eyes, a nose and small, white lips. She even thought she could see cheekbones and a little chin.

'Oh.'

'You don't like it?' He sounded disappointed.

'No. Oh no. She's beautiful. I just didn't know . . .'

How could she speak her surprise? Such delicate features, formed by his calloused hands, a glimpse at his longing. Surely he, too, had wanted children. They had talked about it so often when they first married, joking they would have a baker's dozen but really planning on only three or four. What fun Christmas would be with a household full of little ones, they told each other their first quiet winter together. There was an air of solemnity as they opened each other's presents, but they believed someday their Christmas mornings would reel with running children and squeals of delight. She sewed a small stocking for their firstborn and he sketched plans for a rocking horse he would build. Maybe the first would be a girl, or would it be a boy? How could they have known that twenty years later they would still be childless, just an old man and an old woman alone in the wilderness?

As they stood together, the snow fell heavier and faster making it difficult to see more than a few feet.

'She needs some hair,' he said.

'Oh. I've thought of something, too.'

Jack went toward the barn, Mabel to the cabin.

'Here they are,' she called across the yard when she came back out. 'Mittens and a scarf for the little girl.'

He returned with a bundle of yellow grass

from near the barn. He stuck individual strands into the snow, creating wild, yellow hair, and she wrapped the scarf around its neck and placed the mittens on the ends of the birch branches, the red string that joined them across the snow child's back. Her sister had knitted them in red wool, and the scarf was a stitch Mabel had never seen before — dewdrop lace, her sister called it. Through the broad pattern, Mabel could see white snow.

She ran to a corner of the cabin where a wild cranberry bush grew. She picked a handful of the frozen berries, returned to the snow girl, and carefully squeezed the juice onto her lips. The snow there turned a gentle red.

She and Jack stood side by side and gazed at their creation.

'She's beautiful,' she said. 'Don't you think? She's beautiful.'

'She did turn out, didn't she?'

Standing still, she became aware of the cold through her damp clothes and trembled.

'Chilled?'

She shook her head.

'Let's go in and warm up.'

Mabel didn't want it to end. The quiet snow, the closeness. But her teeth began to chatter. She nodded.

Inside, Jack added several birch logs to the woodstove and the fire crackled. Mabel stood as close as she dared and peeled off wet mittens, hat, coat. He did the same. Clumps of snow fell onto the stovetop and sizzled. Her dress hung heavy and wet against her skin, and she unbuttoned it and stepped out of it. He unlaced his boots and pulled his damp shirt off over his head. Soon they were naked and shivering beside each other. She was unaware of their bare skin until he stepped closer and she felt his rough hand at the small of her back.

'Better?' he asked.

'Yes.'

She reached up over his shoulders where his skin was still cool to the touch, and when she pressed her nose into the crook of his neck, melted snow clung in droplets to his beard.

'Let's go to bed,' Jack said.

After all these years, still a spot within her fluttered at his touch, and his voice, throaty and hushed in her ear, tickled along her spine. Naked, they walked to the bedroom. Beneath the covers, they fumbled with each other's bodies, arms and legs, backbones and hip bones, until they found the familiar, tender lines like the creases in an old map that has been folded and refolded over the years.

After, they lay together, Mabel's cheek against his chest.

'You won't really go to the mine, will you?'

He put his lips to the top of her head.

'I don't know, Mabel,' he whispered into her hair. 'I'm doing the best I can.'

5

Jack woke to the cold. In the few hours he'd slept the weather had changed. He could smell it and feel it in his arthritic hands. He propped himself on an elbow and grabbed at the nightstand until he found a match and lit the candle. His back and shoulders were stiff as he eased his legs over the side of the bed. He sat on the edge of the mattress until the cold was unbearable. Not far from the pillow where Mabel slept, frost crept between the logs with its feathery crystals. He swore quietly and pulled the quilt up over her shoulder. A warm, secure home — he couldn't even give her that much. He carried the candleholder into the main room. The heavy metal door on the woodstove clanged noisily as he opened it. A few coals smoldered in the ash.

As he reached for his boots, through the window he saw a flicker. He stood at the frost-edged glass and peered out.

Fresh snow blanketed the ground and glittered and glowed silver in the moonlight. The barn and trees beyond were muted outlines. There, at the edge of the forest, he saw it again. A flash of blue and red. He was groggy with sleep. He closed his eyes slowly, opened them again and tried to focus.

There it was. A little figure dashed through the trees. Was that a skirt about the legs? A red scarf at the neck, and white hair trailing down the back. Slight. Quick. A little girl. Running at the edge of the forest. Then disappearing into the trees.

Jack rubbed his eyes with the heels of his hands. Not enough sleep — that had to be it. Too many long days. He left the window and stepped into his boots, leaving the laces untied. He opened the door and the chill air sucked the breath out of him. The snow crunched beneath his boots as he walked to the woodpile. It was only as he was returning with an armload of split birch that he noticed their little snow girl. He set the wood on the ground and with empty arms went to where it had stood. In its place was a small, broken heap of snow. The mittens and scarf were gone.

He pushed at the snow with the toe of his boot.

An animal. Maybe a moose had stumbled through. But the scarf and mittens? A raven or a whiskey jack maybe. Wild birds had been known to snatch things. As he turned away, he caught sight of the tracks. Moonlight fell in the hollows. The prints ran through the snow, away from the cabin and into the trees. He bent over them. The silvery blue light was weak, so at first he didn't trust his eyes. Coyote, or maybe lynx. Something other than this. He bent closer and touched the track with the tips of his bare fingers. Human footprints. Small. The size of a child's.

Jack shivered. His skin prickled with goose

bumps, and his bare toes ached cold inside his boots. He left the tracks and the pile of snow, stacked the wood in the crook of his arm, and went inside, quickly closing the door behind him. As he shoved each piece of wood into the stove, he wondered if the racket would wake Mabel. Just his eyes playing tricks. It would come to sense in the morning. He stayed beside the woodstove until the fire roared again, and then he closed the damper.

He eased himself beneath the quilt and against Mabel's warm body, and she moaned softly in her sleep but did not wake. Jack lay beside her, his eyes wide and his brain spinning until finally he drifted into a kind of sleep that wasn't much different than wakefulness, a mystifying, restless sleep where dreams fell and melted like snow-flakes, where children ran soft-footed through the trees and scarves flapped between black raven beaks.

When Jack woke again it was late morning, the sun was up, and Mabel was in the kitchen. His body was tired and stiff, as if he had never slept at all but instead spent the night splitting wood or bucking hay bales. He dressed and in socked feet made his way to the table. He smelled fresh coffee and hot pancakes.

'I think it worked, Jack.'
'What?'
'The sourdough starter Esther gave me. Here, try them.'

Mabel set a plate of pancakes on the table.

'Did you sleep all right?' she asked. 'You look positively worn out.' With a hand on his shoulder, she reached over him to pour coffee from the blue enamel pot into his cup. He picked up the cup, held it warm between his hands.

'I don't know. I guess not.'

'It's so cold out, isn't it? But beautiful. All that white snow. It's so bright.'

'You've been outside?'

'No. Not since I dashed to the outhouse in the middle of the night.'

He got up from the table.

'Aren't you going to eat breakfast?' she asked.

'Just going to get some wood. Nearly let the fire go out.'

He put on his coat this time, and some gloves, before opening the door. The snow reflected sunlight so brilliantly he squinted. He walked to the woodpile, then turned back to the cabin and saw the snow child, or what was left of it. Still just a shapeless pile of snow. No scarf. No mittens. Just as it had been last night, but now exposed as truth in the light of day. And the footprints still ran through the snow, across the yard and into the trees. Then he saw the dead snowshoe hare beside the doorstep. He stepped past without pausing. Inside, he let the wood fall to the floor beside the stove in a clamor, then stared without seeing.

'Have you noticed anything?' he finally said.

'You mean the cold snap?'

'No. I mean anything out of the ordinary.'

'Like what?'

60

'I thought I heard something last night. Probably nothing.'

After breakfast Jack left to feed the animals. On the way to the barn, he scooped up the dead hare and held it close to his side so Mabel wouldn't notice out the window. Once in the barn, he looked at it closely. He could see where it had been strangled, most likely with a thin snare that cut into its white coat and soft underfur. It was frozen stiff. Later, after he had taken care of the animals, he went behind the barn and threw the dead hare as far as he could into the trees.

When he returned to the cabin, Mabel was heating water to wash.

'Did you see the tracks?' she called over her shoulder.

'What tracks?'

She pointed out the window.

'Those?' he asked. 'Must have been a fox.'

'Are the chickens safe?'

'Fine. They're all fine.'

Jack took his shotgun down from over the door and told her he would go after the fox. He knew now what unsettled him about the tracks. The trail began at the heap of snow and led in only one direction — away and into the woods. There were no prints coming into the yard.

The trail wove among the birch trees, over fallen logs and around bare, thorny wild rose branches. Jack followed the loops and turns. They didn't seem like the tracks of a lost child. More like a wild animal, a fox or ermine. Dashing here and there, running across the top of the snow, circling back and around until Jack wasn't sure if he was still following the original trail. If she were lost, why hadn't she come to the door? Why didn't she ask for help? And the tracks did not lead down the wagon trail, toward the south, toward town and other homesteads. Instead, they moved through the trees without direction, but when he looked back over his shoulder, he could no longer see the cabin and he understood that the trail was winding north, toward the mountains. The boot prints were joined here and there by another, different set of tracks. Fox, crisscrossing the child's footprints, then slipping away. He continued to follow the child's trail. Why would a fox stalk a little girl through the trees? He looked down from time to time, then doubted himself. Maybe the girl was following the fox. Maybe that was why her trail was so erratic.

Jack stopped at a fallen cottonwood, leaned back against its thick trunk. He must have gotten off the trail. He wiped sweat from his forehead. It was cold, but the air was dry and calm and he was overheating. He wondered if he hadn't looked closely enough. Maybe he had been following fox tracks this entire time. He returned to the prints and stooped down next to them, half expecting to see pad and claw prints. But no, they were still the smooth, child-sized footprints.

He followed the trail for a while longer, until it meandered down into a small ravine and a dense forest of black spruce. He could not easily fit through those trees. He had been gone for some time now. He turned back and felt a momentary rush of panic — so intently had he stared down at the footprints as he followed them, he had paid little attention to the landscape. The trees and snow were the same in all directions. Then he remembered his own boot tracks in the snow. It would be a long, looping way home, but it would get him there.

Mabel was anxious at the door when he returned. She wiped her hands on her apron and helped him take off his coat.

'I was beginning to worry.'

Jack warmed his hands at the woodstove.

'Well? Did you find the fox?'

'No, just more tracks, all over the place out there.'

He wouldn't tell her about the child, or the dead hare on their doorstep. Somehow, he thought they might upset her.

6

Mabel nervously eyed the trail across the snow as she returned from the outhouse. Never before had a fox come so close to their cabin. She knew they were small creatures, but all the same they frightened her. She stepped over the tracks, but then their smooth, oblong shape caught her eye. They weren't animal tracks at all. Each was a perfect print of the sole of a small boot. She brought her head up and with her eyes followed the trail back to the snow child she and Jack had built the night before. It was gone.

She hurried breathless into the cabin.

'Jack? Someone's ruined our snow child. Someone's been in our yard.'

He was at the counter, sharpening his pocket-knife on a steel.

'I know.'

'I thought you said it was a fox.'

'There are fox tracks, too, in the woods.'

'But those out there?'

'A child's.'

'How can you know?'

'The size of the tracks. And I'm pretty sure I saw her. Last night. Running through the trees.'

'Her? Who?'

'A little girl. She was wearing your red scarf.'

'What? Why didn't you tell me? Did you go after her?'

'This morning, when I told you I was going to look for the fox, I tried to see where she went, but I lost the trail.'

'Last night . . . there was a little girl alone outside in the freezing winter and you didn't see if she needed help? She must have wandered away from somebody's cabin.'

'I don't know, Mabel.'

She went back outside and stared at the little tracks. Just one trail, leading across the snow, away from their cabin and into the trees.

During the next several days the skies cleared, a deep cold settled on the valley, and the child's tracks became edged in frost. They trailed sparkling and delicate through Mabel's thoughts, and left her feeling as if she had forgotten something.

One evening she went to the shelf where a dozen of her favorite books were held in place by mahogany bookends — Emily Dickinson's *Poems*, Henry David Thoreau's *Walking*, Frances Hodgson Burnett's *Queen Silver-Bell*. As she absent-mindedly ran her fingers across the spines, she thought of a fairy tale her father had often read to her. She remembered the worn blue leather of the cover and the golden hue of the illustrations. In one picture, she recalled, a child reached with her mittened hands down to the old man and woman who knelt before her, the old man and woman who had formed her from snow.

The next day when Mabel went to feed the chickens in the barn, she passed the little boot prints.

※

She woke to a silent cabin and sensed the change before she looked out a window or opened the door. It was a muffled quiet, a dense cold pressing at the cabin walls, though it was warm inside. Jack had left her a crackling fire before going to hunt moose again. Her senses were confirmed when she looked out the window and saw a shining new landscape. The snow had come again, and this time it was a fine, driving snow that had accumulated quickly overnight and blanketed the cabin and outbuildings. It transformed boulders and stumps into soft, white lumps. It gathered in deep pillows on spruce boughs, it hung heavily over the cabin's eaves, and it had erased the tracks across their yard.

She carried a basket of bread crumbs and dried apple bits left over from a pie to the barn for the chickens. The hens comforted her, the way they roosted along their spruce pole, their feathers ruffled against the cold. When she came in, they hopped to the straw-strewn ground and clucked like old women welcoming a neighbor. They bustled and stretched their wings. One of the black-and-white hens pecked a scrap from Mabel's fingers, and she stroked its feathered back as it waddled away. She reached into each nesting box. Finally, beneath the soft belly of a red hen, she found two warm eggs.

Mabel put them in her basket as she left the barn. When she turned to pull the door closed, she glimpsed blue in the snow-laden spruce trees beyond the yard. She strained her eyes and no longer saw blue, but instead red fur. Blue fabric. Red fur. A child, slight and quick in a blue coat, passing through the trees. A blink, and the little coat was gone and there was slinking fur, and it was like the flipping black-and-white pictures she had seen in a coin-operated illuminated box in New York City. Appearing and disappearing motion, child and woodland creature each a passing flicker.

Mabel walked toward the forest, slowly at first and then more quickly. She watched for the girl but had lost sight of her.

When she neared the edge of the woods and peered through the snowy boughs, she was startled to see the child only a hundred yards or so away. The girl was crouched, her back to Mabel, white-blond hair fanned down her blue wool coat. Wondering if she should call out, Mabel cleared her throat, and the sound startled the child. The girl stood, snatched a small sack from the snow, and sprinted away. As she disappeared around one of the largest spruce trees, she looked back over her shoulder and Mabel saw her glancing blue eyes and small, impish face. She was no more than eight or nine years old.

Mabel followed, struggling through the knee-deep snow and bending to crawl beneath the boughs. Snow toppled onto her knit hat and trickled down the collar of her coat, but she pushed through the branches. When she emerged and wiped the snow from her face, she discovered a red fox where the child had been. Its muzzle was pressed into the snow and its back was hunched, like a cat licking milk from a bowl. It jerked its head to the side and tore something with its teeth. Mabel was transfixed. Never had she been so close to a wild animal. A few strides and she could have touched the black-tipped, auburn fur.

The creature looked up at her, its head still low, its long black whiskers brushed back along the tapered snout. Then Mabel saw the blood and fought the urge to gag. It was eating some dead thing, and blood splattered the snow and smeared the fox's muzzle.

'No! You get! You get out of here!' Mabel waved her arms at the fox and then, feeling angry and brave, moved toward it. The animal hesitated, perhaps unwilling to abandon its meal, but then turned and trotted along the girl's path into the trees.

Mabel went to the place in the snow and saw what she hoped she wouldn't. A horrifying uncoiling — silvery intestines, tiny bones, blood and feathers.

She had not counted the chickens this morning. She looked more closely and saw it wasn't one of her hens after all, but instead a wild bird of some kind with mottled brown feathers and its head small and torn away.

She left the half-eaten thing and followed the tangle of child and fox footprints into the trees.

As she walked, a gust of wind knocked snow from the branches and blew cold into Mabel's face. It made breathing difficult, so she turned her head and went on into the woods. The wind flurried again, churning snow from the ground and trees into the air. Then it began to blow steadily, and Mabel leaned into it, her eyes downcast, but she could no longer see where she was going. A small blizzard whipped out of nothing. Mabel turned her back to the wind and snow and set out for home. She wasn't dressed for such an expedition, and surely the girl was too far away now. Even as she neared the barn, the blowing snow filled in her tracks, and those of the child and fox. She did not see the dead bird or flecks of blood as she passed by — they had vanished as well.

'I saw the child,' Mabel told Jack when he came in for dinner. 'The girl you described from the other night — I saw her behind the barn.'

'You sure?'

'Yes. Yes. There was a fox following her, and I thought it had killed one of our chickens, but it was something else, a wild bird.'

Jack squinted, as if cross.

'I did see her, Jack.'

He nodded and hung his coat on the hook beside the door.

'Have you heard anything about someone missing a child?' she asked. 'When you were in town yesterday, did you hear any news?'

'No. Nothing at all.'

'Did you ask? Did you tell anybody about her?'

'No. I didn't see much point. I figured she'd gone home or they would have gotten together a search party.'

'But she was here again today. Right near our barn. Why would she come here? If she is lost or needs help, why doesn't she just come to the door?'

He nodded sympathetically, but then changed the subject. He said he hadn't spotted anything but a cow moose with a calf. They would have to kill the chickens as soon as the sack of feed ran out; they hadn't enough money to buy more. The good news, he went on, was that he'd run into George at the hotel restaurant yesterday and had invited the Bensons to dinner the coming Sunday.

It wasn't until this last part that Mabel listened attentively. She was glad the Bensons were coming. Certainly Esther could tell her something about the child; she knew the families in the valley, and maybe she would know why a little girl would be wandering alone through the forest.

7

At night when Jack closed his eyes to sleep, tree branches and game trails and snowy cliffs were imprinted on his eyelids so that sleep merged with his long days spent hunting. For days now he had risen most mornings before light and gone out with his rifle and pack to look for moose, feeling like an imposter every time. He wasted most of one afternoon stalking what turned out to be a porcupine chewing on a low-hanging branch. He'd hiked up and down the Wolverine River, into the mountains, back and forth over the foothills, and he was sick to death of it.

He lay in bed longer than usual and considered not getting up at all. But George was right — if he managed to get a moose, he and Mabel could live off meat and potatoes until harvest. They'd run out of coffee, sugar, dried apples, powdered milk, lard. They'd have to kill the chickens and let the horse go thin. There would be no bolts of new fabric or little trinkets from town. It would be a miserable winter, but they wouldn't starve.

He got up and dressed and decided that tomorrow he would go to town to inquire about the mining job. It might be hard on his old body, but at least he would have something to show for it at the end of the day. Despite the snow, Betty had told him, the train was running and the mine was open. The Navy had upped its coal order, and the railroad had hired a crew of men to keep the tracks clear. No one knew how long the work would last, but for now they were still hiring.

Town was closed up on Sundays, though, so he might as well throw another day to the woods. He had until afternoon, when the Bensons would arrive for dinner. He left the cabin with his rifle and pack and walked the wagon trail toward the far field. The snow was well over the tops of his boots. He had no intention of hiking up toward the mountains, where it would be even deeper. He'd stick close to home and hope the snow had forced the animals down along the river.

The sky was overcast and leaden, and Jack was weighed down by it. He walked through the field, the snow slowing his way, and entered the woods, but his heart was not in it.

He had never thought himself a city boy. He'd worked hard all his life on the family farm in the Allegheny River valley. He knew how to handle tools and work animals and plow the earth. But back home the land had been farmed for generations and it showed in its soft curves and stately trees. Even the deer were half tamed, lazy and well fed as they grazed in the fallow fields. As a boy, he had strolled along the creek down by the family orchard. He picked stalks of grass and chewed on their tender ends. The very air had a soft greenness to it, not too cold, not too hot, a gentle breeze. He climbed the friendly branches of oaks and wandered along the backs of grassy knolls. Those aimless walks as a child were among his most peaceful memories.

This was nothing like back home. He didn't enjoy his solitude in these woods but instead was self-conscious and alert, fearing most of all his own ineptness. When he worked the ground, he stumbled over sprawling roots, axed tree after tree to extend his clearing by a few feet, and uncovered boulders so large he had to use the horse to drag them from the field. How could this land ever be farmed?

Wherever the work stopped, the wilderness was there, older, fiercer, stronger than any man could ever hope to be. The spindly black spruce were so dense in places you couldn't squeeze an arm between them, and every living thing seemed barbed and hostile — devil's club thorns that left festering wounds, stinging nettles that raised welts, and at times swarms of mosquitoes so thick he had to fight panic. In the spring when he first began felling trees and turning over the soil, mosquitoes rose from the disturbed earth in clouds. He wore a head net; it was hard to see, but without it he couldn't have endured. When he wiped the horse's flank with his hand, his palm came away bloody with engorged insects.

That was one blessing — it was too cold for mosquitoes now. Gone, too, was the lushness of summer, the thick green of cottonwood boughs, the broad leaves of cow parsnip, the flare of fireweed. Bare of foliage, the snowy benches and ravines rose to the mountains like a weather-bleached backbone. Jack watched through the naked trees and saw no sign of life. No moose, no squirrels, not a single songbird. A mangy raven passed overhead, but it flew steadily on as if seeking richer grounds.

When Jack told his brothers he was moving to Alaska, they envied him. God's country, they'd said. The land of milk and honey. Moose, caribou, and bears — game so thick you won't know what to shoot first. And the streams so full of salmon, you can walk across their backs to the other side.

What a different truth he found. Alaska gave up nothing easily. It was lean and wild and indifferent to a man's struggle, and he had seen it in the eyes of that red fox.

Jack came to a log and made a halfhearted attempt to brush the snow away before sitting on it. He laid the rifle across his knees, took off his wool hat, and ran his fingers through his hair. For some time he sat bent over, his elbows on the rifle, head in his hands. Doubt crouched over his shoulder, ready to take him by the throat, whispering in his ear, You are an old man. An old, old man.

If he were to fall dead in these woods, nothing would rush to his aid. The north wind would blow down from the glacier, the ground would stay frozen, and a red fox like the one he had looked in the eye might be the first to sniff at his dead body and take a nibble here and there. The ravens and magpies would come to tear away at his frozen flesh, maybe a pack of wolves would eventually find its way to his carcass, and soon he'd be nothing but a strewn pile of bones. His only hope would be Mabel, but then he thought of her struggling under his dead weight. He stood and shouldered his rifle.

He had only cried a few times in his adult life — when his mother died, and when he and Mabel lost that little baby. He wouldn't let himself now. He put one foot in front of the other and walked without seeing or feeling.

It was the quiet that pulled him out of his gloom. A quiet full of presence. He brought his head up.

It was the child. She was before him, just a few yards away. She stood atop the snow, arms at her sides, the hint of a smile at her pale lips. White fur trimmed her coat and leather boots. Her face was framed by the velvety brown of a sable hat, and she wore Mabel's red scarf and mittens. The child was dusted in crystals of ice, as if she had just walked through a snowstorm or spent a brilliantly cold night outdoors.

Jack would have spoken to her, but her eyes — the broken blue of river ice, glacial crevasses, moonlight — held him. She blinked, her blond lashes glittering with frost, and darted away.

'Wait!' he called out. He stumbled after her. 'Wait! Don't be afraid!'

He was clumsy, tripping over his own boots and kicking up snow. She sprinted ahead, but stopped often to look back at him.

'Please,' he called again. 'Wait!'

A sound came to Jack's ears like wind stirring dried leaves or snow blowing across ice, or maybe a whisper from far away. *Shhhhh*.

He did not call out again. He ducked beneath tree branches and waded through the snow as the girl led him farther and farther into the forest. He had to watch his feet to keep from tripping, but each time he looked up, she was waiting.

And then she wasn't. He stopped, squinted, and scanned the snow for her tracks. He saw no sign. Once again he became aware of the quiet, the strange calm of the forest.

From behind him came a high, chirpy whistle like a chickadee's call, and he turned, expecting to see a bird, or maybe the child. Instead, a bull moose stood not fifty yards away. It raised its head slowly, as if the massive, many-pointed antlers were a ponderous burden. Snow sprinkled its long nose and brown hackles. It swayed its antlers slowly side to side. Never had Jack seen such a magnificent animal. On lanky legs, it must have stood more than seven feet at the withers, and its neck was as stout as a tree trunk.

In his wonder, Jack nearly overlooked the obvious — this was his quarry. He had hunted only a few times as a boy, mostly rabbits and pheasants, although he had a vague memory of deer hunting with his cousins one cold, wet morning. This was different, though. This wasn't sport or boyhood adventure. This was livelihood, and yet he was so ill prepared. He couldn't remember much of that deer hunt, but he knew he had never taken a shot.

He expected the animal to spook as he chambered a cartridge in the rifle, but it was only mildly interested and went back to eating the tips of willow branches.

Jack rested his cheek against the wooden stock and tried to steady his grip. His exhalations rose as steam in the cold air and clouded his vision, so he held his breath, aimed for the moose's heart, and pulled the trigger. He never heard the explosion or registered the rifle's recoil. There was only the moment of impact, the animal staggering as if a great weight had come crashing down upon it, and then its fall.

He lowered the rifle to his side and took a few steps toward the moose. It kicked its legs and twisted its neck at a miserable angle. He chambered another round. The moose flailed in the snow, and for a second Jack looked into its rolling, wild eyes. He raised the rifle and shot a bullet into the animal's skull. It did not move again.

Jack's knees were unsteady as he leaned his rifle against a tree and went to the dead moose. He put his hands on its still-warm side and at last understood its size. Its antlers could have held Jack like a cradle, and his arms could not have circled its barrel chest. It had to weigh more than a thousand pounds, and that meant hundreds of pounds of good, fresh meat.

He'd done it. They had food for the winter. He would not go to the mine. He wanted to jump up and whoop and holler. He wanted to kiss Mabel hard on the lips. He wanted someone like George to smack him on the back and tell him well done.

He wanted to celebrate, but he was alone. The woods had a solemn air, and beneath the thrill in his own chest, there was something else. It wasn't guilt or regret. It was trickier. He grabbed the base of each antler to reposition the head. It was heavy, but by leaning into the antlers he was able to jostle the head and neck around. Then he took his knife out of his pack and sharpened it on a steel, all the while considering the feeling in his gut. At last he knew — it was the sense of a debt owed.

He'd taken a life, a significant life judging by the animal laid out before him. He was obliged to take care of the meat and bring it home in gratitude.

But it was something about the child, too. Without her, he never would have seen the moose. She led him here and alerted him when, like a clod, he had passed by the animal. She moved through the forest with the grace of a wild creature. She knew the snow, and it carried her gently. She knew the spruce trees, how to slip among their limbs, and she knew the animals, the fox and ermine, the moose and songbirds. She knew this land by heart.

As Jack knelt in the bloody snow, he wondered if that was how a man held up his end of the bargain, by learning and taking into his heart this strange wilderness — guarded and naked, violent and meek, tremulous in its greatness.

The work was beyond Jack's strength and experience. He had carved up chickens and a few sides of beef, but this wasn't the same. This was a colossal, fully intact wild animal sprawled in its own blood in the middle of the woods. His shot had been good, through the front shoulders and lungs. He needed to open the gut to let the viscera and heat escape before the meat spoiled, but it would be no easy task. The moose's legs, each weighing more than a hundred pounds, were cumbersome and in the way. He tried to lodge his shoulder beneath a hind leg to expose the belly, but it was too unwieldy. He took a section of rope from his pack and wrapped it around the moose's hind ankle. Using all his strength, he pulled it up and away, and then tied the rope to a tree behind the moose. This exposed the abdomen, though Jack feared that if the rope gave way, the leg could deliver quite a blow to the back of his head.

He sharpened his knife again, only because he wasn't sure how to begin. Daylight was wasting, so he plunged his knife into the belly, remembered he didn't want to puncture the gut sack and contaminate the meat, and pulled his knife back out slightly before cutting from stem to stern.

He was up to his elbows in blood and bowels when he heard something approaching through the forest. He thought it might be the child, but then he recalled how silently she traveled. A horse nickered. Jack stood, stretched his back and wiped his knife on his pants.

It was Garrett Benson, walking a horse through the trees.

'Hello there,' Jack called to him.

'I heard shots. You got one down?'

'Yep.'

'A bull?'

Jack nodded.

The boy tied the horse to a nearby tree. As he neared, his eyes widened.

'Holy Moses! That's one big moose.' Garrett went to the antlers, tried to stretch his arms from one side to the other and failed. 'Ho-ly Moses,' he said again more softly.

'Is he big?'

'Hell yeah.' A boy trying out a man's language. 'Hell yeah!'

'I didn't know. This is the first bull I've seen up close.'

Garrett took off his glove and held out his hand. 'Congratulations! He's a dandy!'

Jack wiped some of the blood onto his pant legs, and took the boy's hand.

'Thanks, Garrett. I appreciate that. I have to say, I wasn't expecting this.'

'No kidding. I mean, he's a jim-dandy!'

This was an aspect of Garrett he hadn't seen. The sulky smirk was gone and his boyish face beamed.

'I was riding the river, looking for places to put out traps, when I heard your rifle,' Garrett said. 'Bam. Bam. Two shots. That's always a good sign. I figured you had something down. But boy howdy, I sure didn't think it would be something like this.'

'He seemed good-sized to me,' Jack said.

The boy was quiet, reverent as he ran a hand down the antler bone.

'It's bigger than any I've ever seen,' he said. 'Sure bigger than anything I've ever shot.'

His opinion of Garrett improved. Not many thirteen-year-old boys could win a wrestling match with envy.

'Guess I've got my work cut out for me,' Jack said.

'It's a lot. But with two of us, it'll go all right.'

'Don't feel you're under any obligation to lend a hand.'

The boy took a knife from a sheath at his belt. 'I'd like to.'

'Well, it'd be much appreciated. Maybe you can just give me a few pointers, walk me through some of it. The truth is, I'm in over my head.'

'Looks like you're starting fine, pulling those guts out.' And the boy drew back the hide and peered inside the ribcage. 'Yeah, see there? You can just cut that away and it'll all come out slick.'

When they sliced away the heart and liver, each broader than a dinner plate, Jack slid them still wet into a gunnysack.

❋

For the next several hours, Jack and the boy worked at the moose. It was wearying. Jack's hands were cold and numb, and several times he nicked himself with the knife. His back and knees pained him. The sun slithered through the trees, the air cooled, the dead animal stiffened, but they kept at it. Sometimes Garrett offered advice about where to make a cut or how to separate a joint. He held the legs in place or pulled back the hide so Jack could work more easily. They joked some and talked some, but mostly just worked, and it was comfortable.

When they had cut away the legs and ribs, the tenderloin and backstrap and neck meat, Garrett fetched a handsaw from his saddlebags and they sawed the antlers from the skull.

'You've got to bring these back tonight,' Garrett said, 'so we can show everybody. They'll never believe it if we just tell them.'

Jack would have rather left the antlers and hauled more of the meat home, but he decided the quarters would be safe enough hanging in the trees for the night, until he could come back with the horse and wagon in the morning. He hated to disappoint the boy after all he'd done to help, so they strapped the antlers, vital organs, and some of the finest cuts of meat to Garrett's saddle.

'That's a good horse you got there,' Jack said as they secured the load. 'Doesn't balk at meat being strapped on.'

'I bought him myself, from a miner who used him for packing. I'm going to make him into a trapping horse.'

Bloody and tired, they made their way through the trees, Garrett leading the horse by a rope. Jack hadn't realized how close he was to his field, and from there they followed the wagon trail. It was nearing dark as they came into the yard.

'I sure am grateful for your help,' Jack said.

84

'I'd still be out there hacking away by myself.'

'Sure. Sure,' Garrett said. 'Wait 'till Mom and Dad see it.'

With Jack hobbling after him, Garrett rushed ahead.

'Looks like your folks beat you here,' Jack called out when he saw the sleigh in the yard. Just then, George and his two older sons came out of the barn.

'You're not going to believe this!' Garrett hollered. 'Jack shot the biggest damn moose you ever saw!'

8

As she prepared that morning for the Bensons' arrival, Mabel reminded herself of how it had been at their house for Thanksgiving. She would not fret about the stains on the tablecloth or the rough-plank floor that could never be scrubbed clean. Dinner would be well made, but not so much that it seemed she was trying to show them up. She didn't own any men's overalls and never intended to. Her long skirt and formal sleeves might be overdone, but they were all she had.

By late morning, the cabin was clean and the table set. She spent an hour or so fussing with her hair and rearranging the place settings. She was relieved when dusk came and the Bensons arrived on a sleigh pulled by one of their draft horses. George and the two older boys took the horse to the barn, while Esther unloaded some things from the sleigh and came to the door. There was no knock or opportunity to invite her in as Esther pushed past Mabel.

'Thank God, we're finally here.' She tossed a dusty grain sack on the table, nearly knocking a plate to the floor. 'I thought you could use some onions. We ended up with more than we need.'

She opened her coat and unloaded Mason jars from her oversized pockets. 'This one here's rhubarb jam. Terrific on sourdough pancakes. Did you get that sourdough to take? You've got to baby it some. Don't let it get too hot or too cold. Oh, this one here is blueberry-raspberry, I think. Might have some currants in there. Hard to tell. Sure it will be good, though. Oh, and here's some spicy pickled peas. George's favorite. Don't tell him I snuck you some.'

She took off her coat and threw it across the back of a chair. 'I feared those were going to freeze on the way over. I had to keep them up next to me, just to be sure.' She laughed and looked up at Mabel as if finally taking notice of her. She flung her arms around Mabel's shoulders, squeezed her tightly, and pressed her cold cheek up against Mabel's.

'Oh, it's so good to see you. I've been after George ever since Thanksgiving to get us over here. It's no good being a woman in this country, is it? Too many men, in my opinion. And of course I go off and have all boys myself, as if there weren't enough already.' Esther laughed and shook out her long braid. Then she looked around the cabin and Mabel felt a mixture of pride and shyness, sure that Esther was inspecting the curtains and clean kitchen and assessing her skills as a homemaker.

'Nice tight cabin you've got here. George says you've got some problems with the frost coming through, but that happens to us all on those cold days. Just crank up the fire, I say. Looks like you've got a sturdy woodstove. That makes all the difference.'

Esther stood next to the stove much the way

Jack did, with her hands spread wide to the heat. Mabel realized she had never really studied the stove before, just as she knew that Esther had yet to notice the carefully set table or the few photographs hanging on the walls. It was as if she were seeing a different cabin altogether.

'Jack hasn't come home yet. He should be here anytime, and then we can have dinner. Would you like some tea? I put some water on.'

'Oh, that would be terrific. I'm cold and damp from the ride over. I'm not complaining, though. I've always liked the snow.'

'I do know what you mean. Or at least I can say I am finally getting accustomed to it. There's been a lot to get used to here.'

Esther laughed. 'Isn't that the truth. I don't know if you ever get used to it really. It just gets in your blood so that you can't stand to be anywhere else.'

The women sat at the table, Mabel sipping her tea and Esther talking. Mabel waited for a chance to ask about the child, but Esther never seemed to take a breath.

'I know I'm going to talk your ear right off tonight. It's just so good to have a woman to visit with. Those boys, they do their best, but really they're happier if I keep quiet. Around the dinner table it's always grunt, harrumph, give me some more of this and that. Me, I like to have a good sit-down and talk. That's about all I really miss about town sometimes. Just a good conversation now and then. I don't even care too much what we talk about.'

She then went on to talk about last year's

crops and the railroad's plans to expand, how the bigwigs from back in Washington had come all the way to the Territory to inspect the tracks and pose for photographs, and how all of this mining and expansion would mean more demand for farm goods. Then she talked about the wolves that were running the river and how their younger son wanted to trap a few for the bounty money.

'That boy of mine hasn't showed up yet, has he? He's supposed to meet us here, coming by horse on the river.'

Then Esther asked about the fox Jack had seen in the fields. 'They'll snatch your chickens as soon as they get a chance,' she said. 'You ought to shoot him next time you see him.'

Never in her life had anyone suggested Mabel shoot something. She didn't mention she had never even picked up a gun. It seemed an embarrassing fact in front of Esther.

'Oh. Yes,' she said. 'I suppose so.' She was preparing to say that she had indeed seen the fox, with a little girl, right near their barn, but just then the door burst open.

'Well, call it beginner's luck,' George said. 'Jack's gone and shot the biggest moose in the entire valley. Gals, you've got to come and see this.'

Mabel tried to imagine what she would see in the barn as she followed George and Esther through the snow. She expected an entire animal, still in its skin and fur, still a moose. When she stepped into the lantern light and saw the disembodied antlers atop their bloody stump, she drew in a breath.

'Holy Moses!' Esther said.

'That's exactly what I said, Mom. Isn't it?' The boy turned to Jack. 'Ho-ly Moses.' His excited, youthful voice startled Mabel nearly as much as the scene before her.

'Those antlers got to go seventy inches across,' Garrett said, posing behind them like an African hunter with his trophy.

Suddenly Jack grabbed her about the waist from behind, swung her around to face him and for a second lifted her off her feet.

'I did it, love. I got our moose!' He kissed her quick and hard on the neck, like he was a much younger man, and she a younger woman. He smelled of wild animal and moonshine, and his eyes twinkled from drink. When he set her back down on the straw floor, she was disoriented.

'Oh,' was all she could manage.

The barn was a garble of talk and cheers while Jack told how he had heard something behind him, turned around and here was this bull moose just a few strides from his own field, and he had shot it, and then Garrett came along and he couldn't have done it without him. A bottle was passed none too discreetly among the men and the two older sons, and each held it up and called out 'Cheers!' while Garrett begged in vain for a swig.

'Not just yet, sprout,' Esther said, and then she took a drink herself, and the men all laughed.

Mabel kept quietly to herself. But Esther turned to her and held out the bottle.

'Oh come, come,' she said playfully. 'Drink a toast to your hunter!' So Mabel took the moonshine and held the cold glass to her mouth. The vapor alone was enough to make her cough, but she tipped it back and let the icy-hot liquid splash against her lips, and then she coughed and coughed and handed the bottle back while everyone laughed merrily.

'So no coal mine for you this year, eh, Jack?' George asked.

'Suppose not. I guess we'll have an old-fashioned Alaskan winter — moose and potatoes until we can stand them no more.'

Mabel smiled up at Jack and knew she should be glad, but she couldn't rid her mind of the sawed edge of skull bone at her feet.

Just when her hands were going numb with cold, everyone decided to go back to the cabin for dinner. Jack took the lantern down from its hook on a beam and wrapped an arm around Mabel's shoulders as they walked through the snow. Suddenly she was married to a northern hunter, a woodsman who gutted moose and toasted moonshine in a barn. Everything was topsy-turvy and unfamiliar.

The raucous party made its way into the cabin, all of them talking at once and shaking snow from their clothes. When Jack took off his coat, his arms were plastered with cracked, dried blood, and it was smeared across his shirt and pants. No one else noticed, but he looked at Mabel and down at himself. 'Suppose I should wash up before dinner.'

Garrett brought in a gunnysack and set it on the kitchen counter. From it Esther took a veined, rounded muscle the size of a bread loaf and Mabel realized it was the animal's heart. Esther began to slice it thinly with a knife.

'Heat up a pan, dear,' she said over her shoulder to Mabel. 'We'll have some of this with dinner. Fresh like this, there's nothing better than moose heart.'

Before Mabel could think or move, Esther had a cast-iron pan heating on the woodstove. 'Hand me one of those onions, will you? I'll cut one up to throw in the pan.'

The next hour was a blur to Mabel, her head swimming in the smell of frying meat and onions and the noise of boisterous talking. Someone must have mashed the boiled potatoes. Someone must have put out the bread and sliced carrots and opened a jar of onion relish. Before she understood all that had happened, they were crowded at the table, Garrett with his plate on his lap, and Mabel was cutting a piece of moose heart with a steak knife and taking her first bite.

'Tasty, isn't it?' Esther asked.

Mabel nodded and chewed and tried not to think about the muscle contracting and beating inside a moose's ribcage. She tasted seared flesh and blood like copper, and it wasn't as awful as she had feared.

As the talk dwindled and everyone finished

their meals, Esther looked across the table and said, 'Weren't you getting ready to tell me something? When George came busting through the door.'

'Oh, I can't recall just now.'

'We were saying something about the fox . . . ' Mabel was flustered.

'I did mean to ask you . . . but it can wait until later,' she said.

'Oh, no one's paying any attention. Out with it, then.' Esther waved impatiently. Mabel saw she was right, the men were telling hunting stories and oblivious to them.

'Well, I did mean to ask — do you know if there's a little girl living anywhere near our place? A little blonde girl?'

'A little girl? Let me think. There are only a few families in the valley right now. Most of the homesteads are run by single men who struck out with gold and such. The Wrights have a couple of girls, but they're redheads. Curly red hair, and cheeks like little apples. And they're nowhere near here. They're more the other side of us. Out your way here, well there are a couple of Indian camps up the river but they're usually there only in the summer, when the salmon are running. And, of course, there's not a single blonde among them.'

Esther rose and began gathering the dishes and stacking them on the table. The men paused in their conversation to hand her silverware and knives, but went back to their talk.

'The reason I ask,' Mabel said, leaning toward Esther and speaking quietly, 'is we had a child on our place the other night. Jack got up in the middle of the night and he saw a girl run through the trees. The next morning — we had built this little snowman, well, a little snow girl actually — and it was knocked over and the scarf and mittens were gone. It sounds silly, but I think the child must have done it. It's not that I mind, really. I would have given them to her if she needed them so. I'm just worried she was lost or something. Imagine, a little girl out in the woods in winter like that.'

Esther stopped gathering the dishes and focused on Mabel. 'Here, at your place, you're saying? You saw a little blond child just sprinting about?'

'Yes. Isn't that odd?'

'You're sure about that? Sure it wasn't just an animal or something?'

'No, I'm certain. We even saw her tracks. Jack tried to follow them for a while, but they just went around and around in the woods. Then the other day I saw her, in the trees beyond the barn.'

'That's the dardnest thing. I mean there's the Wright girls, but that's a good ten miles off, probably more . . . ' Esther's voice trailed off as she sat down. Then she looked across the table into Mabel's eyes and smiled gently.

'I don't mean to speak out of turn, Mabel, but this isn't an easy place to get along. The winters are long, and sometimes it starts to get to you. Around here, they call it cabin fever. You get down in the dumps, everything's off kilter and sometimes your mind starts playing tricks on you.' Esther reached across the table and put a hand over Mabel's. 'You start seeing things that you're afraid of . . . or things you've always wished for.'

Mabel let Esther hold her hand for a moment, but then pulled away.

'No, you don't understand. We saw her. And we both saw the tracks, and the mittens and scarf are gone.'

'Maybe it was an animal, or the wind. All sorts of explanations.'

The men had stopped talking. They were all looking at her.

'It's true. Isn't it, Jack? We saw her. In her little blue coat.'

Jack shifted in his chair and shrugged. 'It could have been anything,' he said.

'No. No.' Mabel was angry. 'It was a little girl. You saw her, too. And there were her footprints in the snow.'

'Well, maybe you could show us the tracks,' Esther said. 'Garrett here is a good tracker. He'd be able to tell something.'

Mabel wanted to yell or cry, but she spoke each word carefully.

'The tracks are gone. The blizzard last week covered them all.'

'Blizzard? It hasn't snowed in — ' Esther stopped and pinched her lips together.

Mabel stood and took the dishes to the counter, glad to be free of the table. Jack avoided her eyes as he went to the woodstove and added another log. She busied herself with dessert — sourdough biscuits topped with Esther's homemade jam. As Mabel worked, Esther came up behind her and gently squeezed her elbow. It was an expression of friendship and sympathy, but it left Mabel miserable.

Soon the cabin was again full of lighthearted talk about the seasons, working the land and storing food for the winter. George and Esther had Jack and the boys laughing with their wild stories of ill-mannered black bears, outhouse pranks, and stubborn horses. No one talked about the little girl, or the footprints that had vanished in the snow.

Darkness settled around the cabin and Mabel glanced out the window occasionally with the thought that she might see the child, but there was only her own reflection in the lamplight.

9

Jack started with a biscuit, one of Mabel's sourdough biscuits.

He had risen early to haul the meat home in the wagon, and after he'd hung it from a beam in the barn and put away the horse, he went in for lunch. When Mabel wasn't watching, he slipped a biscuit in his pocket and told her he was going out to work in the barn. Instead he went to the edge of the woods.

It seemed wrong to bait a child this way. As a boy he had enticed deer and raccoons with morsels of food, and his long patience often paid off. He once had a doe take a carrot right from his fingers before it fled to the trees. He never forgot the moment, after what seemed like hours of crouching and waiting, when the doe bent her long neck down to him and took the carrot. He'd felt the touch of her soft muzzle on his fingers.

He dusted the snow from a stump and set the biscuit down, wondering if the same curiosity was driving him. The child was not a raccoon to bait and trap. He worried about her. He'd felt foolish to admit it in front of the Bensons, but the little girl had come again and again to their homestead, and he did not know what brought her. Maybe she was in need but too shy or too frightened to knock on their door. Perhaps she was lonely and sought only companionship, but maybe it was something more urgent. Shelter. Clothing. Food. Help of some kind. The thought preoccupied him, and so he reached out to her the only way he knew how. For the next several hours, Jack worked outdoors, stacking wood and shoveling paths. All the while he watched out of the corner of his eye, but the biscuit went untouched and the forest remained quiet.

The next morning, he saw where tracks approached the stump, wove this way and that where the girl must have hidden behind a spruce tree, a bush. The biscuit remained on the stump.

That evening, he searched the cabin, looking for other possible bait. He picked up tins and opened boxes until Mabel finally asked what he was up to.

'Nothing,' he mumbled, guilty with his lie. She would disapprove of his efforts, or make suggestions of her own, but he must do it his own way. As a youngster, he had never had a deer or wild bird come within reach when his friends were milling about.

More than that, talk of the child seemed to upset Mabel. She had some spirit these days and a brightness in her eyes that eased Jack's heart. The time she spent with Esther was good. But whenever they discussed the little girl, she became agitated. He often caught her looking out the window.

The same traits that as a young woman had made her so alluring now made her seem unwell. She was imaginative and quietly independent, but over the years this had settled into a grave melancholy that worried him. Until he knew more about this little girl and her situation, he felt it best to keep it under his hat.

❄

When the sourdough biscuit, bits of peppermint candy from town, even a piece of one of Mabel's pies that Jack had pilfered, had all failed, he was at a loss for what to try next. He thought back to the scarf and mittens the girl had taken, and wondered if she was cold and in need of more clothes. His brief glimpses of her made him doubt this. She seemed at home in the snow in her furs and wool.

Then, on a trip to town, he saw a miniature porcelain doll on a shelf in the general store. The doll had long, straight blond hair, not unlike the girl's, and it wore the brightly colored dress of a European villager, perhaps Swedish or Dutch. It was too much money for something so frivolous, but he ignored his conscience, bought it on credit, and hid it in his coat pocket. When he got home, he found he couldn't wait until the next morning, so, although it was after dark, he took it with him when he went to feed and water the animals.

He brought the lantern from the barn and walked to the stump where the other offerings had gone untouched. He took the doll from his pocket. Maybe he and Mabel had truly lost their minds. Cabin fever — wasn't that what Esther called it?

Jack raised his voice to the cold night and

101

called out as gently as he could manage.

'This is for you. Are you out there?'

His voice was soft and croaky. He cleared his throat, and called out again.

'I don't know if you're out there or if you can hear me, but we want you to have this. Just something I picked up in town. Well, then, good night.'

He hoped he might see her, or hear a birdsong from the trees, but there was only the cold and dark. He shifted from one foot to the other, shoved a hand into his coat pocket, and at last turned his back, leaving the porcelain doll propped in the snow on the stump.

When he returned to the cabin, Mabel had warmed water on the stove for him to wash. Steam rose as she poured the water into a basin. Jack took off his shirt, put a towel over his shoulders, splashed water onto his face, and soaped up his beard. Behind him he could hear Mabel bustling in the kitchen.

'Oh,' she said quietly.

Jack brought his head up from the basin and wiped his face with the towel.

'What is it?'

'The window. Do you see?'

As they watched, thick frost unfurled in feathers and swirls across the glass, slowly spreading from the center toward the corners. Lacy white vines grew in twists and loops, and icy flowers blossomed. Within seconds the window that had been clear glass was covered in patterns of overlaying frost like fine etching.

'Maybe it's from the steam,' Mabel said in a near whisper. She pressed the palm of her hand against the glass, and her warm skin melted the ice. She curled a fist, rubbed a small circle in the center of the window, and looked through.

'Oh. Oh,' she gasped and leaned closer.

'What, Mabel? What is it?'

'It's her.' She turned, her hand at her throat. 'Her little face, right there in our window. She had fur all around her head, like a wild animal.'

'It's her hat. Her marten hat, with the flaps tied under her chin.'

'But she's there now. Go look.'

'She runs fast, even on the snow,' he said, but Mabel was handing him his boots and coat and opening the door.

When he stepped outside, his wet beard and hair stiffened with ice. He walked around the side of the cabin, but saw only what he expected — snow and trees and night. The child was gone.

The next morning Jack nearly stepped on the small basket outside their door.

'Jack? What's that you — '

'I'm not sure.' He set it on the table, and he and Mabel stood over it. It was made of birch bark, its seams crudely sewn with some kind of dried plant root. The basket fit perfectly in two cupped hands and it was heaped with purple berries. Jack took one, rolled it between his finger and thumb, sniffed it, then put it to his tongue.

'Oh, Jack, you don't know what it might be.'

'It's a blueberry. Tastes like a blueberry.'

She frowned, but he put one to her mouth and she hesitantly tasted it.

'You're right. They're wild blueberries. Frozen like little marbles,' she said.

She sat at the table and touched the bark edges tentatively, as if the basket might break beneath her fingers. 'Was it her?' she asked. 'Did she bring these for us?'

'I guess she knew we were having pancakes for breakfast,' Jack said. Mabel did not smile.

'I'll get some wood for the fire,' he said.

Jack followed his old tracks past the woodpile to the stump at the edge of the forest. The doll was gone. The child's small footprints came toward the stump, went once around, and then straight back into the trees. Each track barely dented the snow, as if she weighed no more than a feather.

When he brought an armload of wood inside, Mabel was cooking pancakes. She dotted a few of the wild blueberries in each one, and they ate them at the table, the small basket between them. They did not talk about the child, not until the table was cleared and Jack was preparing to go back outdoors.

'I'm going to haul some wood from the east field. Everyone says we'll have a cold spell soon.'

'How can you?' Mabel's voice was hushed and trembling. 'How can you eat your breakfast and go into the day as if none of this has happened?'

'It's winter, and we need firewood.'

'She's a child, Jack. You might not be able to admit it to the neighbors, but you've seen her, too. You know she's out there.'

He sighed. He finished lacing up his boots, and then went to Mabel and put his hands on her shoulders.

'What can we do?'

'We must do something.'

'I just don't know what. I think she's all right.'

Mabel narrowed her eyes. 'How can she be all right? A child, wandering around in the middle of winter?'

'I think she's warm. And she must know how to get food. Look at the berries, and that little basket. She knows her way out there, probably better than either of us.'

'But she's just a child. A little girl.'

He thought Mabel would cry, and he wanted to be anywhere else. It was wrong and cowardly, and he'd done it before — when Mabel lost the baby and shook with grief, when the relatives whispered harsh words, when the Bensons asked about the child in the woods. But it was like the need to take a breath. The urge was too strong, and without saying another word, Jack left the cabin.

10

Snowflakes and naked babies tumbled through her nights. She dreamed she was in the midst of a snowstorm. Snow fell and gusted around her. She held out her hands and snowflakes landed on her open palms. As they touched her skin, they melted into tiny, naked newborns, each wet baby no bigger than a fingernail. Then wind swept them away, once again just snowflakes among a flurry of thousands.

Some nights she woke herself with her own crying. Others, Jack gently shook her. 'Wake up, Mabel. You're having a nightmare. Wake up.'

In the light of day, her dreams were drained of their nightmarish quality, and they seemed whimsical and strange, but the taste of loss remained in her mouth. It was difficult to focus on her tasks and she often drifted aimlessly through her own mind. A faint memory emerged again and again — her father, a leather-bound fairy-tale book, a snow child alive in its pages. She couldn't clearly recall the story or more than a few of the illustrations, and she began to worry over it, letting her thoughts touch it again and again. If there was such a book, could there be such a child? If an old man and woman conjured a little girl out of the snow and wilderness, what would she be to them? A daughter? A ghost?

She had sought reasonable explanations. She asked Esther about children who lived nearby. She urged Jack to inquire in town. But she had also taken note of those first boot prints in the snow — they began at the vanished snow child and ran from there into the woods. No tracks came into the yard.

Then there was the frost that crystallized on the window as she and Jack had watched, and the snowstorm that had blown her back toward home when she found the dead bird. Most of all, there was the child herself, her face a mirror of the one Jack had sculpted in the snow, her eyes like ice itself. It was fantastical and impossible, but Mabel knew it was true — she and Jack had formed her of snow and birch boughs and frosty wild grass. The truth awed her. Not only was the child a miracle, but she was their creation. One does not create a life and then abandon it to the wilderness.

A few days after the basket had appeared on their doorstep, Mabel decided to write to her sister, who still lived in the family home in Philadelphia. Perhaps the book was in the attic along with the trunks of clothes and keepsakes that had accumulated there over the years. She sat down at the table, a loaf of bread baking in the oven, and was comforted by the act of writing. It gave her a rational purpose. Either the book was there or it wasn't, but if her sister found it and sent it to her, Mabel was certain it would be of consequence. The book would tell her the fate of the old man and woman, and the child they had borne of snow.

'Dearest sister, I hope this letter finds you well. We are settling into winter here at the homestead,' she began.

She went on to describe the snow and mountains and their new friends the Bensons. She asked about her sister's children, now grown, and the family home. Then, as casually as she could, she inquired about the book.

'Do you remember it, dear Ada? It was one of my favorites for some years of my childhood. I believe it was bound in blue leather, but I remember little of the story — not even the title. I am sure it is an impossible task I am asking of you, but trying to recall the details of the book has become such a distracting nuisance to my mind. It's like having a person's name on the tip of your tongue, nearly remembered but not quite. I only hope by some chance you know the book I am thinking of, and better yet know where to find it in all that jumble of trunks in the attic.'

Mabel also asked if her sister could send some new pencils, as she intended to pick up her former pastime and had only a few stubs in her drawing box.

She sealed the letter, set it aside, and went to the stove. She pulled the loaf of bread from the oven, thumped it softly to see if it was done, then slid it back into the heat. She glanced toward the window and saw Jack at the woodpile. And then she saw the little girl.

She stood in the trees just beyond. Jack hadn't noticed her. He had taken off his coat and was splitting log after log, swinging the heavy maul above his head and bringing it down with a loud crack into the wood. The girl watched and then crept closer, hiding behind a birch tree and peeking around it. She wore the same coat of blue wool trimmed in white fur. Beneath the coat, Mabel could now see, was a light blue flower-print dress that came to below her knees, and high boots or moccasins made of some kind of animal skin and fur.

Mabel paced at the window. Should she go to the door and call out to Jack, or wait until he saw the girl himself? She was so near she hated to frighten her away. Then she saw Jack raise his head and look at the girl. The child was less than a dozen yards from him. Mabel held her breath. She could see Jack speaking, but couldn't hear his words. The child was motionless. Jack stepped closer, a hand extended toward her. The girl stepped back, and then Jack was speaking again. It was difficult to see from the window, but Mabel thought she saw the girl raise a hand in a red mitten, and give a small wave. Mabel's breath fogged the glass. She rubbed it with her hand just in time to see the girl turn and run into the trees. Jack stood with his arms at his sides, the maul at his feet, not moving. Mabel hurried to the door and pulled it open.

'Go, Jack! Go! Go after her!' Her voice was louder and shriller than she'd meant. He startled, then looked from Mabel to the woods and back again. At last he charged after the girl,

110

first at a steady walk, then picking up his pace and trotting through the snow. His legs looked long and awkward as his big boots thumped beneath him. Nothing like the nimble sprint of the girl.

She waited at the window. Occasionally she went to the door, opened it, and looked out in all directions, but the yard and woods beyond were empty. Minutes went by, then an hour and another. She considered dressing in her winter boots and coat and going after them, but she knew that was not wise. Night came quickly on these short winter days.

As the cabin darkened, Mabel lit the oil lamps, put more wood on the fire, and tried to stop her rhythmic pacing. She thought of her mother, how often she had paced and wrung her hands when Mabel's father didn't come home from some late meeting at the university. She thought of the wives of soldiers, gold miners and trappers, drunks and adulterers, all waiting long into the night. Why was it always the woman's fate to pace and fret and wait?

Mabel finally made herself sit by the wood-stove with her sewing and tried to lose herself in the stitches. She didn't know she had fallen asleep in the chair until Jack came in. His beard and moustache were caked with ice and his pant legs were stiff and snow-covered. He didn't bother to take off his boots or stomp the snow from them but stumbled to the woodstove and held out his bare hands. He hadn't been wearing gloves when she'd sent him after the girl. She took his hands in her own. Jack cringed at her touch.

'Are you frostbit?'

'I don't know. Cold, that's for sure.' His words slurred together, either from the ice in his moustache or from fatigue. Mabel rubbed his hands to move warm blood to the tips of the fingers.

'Did you catch up with her? What did you see?'

He slid his hands out of hers and pulled some of the ice from his moustache and beard. He took off his boots and then his coat and pants, which he hung from nails behind the woodstove to dry. The cabin smelled of warm, wet wool.

'Did you hear me? What did you find?'

He didn't look up when he spoke, but instead turned from her and stumbled to their bedroom. 'Nothing. I'm tired, Mabel. Too tired to talk.'

He climbed beneath the covers and was soon snoring softly, leaving Mabel alone again by the woodstove.

11

Jack had always considered himself if not brave then at least competent and sure. He was wary of true danger, of flighty horses that could break your back and farm tools that could sever limbs, but he had always scoffed at the superstitious and mystical. Alone in the depths of the wilderness, however, in the fading winter light, he had discovered in himself an animal-like fear. What shamed him all the more was that he could not name it. If Mabel had asked what terrified him when he followed the girl into the mountains, he could only have answered with the timid uncertainty of a child scared of the dark. Disturbing thoughts whirled through his brain, stories he must have heard as a boy about forest hags and men who turned into bears. It wasn't the girl that frightened him as much as the strange world of snow and rock and hushed trees that she navigated with ease.

The girl had deftly jumped logs and scampered through the woods like a fairy. He had gotten close enough to notice the brown fur of her hat and the knee-high leather moccasins that bound her feet. By the woodpile, when he had spoken to her, he had even caught sight of her blond eyelashes and the intensely blue eyes and, when he asked if she liked the doll, he saw her smile. The shy, sweet smile of a little girl.

But then she had become a phantom, a silent blur. As Jack tried to follow her, an icy fog moved through the forest. Minute crystals of ice filled the air and gathered as hoar frost along the tree branches and on his lashes. He could see only a few feet into the mist. He stopped occasionally, bent with his hands on his knees while sweat froze at his brow. He tried to silence his heavy breathing, but then all he heard was the snow creaking beneath his boots. The child made no sound. He heard twigs crack, only to watch a snowshoe hare bound through the alders, and later, as night closed in, an owl hooted from far away. He never heard the girl. At times he wasn't sure he was even following her anymore but instead blindly thrashing through the trees like a bewitched, crazy man. Then he would see her, just ahead, as if she wanted to be seen.

He lost track of how far he had come or how long he had been gone, yet he kept on, past their 160-acre homestead, up into the foothills of the mountains where he had hunted moose and beyond, to where the trees dwindled to alpine birch shrubs and Labrador tea. He followed a ridge that looked down over the snowy river valley and followed her still higher until he crested a rise and found himself in a narrow mountain gorge with steep shale cliffs.

An eerie gust of wind came down the gorge. Farther up he could see a waterfall of ice pouring off the mountain between the rocky cliffs. Below him, the creek trickled and bubbled beneath ice

114

and wound its way through rock and willow. The girl, though, was nowhere to be seen.

He cautiously followed her tracks up the ravine, and then they disappeared into the snowy hillside. It didn't make sense, yet that is what he saw — her trail didn't continue up the hill or along the creek; it ran into the side of the mountain. Then he noticed what looked like a small door set into the hillside beneath a rounded dome of snow. Jack crouched behind a boulder, a cold sweat on the back of his neck. He could go to that little door and call out to the girl, but he didn't. What did he expect to find? A fairy-tale beast that holds young girls captive in a mountain cave? A cackling witch? Or nothing at all, no child, no tracks, no door, only insanity bared in the untouched snow? That is perhaps what he feared the most, that he would discover he had followed nothing more than an illusion.

Rather than face that possibility, Jack turned his back on the little door and set out for home. For a while, he followed the tracks. At times there were two sets — the child's small prints and his larger ones. Other times there were just his own, and Jack knew he had probably destroyed the child's with his big boots as he followed her. Still, the sight of his solitary tracks winding through the trees left him uneasy. As it grew darker, he feared the meandering trail would keep him in the woods into the coldest, blackest hours of the night, so he left the trail and headed directly toward the riverbed below. From there he could follow the Wolverine back to their homestead and, he hoped, be at the cabin within an hour.

But the route proved difficult as it pulled him down into steep ravines where the snow was well over his knees and forced him through a dense forest of black spruce that threatened to disorient him. He didn't recognize the river when he reached it, not until he had walked partway out onto the ice and heard the roar beneath him. He eased backward until he was sure he was on firm ground, and then he walked downstream, relying on the vague outline of the riverbed to guide him toward their homestead.

He expected Mabel would be waiting for him and wanting answers. It was reasonable, and yet it grated on him. He was tired, aching and surely frostbit, and he had nothing to offer her but a tired old man who quaked in his boots at a child's door.

The next morning Jack woke to the sound of Mabel's knocking about the cabin. Dishes clattered, a broom swished, bumps and thumps — these were the unmistakable sounds of her irritation. Jack eased himself out of bed.

They each went about their chores, but Mabel's anger seemed only to grow, and her footsteps fell heavier and her sighs more audible. Eventually, she would relent, but the breach would become wider and deeper. Jack knew this, yet he could not find the strength to stop it. He escaped to the barn and the woodpile and left Mabel with her sighs.

For the next several days, he worked in the barn or yard, though he knew he should be burning stump piles in the fields. He watched the trees and searched the snow for tracks. If the girl comes back, he told himself, I won't run after her. I won't frighten her away.

So when the girl appeared at Jack's elbow nearly a week later, he did not give chase but instead went about his work as if she wasn't there. He stacked split wood beside the barn, one piece after another. Eventually the girl sat on a round of spruce and watched. When dusk fell, Jack went into the barn to put away the maul and ax. The girl followed, just a few steps behind, and stopped at the barn door. When he came back out, she was there, watching him with her wide blue eyes. He walked past without acknowledging her. Over his shoulder he called, 'Time for supper. Let's go in.'

And the girl followed. Jack held the cabin door open for her. She entered gingerly, as if the floor might fall out from under her, but all the same she came in. As she stepped across the threshold and into the warmth, the thin layer of frost on her coat and hat melted. Jack watched the bits of ice on her moccasins dwindle to nothing and the frost on her eyelashes turn to droplets. The child's eyes were left wet, as if she had been crying.

Mabel was working at the kitchen counter, her back to them. Jack closed the door.

'I think we might need some more wood on

the fire — ' she said, turning with a pot of boiled potatoes in her hands. She looked up and saw the little girl beside Jack and her mouth formed a little circle as if she might make a sound, but instead she dropped the pot of potatoes.

'Oh, oh.' Mabel stared at her feet, soaking wet and covered in bits of potato. 'Oh dear.' The girl had stepped back, startled at the clamor of the pot hitting the floor but now, in the silent cabin, she let out a little giggle and put her red mittens over her mouth.

Mabel quickly scooped the potatoes back into the pot and used a towel to soak up the water. All the while her eyes never left the child.

'I'll take your coat for you,' Jack said.

The girl took off her mittens, and as he reached to take them, she drew something out of her coat pocket. It was a small animal, white fur and black nose, and Jack was prepared for it to writhe and jump. But it was a lifeless pelt, less than a foot long snout to tail.

'An ermine?'

The child nodded and held it out to him. Beneath the fur its dried skin crinkled like thin parchment paper. Mabel came to his side and touched the tiny empty eyelids and the bristly whiskers. She ran her fingers down the white fur to the black-tipped tail.

'That's a nice little pelt,' he said and went to give it back to the child. But she shook her head.

'Put it back in your pocket so you don't forget it.'

Again the barest shake of her head, a small smile.

'She wants us to have it,' Mabel whispered.

'Is that it? Is it for us?'

A smile.

'Are you sure?' he said.

A vigorous nod.

Jack hung the ermine from a hook by the kitchen window and smoothed the back of his hand down the white fur. Mabel bent down toward the child. 'Thank you,' she said.

'Here you are.' He pulled a chair out from the table. 'You can sit here.'

The girl sat, coat and mittens piled on her lap, the marten-fur hat still on her head.

'Are you sure I can't take those for you?' he asked.

The girl didn't speak.

'All right. Suit yourself.'

As Mabel put a plate of moose steaks in the middle of the table, she glanced at Jack, widened her eyes questioningly and raised her eyebrows. He shrugged almost imperceptibly.

'I suppose we won't be having potatoes, will we?' Mabel said. She looked at the girl and smiled. 'We do have some of those awful sailor biscuits. I guess that'll have to do. And some boiled carrots.'

12

Never had Mabel imagined the little girl would be sitting before them, at their own kitchen table. How had this come to be? The moment had the surreal fast-and-slow movement of a dream. She set an empty plate in front of the child and fought the urge to grab her hand, to touch her and see if she was real. She and Jack sat in their chairs. He folded his hands in his lap and bowed his head. Mabel did as well, but could not stop looking at the girl.

She was even smaller than she had appeared at a distance, and the chair back towered around her. With her coat on, the child had looked almost roly-poly as she sprinted through the trees, but now Mabel saw her thin arms and small shoulders. She wore that same cotton dress with tiny flowers on it, but Mabel could see now that it was a summer dress for a grown woman. Beneath it, she wore a long-underwear shirt that was too small; the sleeves did not reach her thin wrists. The girl's hair was white-blond, but when Mabel studied it, she saw that woven and twisted among the strands were gray-green lichens, wild yellow grasses, and curled bits of birch bark. It was strange and lovely, like a wild bird's nest.

'Dear Lord,' Jack began. The girl did not close her eyes or bow her head but, unblinking, watched Jack. Delicate lips, the hint of bones beneath rounded child cheeks, a small nose — Mabel found herself recalling the face Jack had carved into the snow. The child's face was gentle and young, but there was a fierceness as well, in the flash of blue in her eyes and the point of her little chin.

'We thank you for this food and for this land . . . ' Jack paused. Mabel couldn't remember him choosing his words so carefully for a blessing. 'We ask you to be with us as we . . . share this meal, with each other and with . . . with this child who has joined us.'

The girl opened her eyes wider and glanced from Jack to Mabel, her lips pressed together.

'Amen.'

'Amen,' repeated Mabel. The girl watched, her hands bundled in her coat, as Mabel served moose steaks onto each plate. Then she leaned forward slightly, as if to inspect the meat.

'Oh. Let me get those awful crackers.' Mabel stood and walked behind the girl, pausing for a moment to take in her fragrance — fresh snow, mountain herbs, and birch boughs. Mabel allowed her hand to slide along the back of the chair, her fingertips barely touching the girl's hair. Perhaps it was not a dream after all.

As soon as Jack and Mabel began to eat, the girl did as well. She picked up the sailor cracker, sniffed it loudly, and then set it down again. Mabel laughed. 'I agree wholeheartedly,' she said and set her own cracker aside.

The girl then picked up the meat with her hands, smelled it, and bit into it. When she saw

Jack and Mabel watching, she put it down. Jack used his knife and fork to slice pieces off his own steak and eat them.

'It's all right, dear,' Mabel said. 'You eat it any way you want.'

The girl hesitated, then picked it up in her hands again. She didn't devour it the way Mabel expected, like a starving pup, but instead ate it daintily, little nibbles here and there, but eating every bit, even a line of gristle that ran through it. Then the child picked up each slice of boiled carrot and carefully ate it. Her plate was clean even as Jack and Mabel continued to cut their meat.

'Would you like some more? No? Are you sure? There's plenty here.'

Mabel was alarmed to notice how flushed the child's cheeks had become. Her eyes had gone glassy as if from fever.

'You're too warm, child,' Mabel said. 'Let me take your coat. Your hat.'

The girl shook her head firmly. Along the bridge of her nose, tiny beads of sweat formed and, as Mabel watched, a large droplet slid down the child's temple.

'Open the door,' Mabel whispered to Jack.

'What?'

'The door. Prop it open.'

'What? It's well below zero.'

'Please,' she begged. 'Can't you see? It's much too hot in here for her. Go — open the door!'

So Jack did, and he wedged a piece of firewood in the doorway to keep it open.

'There, child. That will cool you. Are you well?'

The girl's eyes were wide, but she nodded.

'Do you have a name?' Mabel asked. Jack frowned. Perhaps she pushed too quickly, but she couldn't help herself. She was desperate to seize the child, to hold her and not let go.

'I'm Mabel. This is Jack. Do you live nearby? Do you have a mother and father?'

The girl seemed to understand but gave no expression.

'What's your name?' Mabel asked.

At this the child stood. Her coat was on before she reached the doorway.

'Oh, don't leave. Please,' Mabel said. 'I'm sorry if I asked too many questions. Please stay.'

But the girl was already out the door. She did not seem angry or frightened. As her feet hit the snow, she turned back to Mabel and Jack.

Thank you, she said, her voice a quiet bell in Mabel's ear. And then she slipped away into the night with her long blond hair trailing down her back. Mabel remained in the open door until the cold air seeped in around her feet.

13

The girl appeared and disappeared without warning, and it unnerved Jack. There was something otherworldly in her manners and appearance, her frosty lashes and cool blue stare, the way she materialized out of the forest. In ways she was clearly just a little girl, with her small frame and rare, stifled giggles, but in others she seemed composed and wise, as if she moved through the world with knowledge beyond anything Jack had encountered.

The child had not shown herself for several days when Garrett came to visit. It was a snowy afternoon, nearly dark even at midday, when the boy rode his horse in from the river.

'Hello!' he called out to Jack. The boy dismounted and dusted snow from his hat brim.

Several times now Garrett had ridden through on his way home from his trapline. If he'd caught anything, he'd show it to Jack, and then for an hour or so he would follow Jack around while he worked. He would help stack wood or move pallets. Jack would ask him about trapping and hunting, but mostly the boy just talked without prompting. Ever since they'd field dressed the moose together, the boy was different, as if eager to be friends. He even seemed to seek Jack's approval.

'You bringing anything home today?' Jack asked with a nod toward Garrett's horse.

'Naw. Nothing. Missed a coyote that was too smart to come into my set. You leave any bit of scent behind, anything that rouses their suspicion, and you might as well call it a day. They won't come near your trap. Sometimes I think they're harder to catch than just about . . . '

But Jack wasn't listening. Over Garrett's shoulder, through the falling snow, he spotted the little girl at the edge of the trees. She peered around the thick trunk of a cottonwood.

'You see something?' Garrett asked. He turned to follow Jack's eyes, but the girl was gone.

'Thought I did,' Jack said, 'but it was just my old eyes playing tricks on me.'

The next day when Jack was alone in the yard, the child approached silently and sat on a stump while he worked. A few times she opened her mouth as if to speak, but then closed it again.

Jack was certain her visits were driven by more than just curiosity or hunger. It was something akin to sorrow or weariness, like a bruise in the skin beneath her eyes.

While Mabel continued to prod at the dinner table, sneaking in questions here and there that went unanswered, Jack chose to watch and wait. Eventually she would make her purpose known. For now, he enjoyed her company. Only a few times did she venture into their cabin, and always she refused to stay the night. But she

126

brought them her little gifts: the white ermine pelt, the basket of berries, an arctic grayling cleaned and ready for the frying pan. Jack came to see that the dead snowshoe hare, strangled and left on their doorstep — that, too, had been a gift from the child. He regretted throwing it into the woods.

Then the day came when she appeared without gifts but instead with the questions Jack had seen in her eyes. She arrived early, just after he had finished breakfast and stepped outside into the dim morning, and she followed him around the barn and yard like a shadow.

As he closed the barn door, he felt her small cool hands clasping at his wrist. She tugged at his arm so that he bent to her.

Will you promise?

Her voice small and frightened.

And before he knew the implications of such a promise, he was following her through the snow. The child ran as if alarmed, as if pursued, but when Jack fell behind, she slowed and led him toward the mountains and up the alpine slopes.

He followed as best he could. He was a huffing, slow-footed oaf next to her. Her steps were so light and sure. The way seemed much longer than before, when he had chased her through the woods at night. He sensed the girl's impatience. She paused just until he reached her, then sprinted away again before he had a chance to catch his breath. He no longer paid attention to where they were going, but only knew it was up. The long, slow climb cramped his calves and ached in his lungs. The solid gray sky pressed down on him. He was weak and heavy. Each time they reached the top of a ridge he thought, This is it. We've finally arrived. But then they would continue higher, to the next ridge, and on again. The snow was deeper than before and he slogged through while the girl seemed to float across it.

Are you well?

She stood above him.

We're almost there, she said.

Fine, he said. I'm fine. Lead the way.

He tried to smile but knew it was more like a grimace.

I'm not as young as I once was, but I'll get there.

The girl seemed to make an effort to go slower, to show him where he could place his feet and where he could grab at a tree branch to pull himself up a ledge.

Then he saw rocky cliffs ahead of them and heard the trickle of a creek beneath the ice. He followed the girl up the ravine. Soon they were among a clump of large spruce trees that seemed out of place so high up the mountain, and the large boughs and immense trunks gave a sheltered feeling to the narrow valley. She slowed here without looking at Jack and seemed reluctant to go on. Then she stopped and pointed toward a snow-covered heap beneath one of the trees.

What is it?

The girl didn't answer. She only pointed, so Jack walked past her to the heap. He brushed away some of the snow and uncovered a canvas tarp. He looked at the girl again, questioning, but she turned away.

When he pulled back the tarp, a dozen voles scuttled away into the snow, and he saw a man's neck where blond hair met a woodsman's wool coat. Jack's heart beat loudly in his ears. He put his hand to the broad shoulder, and it was like shoving a cottonwood log, cold and frozen to the ground. Jack stepped around the corpse. He saw now where the voles had made their small tunnels through the snow, spreading in a maze in all directions from the dead man. He didn't want to, but he dusted the snow off the face and head, then off his side and chest. The corpse lay on its side, curled up like a child, but it was no child. He was a big man, much taller and broader in the shoulders than Jack, and there was no doubt he was gone to this world. His milky eyes, sunk back into his skull, stared blankly ahead. His skin was a ghastly blue. Ice crystals grew on his face and clothes and along his blond hair and long, bushy beard. The rodents had begun to gnaw away his frozen cheeks and nose and the tips of his fingers, and their droppings were everywhere.

Jesus. Christ almighty.

Then Jack remembered the girl. He turned and she was there at his elbow, peering down at the frozen man.

Who is he? Jack asked.

My papa, she whispered.

What happened?

I tried. I tried and tried.

Jack looked into her eyes, and it was like watching water gather on lake ice. No sloppy dribble, no sobs. Only a quiet pool on the blue.

I pulled on his arm and said, Please, Papa. Please. But he wouldn't come. He only sat in the snow.

Why wouldn't he move?

The girl's chin trembled as she spoke.

He told me Peter's water kept him warm, but I knew it wouldn't. I wanted to make him warm. I held his hands and then I held his face, just like this.

And the girl reached down and cupped the dead man's cheeks in her small hands with the tenderness of a daughter's touch.

I tried, but he was colder and colder and colder.

Jack went to one knee beside the corpse and caught the strong smell of liquor. A green glass bottle was clenched in a frozen claw of a hand. Jack's stomach turned. How could a man do this, drink himself to death in front of his child?

Why couldn't I make him warm? the child asked.

Still on one knee, Jack reached up and took hold of her small shoulders.

You aren't to blame. Your papa was a grown man, and no one could have saved him but himself. This is not your fault.

He pulled the canvas back over the dead man.

When did this happen?

The day the snow first came, the child said.

He knew when. It was the night he and Mabel had built the little snow figure in the yard.

130

Nearly three weeks ago.

Why didn't you ask for help?

I kept Fox away. I threw stones and yelled. And I wrapped Papa so the birds wouldn't peck at him. But now . . . the voles are eating him.

What choice did he have? He stood and dusted the snow from his knee.

I might have to get some help, from town, he said.

The girl's eyes flashed with anger. You promised. You promised.

And so he had. Jack sighed heavily and kicked the sides of his boots together. It was more than he had bargained for.

This isn't all going to happen today, he said. I've got to think about this, about how we're going to take care of . . . your papa.

All right.

The girl was tired and calm, the fight drained out of her.

You will stay with us until we can sort things out.

Jack spoke as he had that first day when he'd told her it was time to go in for dinner, as if this were the last word.

The girl stood straight, her eyes sharp again.

No, she said.

I can't leave you here in the woods. This is no place for a child.

It's my home, she said.

She stood with her head high. The mountain wind blew through the spruce trees and stirred her blond hair.

This was her home. Jack believed it.

In Alpine, he asked around, saying he'd seen ax blazes on several trees, signs of marked trails. Had anyone been trapping near his homestead over the years? Anybody living up toward the mountains?

'Yeah. Yeah. Funny you ask 'cause I haven't thought of that fellow in a coon's age,' George said. 'We called him 'Swede' and he never told us different. Didn't give a name, now that I think of it. More likely Russian, I'd guess — judging from the way he said his words.'

'What did he look like?' Jack asked. 'Just curious if I ever met him along the way.'

'Big, strapping man. Built like a lumberjack. Light-colored hair. A beard. A little off, if you ask me. Not the friendly, talkative sort. Esther's known for inviting the bachelors over for Sunday dinner once in a while, but she never asked him. I wonder what happened to him. You think he's trapping around your place?'

Betty remembered the man, too.

'Oh, he was an odd duck, that one,' she told Jack as she poured him a cup of coffee. 'Like a lot of 'em, he panned gold in the summers, trapped in the winters. Probably thought he'd strike it rich and go back to wherever he came from. Couldn't understand him half the time, always mixing another language in with his English.'

'You seen him lately?' Jack asked. 'I just want to know who I'm dealing with, if he's trapping out my way.'

'Nope. Can't remember the last time he was in here. But then he only came into town a few times a year. Spent all his spare time drinking with the Indians upriver, from what I heard.'

'Wonder what 'came of him.' Jack casually stirred his coffee.

'Who knows? Maybe he went back to wherever he came from. Or the river drowned him, or a bear ate him. Happens all the time. Men come and men go. Sometimes they just walk off the face of the earth.'

'You recall him having any children? . . . Or a wife? I was just thinking Mabel might want to get to know her.'

'Can't say that I do. Seemed a pretty solitary type to me.'

A tired sadness settled over Jack as he rode back to the homestead. The horse trotted sharply and tossed its head, as if invigorated by the brisk weather. Jack's hands stiffened in the cold as he held the reins. He thought of the girl on the side of the mountain with her dead, frozen papa and wondered if he was doing the right thing. She had made him promise not to tell anyone, especially Mabel, and Jack understood. Most any woman wouldn't allow a child to stay in the wilderness alone with her father's corpse. The girl feared being yanked away from what was familiar. Jack had watched when Mabel once or twice reached out to brush hair away from the girl's eyes or to help button her blue wool coat.

133

The girl flinched and pulled back. She clenched her teeth and pursed her lips as if to say, I can take care of myself.

Jack was fairly certain it was true. The girl knew the woods and trails. She found food, shelter. Was that all a child needed? Mabel would say no. She'd say the girl needed warmth and affection and someone to look after her, but Jack had to wonder if that didn't have more to do with a woman's own desires than the needs of a child.

Besides, he had promised the girl. He made few promises, but those he made, to the best of his abilities he kept.

The secret clung to Jack in the scent of black woodsmoke and melting snow. At night, Mabel pressed her face into his beard and touched his hair with her fingers.

'What have you been burning?'

'Just some of those stump rows from last summer. Good weather to burn. Not too windy or dry.'

'Yes. I suppose so.' She didn't seem altogether convinced.

The ground was taking longer to thaw than he had predicted. He dragged the dead man out from under the tree and cut it down. Then he cut up the wood where it lay, and built a fire from its tinder-dry branches. The girl watched the tree burn. She stood well back and the flames flickered in her eyes. Jack asked her if she could tend the fire, while he was gone, but she shook

134

her head. So when the short day ended and night fell, he piled the wood as high as he dared and then climbed down the mountain. Behind him, the fire crackled and popped and flamed in the night.

The next day he scraped at the frozen earth beneath the smoldering wood, digging as far down as he could with a shovel. A December grave was hard earned in this place, but it would come. He left the man beneath a tarp, far from the fire. It was a gruesome thought, but he didn't want the body to thaw. It was keeping well frozen.

❄

On the third day, Jack trudged home covered with soot and weary to the bone. Mabel was waiting.

'George came by,' she said. 'I told him you were out in the new field, burning stumps.'

'Oh?'

'He said you weren't out there. He couldn't find you.'

'Hmm.' He didn't look into her face.

She took hold of his forearm and squeezed gently. 'What is it? Where have you been?'

'Nothing. I've just been working. George must have missed me somehow.'

❄

The next morning Jack returned to dig in the softening earth and build the flames back up. He

135

was drenched in sweat and coated in dirt and charcoal from the half-burned logs. The girl was nowhere to be seen, but at times Jack felt something watching him from the trees and wondered if it was the girl or the red fox he had seen slip now and then between snow-covered boulders.

By mid-afternoon the pit seemed deep enough to bury a man. Jack scraped the last coals out of the hole and then leaned on the shovel, his cheek resting on his hand. This wasn't the first grave he'd dug alone. He thought back to a small grave, a tiny lifeless body, not much bigger than a man's heart.

Jack called for the child. It's time, he said. Time to put your papa to rest.

She appeared from behind one of the spruce trees.

Is it gone? she asked.

You mean the fire? Yes, it's gone.

There was no coffin. He didn't have the lumber to build one and didn't want to attract too much attention by inquiring in town. The tarp would have to do. Jack shoved and pulled at the canvas until it broke free of ice, and then he dragged the body across the snow to the grave.

Have you said your goodbyes?

The girl nodded. Jack felt ill. It could have just been the long day of sweating and freezing and no stomach even for lunch. But it didn't seem right, burying a man without notifying the authorities or signing some piece of paper or at least having a man of the cloth read something from the Bible. He didn't see a way out. The worst that could happen to this child, besides her father dying in front of her, would be for the authorities to be involved. She'd be shipped off to some orphanage far from these mountains. She seemed to him both powerful and delicate, like a wild thing that thrives in its place but withers when stolen away.

Without another man to help him lower it slowly, Jack shoved the tarp-wrapped body into the hole where it fell with an ungodly thump.

Shall I cover him up then? he asked.

The girl nodded.

He began shoveling in dirt and black, dead coals. He wondered if he had the strength to finish, but he kept at it, shovelful after shovelful, the girl silent behind him. Occasionally he stamped his feet on the dirt to settle it and the girl joined him, hopping up and down on the grave, her small face frowning, her marten-fur hat hanging down her back by strings tied at her neck.

So it's done, then, Jack said.

He scraped a few last piles of dirt over the grave.

The girl came to Jack's side. She closed her eyes, then flung her arms into the air. Snowflakes lighter than feathers scattered across the grave. It was more snow than a child could possibly hold in her arms, and it filtered down as if from the clear sky above. Jack was silent until the last flakes settled.

When he did speak, his voice was hoarse from the smoke.

In the spring, he said, we can put some pretty rocks here, maybe plant flowers.

The girl nodded and then wrapped her arms around his waist, pressed her face into his coat. Jack stood motionless for a moment, awkward with his arms at his sides, and then he slowly reached around her and patted her softly on the back, smoothed her hair with his rough hand.

There, there. All right. It's going to be all right. It's done now.

Part 2

Then one morning, when the last of the snow had melted, she came to the old couple and kissed them both.

'I must leave you now,' she said.

'Why?' they cried.

'I am a child of the snow. I must go where it is cold.'

'No! No!' they cried. 'You cannot go!'

They held her close, and a few drops of snow fell to the floor. Quickly she slipped from their arms and ran out the door.

'Come back!' they called.

'Come back to us!'

'The Snow Child' retold by
Freya Littledale

14

It was unexpected, to look forward to each day. When Mabel woke in the mornings, happy anticipation washed over her and for a moment she would not know its cause. Was this day special for some reason? A birthday? A holiday? Was something planned? Then she would remember — the child might visit.

Mabel was often at the window, but it wasn't with the melancholy weariness of the previous winter. Now she watched with excitement and hope that the little girl in the fur hat and leather moccasins would appear from the woods. The December days had a certain luminosity and sparkle, like frost on bare branches, alight in the morning just before it melts.

Mabel tempered herself. She imagined running to the girl when she appeared at the edge of the trees and throwing her arms around her, spinning her in circles. But she didn't. She waited patiently in the cabin and pretended not to notice her arrival. When the child came indoors, Mabel did not scrub her clean, brush the leaves and lichen from her hair, wash her clothes and dress her anew. It was true — she sometimes pictured the child wearing a lovely ruffled dress and pretty bows in her hair. Sometimes she even daydreamed about inviting

Esther over for tea to show off the girl as if she were her own.

She did none of these things. They were silly fancies that had more to do with her own romantic ideas of childhood than with this mysterious girl. The only real desire she had, once she stripped away the vain and the frivolous, was to touch the child, to stroke the girl's cheek, to hold her close and deeply breathe in her scent of mountain air. But she contented herself with the child's smiles, and each morning she watched at the window, hoping this day she would come.

Mabel had not been able to find a pattern in the visits. The child came every other evening for a week or so, but then for two or three days she wouldn't appear.

One morning she came and stayed with Mabel in the kitchen instead of following Jack around the barn. She watched Mabel mix bread dough, and it was as if a songbird had landed on a bedroom windowsill. Mabel did not want to frighten her away by moving too abruptly, so she emulated Jack's quiet, accepting manner. She spoke softly to the girl. She described how you had to dust the dough in flour and knead it again and again until it was right in the hands, even and elastic. She told the child that Jack's aunt had taught her how to bake bread, that she had been astounded a woman could be grown and married and not know how.

That evening, the girl stayed for dinner. Jack came in from the barn, and Mabel and the child joined him at the table. The girl bowed her head before he had even begun saying the blessing, and Jack and Mabel's eyes met. She had grown accustomed to their ways.

Jack seemed in an uncommonly good mood, making jokes and talking about his day's work as they passed the food around the table. At one point, he turned to ask the girl to hand him the salt. She was focused on her own plate and didn't notice. Jack cleared his throat, then tapped lightly on the table.

This is getting silly, he announced.

The child startled. He quieted his tone.

We must call you something. Will it be 'girl' for ever?

The child was silent. Jack reached over her for the salt, apparently giving up on getting a name from her. Mabel waited, but Jack went back to eating.

Faina, the girl whispered.

What's that, child? Mabel asked.

My name. It's Faina.

Will you say it again, more slowly?

Fah-EE-nah.

Each syllable a quiet whisper. Mabel at first could make no sense of the foreign sounds, so many vowels without their consonants, but then she heard a gesture toward words like 'far' and 'tree' and a breath of air at the end, sounds that were indeed this little girl sitting at their table. Faina.

What does it mean? Mabel asked.

The girl bit her lower lip and frowned.

You must see it, to know.

Then her face brightened.

But I'll show you. Someday I'll show you what it means.

Faina. It is a lovely name.

Well there, Jack said. That simplifies things, doesn't it?

That night, after the child left, they said her name again and again. It began to roll easily off their tongues, and Mabel liked the way it felt in her mouth, the way it whispered in her ear — Did you see how Faina bowed her head at dinner? Isn't Faina a beautiful child? What will Faina bring next time she visits? They were like children pretending to be mother and father, and Mabel was happy.

Dawn broke silver over the snowdrifts and spruce trees. Mabel was at the kitchen table trying to sketch the birch basket the girl had brought them. She had it propped against her wooden recipe box so that it tipped toward her, and she tried to remember how it had looked full of wild berries. It had been too long since she had drawn, and the pencil was awkward in her hands, the shading and angles of the drawing all wrong. Frustrated, she put a hand to the back of her neck and stretched.

At the sight of the girl peeking in the window, Mabel startled, but then smiled and raised her hand in greeting. When the child waved back, affection surged through her.

Faina, child. Come in, come in.

The child brought the smell of snow in with her, and the air in the cabin cooled and brightened. Mabel unwrapped the scarf from her neck, took her mittens, fur hat, and the wool coat. The child let her do this, and Mabel hugged the clothes to her breast, felt the chill of winter, the coarse wool, and the silky brown fur. She draped the scarf over the back of her hand and marveled that her sister's dewdrop stitch would adorn this little girl.

What were you doing?

The child stood at the table with one of the pencils in her hand.

I was drawing, Mabel said. Would you like to see?

She set the child's outdoor clothing on a chair and left the door cracked open, so a draft could move through the cabin and cool the girl. Then she pulled a chair out for her and sat beside her.

This is my sketchpad. And these are my pencils. I wanted to draw a picture of the basket you gave us. See?

Mabel held up the drawing.

Oh, the child said.

It's not very good, is it? I'm afraid I've lost any skill I might have had.

I think it is very nice.

The child skimmed her fingers across the paper surface and rounded her lips in wonder.

What else can you draw? she asked.

Mabel shrugged.

Anything I set my mind to, I suppose. Although it won't necessarily look the way it ought.

Could you draw a picture of me?

Yes. Oh, yes. But I must warn you, I've never been very good at portraits.

Mabel put the child's chair near the window so the winter light shone on the side of her face and lit up her blond hair. For the next hour, Mabel glanced from sketch paper to child and back again, and waited for the girl to protest, but she never complained or moved. She was stoic, her chin slightly raised, her gaze steady.

With each stroke of the pencil, it was as if Mabel had been granted her wish, as if she held the child in her arms, caressed her cheek, stroked her hair. She drew the gentle curve of the child's cheekbones, the peaks of her small lips, the inquisitive arch of her blond eyebrows. Self-contained, wary and brave, innocent and knowing . . . something in the turn of her head, the tilt of her eyes, hinted at a wildness Mabel wanted to capture, too. All these details she took in and memorized.

Would you like to see?

Is it finished?

Mabel smiled.

As well as I can for today.

She turned the sketchpad toward the child, not knowing what reaction to expect.

The child took in a breath, then clasped her hands in delight.

Do you like it?

Oh, yes! Is that me? Is that what I look like?

Have you never seen yourself, child?

The girl shook her head.

Never? Not in a mirror? Well, I have just the

thing. Much better than any drawing I can manage.

Mabel went to the bedroom and came back with a hand mirror.

Do you know what this is? It's a little glass, and you can see yourself in it.

The child shrugged her small shoulders.

There, do you see? That's you.

The girl peered into the mirror, her eyes wide and her face somber. She reached out and touched the shining surface with one fingertip, then touched her own hair, her face. She smiled, turned her head side to side, brushed her hair away from her brow, all the while watching in the mirror.

Would you like to have the picture I drew of you?

Faina smiled and nodded.

Mabel folded the portrait until it was a square small enough to fit in the child's pocket.

When the little girl was gone and dinner finished, Mabel knitted by the woodstove. Outside, the wind tore down the river valley and she thought she could hear another sound, too. A mournful baying.

'Is that the wind, Jack?'

He stood at the window, looking out into the blackness.

'Nope. I think it's those wolves upriver. I heard howling the other night, too.'

'Would you stoke up the fire? I feel I've caught a chill.'

She watched him put birch logs to the fire, the flames catching on the papery bark and flickering light against the cabin walls. Then he went to the window and looked for some time out into the night, the way she always did.

'Is she safe?' Mabel asked. 'That wind's blowing so savagely. And the wolves.'

'I expect she's all right.'

They stayed up unusually late. Jack went outside several times to get more wood, despite the stack of logs just inside the door, and Mabel continued to knit, though her hands were tired and her eyes burned. Finally they could stay awake no longer and crawled into their bed together. They fell asleep to the sound of the wind blowing down the valley.

15

It was mid-February when a parcel addressed to Mabel arrived, wrapped in brown paper and delivered via train to Alpine. Jack brought it from town, along with a few supplies bought with the last of their credit at the general store.

Mabel waited until he went back outside before she sat at the table to open it. Could this be it at long last? It seemed ages ago that she had written her sister to ask about the book. For several weeks she had been hopeful, but when it hadn't come she assumed either her sister couldn't find it or was not interested in the query.

She was tempted to tear open the package but felt the need to be calm and collected. She heated a kettle of water and steeped a cup of tea. When it was ready, she sat at the table and unknotted the packing twine and carefully unfolded the paper. Inside were two separately wrapped packages. The larger one looked distinctly like a book, but Mabel chose to open the smaller first. It contained several fine drawing pencils as well as sticks of charcoal. She turned to the larger package and unfolded the brown paper slowly.

The book was just as she had remembered it — oversized and perfectly square, a shape unlike any children's book she had ever seen. It was bound in blue morocco leather. An exquisite snowflake design was embossed in silver on the front cover, and the same silver gilding decorated the spine. She placed the book flat on the table in front of her and opened it. 'Snegurochka, 1857' was written lightly in pencil in the upper corner of the blue marbled endpaper. 'The Snow Maiden.' It was her father's neat writing. He had collected many books on his travels, and some he brought back especially for her. He kept them on a shelf in his study, but whenever she wanted to look through them, he would pull them down and sit her on his lap while he turned the pages.

With the book in front of her, Mabel could have been back in her father's study with its scent of pipe tobacco and old books. She turned the first page. On the left was a full-color plate overlaid with a sheet of translucent paper, on the other the story, written in blocky, illegible letters. It was in Russian! How could she have forgotten? Maybe she had never noticed. Although this had been one of her favorite childhood books, she realized now that she had never actually read it. Her father had told her the story as she looked at the illustrations. Now she wondered whether her father had known the words or had invented the story based on the pictures.

It had been many years since her father had died, but now she recalled his voice, melodic and rumbling.

'There once was an old man and woman who loved each other very much and were content with their lot in life except for one great sadness

150

— they had no children of their own.'

Mabel shifted her eyes back to the illustration. It was similar to a Russian lacquer painting, the colors rich and earthy, the details fine. It showed two old people, a man and a woman, kneeling in the snow at the feet of a young girl who seemed to be made of snow from the ground to her waist, but to be a real child from her waist up.

The snow child's cheeks glowed with life and jewels crowned her blond hair. She smiled sweetly down at the old couple, her mittened hands held out to them. Her embroidered cloak spilled from her shoulders in a shimmer of white and silver, with no clear distinction between the cloak and the snow. Behind her the snowscape was framed by a stand of black-green spruce trees and, in the distance, snowy, sharp-peaked mountains. Between two of the trees stood a red fox with narrow, golden eyes like a cat's.

She reached for her cup of tea to find that it had gone cold. How long had she stared at that single illustration? She sipped the cool tea and turned the page. It was night. The little girl ran into the trees. Silver stars glittered in the blue-black sky above her as the couple peered sadly out of their cottage door.

With each turn of the page, Mabel felt light-headed and torn from herself.

She picked up the book and held it closer to her eyes. The next illustration had always been her favorite. In a snowy clearing, the girl stood surrounded by the wild beasts of the forest — bears, wolves, hares, ermines, a stag, a red fox, even a tiny mouse. The animals sat on their

151

haunches beside the girl, their demeanor neither menacing nor adoring. It was as if they had posed for a portrait, with their fur and teeth and claws and yellow eyes, and the little girl gazed plainly out at the reader without fear or pleasure. Did they love the little girl, or did they want to eat her? All these years later, Mabel still could find no answers in the wild, gleaming eyes.

She closed the book and traced the embossed snowflake with her fingertips. She began to gather the brown wrapping and it was then that she saw her sister's letter, tucked into the folds of paper and nearly discarded.

Dearest Mabel,

What a joy to read your letter, to see your lovely handwriting once again and know you are alive and well. It must sound terribly outlandish to you, but to all of us here it is as if you have been banished to the North Pole. It was a relief to know you are warm and safe and even have welcoming neighbors. They must be a rare blessing in that wilderness. I am pleased, too, to know you will once again pick up your sketchpad. I have always known you to be a talented artist. Won't you send us some little drawings of your new homeland? We are anxious to share in your adventures.

As to your request for this book, it is a pure stroke of luck that I was able to send it to you. A student from the university, a Mr Arthur Ransome, has been sorting through Father's collections and was particularly enamored with this book. Of all subjects, he is studying fairy tales of the Far North. I had no attachment to the book, so allowed him to have it for his studies. When I received your letter, I was thrilled to recall that I knew precisely where it was. Of course, I practically had to pry it from the young man's hands. He cautioned me that it was a rare find and should be treated with great care. He was appalled to learn that I would be mailing it to you in the farthest outreaches of civilization.

As I prepared to send the book to you, I happened to notice that it is all written in Russian. Unless you have learned the language while in Alaska, I was afraid you might be at wit's end to discover the book is unreadable. Before I wrapped it, I asked the young man to tell me something of Snegurochka, the Snow Maiden.

Mr Ransome says the story of the snow child is of similar import in Russia as Little Red Riding Hood or Snow White in our own country. Like many fairy tales, there are many different ways it is told, but it always begins the same. An old man and an old woman live happily in their small cottage in the forest, but for one sorrow: they have no children of their own. One winter's day, they build a girl of snow.

I am sorry to say no matter which version, the story ends badly. The little snow girl comes and goes with winter, but in the end she always melts. She plays with the village children too close to a bonfire, or she doesn't flee the coming of spring quickly enough, or, as in the version told in Father's book, she meets a boy and chooses mortal love.

In the most traditional tale, according to Mr Ransome, the snow child loses her way in the woods. She encounters a bear, which offers to help her find her way. But she looks at the bear's long claws and sharp teeth, and fears he will eat her. She refuses his assistance. Then along comes a wolf, which also promises to lead her safely to the cottage, but he is nearly as ferocious looking as the bear. The child again refuses.

But then she meets a fox. 'I will take you home,' he vows. The child decides the fox looks friendlier than the others. She takes hold of his fur scruff, and the fox leads her out of the forest. When they arrive at the old couple's cottage, the fox asks for a fat hen in payment for her safe return. The old people are poor and so decide to trick the fox by instead giving him a sack with their hunting dog inside. The fox drags the sack into the woods and opens it. The dog lunges out, chases the fox and kills it.

The snow child is angry and saddened. She bids the old couple farewell, saying that since they do not love her even as much as one of their hens, she will return to live with her Father Winter and Mother Spring.

When the old woman next looks outside, all that remain are the child's red boots, red mittens, and a puddle of water.

What a tragic tale! Why these stories for children always have to turn out so *dreadfully*

154

is beyond me. I think if I ever tell it to my grandchildren, I will change the ending and have everyone live happily ever after. We are allowed to do that, are we not Mabel? To invent our own endings and choose joy over sorrow?

16

'Couldn't we keep just one?' Mabel pleaded. 'The red hen. She's such a dear, and we could feed her table scraps.'

'Chickens aren't solitary creatures,' Jack said. 'They like a flock. It wouldn't be right.'

'Won't Mr Palmer allow us a little more credit, just to buy some feed for the rest of the winter? It wouldn't cost so much, would it?'

Jack's shirt collar tightened at his throat, and the cabin was too warm and too small. Chicken feed, for Christ's sake. What kind of man can't afford chicken feed? They had already run out of coffee, and the sugar wouldn't last much longer.

'It's got to be done.' He went to the door and had nearly shut it on his way out when he heard Mabel.

'Esther says it's best to dip them in boiling water to pluck them. Shall I heat a pot?'

'That'd be fine.' And he closed the door.

Jack took no pleasure in slaughtering the chickens. If he'd had his choice, he would have kept them alive and plump in the barn for all the days of their lives. During the summer, they were

157

good layers, most of them, and he knew Mabel had some attachment. But you couldn't let an animal starve under your care. Better to kill it and be done with it.

He eyed the ax by the woodpile as he walked to the barn. He wished now that he'd thought to ask George for some advice as well. His grandmother had been known to strangle a chicken with her bare hands, but mostly he'd heard of cutting their heads clean off and letting them bleed out. An unpleasant task, no matter how it was to be done.

A dozen headless chickens, and soon he would be bringing them into the kitchen to poor Mabel, who had doted on them. She would do it, though. She'd gut the birds and pluck the feathers and never once complain, just as she hadn't complained about the dwindling supplies or the endless meals of moose meat and potatoes. The past few weeks, she had gathered frozen wild cranberries and rosehips and jarred some jam, and she'd figured out how to make an eggless cake that wasn't all that bad. She was making do, and somehow it suited her. She had a rosiness to her cheeks and laughed more than she had in years, even as she served yet another plate of fried moose steak.

She'd picked up her books and pencils again, too. Jack took note of that. The child was always bringing something new for her to draw — an owl feather, a cluster of mountain ash berries, a spruce bough with the cones still attached. The two of them would sit at the kitchen table, the cabin door propped open 'so the child won't get too warm', their heads together as she drew. It was good to see.

But it also scared him how much the girl was growing on Mabel. On him, too. He could admit that. He might not watch out the window, but he waited just the same, and hoped for her. Hoped she wasn't lonely or in danger. Hoped she would appear out of the trees and come running, smiling, to him.

Sometimes he wanted to tell Mabel the truth. It was a burden, and he wasn't sure he carried it right. He wanted to tell Mabel about the dead man and the lonely place in the mountains where he had buried him. He wanted to tell her about the strange door in the side of the mountain. The knowledge of the child's suffering sat heavy and cold in his gut, and sometimes he could not look at her small, wan face for fear of choking.

He had promised the girl, but maybe that was just an excuse. The awful truth of what the child had witnessed would wrench Mabel's heart, and the last thing on earth he wanted to do was cause her any more sadness. Her capacity for grief frightened him. He'd wondered more than once if she had ventured onto the river ice in November knowing full well the danger.

Jack grabbed a hen by her feet and carried her, squawking and flapping her wings, out to the chopping block by the woodpile. The racket didn't stop for some time, even well after the head was cut off. Only eleven more to go, Jack thought grimly as he laid the dead bird in the snow.

He hadn't planned on helping with the plucking, but then he saw what a long, unpleasant chore it would be for a person alone. Side by side at the kitchen counter, covered in feathers and their sleeves rolled up, Jack and Mabel took turns dipping a chicken in the boiling water, then pulling handful after handful of feathers. They tried to gather the red and black and yellow feathers into burlap sacks, but soon more were stuck to the floor and floating around the cabin than in the bags.

'Maybe we should have done this outside,' Mabel said as she tried to wipe a wet feather from her forehead with the back of her hand.

Jack chuckled.

'I'd get that for you, but I'm afraid I'd only leave more,' he said and held up his feather-coated hands.

'And this horrid smell,' Mabel said. The steam that rose from the boiling water smelled of scalded feathers and half-cooked chicken skin.

'I was thinking — maybe we should have chicken for dinner,' Jack said, trying to keep his face stern.

'No, no. I couldn't bear . . . Oh, you're teasing me,' and she flicked a feather in his direction.

As he began plucking another bird, Mabel sighed beside him.

'What is it?'

'It's dear, sweet Henny Penny,' she said and looked sadly down at the dead hen in her hands.

'Told you it was best not to name them.'

'It's not the names. I would have known them no matter what I called them. Henny Penny used to follow me about while I gathered the eggs, clucking like she was giving me advice.'

'I am sorry, Mabel. I don't know what else to do.' He flexed his hand, felt the tendons give and take, and wondered how he could again and again disappoint her.

'You think I blame you?' she said.

'Nobody else to. It's on my shoulders.'

'How is it that you always arrive at that conclusion? That everything is your fault and yours alone? Wasn't it my idea to come here? Didn't I want this homestead, and all the hard work and failure that would come with it? If anything, I'm to blame because I've done so little to help.'

Jack still looked at his hands.

'Don't you see? This was to be ours together, the successes and the failures,' Mabel said, and as she spoke she gestured grandly as if to encompass everything, the plucked chickens, the wet feathers.

'All of this?' he said, and couldn't help a smile.

'Yes, all of this.' Then she too smiled. 'Every blasted feather. Mine and yours.'

Jack leaned over and kissed her on the tip of her nose, then stuck a chicken feather behind her ear.

'All right then,' he said.

When they had finished the last chicken, they attempted to sweep the feathers out of the cabin, but the impossibility of the task left them both laughing until Mabel gave up and collapsed in a kitchen chair, legs stretched out in front of her. Jack used his forearm to wipe sweat from his forehead.

'Who would have thought it would be so much work, getting chickens ready to eat?' Mabel fanned herself with a hand. Jack nodded in agreement, then took the birds to hang in the barn with the moose meat. They would stay frozen until they could bring themselves to eat them.

When he returned, he saw that Mabel had set one aside.

'We were joking, weren't we? About cooking one for dinner tonight?'

'It's not for us.'

'Then what?'

Mabel put on her coat and boots.

'I'm taking it to a place in the woods.'

'What place?'

'Where you left her the treats and the doll.'

So she'd known all along.

'But a dead chicken?' he asked. 'For the child?'

'Not for her. For her fox.'

'You're going to feed one of our chickens to a wild fox?'

'I need to do this.'

'What for?' Jack's voice rose. 'How in God's name does it make a bit of sense, when we're just barely getting by, to throw a dinner out into the woods?'

'I want her to know . . . ' and Mabel held her chin up, as if what she said took some courage. 'Faina needs to know that we love her.'

'And a chicken will tell her that?'

'I told you, it's for her fox.'

As Mabel carried the naked, dead bird into the night, Jack wanted to laugh at the absurdity of it. Instead he found himself thinking of what Esther had said about a dark winter's madness.

17

As he neared the cabin, Jack heard the chatter of women's voices, and when he came through the door with an armload of firewood, he found Esther with her feet propped indecorously on a chair in front of the woodstove. She wore men's navy wool pants with the cuffs tucked into long red-striped socks. A big toe stuck out through a hole in one sock, and as Jack loaded more wood into the stove, she wiggled her toes toward the heat.

'I was just telling Mabel, I hope that boy of mine don't pester you too awful much. I know he's coming around a lot this winter, talking your ear off I'm sure,' she said.

Mabel handed her a cup of tea and she slurped at it.

'No. No.' He tried not to look at the bare toe. 'Not at all. Truth be told, I kind of enjoy his company. I could learn a lot from him.'

'Don't you dare tell him that. It'll go straight to his head, and we'll never hear the end of it. That boy knows a lot, but not half as much as he thinks he does.'

'Ah well. Suppose that was true about most of us at that age.'

'He's taken a liking to you, though. He's always talking about you. Jack says this and Jack says that.'

Mabel handed Jack a cup of tea. 'There are johnnycakes, too. Esther brought them.'

The two women had spent most of the day sharing recipes and patterns, and even out in the yard he had heard their laughter. He was glad for Mabel to have the company.

Esther stood and stretched and took a johnnycake from the plate.

'I was also dispensing a little advice. I told Mabel here she's got to get out of the cabin more. All this talk about little girls running around in the trees. Next thing you know she'll be holding tea parties in the front yard wearing nothing but her skivvies and a flowered hat.'

Esther nudged Mabel with an elbow and winked, but Mabel did not smile.

'Oh look at you, white as a ghost. I'm not telling you anything you don't know. This is nonsense, all this talk about a little girl.'

'I'm not crazy, Esther.' Mabel's voice was tight, and she caught Jack's eyes with her own.

'So you do have some fight in you, my girl.' Esther hugged her waist. 'You'll need every bit of that to survive around here.'

Jack expected Esther to find some reason to leave then, but either she took no notice of Mabel's cross silence or she had more strength in the face of it than he could ever muster. She plopped herself into a chair at the table and swished tea around in her mouth.

'Good tea. Real good tea,' she said. 'Did I ever tell you about the grizzly tea?'

'No. Can't recall that you did,' Jack said. He had intended to work outside for another hour or two, but he pulled up a chair across from her and Mabel and took another johnnycake.

'Danny . . . Jeffers. Jaspers? Ah hell, my mind's going. Anyway, Danny carried around a nasty-smelling burlap bag filled with . . . well, let's just say the less-than-desirable parts of grizzly bears. He swore you could brew a tea with it that would improve your love life.'

Esther's eyes sparkled mischievously. 'Soooo, you always knew who was having trouble in the sack, based on who was talking to old Danny.'

'Oh, you had to drink the stuff? How dreadful.' Mabel wrinkled her nose.

'I was thinking more about those poor grizzly bears,' Jack said. 'Imagine enduring that!'

Esther laughed and held her belly.

'Now that would be a sight, wrestling a grizzly bear to the ground.'

'Well you don't mean . . . ' Mabel wore an appalled expression.

Esther could barely speak for laughing so hard. 'No, no . . . The bears weren't alive. He killed them first.'

'Oh,' Mabel said quietly, and Jack couldn't tell if she was embarrassed or thinking of all the dead bears.

'I suppose a lot of characters have come through here over the years,' he said.

'Oh sure. This place draws kooks like flies. We count ourselves among the sane ones, and that tells you something.'

Mabel did smile then.

'You must have heard about the fellow who painted his cabin bright orange?' Esther asked.

'No, no.' Mabel laughed and shook her head. 'I won't believe you anymore. You're making it up.'

Esther solemnly held up her right hand. 'I swear it's the truth. Orange as a piece of fruit. Said it would help him keep cheerful during the black winters. His place was down just the other side of the tracks. I thought it was kind of pretty myself, but all the men in town teased him no end.'

'Did it work?' Jack asked.

'Can't say that it did. He burned up in his cabin that winter, the whole thing down to the ground. I always kind of wondered — he complained about the cold more than any man I've ever known. What in the Sam Hill he was doing in Alaska is beyond me. Everyone said the fire was an accident, and that all the paint fueled the flames, but maybe he was just sick of being cold. Wanted to go out in a blast of heat, like old Sam McGee.'

'Sam who?' Mabel asked. 'Did he live around here?'

'Sam who! And your own father was a literature professor?' Esther went on to recite some verses by a Yukon poet named Robert Service that told of all the strange things done under the midnight sun.

As light faded, Mabel asked her to stay for dinner, but she said no, she had to get home and cook for her houseful of men. Once she had dressed in her coat and boots and was ready to leave, she hugged Mabel again.

'Darn it if you haven't become my very best

friend,' she said. 'Take care, won't you?'

'I will,' Mabel said. 'It was good to see you.'

Jack followed Esther into the yard and offered to hitch the wagon.

'I got it just fine, Jack,' she said. She leaned in close to him and looked back toward the cabin.

'But I do worry about her,' she said. 'She's got a bit of the sadness about her, like my own mother did. Keep a close watch over her.'

Jack expected Mabel to be sullen and quiet when he went back inside, but she was humming to herself at the kitchen sink.

'You two have a good visit?'

'We did. I've never met anyone like her. She is full of surprises, and I rather enjoy it.'

She poured water into a pot and didn't look at him. 'Why don't you ever speak up for me, tell her that you've seen the child as well?'

So he was the one, not Esther, who had angered her.

'It completely baffles me, Jack. She's real. You've seen her with your own eyes, sat with her at this very table. And yet never once have you acknowledged it to the Bensons.'

'I don't know,' he said. 'Maybe I'm not as brave as you.'

'You're mocking me.'

'No. You're different. True to yourself, even if it means people will say you're crazy. Well, me . . . I guess I just . . . '

'You don't say a word.' But there was more

bemusement than anger in it.

She went back to sorting through a sack of potatoes.

'Should I get a pair of those wool pants like Esther was wearing?' she asked.

'Only if you wear the holey socks as well.'

'But didn't they look warm and practical?'

'The socks?' he teased.

'No, no. Those socks were something else.'

As she began to peel potatoes, he stood behind her and touched the tendrils of hair that had fallen from their clips and curled at the nape of her neck. Then he reached around her waist and leaned into her. All these years and still he was drawn to the smell of her skin, of sweet soap and fresh air. He whispered against her ear, 'Dance with me.'

'What?'

'I said, let's dance.'

'Dance? Here, in the cabin? I do believe you're the mad one.'

'Please.'

'There's no music.'

'We can remember some tune, can't we?' and he began to hum 'In the Shade of the Old Apple Tree'.

'Here,' he said, and swung her around to face him, an arm still at her waist, her slight hand in his.

He hummed louder and began to twirl them around the plank floor.

'Hmmm, hmm, with a heart that is true, I'll be waiting for you . . . '

' . . . in the shade of the old apple tree.' She

kissed him on the cheek, and he swept her back on his arm.

'Oh, I've thought of one,' she said. 'Let me think . . . ' and she began to hum tentatively. Jack didn't know it at first, but then it came to him and he began to sing along.

'When my hair has all turned gray,' a swoop and a twirl beside the kitchen table, 'will you kiss me then and say, that you love me in December as you do in May?'

And then they were beside the woodstove and Mabel kissed him with her mouth open and soft. Jack pulled her closer, pressed their bodies together and kissed the side of her face and down her bare neck and, as she let her head gently lean away, down to her collarbone. Then he scooped an arm beneath her knees and picked her up.

'What in heaven's — you'll break your back,' Mabel sputtered between a fit of laughter. 'We're too old for this.'

'Are we?' he asked. He rubbed his beard against her cheek. She shrieked and laughed, and he carried her into the bedroom, though they had not yet eaten dinner.

18

The cranberries were tiny red rubies against the white snow and Mabel's eyes searched them out. She had thought them inedible, but Esther told her they were actually sweeter once they'd frozen and perfect for sauces and ˉjellies. The late February weather had warmed to just below freezing. The sky was blue, the air was calm, and it was surprisingly pleasant to be outside. Mabel waded through the deep snow near the cabin, carrying the birch basket Faina had given them. The berries were small and scattered among the bare, spindly branches, but Mabel was beginning to fill the basket a few at a time. She planned to make a savory relish with the cranberries, Esther's onions, and spices. Maybe it would make the moose meat taste like something other than the same meal they'd eaten every day for weeks on end. She was smiling to herself, thinking of how necessity truly is the mother of invention, when she looked up to see the child and the fox.

Faina never ceased to startle Mabel. It wasn't just the way the girl appeared without warning, but also her manner. She stood with her arms at her sides in her wool coat, mittens, scarf, fur trim, and flaxen hair. Her brown fur hat was dusted in snow, as were her eyelashes. Her expression was calmly attentive, as if she had been waiting, for minutes, perhaps years, knowing it was only a matter of time before Mabel came to this place in the woods.

Mabel was no longer sure of the child's age. She seemed both newly born and as old as the mountains, her eyes animated with unspoken thoughts, her face impassive. Here with the child in the trees, all things seemed possible and true.

Just as startling was the fox. It sat beside Faina with its silken red tail curled around its feet and its ears pricked forward. Something in its predatory eyes and thin black mouth told of a thousand small deaths, and Mabel could not forget its muzzle smeared with blood.

Is he your friend? she asked the child.

Faina shrugged her small shoulders.

We hunt together, she said.

Who does the killing? Mabel asked.

Both of us.

Do you ever pet him?

The girl shook her head.

Once I did, she said. When he was a kit, he took pieces of meat from my fingers, and he never bit me. At night he sometimes slept beside me. But he is too wild now. We run and hunt together, but that is all.

As if to show the truth of what she had said, Faina reached her mittened hand down toward the fox. It swiftly ducked and darted around the child's legs and into the trees. The girl watched, and Mabel thought she saw a look of wonder and longing on her face.

Have you picked many berries? Faina turned back to her.

A few, Mabel said. Not as many as I should have. But it's a lovely day. I don't mind that it has taken me most of the morning.

The girl nodded, then pointed past a stand of spruce.

There are more just over there, she said.

Thank you. Won't you come with me?

But the girl was already running away, toward the cabin. She flickered through the trees and skimmed across the top of the snow, until Mabel was alone again in the forest. Sunlight sparkled on the snow and she could hear the wind blowing down from the glacier, but here it was quiet, so quiet Mabel was left to wonder if she had always been alone. She walked through the snow and into the spruce trees.

It took some time to identify what she was hearing. Mabel had filled her basket to overflowing with the cranberries Faina had pointed her toward. She pulled her mittens back on and held the basket carefully, not wanting to spill a single berry into the snow. As she neared the cabin, she thought she heard shouts. Or maybe it was singing. Then, as she broke through the trees and out into the yard, she heard it clearly — laughter.

Jack and the child stood side by side, their arms outstretched and their hands nearly touching. Then, without warning, they threw themselves backward into the deep snow.

Come see! Come see! the child called out to Mabel.

Jack? Faina? What on earth . . .

We're snow angels, Jack called out, and the girl giggled.

Mabel walked to them, the basket in her hands, and looked down. Jack had sunk nearly a foot into the snow and he was waving his arms and legs like a drowning man. He grinned, and Mabel saw that his beard and moustache were caked with snow.

Nearby, the child lay on top of the snow, smiling, her blue eyes wide.

She saw now that they were surrounded by angels in the snow — Jack's large, deep-set figure and the child's, smaller and lighter. A dozen or more were sprinkled across the yard two at a time, and they shone in the sunlight. Mabel had never seen anything more beautiful, and she walked among them.

Jack struggled to his feet. Then he reached down to Faina and grabbed her hands.

Watch, the child called to her.

Jack plucked Faina from the snow, both of them laughing.

What Mabel beheld in the snow took her breath away. The angel was so delicate, and its wings perfectly formed, like the print left on snow where a wild bird has taken flight.

Isn't that something? Jack asked.

I don't understand. How . . .

Don't you remember doing this when you were a little girl? Jack said. You just wave your arms and legs around. Come on. Give it a try.

Mabel hesitated, held up her basket of berries.

Oh, please. Won't you? the child begged.

Jack took the basket and handed it to Faina.

176

I don't know. With my long skirts and all.

But he took her by the shoulders and, before she knew his intentions, gently shoved her backward. She expected it to hurt, but the powdery snow was like a thick duvet that softened her fall and muffled all sound. She saw Jack and the child grinning down at her and above their faces the brilliant blue sky. Closer, she could see the individual snow crystals that encased her.

Go on then, Jack called down to her. You've got to flap your arms to make the wings.

Mabel swept her arms up and felt the drag of the snow, then back down again. Then she moved her legs side to side.

All right? she asked.

Jack reached down to her, they clasped hands, mittens and work gloves, and he grunted as he pulled her to her feet.

Oh, look! Look! the child cried out. Isn't it perfect?

Mabel looked down at her own snow angel. Like Jack's, it was set deep into the snow and the wings weren't feathery. But it was lovely, she had to agree.

Yours is the most beautiful of all, Faina said, and she threw her arms around Mabel's waist and hugged her tightly, and Mabel felt as if she were falling again, tumbling, laughing, backward into the powdery snow.

The snow angels remained in the yard, even as the little girl came and went from the forest, and

Mabel smiled at them. It wasn't just their whimsical presence, dancing from barn to cabin, cabin to woodpile. It was also the memory of Jack flinging himself back into the snow like a little boy, and giggling Faina at his side. And then the child's arms around her, hugging her as a daughter hugs her mother. Joyfully. Spontaneously. The most beautiful of all. The most beautiful of all.

Mabel left the kitchen window and returned to the woodstove. Wait until Esther sees that display, she thought. If she considered us half mad before, once she sees we've spent our days making snow angels in the yard, she will surely have us both committed. She stirred the bubbling cranberries. The musky, sour smell permeated the cabin and, Mabel realized, smelled much like the Bensons' cluttered home had that first day she visited.

She glanced out the window again. Lovely, crazy snow angels! And then it struck her — among all those snow angels were Faina's. Her delicate imprints with their feathery wings. Surely their existence could not be denied.

When Esther sees them, she will know it's true, the child is real. How could she and Jack make a dozen little angels the shape and size of a little girl?

Though the child had at first been a source of gentle teasing, as winter progressed Esther had become kind and cautious in her doubt. She asked if Mabel was getting enough fresh air, if she was sleeping too much during the day. She encouraged her to come visit, and when Mabel said she wasn't comfortable driving the horse alone, Esther began to show up regularly.

There was no guarantee Esther would come any time soon, but she did visit every few weeks, weather depending, and often on a Sunday afternoon. It had been more than two weeks since her last visit and Sunday was just a few days away. As long as it didn't snow, she would see proof of the little girl from the forest, and Mabel would be vindicated.

Esther's disbelief was all too familiar. It brought to mind the many years Mabel had spent as a child, looking for fairies and witches and being teased by her older siblings. Her head is stuffed full of nonsense, one teacher had warned her father. You let her read too many books.

Once Mabel was certain she had caught a fairy. When she was eight years old, she built a trap box out of twigs and hung it in the oak tree in their backyard. In the middle of the night she spied it out her bedroom window, rocking back and forth in the moonlight, and when she opened the window she could hear a high-pitched twittering, just how she imagined a trapped fairy would sound.

Ada! Ada! she had called to her sister. I've caught a fairy. Come and look. Now you'll see they're real.

And Ada came, sleepy-eyed and grumbling, and they walked in their bare feet and nightgowns out to the oak tree. But when Mabel lowered the box from the branch and peeked inside, what she saw wasn't a fairy but a trapped songbird, quivering in fear. She opened the little door, but the bird would not fly out. Ada shook the stick box, and when the bird fell to the grass, Mabel could see that it was failing. Before she could make it a nesting box in the house, it had died.

The memory made her ill. Wrapped tightly in its hold were shame and humiliation, and the terrible guilt of having caused the bird's death. But at the core was the truest emotion — an angry disappointment. If she couldn't convince anyone else, how could she go on believing?

The next days were bright and calm. Mabel guarded the snow angels, and they didn't fade. They glittered and shone beneath the blue sky as the days lengthened. When the sun glared down, she feared they would melt, but the air stayed cool and the snow fluffy and dry.

It wasn't until Sunday morning that the wind began to blow down from the glacier. Mabel could hear it gust along the riverbed, and she watched it stir the treetops, knocking snow to the ground. Please, Mabel thought. Come quickly. Come see, and you'll know she is real.

Mabel did not hear the horse trot into the yard that afternoon — the wind was blowing too violently. She didn't know Esther had arrived until the door burst open and she came tripping into the cabin.

'Look what the wind blew in!' Esther said. She laughed boisterously and slammed the door closed.

'Oh, Esther! You came. And in this weather!'

'It wasn't this bad until I was halfway here, and then I figured I was damned either way, so here I am.'

'I'm so glad. Wait! Don't take off your coat. I want to show you something.' She wrapped a scarf around her face and pulled a hat low on her head.

True to her adventurous nature, Esther didn't ask why, only turned on her heels and followed Mabel back out into the blustery afternoon. Although the sun was still shining and the sky was clear, the wind swept the powdery snow off the ground, swirled it through the air. Half blind, they stumbled across the yard.

'Over here,' Mabel called to Esther.

'What?'

They couldn't hear each other over the wind, so Mabel waved for her to follow and they went toward the barn. Maybe on the lee side the snow angels would be protected.

When they arrived, however, only the faintest suggestion remained, just a few shapeless dents in the drifting snow.

'Do you see?' Mabel yelled into the wind.

Esther shook her head, then raised her eyebrows and held up her hands questioningly. The wind slacked for a moment, though they could still hear it in the distance.

'Do you see anything?' Mabel pointed to where the snow angels had been.

'No, Mabel. All I see is snow. What am I supposed to be seeing?'

'It's just . . . They were here.'

'What was here?' Esther spoke quietly, concerned.

Mabel forced a smile.

'Nothing. It was nothing.' She hooked her arm into Esther's. 'Come on. Let's get back inside, before the wind begins to blow again. I want you to try my cranberry relish.'

19

Jack had shoveled a path through the snowdrifts and was splitting kindling when Garrett rode into the yard with a dead fox slung across the front of his saddle. Jack stood beside the chopping block and watched the boy ride in. He sat the horse with ease, his head low, his shoulders moving with the shift and give of the animal and land beneath him. It wasn't until he looked up and saw Jack that his youth shone. He sat up straight with a grin, swept his hand overhead in greeting, and then pointed to the dead fox.

'What did you bring in today?'

'Isn't it a beaut?' Garrett said as he jumped down from the horse. He reached up and took the fox by the scruff and lifted its limp head.

'A silver fox,' the boy said with some pride.

Jack set down his hatchet and walked to the horse. The fox's ears and muzzle were as pure as black silk, but along its back and sides, the fur was a frosted silver.

'Is it iced up?'

'No sir,' Garrett said. 'That's the way they come — silver tipped.'

'It's splendid all right,' Jack said. 'You catch many?'

'This is my first ever. They're not real

common,' Garrett said. 'Mostly bring in reds and cross foxes. You ever see one of those crosses? They're a mix of red and black, and they've got a black cross along their back.'

Jack went back to his pile of kindling and sat on the chopping block. 'Get yourself any of those recently? Any reds?'

'About a month ago, pulled a cross fox out of a snare. I missed another one when it stepped over my trap. 'Course I don't know what color that one was,' Garrett said and laughed at his own joke.

'No, I guess you wouldn't. What'll you do with this one?'

'I was thinking of a ruff for mom's parka. Don't mention it though. I'd like it to be a surprise.'

'That'd be a fine gift.'

'I got her a pair of lynx mittens made last year. Betty down at the hotel — she'll sew you something if you give her a few pelts for the work. Hats, mittens. She's pretty good, too. I'd like a wolverine ruff, if I ever catch one.'

Jack was ready to go back to chopping kindling, but the boy wanted to talk, so he let him. While he set another spruce log on the block, the boy stacked kindling and told him about the tracks he'd seen that day — a pile of rabbits, a porcupine, a few lynx, and a lone wolf heading upriver.

'Is that unusual, a wolf by itself?'

'Probably a young 'un, kicked out of the pack and looking for his own way. I set some snares around an old moose kill. Hope I get him.'

Jack whittled down the spruce log with the hatchet and slivers of kindling fell neatly to the ground.

'You like that life, do you?' he said and picked up another log. 'Trapping wild animals.'

The boy shrugged.

'Beats dirt farming,' Garrett said. His look was quick. 'No offense.'

'Ah well. I'm none too keen on it myself sometimes. But it's a living. Trapping, though — that's got to be tough work. Kind of lonely, too.'

'I like it. Traveling the river. Just me, the wind and the snow. I like to watch the tracks, seeing the animals come and go. When I get older, I'm going to build myself a cabin up the river. Buy myself some dogs. I'd get a team now if Mom would let me, but she can't stand the barking and howling and she says they'll eat us out of house and home. But once I leave the homestead, then I'll get a team and push my line all the way up to the glacier.'

'You won't stay on and farm?'

'Nah. My brothers — they can have it.'

Jack felt for the boy. It wasn't easy to make your own way with brothers already busting ahead of you. He'd watched the older boys hassle Garrett, the way they bossed and teased him. It was no wonder he'd taken to the woods.

'You seem to know your way around. Your dad brags about you.'

The boy shrugged and kicked the toe of his boot into the snow, but Jack could tell he was pleased.

'Guess I'd better be going before it gets too late,' Garrett said. 'Do you think your wife might like to see the fox before I go?'

'Maybe another time,' he said.

Garrett nodded, pulled himself up into the saddle, and rode toward home.

'What did Garrett bring to show you today?' Mabel asked when Jack went in for the night. She was setting dinner on the table.

'A fox.'

She stopped what she was doing.

'A fox?'

'I know what you're thinking, but it wasn't Faina's. This was a silver fox. Nothing like that red one she runs with.'

It should have been the end of it, but it wasn't. All through dinner, she came back to it.

'Does he have to trap fox? Does he try to catch the red ones, too?'

'It's what he does, Mabel. And he can't pick and choose the colors.'

A bit of quiet, and then, 'But he could catch Faina's, couldn't he? He could kill her fox?'

'I wouldn't worry yourself about it. Her fox seems a wary sort. It won't find its way into one of Garrett's traps.'

'But what if it did? Can't we tell him to stop?'

'Stop trapping? Don't see we have that kind of authority. And Garrett's not the only one out there. Up and down this river, men are trapping.'

But Mabel seemed rattled by his assertion.

She hardly touched her meal, and she paced in front of the bookshelf several times before taking a letter from one of the books. He was relieved when she at last sat in the chair by the fire to read.

20

It was a tangled, sickening kind of vigil. Mabel watched for the boy, but it was the fox and the little girl that occupied her thoughts. Any sound that could be horse hooves in the snow brought Mabel to the window, pulled her eyes into the trees. Sometimes she even walked to the river to look up and down the ice.

If Garrett were to ride onto their homestead with a red fox dead in his arms, Faina would be lost to them. That was how the story went. Mabel had reread her sister's letter until the creases were worn, and it was there, in Ada's lovely, educated handwriting — the fox is killed, the one that brought the child safely out of the wilderness and to their cabin door. Love doubted. Boots and mittens abandoned. Snow melted in clumps. Another child gone from their lives.

It was a possibility she could not bear. She wound herself tightly, as if within her girdled ribs she could contain all possibilities, all futures and all deaths. Perhaps if she held herself just right. Maybe if she knew what would be or could be. Or if she wished with enough heart. If only she could believe.

She hadn't before, when a life kicked inside her very womb. In a closed-up place in her heart, she knew it was her fault. During the pregnancy she had wondered, Am I meant to be a mother? Am I capable of so much love? And so it had died inside her. If only she hadn't doubted, she could have born the baby wailing to life, ready to nurse at her breast.

This time she would not let her love slacken, even for a moment. She would be vigilant and wish and wish. Please, child. Please, child. Please don't leave us.

But then she would think of Faina running through the trees with the wild fox at her heels, and of Garrett with his steel traps and snares, and she would wonder if one can truly stop the inevitable. Was it as Ada had suggested, that we can choose our own endings, joy over sorrow? Or does the cruel world just give and take, give and take, while we flounder through the wilderness?

Either way, Mabel could not stop herself. She paced and watched and held herself tightly. She pestered Jack with questions. How much longer would the boy trap? Where did he go? What had he caught this time? When Garrett led his horse past the cabin window and waved cheerfully, a dead wolf strapped to the back of the saddle, Mabel held her breath. And when Faina appeared at their door the next day, she let out that breath to ask, How is your fox? And the child said, He's fine.

At last, when March came and Jack said the boy would soon pull his traps, Mabel began to breathe more freely. The first signs of spring arrived in fits and starts, snow that melted, and then rain and snow again. The drifts in the yard dwindled to small patches, but in the woods the snow was still deep. Each morning ice formed on the puddles, and water dripped from the eves and froze into long, glassy icicles.

When Garrett passed through on his way home, Mabel asked him into the cabin for a hot drink and a piece of bread.

'So how many more fox have you caught?' she asked, as if idle curiosity, not desperation, drove her. She set a few slices of fresh bread on the table in front of him.

'None,' he said. 'Not since that silver. I did pick up a wolf, though. And a couple more lynx and coyotes.' The boy was awkward, keeping his hands first at his side, then resting his forearms on the table. He shifted his legs nervously, and picked up a piece of bread.

'How much longer will you trap?' Mabel asked as she put a cup of tea in front of him and lingered behind his chair.

'The river ice is going soft,' he said around a mouthful of bread. 'Few days, I'll snap my traps and call it a year.'

Mabel reached down with one arm and hugged him around the shoulders.

'We worry about you,' she said. She straightened, embarrassed by her outburst, and adjusted her dress. 'Jack and I wouldn't want you to be out on the river if it wasn't safe. And you've done well, haven't you?'

He seemed taken aback by her affection, but

grinned all the same. 'I'll get some fur money this year.'

'Good for you,' she said, and went back to the kitchen counter.

Mabel dozed by the woodstove just before noon, a book propped open in her lap. Most of the winter she hadn't allowed herself to sleep in the middle of the day, if for no other reason than to prove she had not even a touch of cabin fever. But, tossed about by nightmares, she hadn't slept well the night before. Now, soothed by the light of day and the warmth of the fire, she drifted off.

She woke to a small, cool hand atop hers and opened her eyes to Faina.

I have something, the girl said and pulled at Mabel's hand.

Oh, child, you surprised me.

Please hurry, she said.

Is it something to draw?

The child nodded and tugged at her.

Where?

Faina pointed out the window.

Outside? All right. All right. Let me get my boots and coat.

Your pencils, too?

Yes, yes. And my sketchbook.

When Mabel opened the door, the falling snow amazed her. The first week of April, and it was snowing.

Faina took Mabel's hand again and together

they walked into the yard. Even with snow, it smelled of spring, of thawing creek banks and moist earth, of old leaves and new leaves and roots and bark. Mabel became aware of how they stood together, she and the child, still holding hands, and Faina's was so slight and cool, and Mabel's heart was a hole in her chest filling like a well with icy, sweet water.

Will you draw? Faina said quietly.

The snow? I wouldn't know how to go about it.

Faina let go of Mabel and put her palm to the sky, her mitten hanging from a red string at her wrist. A single snowflake lit upon her bare skin. Faina turned and held it to Mabel.

Now can you draw it?

The snowflake was no bigger than the smallest skirt button. It was six pointed with fernlike tips and a hexagonal heart, and it sat in the child's palm like a tiny feather when it should have melted.

It was as if time slowed so that Mabel could no longer breathe or feel her own pulse. What she was seeing could not be, and yet it did not waver. There in the child's hand. A single snowflake, luminous and translucent. A sharp-edged miracle.

Please, will you draw it?

The child's blue eyes were wide and rimmed in frost.

What else was there to do? Mabel fumbled to open her sketchbook. She took the pencil into her weak fingers and began to draw. Faina stood motionless with the snowflake in her hand.

Perhaps we should go inside and sit down to do this, Mabel said, but then realized her mistake. The child smiled and shook her head.

No, no. I guess we can't go inside the warm cabin to draw snow, can we?

The sketch was too small, and Mabel saw it would be impossible to capture every groove and line. She wished for a magnifying glass and flipped to a new page.

I have never been any good at symmetrical drawings, she said more to herself than to the child. I'm too impatient. Too imprecise.

She began again, drawing with broader strokes and filling the entire page with the single geometric shape. She propped the sketchbook on one hand and drew with the other, bending slightly to look more closely. But her breath — that alone could reduce the snowflake to a droplet. She turned her face to the side so as not to exhale on it.

Snow began to land as wet spots on her paper. Mabel worked faster and let out frustrated sighs. If only she were a better artist.

It's perfect, Faina whispered. I knew it would be.

Mabel looked from her drawing to the snowflake in the child's hand.

I can always work on the details later. Shall we call it finished for now? she asked.

Yes, Faina said.

The child put the heel of her hand to her lips and blew on the snowflake and it fluttered into the air like dandelion down.

Oh, Mabel said. Tears came to her eyes, and

she didn't know why.

Faina took her hand again, leaned into Mabel and held tightly to her. The wet snowflakes landed all around them. The world was silent. The snow fell heavier and wetter, and Mabel's coat turned damp.

Faina pulled on her sleeve. Mabel leaned down, expecting her to whisper something in her ear, but instead Faina put her cool, dry lips to Mabel's cheek and kissed her.

Goodbye, the child said.

When Faina let go of her arm and ran into the snow that was now rain, Mabel knew. She tucked the sketchbook under her coat and stood in the rain until her hair was dripping wet and her coat was soaked through and her boots were in mud. She stood and stared through the rain and tried to see into the forest, but she knew.

21

Winter had been a foolish waste of time. He had tinkered in the barn, sorted tools, plucked chickens, played in the snow. He should have done more in the cold months to prepare, but what? It was true what they said about this land — all the work was done in a few frenzied months. The only reason a man could farm here at all was because the sun lasted twenty hours a day during the height of summer, and vegetables grew overnight to enormous sizes. George said he'd seen a cabbage come out of the fields at nearly a hundred pounds.

But here it was May, and Jack couldn't till a row without the horse nearly drowning in mud. Back home the crops would already have been in the ground a month. As he waited for the soil to thaw and dry, he heard a ticking clock, not just the one marking the minutes of each day, but another, more resounding thump that counted down his own days.

This season the homestead had to support itself. He was banking on the fact that several farmers had given up, walked out on their land, even as the market seemed to open up with the railroad expansion. He would throw everything into this year. He'd plant not just potatoes but also carrots, lettuce, and cabbage, and sell vegetables throughout the summer to the mining camps.

He and Mabel talked little, but when they did, they argued. He mentioned that he needed to hire a crew of boys from town to help plant, but they had no money for it.

'We'll have to find some other way,' Mabel said, absently staring at her hands.

'What way? How, in God's name?' His voice was angry, too loud. 'I'm not a young man,' he said more gently. 'My back aches and I can hardly make a fist in the morning. I need help.'

'Who says you have to do this alone? What am I?'

'You're not a farm hand, Mabel. And I won't let you become one.'

'So you'd rather beat yourself to death out there, and leave me in here, so we can each suffer alone.'

'That's never been what I wanted. But the truth is, it's just the two of us. Someone's got to care for the home, and someone's got to earn us a living.' So once again it circled back to the void between them where a child should have been. A girl to help Mabel with the housework. A boy to work in the fields.

'What about the hotel? Maybe I can bake for Betty again.'

'I thought we came here to farm, not to peddle pies and cakes like gypsies. This is it. If this land is ever going to support us, this is the year we've got to do it. And I just don't see how I can do it on my own.' He walked out, but kept himself from slamming the door.

Even as a boy Jack had loved the smell of the ground softening in the thaw and coming back to life. Not this spring. A damp, moldy dreariness, something like loneliness, had settled over the homestead. At first Jack did not know its source. Maybe it was only his own mood. Perhaps it was the spring weather, with overcast skies and freezing rain that soaked through the cabin walls. Mabel, too, seemed beset by a morose restlessness.

Then Jack counted the days — nearly three weeks since the girl's last visit, the longest absence since she'd come into their lives. He tried to train his thoughts on the planting season before him, but he was troubled.

The child's name had gone unspoken. Her chair sat empty, and Mabel no longer put a plate in front of it. Jack worried as much for his wife as for the girl. Mabel no longer watched out the window for her, and he often found her gazing into a basin of dirty dishwater as if she'd lost track of the hours. Sometimes she didn't seem to know he'd entered the cabin until he put a hand on her arm.

The past winter had been so different. Jack had looked forward to their meals together, even when Faina wasn't there. He and Mabel had talked, then, of their plans for the homestead and their future. Jack did not fall asleep right after dinner but helped clear the table. The first time he stepped in and began to wash the dishes, she had pretended to swoon, the back of her hand to her brow, peering through half-closed lids until he kissed her smile. They laughed and danced and made love.

That joy was gone with the child.

He walked past the barn toward the new field. Mud sucked at his boots. He stepped off the trail to walk on the moss and grass of the unbroken ground. Tiny green buds were just beginning to open on the birch trees. Something moved through the forest.

'Faina?'

Movement again, dark and quick, but it was too deep in the trees for him to make out anything more. A path led away from the field, and he followed it. Three days ago he had seen bear tracks in the mud and scat in the trail. He didn't have his rifle, but he wouldn't turn back now.

A week could be explained, she could have gone hunting. Three weeks — that was something different. Illness, an avalanche of wet spring snow, rotten river ice. Jack ticked off the grim possibilities as he strode through the trees.

The land was naked without snow or summer greenery. At his feet, fiddlehead ferns unfurled and tiny shoots pushed up through last year's dead leaves. He climbed as fast as his old heart would allow him. After some time, he arrived at the cliff face and realized he had veered off course and missed the creek. He followed a game trail along the base of the cliffs, ducking under alders, until he heard rushing water. The sound led him to the creek, swollen with spring runoff. It was deafening.

He walked up the creek until he crested a rise and saw the familiar stand of large spruce. There was the stump of the tree he had cut and burned. A heap of rocks had been arranged on the man's grave. Faina must have brought them from the creek bed.

'Faina? Faina! Are you here?' His shouts were lost to the roaring water. 'Faina? It's Jack. Can you hear me?'

He recalled the door in the mountain where he had watched the girl disappear. He scanned the hillside several times before he saw it. It was like any other cabin door, made of rough-hewn boards, except it was cut short enough so that a grown man would have to stoop to enter, and it wasn't hung in the frame of a cabin but set into a grassy knoll. He saw no tracks leading in or out. When he rapped with his knuckles, the door swung inward on leather hinges.

'Faina? Dear child, are you here?'

He dreaded finding her huddled in a bed, sick or starving or worse. Inside it was not as dim as he'd anticipated. Daylight came from somewhere overhead.

'Faina?'

There was no answer. His eyes adjusted. The walls around him were made of logs that had been squared off with an ax. Above him was a wooden ceiling, with a square opening to the sky not much bigger than a stovepipe. Directly below this hole, a large fire pit held the cold, charred remains of a few small logs. The fire pit was also square, set into dirt but framed by the wooden planks that formed the floor.

The builder had dug into the side of the hill and framed the room inside, then replanted sod over the top. The effect was that the small cabin looked like a grassy knoll, just another part of the mountainside. It probably provided better insulation, particularly in winter when the hill was covered in snow, but it didn't seem solely a practical matter. There was something foreboding about the structure. Whoever lived inside these walls would dwell in darkness and secrecy.

The air was musty, like that of an abandoned attic, but as he walked around the small room he caught specific scents — wood, dried meat and fish, tanned furs, and wild herbs. Overhead, dried plants hung in bunches from the roof frame. When Jack stood upright, his head was less than a foot from the ceiling.

The door behind him swung shut with a thump.

'Faina?'

He pushed it open again, but no one was there.

Now that he was in this dank, lonely place, he was more anxious about the child. He paced the small quarters. If he hadn't seen her go through the door, he wouldn't believe a young girl had ever lived here. There were no toys, no dresses or child-sized clothes of any kind. Perhaps she had gone somewhere and taken all that with her — it was impossible to know what had been here and now wasn't. He kicked at the charred wood in the pit. No sparks, no smoke. The fire had been out for days, if not weeks.

There was a bunk made of peeled spruce logs.

Instead of blankets and sheets, the bedding was caribou hides and other tanned furs. One corner formed a makeshift kitchen of sorts, with a counter and shelves lined with odds and ends — jars of beans and flour, but not much food to speak of. The opposite wall held wooden pegs from which hung snowshoes, axes, saws, woodworking tools, things a grown man would use. The tools were grimy and beginning to rust. There were also a few items of clothing, including a fur-ruffed parka that would have been too large even for Jack. He took it off the peg and heard a clinking sound. In the pockets were half a dozen empty glass bottles. He held each to his nose. Some smelled of animal urine and glandular lures, others of a potent moonshine. Peter's water, the child had called it. He shook his head to clear his nostrils and hung the parka back on its peg. In another corner, Jack spotted a stack of dried pelts: beaver, wolf, marten, mink.

He headed toward the door, then remembered the doll. It could be here somewhere. He tossed aside the furs on the bed but found nothing. Then he noticed a wooden box underneath the bunk. He got on his knees and pulled it out.

Inside was a pink baby blanket, worn and dirty but neatly folded. Beneath it were scattered a few black-and-white photographs. Jack picked them up. One showed a nicely dressed couple standing on a dock, suitcases and trunks stacked beside them, as they embarked on a journey. He didn't recognize the man at first — in the photograph he was much younger, with a dapper haircut and clean-shaven face. The woman beside him wore a stylish dress, and in her fine-featured face and blond hair Jack saw Faina. These must be her parents, perhaps leaving Seattle on a ship for Alaska. In another photograph, the woman held an infant swaddled in a blanket that looked new and clean, but Jack was fairly certain it was the same one folded in the box. Another showed the man posing with snowshoes, parka and a lopsided grin. He barely resembled the grizzled corpse Jack had pushed into a hole in the ground, but it was him.

Jack clenched his jaw. How could a man abandon his young daughter to the wilderness? He put the photographs and blanket back in the box and slid it under the bed. Standing up, his knees creaked and he felt old and afraid. The child was gone. This place had swallowed her.

He thought again of the doll and took one last look around the room, but knew he wouldn't find it. It was small comfort. Faina was lost to them, but wherever she was, whatever had befallen her, the doll had been with her.

When he stepped outside, he blinked hard against the daylight and fumbled to close the door. He stood there a moment, listened to the creek and let the mountain air blow against his face. Even with all this heartache, it was beautiful here. He could see across the entire river valley, could almost make out their homestead far below.

22

The next day, when afternoon came and went and Jack did not return from the fields, Mabel was only vaguely puzzled. He must have worked through without a break. When evening came and dinner sat cold on the table, she knew something was wrong. Panic constricted her throat, but she dressed calmly in her coat and boots. At the last minute, she took the shotgun down from the wall and filled her pocket with shells. She vowed to learn to shoot it.

Her hem dragged in the muck as she followed the trail to the fields. Her father-in-law had died in the orchard of a heart attack, and Mabel pictured Jack collapsed in a field. She would be left alone, with little choice but to return to her parents' home where her sister now lived, or go to Jack's family.

Her eyes scanned the first field she came to, but she saw no sign of Jack or the horse. Evening shadows darkened the edge of the forest and in the sky a handful of stars were scattered across the pale blue. A flock of sandhill cranes rose up from a meadow, their calls as ghostly as their gray, slow-beating wings. The mud was beginning to stiffen in the cold. Mabel followed the trail and trembled uncontrollably.

Through the trees she heard the horse whinny.

The trail circled around to the new field, and there she could see the silhouette of the horse, lifting one hoof, then another, still harnessed to the overturned plow.

'Jack? Jack?' she called.

She made out only shapes in the gloomy half-light, but she walked toward the horse. There was a muffled groan.

'Mabel?'

She wanted to run toward the voice, but the rough ground wouldn't allow her. Still she saw no sign of him.

'Here, Mabel. Here.'

She followed the sound, her head bent toward the ground until she nearly stepped on him. He lay flat on his back, his face to the darkening sky.

'What happened?'

'The horse. Dragged me along. Hours ago.' His words came through a slurry of dirt and blood. Mabel knelt beside him and with her sleeve tried to wipe the mess away from his mouth.

'How did this happen?'

'Black bear.'

'Here?'

'By the woods. I busted a bolt on the damned plow, was trying to fix it. The horse saw the bear first and started prancing.'

Mabel looked toward the forest.

'Gone now. Don't think it meant us harm. Just ambled out, like he didn't see us. I tried to get free of the plow. The horse spooked and flipped around on me, caught my leg up in it. Pulled me through the dirt, 'til I fell free. Hoped he'd bring the damned plow all the way home, so you'd know. But he stopped just there.' Jack tried to sit up, but grimaced in pain.

'Where do you hurt?'

'Damn near everywhere.' Jack tried to laugh, but it came out as a gravelly cough. 'It's my back.'

'What can I do?'

'Unhitch the horse. No, don't be nervous. He's all run out now.'

'Then what?'

'Then we've got to get me on him so you can walk us home.'

'Can you stand?'

'I don't know.'

After Jack talked her through it, she unhitched the horse and led it to where he lay. Slipping her arms beneath his, she tried to help him off the ground. He was heavier than she expected, and she sank in the cold mud under his weight. He wrapped his arms around her shoulders and, groaning, got to his knees.

'Christ.' He squinted tears from his eyes.

'I should go for help. I'll get George.'

'No. We can do this. Here.' He held her around the shoulders again and she stood with him, her face crushed into his muddy shirt.

'Easy. Easy there. Grab his bridle.'

With one hand Mabel tried to hold the horse steady while it jerked its head away. Jack fell from her and leaned into the animal's side.

'Jack, you can't. How can you mount him like this?'

'I've got to.' He grabbed the mane and cried out as he hauled himself up, sprawling belly-down across the horse.

'Whoa! Whoa!' Mabel fought to keep the horse still. Jack eased one leg around so he straddled the bare back, his head against the animal's neck where the coat was stiff with dried sweat. Jack's breathing gurgled.

'Jesus,' he whispered. 'Jesus.'

'Jack? Should I start walking now?'

'Easy. Easy does it.'

The way home was long and disorienting. Mabel couldn't discern distance or depth in the murky light. She carried the shotgun in one hand and led the horse with the other. Whenever the horse tripped or stumbled, Jack cried out. Mabel wished she had a rope or lead. Several times the animal yanked the halter strap from her hands, and she feared it might throw Jack to the ground and bolt home.

'It's OK, Mabel. Just take it slow.'

She led the horse to the cabin door and helped Jack slide slowly to the ground, down to his hands and knees.

'Go on,' he said. 'Take the horse to the barn.'

'But — '

'I'll get myself inside. Go.'

As she led the horse away, she looked over her shoulder to see Jack crawling up the doorstep.

A focused composure came over her as she heated water and helped Jack out of his clothes. She put a wool blanket on the floor in front of the woodstove so he could lie there while she washed the blood and dirt from his skin and hair. He grunted in pain occasionally, especially as she dabbed at the abrasions across his shoulder blades. What concerned her more was the deep purple that had begun to well up across his lower back.

'I should go for help.'

He shook his head. 'Just get me into bed.'

She decided to leave the superficial wounds unbandaged, hoping they'd heal faster that way, and slid a clean long-underwear shirt over his head. Half naked, Jack went on hands and knees into the bedroom. Mabel helped him onto the bed. Later she brought him a bowl of broth and tried to spoon it into his mouth, but he only gritted his teeth in pain.

She sat up late that night with a candle on the table and a cup of cold tea in front of her. Occasionally she heard the bed creak and Jack moan. He had shattered bones before — caught his hand between pallets at the family farm, broke his leg when a horse rolled on him — but she had never seen him like this. She knew the pain would worsen by tomorrow. She thought of the empty fields and the frantic pace he had been working, often twelve hours at a stretch, and still he said he would never get it done. Even if he healed quickly, this could ruin them.

Mabel never really slept that night. Her agitated mind worked in relentless circles of planting days and calculated earnings, circles that always came back to a place with no answers. Occasionally she nodded in the chair, only to startle awake at the sound of Jack's cries.

Her prediction was correct — his pain doubled up on itself through the night, and by morning Jack could hardly speak. She gently rolled him onto his side and lifted his shirt. The bruises ran deep to the bone.

'My feet are numb, Mabel.' His whisper was desperate.

She smoothed her hand across his forehead and kissed him on the lips. She spoke with a calm assurance she did not feel. 'I'll be right back.' She brought him water and soft bread, then told him she would be outside for a while feeding the horse.

She had saddled a horse only a few times in her life, but she decided it would be faster than the wagon. She did not want to leave Jack alone but, like the problems she had worried over during the night, there seemed to be no other answer. She would go for a doctor.

Despite the summer she had spent in town, she couldn't recall where to find the doctor. He probably had a room in the boarding house or somewhere in the hotel. After the wearying two-hour ride from the homestead, Mabel dismounted and walked the horse along the dirt road to the general store. Jack had always spoken well of Joseph Palmer, the owner. She remembered him as a kind man with a short white beard and quiet manner.

The old man seemed embarrassed on Mabel's behalf when she asked after a doctor.

'No doctor around here. Nearest one would be in Anchorage. You'd have to catch the train in.'

'What?'

'We don't have a doctor, dear. Never have,' he repeated gently.

'You must be joking? No doctor? Isn't this a town, for God's sake?'

Mabel took a slow breath, tried to find some small reservoir of strength inside herself. Mr Palmer nodded as she told him of Jack's injuries. He'd known men who twisted up their backs and doctors never could do much anyways.

'You've just got to let time take its course. It'll either heal, or it won't,' and he said it as if he regretted the truth, as if he knew what hung in the balance.

Aside from train tickets to Anchorage, Mr Palmer could only offer her a brown glass bottle.

'Give him a bit every few hours. It'll ease the pain and help him sleep,' he said. 'And don't worry about giving him too much. I've known men who drink it regularly and don't seem overly affected.'

Mabel paid and thanked him. As she turned toward the door, he spoke again.

'It might not seem proper, but you could consider getting him a few jars of drink. Ted Swanson, on the other side of the tracks, down by the river. He could help you. It might do Jack some good, mix a bit of that in alcohol. I don't usually make such recommendations, but it sounds as if he's in need.'

Laudanum and moonshine — all this place could offer her injured husband. She mounted the horse and galloped toward their homestead, too angry to be frightened.

23

Sticky cottonwood buds cracked open beneath blue skies and the mud in the fields turned to moist, rich soil, but Mabel's grief seemed beaten over and dusty and all too familiar. Something akin to hunger or thirst clung to the back of her throat, and she considered drinking some of Jack's laudanum, but didn't. Backlit by the brilliant sun, the cabin was dark and cool. She didn't light the fire, but kept candles burning. In the bed where she no longer slept, Jack lay in a stupor, calling out only when the painkiller wore off. She thought of what Esther had told her about moose, how they often starved to death just as spring arrives. Having lived through the depths of winter, the long-legged animals wallow in the heavy, wet snow and succumb to exhausted despair.

She was alone. The strong husband who had cared for her was a crumpled man who sobbed in the night and begged her to leave him, to go back home and find a new life without him. The little girl she had begun to love had vanished, another child lost. Sitting upright in the chair, she slept in brief, intense bouts at odd hours and dreamed of a bloody, stillborn infant and puddles of snowmelt. The fairy tale from her sister's letter haunted her dreams. 'Whenever I do know that you love me little, then I shall melt away again. Back into the sky I'll go — Little Daughter of the Snow.'

When Mabel woke, she could not even grieve her dreams. There was too much to be done: caring for the horse, hauling the water, helping Jack to a makeshift chamber pot, cooking meals, even if she alone ate them. Fatigue distorted her sense of time, and often she did not know whether it was day or night, dusk or dawn.

One afternoon, when the nightmares would not leave her, she went outside and blinked against the sun. She threw bread scraps to the wild chickadees and pine grosbeaks and talked to them as if they could understand, but they only scattered at the sound of her voice. She went to the pasture and stroked the horse's soft muzzle. She wandered into the trees and picked the boughs of highbush cranberries, and, with the tiny white blossoms clasped in her hands, she let her eyes search for the girl, but the woods were silent. She thought of the black bear and the wolves. She only had to get Jack well enough to travel, and then they would leave this place. There was nothing for them here.

'Hello! Hello! Anyone at the homestead?'

With the sun in her eyes, she couldn't make out the figure on horseback. The man dismounted and removed a burlap sack from his saddlebags. It was George. Relief nearly buckled Mabel's knees, and when he offered her his arm, she took it gratefully.

'So the old man is laid up, eh?'

He led her indoors to a chair and began taking

clinking Mason jars from the sack. He lined them up on the table, each jar sparkling with clear liquid.

'Now, don't give me that look, Mabel. Never been a better excuse than a broken back. So where is he?'

Mabel pointed to the bedroom where Jack slept.

'He can't walk on his own yet,' Mabel whispered. 'And when the laudanum wears off, the pain is unbearable.'

George shook his head side to side and clicked his tongue softly. 'Damn. He's not up to snuff, is he?'

'No, George. No, he is not.' She stood and began putting the jars of moonshine onto a shelf in the kitchen, as if it made some difference.

'As soon as he is well enough, I'll schedule our travel,' she said. 'And I know he will want you to have any of our tools and equipment, and of course the horse. We won't be able to take any of it with us, I'm afraid.'

'Mabel?'

'We can't stay here. You must see that.'

'You're leaving the homestead? For good?'

'We were barely keeping it going as it was, George. And there's just the two of us. It has been a fantastic adventure, coming here. But now it's time we accepted our lot and went home.'

'You can't just walk away. You've done so much work with the place. There's got to be another way.'

George glanced toward the bedroom. 'How

long's he been like this?'

'More than a week.'

'And how much had he gotten done on the fields before he got hurt?'

'He was still just preparing them.'

'Nothing's been planted?'

Mabel shook her head.

'Goddamned — excuse the French. It's just a helluva blow, isn't it?'

'Yes, George. It truly is.'

He was unusually quiet as he mounted his horse.

'We'll say goodbye before we go,' Mabel called to him from the cabin door. 'Tell Esther thank you, for everything. You were truly the most wonderful neighbors we could have hoped for.'

George glanced back at her, shook his head, and rode off without a word. Mabel was certain his look was reproachful.

She was emptying the basin behind the cabin later that afternoon when she heard a wagon approaching on the dirt road. She hurried indoors and began to hide the linens and underwear she had been washing.

'Don't do that on our account.' Mabel heard Esther's laugh at the door.

'Oh, Esther!' She was surprised to find herself hugging her, then pressing her face into her friend's shoulder and sobbing.

'Go on. Go on. You have yourself a cry.' Esther patted her on the back. 'There you go.'

Mabel pulled away, smiled, and wiped her face. 'Look at me. I'm a mess. What an awful way to greet a visitor.'

'I wouldn't expect anything else. Poor woman, here for days on your own caring for a banged-up man. Strong as they are, they're like children with pain. No birthing to toughen them up, I say.' Esther looked Mabel straight in the eye when she said this, and there was no wince of regret or embarrassment. It was as if Esther knew exactly what memories she conjured, and Mabel understood — she had gone through labor, if only to deliver a dead child. She had survived that, hadn't she? It was as if she had reached into her own pocket and discovered a small pebble, as hard as a diamond, that she had forgotten belonged to her.

'Where the hell am I supposed to put this?'

Garrett stood in the doorway, glaring over a heap of parcels in his arms.

'Watch your mouth. And put it wherever you can find room. Then go get the rest.'

'What is all this, Esther?'

'Supplies.'

'But we don't . . . didn't George tell you?'

'About your harebrained plan to ditch us? Oh, he told me all right. We finally get some interesting friends and you think we're going let you go without a fight.'

'But we are leaving, so we don't need any of this.' Mabel dropped her voice to nearly a whisper. 'And honestly, Esther, we don't have the money to pay for it.'

Garrett stomped by and dropped another

armload onto the table. As the boy marched by, Esther pretended to slap him on the back of the head. Despite herself, Mabel smiled.

'Don't worry about the money. Everybody heard about your predicament and threw some stuff together. Nothing fancy, but it'll keep us for a while.'

'I don't know what to say. It's too much . . . too generous.'

'Well, we might not have a doctor around here, but we do have a few kind hearts among us,' and Esther winked over her shoulder as she began unloading boxes and sacks.

'Oh, I'm appalled at myself! I didn't mean anything by it. I was just so frustrated.'

'No harm done. Old Man Palmer was too impressed by your riding skills to be offended. He said he'd never seen a lady gallop in such a gentlemanly way. Garrett, put those bedrolls over there, behind the woodstove. Keep them out of the way for now.'

'Bedrolls?'

'Didn't I mention? We're moving in. The boy and me. We might be a bossy, ill-tempered pair, but you can't complain about free help.'

'Help? With Jack?'

'With Jack. With the planting. You've got us for the rest of the season, or until you get sick of us.'

'Esther — no, no. We can't allow this.'

'Can't allow it? I don't think you understand who you're up against here, dear heart. We'll be planting those fields, Garrett and me. You can either help or get out of the way, but we'll be doing it.'

Her voice was drowned out by the ruckus of Garrett dragging a horse trough through the cabin door. 'Cripe's sake, Ma. What the hell did we bring this for?'

'If you weren't working your jaw, you'd be getting the job done. Bring it on over here, by the woodstove.'

'Don't you think they've probably got a trough or two of their own?' He sarcastically rolled his eyes toward the barn.

'Not like this one.'

The horse trough was sparkling clean and took up most of the standing room by the woodstove. Mabel had the comic realization that she was watching her house being turned into a Benson home, quarrels and clutter and all.

'Garrett, have Mabel take you out to the field so you can take a look at the plow. See if it needs any fixing. Go on, Mabel. Some fresh air will do you good, and I'll take care of things here.'

The boy was sullen and unresponsive on their walk, and Mabel soon left him in the field to work on the plow. Despite a niggling guilt, she took the long way back to the cabin. She inhaled the green scent of new leaves and studied the sharp line along the mountaintops where white snow met leafy forest. Then she remembered she had missed Jack's dose of laudanum.

'Back already? You should have stayed gone a bit. Your water's not done yet.' Esther dipped a finger into a giant pot on the woodstove. She had propped open the cabin door to let the heat escape. Mabel hurried to the bedroom. Jack's hair was damp and combed, and he smiled meekly up at her from the pillow.

'She gave me a bath,' he said.

'Esther did?'

He nodded as well as he could. Pillows and blankets propped him up in a peculiar position, with his knees bent and separated.

'Are you comfortable?'

He squinted self-consciously and then nodded. 'Believe it or not.'

'I'm sorry I missed your dose of medicine.'

'Esther gave it to me, with a nip of something stronger.'

'Hurry on out here,' Esther called from the other room, 'before the water gets cold or that adolescent son of mine comes back.' She was dumping the pot of steaming water into the horse trough.

'Usually it'd be the other way around, ladies first, but I wanted to get those wounds clean as possible. You're getting some fresh water on top of that, though.'

Mabel wanted to refuse, to tell Esther she had done too much, but she stripped and climbed into the knee-deep hot water while Esther stood guard at the door.

'Take your time. It's not every day you're getting a bath like that.'

Beside the makeshift tub, Esther had placed a chair that held a clean washcloth, a bar of milled soap, and a bottle of lavender-scented shampoo. The water was almost unbearably hot, but Mabel let herself sink until even her head was submerged and her untied hair floated around her. Each time she started to get out of the tub,

Esther ordered her back in, so she soaked until the water was tepid and the skin on her fingers and toes wrinkled. When she finally did get out, the sun had disappeared behind the mountains and left the perpetual twilight of a summer night. Esther wrapped her in a towel and fluffed her hair.

'There. Now we're getting somewhere. Dinner will be ready soon. Get some comfortable clothes on. Nothing fancy. Just something to sleep in. I expect Garrett will be gone until late, looking at the fields. He's not keen on bunking with two old women, but he'll get tired eventually.'

With both of them wearing nightgowns, Esther served Mabel black bear stew, hot from the stove, and fresh biscuits. Then she spread out three bedrolls.

'I figured you'd been sleeping in a chair for days now. I know how it is when you've got a sick one tossing and turning in your bed. But these aren't so bad. I even brought you a clean one. Come on now,' and she crawled beneath her covers and patted the bedroll beside her.

Mabel found it an unexpected relief to rest her head on a pillow, to be clean and fed and not alone.

'So, do you really think we can manage this?' she whispered from beneath her covers. 'You and Garrett and me? Planting our whole farm?'

'I wouldn't be here if I didn't think we could do something.'

'But what about your own place?'

'George's got Bill and Michael there to help, and we'd planned on hiring a couple of the youngsters from town to help with planting. We've got a good portion done already.'

'I don't know how to thank you.'

'We're not there yet.'

The two women were silent a while, and then Esther spoke gently. 'And what of your little girl?'

'She's gone, Esther.'

She reached over and found Mabel's hand and squeezed it once.

'Sweet Mabel,' she said. 'I suppose now that you're getting some sunshine and fresh air, she isn't coming around anymore.'

Mabel didn't answer, only stared at the ceiling for a long time. She thought Esther might have fallen asleep, and she had nearly dozed off herself when she began to laugh, quietly at first, but then louder.

'What's tickled your funny bone?'

'You really gave Jack a bath? I can hardly believe it,' Mabel said. 'His mother. Myself. I don't think another woman has ever . . .'

'I've been married for thirty years and have three sons. When you've seen one, you've seen 'em all.'

The two women were giggling when Garrett walked in the door.

'What? What's so funny?' he asked, but his stern face and blushing cheeks only made them laugh harder.

Voices rolled over Jack in waves that left him nauseous and confused, so he let himself sink back into the thick liquid of laudanum and moonshine. It was a warm, black place, without past or future or meaning. Later, when he woke to quiet shadows, his head was clear and thudding. He didn't understand the laughter he had heard before. Then he remembered Esther, helping him naked into a horse trough of hot water. Pain burned a hole through the center of his back and radiated up through his chest, and he sobbed. He stuffed a fist into his mouth to stifle it, and he sobbed and sobbed. Self-pity. That's what this was. It wasn't the searing nerves and muscle spasms that tore him apart. It was his life reduced to useless burden.

'Jack?' A whisper from the bedroom door. 'You needing something?'

He swallowed hard and wiped his mouth with the back of his hand.

'Time for another dose?'

It wasn't Mabel.

'Esther? You're here?'

'Shhh. Giving your wife a break. Drink this.' She had mixed laudanum and moonshine in a tin cup, and he drank it down in a noisy gulp. She took the cup, then with a handkerchief wiped the wetness from his eyes and cheeks.

'This too shall pass, Jack. I know it doesn't seem like it now, but it will. Me and Garrett are here to help, and Mabel's tougher than she lets on. This isn't all on your shoulders now. You've

223

got some help. You understand? It's going to be all right.'

But Jack was seeking out that deep, opaque place where sound and pain and light are muted, where a man doesn't have to put words to his despair because his numb tongue and useless lips can't speak anything at all.

24

Esther insisted on being Jack's primary nurse, slowly reducing the laudanum doses and increasing the length of his daily walks. First, just to the kitchen table. Then to the outhouse so at least he wouldn't have to use a chamber pot.

'You're too easy on him, Mabel. He's got to get up and move. It's the only way those muscles can start to work again.'

'But he's in so much pain.'

'At some point his hurt is deeper than a sore back. Do you know what I'm saying? It's a more terrible kind of hurt, a kind that opium and drink only make worse. He's got to get on his own two feet. He's got to see his land and help us make some decisions so that he knows it's still his, even if he can't get his hands in the dirt.'

So while Garrett showed Mabel how to cut seed potatoes so each piece had one eye, Esther spent the morning walking Jack around the fields. Mabel couldn't bear to watch his slow shuffle. It was as if he had aged a century in a month. His face was gaunt and his back bent. When his foot caught on a root or rut, he would grunt and stand in one place, his eyes closed and his jaw muscles clenching and unclenching. She would have been ashamed to admit it to anyone, but she was glad to sit in the yard with Garrett, to cut seed potatoes rather than escorting her husband on his agonizing walk.

And the boy wasn't such terrible company. Esther said he was chafing at the humiliation of having to work another man's homestead with two old women. He thinks he wants to be a mountain man, Esther said, that farming is beneath him. But he's a good boy. He works hard when he puts his mind to it.

Mabel observed Garrett's resentment; he stomped in and out of the cabin and sulked when his mother ordered him around. But when she was alone with him, the boy was less petulant. He was, actually, patient and instructive, and did not patronize her. Never once did he say, 'Now, watch that knife' or 'Mind you don't cut yourself'. He assumed Mabel could do the work, and so she could. Soon she was almost as fast as he was with the paring knife.

The sun climbed higher in the sky and warmed the top of Mabel's head while she tossed the cut seed potatoes into the burlap sack between them. It was lunchtime and she didn't know where the morning had gone. The boy followed her inside and helped her fix a meal of cold sliced moose steak and yesterday's bread. After Esther helped Jack back into bed, the three of them ate quickly while standing in the kitchen, Mabel's hands still smudged with dirt and her dress sleeves pushed up.

When they went out to load the wagon with the seed potatoes, Mabel followed. It was only as she handed a heavy burlap sack to Garrett on the back of the wagon that she appreciated what she was doing — farm work. The boy took no notice of her pause, but grabbed the bags and hopped down. As Esther drove the wagon toward the field, Mabel and Garrett followed behind.

'Maybe none of my business,' he said, 'but that dress might get in your way. You don't have any trousers or anything, do you? Mom always wears overalls when she's working.'

'No. I don't have anything like that. The dress will have to do.'

Garrett looked skeptical but kept walking.

Esther dropped sacks of seed potatoes up and down the field, then harnessed the horse to a cultivator to form the rows. Garrett and Mabel followed. The boy showed her how far apart to plant and how deep to dig the hole before dropping in the cut potato, following her to scoop dirt over the top and lightly pat. As they worked, they dragged the burlap sack along with them.

After a time the work became methodical and rhythmic, and Mabel's mind wandered. She planted with bare hands and thought of soil, warm and crumbling between her fingers, and of sprouting plants and decaying leaves. She stood, shook out her skirts, bent again toward the earth, dug another hole, dropped in a potato, then another hole, another potato. She pressed her hand into the dirt mound, like a little grave.

Here in the potato field, the colors were too sharp and full of yellow sun and blue sky. Even the air was different than back in Pennsylvania, drier and cleaner. Time had passed, more than a decade. Yet as she knelt here, Mabel was back there. Pewter moonlight. The paths of the orchard. Rough ground beneath her knees. A dead child two days buried.

She remembered how she had left Jack asleep in bed to wander out of doors in her nightgown. Weakened and bruised by her long labor, she didn't know what led her down the gravel drive to the orchard, where the trees stood brown and leafless in the blue moonlight.

That is where he would have dug the grave, in the ground his family had farmed for generations. She crawled between the trees, her knees and palms scraped. When she found nothing, she stood and felt a painful tingling in her breasts and suddenly milk trickled down her front, wet her nightgown, dribbled onto her belly, spilled uselessly to the ground.

I cannot survive this grief, she had thought.

'Are you OK?'

Garrett's shadow fell across her face and she didn't know how long she had been there, kneeling in the dirt.

'Yes. Yes. I'm fine,' Mabel said. She wiped her dirty hands on her dress. 'I was only recalling something.'

When she looked up at Garrett, the boy's eyes widened.

'Are you sure you're all right? Because

228

. . . well, because you don't look so good.' The boy gestured toward her face. A few tears must have run down her dirt-smeared cheeks and the lines would look ghastly.

'Please forgive an old woman's weepiness,' she said and began to search for something to wipe her face.

Garrett stood staring.

'Surely you've seen a woman cry before.'

He shrugged.

'No? Perhaps not. I certainly cannot imagine your mother blubbering about.'

'Should we go back? Do you need a rest?'

'No. No. Just something to wipe my face.'

The boy searched his pockets for a handkerchief, but finding nothing he unrolled the sleeve of his work shirt and held up the cuff. 'It's kind of dirty, but you're welcome to it.'

Mabel smiled and blotted her eyes with his shirtsleeve. 'Thank you,' she said.

As the boy turned to reach for the burlap sack at his feet, Mabel caught his sleeve again and held his arm with both hands. 'I've been wanting to ask you something, Garrett.'

'Yes, ma'am?'

'Did you ever catch another fox, after that silver one?'

'No ma'am, never did,' he said. He studied her thoughtfully. 'Are you wanting a fox ruff? Because if you are, I've got a few pelts left over from last year. I'm sure Betty could sew you something.'

But Mabel was already bending to the earth to dig another hole.

She had survived, hadn't she? Even when she had wanted to lie down in the night orchard and sink into a grave of her own, she had stumbled home in the dark, washed in the basin, and in the morning cooked breakfast for Jack. She had put away the dishes and scrubbed the table and counters. She had baked bread. She had worked and tried to ignore the painful swell of her breasts and the empty cramp of her womb. And then she had done the unthinkable; she had entered the nursery and put her hands on the oak crib, the one Jack had slept in as a child, and his mother before him. She touched the pastel quilt she had sewn, and then sorrow collapsed her into the rocking chair, where she sat with her arms across her sagging belly and remembered how it had been to have another person growing inside her.

When she had the strength, she began to fold the tiny clothes and blankets and cloth diapers and put them into plain brown boxes. She didn't stop working, but the sobs came and distorted her face, bleared her eyes, made her nose run. She didn't hear Jack come to the door. When she looked up he was watching her silently, and then he turned away, uncomfortable, embarrassed by her unharnessed grief. He didn't put his hand on her shoulder. Didn't hold her. Didn't say a word. Even these many years later, she was unable to forgive him that.

At the end of the row, Mabel stood, put her hands to the small of her back, and stretched. Her hem was soiled, her hands dusty and tired. She looked down the field and saw how much they had done. Garrett slapped his hands on his pant legs.

'One row down,' he said. ''Bout a thousand to go.' And the boy gave her a half-smile, his eyebrows raised as if to ask 'Are you still in?'

Mabel nodded.

'Onward ho?' she asked.

Garrett raised a hand, like a conquering explorer.

'Onward ho!'

As Esther rounded a row and headed back down the field, she slowed the horse and gave a wave to the two of them. Mabel raised her hand and waved back. A breeze stirred the loose strands of hair around her face and wicked away the sweat. The sky overhead was cloudless and brilliant. In the distance, beyond the trees, she could see the white mountain peaks. She lifted her skirts and stepped over the row they had just planted. Garrett pulled the burlap sack to her and they started again.

They worked until dusk and arrived back at the cabin well past dinnertime. Jack had lit the lanterns and was frying steaks.

'What's all this?' Esther said. She inhaled deeply and grinned. 'Something smells mighty good.'

'Can't do much. Thought the least I could do is feed my help.' He smiled like a man at fault.

❇

The next days were a blur of potatoes, earth, sun and aching muscles as each row of planting went by. Jack did what he could but mostly stayed in the cabin and fixed meals. In the evenings everyone was too tired to talk. The boy nodded off at the dinner table with his chin propped up on his dirty hands. By the time night fell, Mabel was numb with fatigue. She had never understood how Jack could fall asleep in a chair without washing up, talking to her about his day, or even removing his filthy boots. Now she knew. Yet for all the sore muscles and monotony, the days of working in the fields filled her with a kind of pride she had never known. She no longer saw the cabin as rough, but was grateful at the end of the day for warm food and a bedroll on which to collapse. She didn't notice if the dishes went unwashed or the floor unswept.

'I think we've done it, Jack,' Esther announced one afternoon, hands on her hips. 'I know you had plans to do more this year, to get some lettuce and such planted along with the potatoes. But I was thinking, we've got the potatoes in the ground and we'll see what happens.'

Jack nodded in agreement. Maybe it would be enough to get them by.

'We wouldn't be here if it weren't for you two.' His voice was gravelly and genuine, but there was a dimness behind his eyes that reminded Mabel of shame. 'I don't know how we'll ever repay you.'

Esther waved him off impatiently, and said she planned on going home that evening.

'It's been a hoot, but I'm ready to sleep in my

232

own bed, snoring husband and all. You're shaping up, Jack, and I think Garrett can manage the fields. Nope — no ifs, ands or buts about it. George and I have talked it out. Garrett works better here than he ever did at home, and our planting's done. You can fix him a place in the barn to get him out of your hair. Then you two can have your place back to yourselves.'

It was time, yet Mabel dreaded it. Jack was a different man, unsteady and unsure. She could not forget how, during the worst of it, he had cried and begged her to leave him. And then, while he hobbled about, she had gone into the fields and worked with a new strength and surety. With Esther and Garrett gone, she and Jack would once again share a bed, and she wondered if it would be like sleeping with a stranger. Jack looked at her sadly, as if he could read her thoughts.

After dinner, Esther left and Mabel showed Garrett to the barn loft. He brought his bedroll, and she overturned a wooden box for him to use as a nightstand. There she set a lantern, as well as an alarm clock and a book.

'*White Fang*, by Jack London. Have you read it before?'

'No, ma'am.'

'Please, just call me Mabel. I think you'll like this one, but if it doesn't suit you, I've got dozens of others to choose from.'

She was going to warn him to be careful with the lantern, but thought better of it. He had treated her as an equal, so she would try to do the same.

'Come inside if you need anything, even if it's just company.'

'Yes, ma'am . . . I mean, Mabel.'

'Garrett, there was one other thing I've wanted to ask you.'

'Yes?'

'When you were out there trapping last winter, did you ever see anything unusual? Tracks in the snow? Anything you couldn't explain?'

'You mean the little girl, don't you? I heard about her.'

'And? Did you ever see any sign of her?'

The boy gave a slow, disappointed turn of his head.

'Nothing at all? Ever?'

'Sorry,' he said.

It was a cold night, and Jack had started a fire. The dirty dishes were left piled in the kitchen, and Mabel sat in a chair in front of the woodstove and stretched her feet to the warmth. She was more tired than she could ever remember being. Her muscles ached and hummed. When she closed her eyes, tilled rows stretched to the horizon. She drifted along the earth.

'Mabel. You're falling asleep. Come to bed.'

Jack rubbed her shoulders. 'This has been too much for you.'

'No, no.' She looked up at him. 'It feels wonderful, to share in the work, to feel like I'm doing something. Today might very well have been one of the best days of my life . . . ' Her voice trailed off as she understood what she was saying. Jack nodded without speaking.

She put on her nightgown and got into bed. Jack, stripped to his long underwear, sat on the edge.

'Jack?'

'Hmmm?'

'We are going to be all right, aren't we? I mean, the two of us?'

He groaned as he eased his feet onto the bed. He rolled onto his side to face Mabel, reached to her and ran his hand down her unbraided hair, again and again, without speaking. Mabel saw tears in the corners of his eyes, and she propped herself on an elbow. She leaned to him and kissed him on his closed wet eyelids.

'We will, Jack. We will be all right,' and she cradled his head in the crook of her arm and let him cry.

25

That summer was a farmer's blessing. Even Jack could see that. At perfect intervals the skies rained and the sun shone. Of his own accord, Garrett planted rows of vegetables to supply the railroad, and the plants flourished in the fields.

Jack's back still gave him trouble, and there were mornings when he had to slide out of bed to the floor and crawl to the bureau to pull himself to a standing position. His hands and feet sometimes went numb, and other days his joints swelled and ached. He suspected a morning would come when he wouldn't be able to get out of bed at all.

But in the evenings, when the snow-capped mountains went periwinkle in the twilight of the midnight sun, he would walk the fields alone, and his step was lighter. He would go down the perfect rows of lettuce and cabbage, their immense leaves green and lush. The earth was soft beneath his boots and smelled of humus. Often he would scoop some of the soil in his hand and run his thumb over it, marveling at its richness, and sometimes he would pull a radish, rub it clean on his pants, and bite into it with a satisfying crunch, then toss the greens into the trees. From there he would walk down to the new field where the potato plants had grown thigh high and had just begun to flower. It hardly seemed the same stretch of lifeless, bone-bruising ground the horse had dragged him across last winter.

He owed this to Esther, he knew, and the boy. Garrett staggered the lettuce and radish crops so they were ready when the railroad needed them week to week. He weeded and hilled the potatoes. He knew which kind of fertilizers worked, and which didn't, so Jack didn't have to trust the salesman in Anchorage but could go on real experience.

Even at just fourteen, the boy was a dependable farmer, but his heart wasn't in it. With permission, Garrett would leave for days at a time, taking his horse, a rifle, and a knapsack. Sometimes he returned with the pack full of rainbow trout or spruce grouse for dinner. Once he brought Mabel a beaded moosehide pouch sewn by an Athabascan woman upriver. Other times he came back with stories of a mountain waterfall he had discovered or a grizzly bear he had seen playing on a patch of snow.

'That bear was just like a little kid, running to the top and sliding down, then back up to the top.'

One evening, the summer sun glinting down the valley, Garrett asked to join Jack on his stroll around the fields.

'I'll bring a gun. Maybe we'll run into a grouse or two.'

Jack was self-conscious about his slow pace

and disinclined to give up his solitude. Also, he didn't care much for the boy shooting game on the farm. Jack had spooked a grouse or two on his walks, and he enjoyed the burst of excitement it gave him when the bird flapped noisily up from his feet and then settled, plump and ruffled, on a spruce branch. He said nothing in hopes the boy would take the hint, but Garrett dashed to the barn to get his shotgun.

'We'll be back in a bit,' Jack said over his shoulder as he walked out the door, but he doubted Mabel had heard. She was bent over the table, working on the sewing project that had consumed her evenings, and he felt a rush of affection for her.

It humiliated him at first, knowing she was working the farm in his place. Now, with summer mostly gone, he knew his step was lighter in part because of her. She was no longer a lost soul — she was right there beside him, the same dirt on her hands, the same thoughts on her mind. How many rows of reds should we plant next year? Do we need to lime the north field? When the new hen starts laying, should we let her hatch a dozen or so? The fate of it all, the farm, their happiness, was no longer his alone. Look what we've done, she said to him one morning as she pointed to the rows of radishes, cabbage, broccoli, and lettuce.

Shotgun in the crook of his arm, Garrett trotted down the dirt road and caught up with Jack.

'We'll probably never see another year like this,' the boy said. He shook his head in disbelief as he looked out over the field. 'Can you believe it? We want rain, it rains. We want sun, the sun shines.'

'It's been good.' Jack bent and pulled two plants. He handed a radish to Garrett. They both wiped them on their pants and silently ate them.

'Can't thank you enough for everything you've done here.' Jack tossed his greens into the trees.

'It's nothing.'

'No, it is something.'

They followed the trail that led to the new field. Garrett led the way, carrying his shotgun and kicking at dirt clods. What are you feeding my boy over there? Esther had joked, and Jack, too, had noticed that Garrett had shot up several inches during the summer. He had lost some of the boyhood softness in his face, and his jawline and cheekbones were more prominent. His mannerisms had matured as well. He looked Jack in the eye, spoke his opinions clearly, and rarely had to be asked to do something. George doubted it, said they were too kind to speak so of his youngest son, but during their visits he eventually saw the change, too. Maybe we should have sent our others over as well, George said and laughed. But Jack suspected the boy could only come into his own without his brothers looming over him. There was even some sign that Garrett took pride in the work he had done here at their homestead.

The trail ran along the edge of the field and past a swath of black spruce. The waning daylight did not penetrate far into the spindly, dense trees and the air was noticeably cooler in their shadow. It was such a thin line, just a wagon trail, that separated the forest from the tidy green of the field, and Jack was thinking of the work that had gone into it when Garrett stopped in the trail and broke down his shotgun as if to load it. Jack looked past him. It took a moment for his eyes to focus, and just as they did, Garrett dug a cartridge from his pocket and thumbed it into the barrel.

'No! Wait.' Jack put his hand on the boy's back. 'Don't.'

Garrett looked at him out of the corner of his eyes, and took aim.

'I said don't shoot it.'

'That fox? Why not?' Garrett squinted in disbelief, then swept his eyes back down the gun barrel, as if he had misheard. The fox ran out of the woods and crouched in the trail. Jack couldn't be sure — one red fox from another. But the markings looked the same, the black ears, near-crimson orange fur, the black-socked feet. It was all he had left of her.

'Leave it be.'

'The fox?'

'Yes, for Christ's sake. The fox. Just leave it be.' Jack shoved the gun barrel down.

The animal took its chance and darted into the potato field. Jack glimpsed the fluffy red tail between the plants and then it was gone.

'Are you crazy? We could have had it.' Garrett broke down the shotgun, pulled out the cartridge and stuffed it in his pocket. Their eyes met, and Jack saw a flash of irritation, maybe even contempt.

'Look, I wouldn't have minded but — '

'He'll be back, you know.' Garrett's short, disrespectful tone surprised Jack.

'We'll see.'

'They always are. Next time he'll be picking through your dump pile or sniffing around the barn.' Garrett walked ahead and as they circled the field, he watched where the fox had run but didn't say anything. It wasn't until they neared the house that he spoke again. 'It doesn't make any sense, letting it get away.'

'Let's just say I know that one. He used to belong to somebody,' and Jack found the words hard.

'Belonged? A fox?' They neared the barn and Jack wanted the talk done and Garrett off to bed, but the boy stopped in front of the door.

'Who did it belong to?'

'Somebody I knew.'

'There's nobody else around here for miles . . . ' His voice trailed off and he turned to the barn, then back again. 'Wait. It's not that girl, is it? The one I heard Mom and Dad talking about? The one Mabel says came around last winter?'

'Yep. That was her fox, and I don't want anyone shooting it.'

Garrett shook his head and exhaled sharply out his nose.

'Is there a problem with that?'

'No. No, sir.' It had been a long time since he had called Jack sir.

Jack walked toward the house.

'It's just . . . there wasn't really a girl, was there?'

Jack almost kept walking. This wasn't a

conversation he wanted to have. He was tired. His evening had been disturbed and he wished he had stayed put at home in front of the woodstove. But he faced Garrett.

'Yes. There was a girl. She raised that fox from a pup. It still comes around sometimes, but it's never done any harm, only taken what we've offered.'

Again there was the shake of the head and the soft snort.

'There's no way.'

'What? Raising a fox from a pup?'

'No. The girl. Living by herself around here, in the woods. In the middle of winter? She wouldn't stand a chance.'

'You don't think a person could do it? Live off this land?'

'Oh, somebody could. A man. Somebody who really knew what he was doing. Not many,' and he said it as if he were one of the few. 'Certainly no little girl.'

Garrett must have seen a look pass over Jack's face, because his confidence seemed to falter. 'I mean, I'm not doubting what you think you saw. Maybe there's just another way to account for it.'

'Maybe.' Jack walked slowly toward the house. He didn't wait for Garrett to say more, but as he neared the door he heard him call out, 'Good night. And tell Mabel good night, too.' Without turning around, Jack held up the back of his hand in a brief wave.

❋

'Nice walk?' Mabel's eyes were on her sewing. She had lit a lantern in the weak light and was bent close to the fabric. Jack eased off his boots and went to the basin to wash his hands. He splashed the cold water over his face, too, and then dried his face and the back of his neck.

'How's the sewing coming?'

'Slow but sure. I just had to rip out a few seams, so I'm pulling my hair out right now.' She put down her work, sat back in the chair and stretched her neck. 'Did you two have a nice walk?'

'It was all right. Quieter on my own.'

'Yes. He's become quite a talker, hasn't he? But I do enjoy him. And he is a hard worker.'

'Yes. He is.'

Jack stoked the woodstove and added a log. Nights were cooler now as autumn approached.

'So what have you been sewing on over there?'

'Oh, just a little something.'

'A secret? A Christmas present, then, is it?'

'Not for you. Not this one,' and Mabel smiled up at him.

'Well, what then?'

'Oh, nothing really . . . ' and he knew she wanted to tell him.

'Come on. Out with it. You're like a cat with a goldfish in its mouth.'

'All right then. It's for Faina. A new winter coat. I think I've figured out how to do the trim.' Mabel stood and held the pieces of the coat in front of her, laying the blue boiled wool across her front and along her arms as if it were sewn together. Then she picked up a few strips of white fur.

'For Faina?'

'Yes. Isn't it beautiful? This is rabbit fur. Snowshoe hare, actually. I asked Garrett for it. I told him I was working on a sewing project. He said this was the softest, and it is. Feel it.'

So this is what she'd spent her time on these past few days. This is what kept her up at night, sketching in her little notebook, smiling and light-hearted. He wanted to yank the thing from her hands and throw it to the floor. He felt sick, light-headed even.

'Don't you like it? You see, I noticed last time we saw her, how her coat was frayed and worn. And she had nearly outgrown it last winter. Her wrists were sticking out. I wasn't sure about the size, but I tried to remember how tall she had been when she was sitting in this chair, and how narrow her shoulders were.'

Mabel spread the coat on the table and picked up some spools of thread. Her face was radiant. 'It'll be lovely. I know it will. I just hope I can finish it in time.'

'In time for what?'

'For when she comes back.' She said it as if it were as plain as the nose on his face.

'How do you know?'

'Know what?'

'For Christ's sake, Mabel, she's not coming back. Can't you see that?'

She stepped back, her hands at her cheeks. He had frightened her, but then her temper flared in her eyes. 'Yes, she is.'

She folded the coat and began sticking pins in the little tomato pincushion, her movements quick and angry. Jack sat in the chair by the woodstove. He put his elbows on his knees and cradled his head in his hands, his fingers in his hair. He couldn't look at Mabel. He heard her in the kitchen, clattering dishes and slamming cups, and then walking to the bedroom door. There she stopped. He did not raise his head. She was out of breath, her voice hushed but sharp.

'She is coming back. And damn it, Jack, I won't let you or anyone else tell me differently.'

She carried the last lit lantern with her into the bedroom, leaving Jack alone in the dark.

26

Snow had come to Mabel in a dream, and with it hope. Her coat as blue as her eyes, her white hair flashing as she skipped and spun down mountain slopes. In the dream, Faina laughed, and her laughter rang like chimes through the cold air, and she hopped among the boulders and where her feet touched rock, ice formed. She sang and twirled down the alpine tundra, her arms open to the sky, and behind her snow fell and it was like a white cloak she drew down the mountains as she ran.

When Mabel woke the next morning and looked out the bedroom window, she saw snow. Just a dusting across the distant peaks, but she knew it had been more than a dream.

The child did not have to die. Maybe she wasn't gone from them for ever. She could have gone north, to the mountains, where the snow never melts, and she could return with winter to her old man and old woman in their little cottage near the village.

Mabel only had to wish and believe. Her love would be a beacon to the child. Please, child. Please, child. Please come back to us.

No matter how she turned it over in her mind, Mabel always traced the child's footsteps back to the night she and Jack had shaped her from snow. Jack had etched her lips and eyes. Mabel had given her mittens and reddened her lips. That night the child was born to them of ice and snow and longing.

What happened in that cold dark, when frost formed a halo in the child's straw hair and snowflake turned to flesh and bone? Was it the way the children's book showed, warmth spreading down through the cold, brow then cheeks, throat then lungs, warm flesh separating from snow and frozen earth? The exact science of one molecule transformed into another — that Mabel could not explain, but then again she couldn't explain how a fetus formed in the womb, cells becoming beating heart and hoping soul. She could not fathom the hexagonal miracle of snowflakes formed from clouds, crystallized fern and feather that tumble down to light on a coat sleeve, white stars melting even as they strike. How did such force and beauty come to be in something so small and fleeting and unknowable?

You did not have to understand miracles to believe in them, and in fact Mabel had come to suspect the opposite. To believe, perhaps you had to cease looking for explanations and instead hold the little thing in your hands as long as you were able before it slipped like water between your fingers.

And so, as autumn hardened the land and snow crept down the mountains, she sewed a coat for a child she was certain would return.

Mabel ordered several yards of boiled wool, and then in a giant kettle dyed it a deep blue that reminded her of the river valley in winter. The lining would be quilted silk, and the trim white fur. It would be sturdy and practical, but befitting a snow maiden. The buttons — sterling silver filigree. They came from a shop in Boston and she had saved them for years in her button jar, never finding a purpose for them until now. The white fur trim she would sew around the hood and down the front of the coat, along the bottom, and around each cuff. Snowflakes, embroidered with white silk thread, would cascade down the front and back of the coat.

She retrieved her sketchbook and a copy of Robert Hooke's *Micrographia: Or Some Physiological Descriptions of Minute Bodies Made by Magnifying Glasses*. It was one of the few natural history books of her father's that she had brought with her and she thought of it one evening as she worked on Faina's coat. The old book contained illustrations of magnified images, and as a child Mabel had been particularly enamored with the foldout copperplate engraving of a louse with all its spindly legs. But she remembered, too, that there had been drawings of snowflakes.

'Exposing a piece of black Cloth, or a black Hatt to the falling Snow, I have often with great pleasure, observ'd such an infinite variety of curiously figur'd Snow, that it would be as impossible to draw the Figure and shape of every one of them . . . ' and beside these words Hooke had included his sketches of a dozen snowflakes, looped and feathered, stars and hexagons. Mabel copied several of the designs. Then, from memory, she tried to re-create the one she had seen on her coat sleeve the night she and Jack made the snow child.

She followed a simple coat pattern she had ordered from a catalog. In the evenings, even when it was still bright outside, the trees and roof eaves kept the sunlight from coming in through the small cabin windows, so she lit a lamp and unfolded the fabric on the table. Following the pattern offered a kind of comfort, a quiet balance to working in the fields during the day. The farm work was coarse, exhausting, and largely a matter of faith — a farmer threw everything he had into the earth, but ultimately it wasn't up to him whether it rained or not. Sewing was different. Mabel knew if she was patient and meticulous, if she carefully followed the lines, took each step as it came, and obeyed the rules, that in the end when it was turned right-side out, it would be just how it was meant to be. A small miracle in itself, and one that life so rarely offered.

As much as she enjoyed the sewing, it was in the embroidery that she would express her new hope, each stitch a devotion, each snowflake a celebration of miracles. The first she chose to create was Faina's, the one the child had held in her bare hand — a star with six perfect points, each with an identical fern pattern. Between the ferns, the points of a smaller star over-lapped, and at its center, the hexagonal heart.

Mabel was bent over the embroidery hoop in her hands, her nose a few inches from the fabric, when Jack came in from feeding the horse. She didn't mind that he stayed out later and later each evening, though she wondered why he avoided her. It was his irritability that gave her pause.

'Is everything all right?' she asked as she looked up from her needle and thread.

He nodded in her direction.

'I see it frosted last night,' she said. 'Will we get all the potatoes out of the ground soon enough?'

Another brusque nod.

'Is Garrett off to bed? I had meant to give him another book to read. I was thinking of another Jack London, or perhaps *Treasure Island*. If he doesn't finish it in time, he can always take it with him.' Mabel bit the thread in half and held the embroidered snowflake at arm's length to inspect it. She could show it to Jack, but it would only make him angry. The coat, the snowflake sketches, all talk of Faina caused him to tighten his shoulders and stop speaking. She could have asked why, but she feared the answer. Leave it be, he was fond of saying, and so she did.

A week later, the last of the potatoes were in burlap sacks and they woke to a skiff of snow across the land, but it was early and thin. By midday, it would be gone, and Mabel was certain it would be several weeks before winter came to stay. All the same, the sight of it delighted her. She quickly fixed breakfast for Jack and Garrett and then put on her coat and boots.

'Where are you off to?' Jack asked as he scraped the last forkful of egg and potato from his plate.

'I thought I'd go out for a walk, just to see the snow.'

Jack nodded, but in the tired creases around his eyes, she saw his misgivings. That she was soon to be disappointed. That Faina would not return. That the child wasn't the miracle Mabel wished her to be.

Mabel buttoned up her coat to the neck and pulled on a hat and work gloves before stepping outside. It was warmer than she had expected. Already the clouds had cleared and the sun was coming through the trees. The cottonwoods and birches had lost their leaves, and the new snow lay along the branches in thin white lines. Her boots tracked the snow as she walked, uncovering dirt, browned grass, and yellowed leaves. Past the barn and the cottonwood, the fields were unbroken white. She thought she would walk to the river or follow the wagon trail to the far fields, but then she remembered it was Garrett's last day. He was going back with his family for the winter and although they would surely see him during the next months, it still seemed a goodbye of sorts. She meant to let him choose a book to take with him.

When she returned, Garrett was washing the dishes.

'No. No you don't. Not on your last day.'

Mabel hung her coat on the hook beside the door. 'What will we ever do without you, Garrett?'

'I don't know. I could stay instead.'

'I don't think your mother would agree to it,' Jack said, stacking the plates beside the washbasin. 'She's ready for her youngest to come home.'

Garrett looked doubtful but seemed to bite his tongue. He had grown and changed these past few months. He had taken on much of the responsibility of the farm, and in the evenings they talked about crop varieties and weather patterns, books and art. Mabel no longer sat outside the circle of conversation. She was as eager to discuss the type of turnips they would plant as to describe the museums she had visited in New York.

Who would think that an adolescent boy would have anything to teach an old woman? But it was Garrett who had led her into the fields and closer to the life she had pictured for herself in Alaska. She could think of no way to explain that to him. With a mother like Esther surely he could not imagine a woman doing anything against her will, or worse yet, not knowing her own will. It was as if Mabel had been living in a hole, comfortable and safe as it might have been, and he had merely reached down a hand to help her step up into the sunlight. From there she was free to walk where she would.

'Garrett, I was thinking you could borrow a book to take home with you. Only if you would like to, of course.'

'Could I? You wouldn't mind? I'll be real careful with it.'

'Of course you will. That's why I'm offering.' Mabel led him into the bedroom and knelt on the floor to pull out the trunk.

'Here, I can get that.' He easily tugged it out from under the bed. 'This is full of books? This whole thing?'

'That one, and a few others as well.' She laughed at Garrett's surprise. 'You should have seen my father's library. A room nearly the size of this whole cabin, lined with shelves and shelves of books. But I could bring only a few of them with me.'

'Do you miss 'em?'

'The books?'

'And your family? And everything else? It must be real different than here.'

'Oh, sometimes I wish I had a certain book or could visit with a certain friend or relative, but mostly I'm glad to be here.' Mabel opened the trunk and Garrett began pulling books off the stacks inside.

'Take your time. Your mother isn't expecting you until dinner.' She stood and dusted off her skirt. She was at the door when she heard Garrett say, 'Thank you, Mabel.'

She thought of expressing her own gratitude, of trying to explain what he had done for her.

'You're welcome, Garrett.'

27

Dearest Ada,

Congratulations on your new grandchild. What a blessing! And to have them all so near. It must be wonderful to hear the pitter-patter of all the children's feet on the old wooden stairs when they come to visit. I was so sorry to hear of Aunt Harriet's passing, but it sounds as if she left the world the best way any of us can, quietly and at an old and respectable age. All your news of the family was a precious gift to me.

We are well here, and I truly mean it. I know you thought us mad to move to Alaska, and for some time I wondered that myself. This past year, however, has made up for it all. I have begun to help more with the farm work. Imagine me — the one they always called 'timid' and 'delicate' — in the fields digging up potatoes and shoveling dirt. But it is a wonderful feeling, to do work that really seems like work. Jack has transformed this untamed stretch of land that we call home into a flourishing farm, and now I can claim a small hand in it as well. Our pantry shelves are stocked with wild berry jams and jars of meat from the moose Jack shot this fall. Oh, I do sometimes miss 'Back East', as they call it here, and certainly my heart longs to see you and everyone else in the family, but we recently decided we are here to stay. It has become our home, and Jack and I have a new way of life here that suits us well.

I am sending you a few of my recent sketches. One is of the strawberry patch I am so proud of and that filled many a strawberry pie this past summer. The other is of fireweed in bloom along the riverbed. In the background you can see the mountains that frame this valley. The last is of a snowflake I had the pleasure of observing this past winter. Several times I have redrawn this single snowflake, as I never seem to tire of its infinitesimal elegance.

Tucked among these pages is also a pressed cranberry bouquet. The small white flowers are easily overlooked now that they are dried, but they are so lovely when they fill the woods in the spring. And I am sending a pair of booties for Sophie's new baby daughter. The fur trim is from a snowshoe hare a neighbor boy provided to me. I hope they reach you before she has outgrown them altogether.

I expect we will soon have snow. The mountains are white and the mornings have a chill, and I look forward to its coming.

Sincerely, your loving sister,
Mabel

28

Winter came hard and fast at the tail end of October. It wasn't the slow, wet snow that marks a gentle end to autumn, but instead a sudden, grainy snowstorm blown by a cold river wind. Just after dinner it was already midnight dark, and Jack and Mabel listened to the storm knock against their cabin. Jack looked up from greasing his boots by the woodstove and Mabel paused in her sewing at the kitchen table. The knock came again and again, louder. At last, Jack went to the door and opened it.

He had the momentary notion that what stood before him was a mountain ghost, a blood-stained, snowy apparition. Faina was taller and, if possible, thinner than he remembered. Her fur hat and wool coat were covered in snow, and her hair hung like damp, fraying rope. Dried blood streaked her brow. Jack could not speak or move.

The girl took off her hat, shook the snow from it, and looked up.

It's me. Faina.

She was slightly breathless, but her voice, even and cheerful, broke his spell. He took the child in his arms and held her, rocking on his heels.

Faina? Faina. Dear God. You're here. You're really here.

He wasn't sure whether he spoke the words

aloud or only heard them in his head. Then he pressed his beard into her hair and smelled the glacier wind that blows over the tops of the spruce trees and the blood that courses through wild veins, and his knees nearly gave way. With one arm still around her shoulders, he pulled the girl into the cabin and closed the door.

My God, Mabel, and he knew he sounded shaken. It's Faina. She's here. At our door.

Oh, child. I wondered when you'd come.

Mabel, calm and smiling. How could she stand so assuredly when he, a grown man, was staggered by the sight of the girl? Why didn't she cry, run to the child, even fall at her feet?

Mabel stood behind her and brushed the snow from her shoulders. Look at you. Just look at you.

Mabel's eyes glistened and her cheeks were bright, but she did not shriek or bawl. Faina began to unbutton her coat, and Mabel helped her out of it, shook off snow.

There. Now let me see.

She held the girl at arm's length.

I knew you'd have grown.

Grown? Surely Mabel had lost her mind. No talk of the blood, the child's desperate appearance, her months-long absence.

Jack touched the girl's chin and turned her face up to his. What's happened to you, Faina? Are you all right?

Oh, this?

The girl looked at her hands.

I was skinning rabbits, she said.

Her eyes were wide, expectant.

I'm here, she said. I've come back.

Of course you have. Of course, and Mabel said it easily, as if there had never been a doubt.

How . . . but Jack's words were lost as Mabel ushered the girl to the table.

I knew it would be soon, she said. That's why I've hurried so. I just finished tonight. But wait. I'm rushing ahead of myself. You need to wash up and get settled, yes?

Faina smiled and held out her hands. They were cold-chafed and stained, each fingernail rimmed with blood, but Mabel merely clucked like a mother hen, as if it were a bit of dirt smudged on a boy who had played in the mud. She tucked her sewing project onto one of the chairs.

Well, let's see, she said. I had water on the stove already for tea. There should be enough to wash with.

Faina smiled shyly. Before long, Mabel was sitting with her, washing her hands in soapy, lukewarm water, wiping her face with a washcloth. Jack stood beside the woodstove, bewildered as much by his wife's calm as by the child's appearance. When Mabel left to get something from the bedroom, Jack strode to Faina's side, knelt at her chair, fought the urge to embrace her again.

He pointed to the bloody water in the basin and spoke more sternly than he intended.

What is all this? Where have you been? What has happened to you?

Jack, don't pester her so, Mabel said from behind him. She's tired to the bone. Let her rest.

Faina started to speak, but Mabel shushed her gently and held the mirror up for the child to see.

Everything's fine now. You're here, safe and sound. And you look beautiful.

It was true. The child was alive and well, here in their cabin. Garrett had doubted it was even possible, and Jack felt a rush of pride in her. She had survived, against all odds.

What do you think? Mabel asked Jack, turning Faina to face him.

The child stretched out her arms and gazed down at the new coat. Jack had never seen anything like it. It was the cool blue of a winter sky, with silver buttons that glistened like ice and white fur trim at the hood and cuffs and along the bottom edge. But the coat's splendor came from the snowflakes. The varying sizes and designs gave them movement, so they seemed to twirl through the blue wool. Its strange beauty suited the child.

Lovely, he said, and he had to choke back his emotion at the sight of the little girl in the snowflake coat, come home at last.

How about you? he asked. Do you like your new coat?

The child didn't speak, but seemed to frown.

Faina? Oh, dear child, it's all right, Mabel said. If you don't like it, it's all right. It's just a coat.

The girl shook her head, no, no.

Really. It's nothing. If it's too tight, I can make another. If it's too big, we can set it aside for another year. Don't fret.

You did this? Faina whispered. You made this, for me?

Well, yes. But it's nothing but fabric and a few stitches.

The girl smoothed her hands down the front, over the snowflakes falling one by one.

Do you like it?

In answer, the girl leapt to Mabel's arms and turned to rest her head against Mabel's shoulder, and in the child's smiling face Jack saw such affection.

I love it more than anything, she said against Mabel's arm.

Oh, you couldn't make me happier. Mabel stood and held the child's hands in her own and looked her up and down.

It does fit well, doesn't it?

The girl nodded, then glanced to where her old coat hung.

I was thinking, Faina. Perhaps I could take your old coat and make it into a blanket for you. That way, you'd still have it. Would that be all right? I'd have to cut it into pieces, but then I could sew them back together into a nice new blanket.

Really? You could? And I'd still have it?

Oh, yes. Most definitely yes.

Mabel was giddy and talkative as she cooked dinner, not allowing Jack or the child to speak of anything except the joy of being together. Maybe that should have been enough. Maybe he should have been grateful without asking for more.

It was only when the cabin became overheated,

with the woodstove and steam from cooking, when the girl seemed to wilt in her chair, only then did Jack sense some ripple beneath the surface, some doubt or fear in Mabel's desperate happiness. She dashed to the door and brought in a handful of snow. She dabbed it to the girl's cheeks and forehead.

There, there. It's much too hot in here. There, there.

Jack put the back of his hand to the child's forehead, but she was cool to the touch.

I suspect she's just tired, Mabel.

But she continued with the snow, putting some to the girl's lips.

Too hot, too hot, Mabel murmured. Please, get some more snow.

Jack opened the door to the swirling storm, driven in all directions by the wind off the river. It was a miserable night. She'd be soaked through in no time, and the wind would suck away any last heat. He would not let the girl leave, not to go back to that cold, lifeless hovel in the mountains.

You'll stay here tonight, he said as he brought in another handful of snow.

Mabel frowned.

Will she?

Yes.

He spoke with more confidence than he felt.

The girl sat forward in her chair, her blue eyes narrowed and fierce.

I will go, she said.

Not tonight, he said. You will stay here, with us.

Oh yes, you must, child. Can't you hear that

wind blowing? You can sleep in the barn.

Jack wondered at his wife. The barn? Why would she suggest such a thing? It was freezing out there, nearly as cold as being outdoors, but she persisted.

You'll be comfortable, she said. We even have a little bedroom made up, for the boy who helped us this summer. It's perfectly cozy and out of the wind.

But Faina was on her feet. When she looked at Jack she didn't speak, but it was as if she were shouting. You promised. You can't keep me here.

He wondered what he could do. Physically hold the child, force her to stay against her will? She would fight like a trapped polecat. She would hit and scream, maybe even bite and scratch, of that he had no doubt, and he would be left feeling a beast himself.

But he could not let her go back to the lonely wilderness after stumbling, bloodstained, into their home. If she were injured or killed, when he could have kept her safe, he would never forgive himself.

Faina had already fastened the shining silver buttons on her new coat.

Please don't be angry, she said.

Can't you hear the wind? Jack said.

The child was already at the door. He waited for Mabel to protest, even to beg.

All right, she said. If you must go, you must. But you'll be back, won't you? Promise to always come back.

Solemnly, as if swearing an oath, the child said, I promise.

Jack watched her leave, and it seemed like a disturbing dream, the child with her blood-smeared brow and twisted blond hair and snowflake coat, and his wife, composed and accepting. He stood some time at the window, staring into the night. Behind him Mabel bustled with the dishes and sewing scraps.

'How could you have known?' he asked.

'Hmmm?'

'How could you have known she was coming back? Now? Ever?'

'It's the first snow. Just like that night.'

Jack looked at her, slowly shook his head, not comprehending.

'Don't you remember? The night when we built the snow child. Snowflakes as big as saucers. Remember? We threw snowballs at each other. Then we made her. You carved her lovely face; I put on her mittens.'

'What are you saying, Mabel?'

She went to her shelves and brought back an oversized book bound in blue leather, adorned with silver gilding.

'Here,' she slid it across the table toward him. 'You won't be able to read it, though. It's in Russian.'

Jack lifted the book. It was surprisingly heavy, as if the pages were made of lead rather than paper. He flipped through the illustrations, impatient.

'What is this?'

'It's a storybook . . . '

'I can see that. What's that to do with — '

'It's about an old man and an old woman.

More than anything they want a child of their own, but they can't have one. Then, one winter night, they make a little girl out of snow, and she comes to life.'

Jack felt a stomach-turning sinking, as if he had stepped into bottomless wet sand and try as he might could not get back onto firm ground.

'Stop,' he said.

'She leaves each summer, and comes back when it snows. Don't you see? Otherwise . . . she would melt.' Mabel looked a little frightened at her own words, but she didn't falter.

'Jesus, Mabel. What are you saying?'

She opened the book to an illustration of the old man and old woman kneeling beside a beautiful little girl, her feet and legs bound in snow and her head crowned in silver jewels.

'See?' she said. She spoke like a nurse at a bedside, calm and knowing. 'You see?'

'No, Mabel. I don't see at all.' He slammed the book closed and stood. 'You've lost your mind. You're telling me you think that little child, that little girl, is some sort of spirit, some sort of snow fairy. Jesus. Jesus.'

He stomped to the other side of the cabin, wanting to escape but unable.

Mabel gently pulled the book back and slid her hands up and down the leather. She was shaking slightly.

'I know it sounds implausible, but don't you see?' she said. 'We wished for her, we made her in love and hope, and she came to us. She's our little girl, and I don't know how exactly, but she's made from this place, from this snow, from this cold. Can't you believe that?'

'No. I can't.' He had the urge to take Mabel by the shoulders and shake her.

'Why not?'

'Because ... because I know things you don't.'

Now she looked frightened. She held the book to her chest, her lips pursed and trembling.

'What do you know?'

'Jesus Christ, Mabel, I buried her father. He drank himself to death in front of that poor child. She begged him to stop. She put her little hands to his face, trying to warm him even as he was dying in front of her. Her own father. All those days I was gone? Where did you think I was? I was up there, in the mountains, trying to help her. Digging a goddamned grave in the middle of winter.'

'But you never told me this.' As if he was lying, inventing this awful tale to prove her wrong. So tightly she held on to her illusions. Jack clenched his jaw again and again, felt the muscle work as he bit back his anger.

'She made me promise not to tell you or anyone else.' It sounded so weak. A grown man making a promise like that to a little girl. He'd been a fool.

'What about a mother?'

'Dead, too. When she was just a baby.' He was old and tired and couldn't holler such things in an argument. 'I think it must have been consumption. Faina said she died of a coughing sickness, in the Anchorage hospital.'

She stared blankly. Her head nodded slightly,

all the blood drained from her face. He went to her, knelt beside her chair, took her hands in his.

'I should have told you. I'm sorry, Mabel. I am. I'd like it to be true, that she was ours, that she was a wilderness pixie. I would have liked that, too.'

She whispered through her teeth, 'Where does she live?'

'What?'

'Where does she live?'

'In a sort of cabin dug into the side of the mountain. It's not that bad really. It's dry and safe, and she has food. She takes care of herself.' He wanted to believe that the child was tough and sure-footed, like a mountain goat.

'By herself? Out there?'

'Of course, Mabel,' he pleaded. 'What could you have thought, that when she wasn't here with us she was some kind of snowflake, a snow child? Is that what you thought?'

She yanked her hands from his and stood with such force she knocked her chair over.

'Damn you! Damn you! How could you?'

Her anger startled him. 'Mabel?' He put his hands on her shoulders, thinking to hold her, but he could feel the heat of her fury through the fabric of her dress.

'How could you? Let her live out there, like a starving animal? Motherless. Fatherless. Starving for food and love. How could you?' She shoved her way past to the coat hooks.

'Mabel? What are you doing? Where are you going?' He took her by an arm, but she pushed him away. She wrapped a scarf around her neck, pulled on gloves and a hat, then took the oil lantern down from its hook above the table.

'Mabel? What are you doing?' He stood there in his socked feet as she slammed the door behind her.

She would come back. It was night, and it was snowing. She couldn't go far. She didn't know the way, had rarely left the homestead except by a wagon he drove.

But the silence of the cabin unnerved him. He lit another lantern, paced at the door. The minutes ticked by on the old wooden clock on the shelf. Finally, he put on his coat and boots and took the lantern. Outside the snow was thick. It fell so densely that he could see no more than a foot or two in front of him, and Mabel's tracks had disappeared.

29

Mabel ran without seeing, her face wet with tears and snow, her feet tripping. The small circle of lantern light swung wildly among the snowy trees. For some time all she did was run toward the mountains, and of that she wasn't even certain, but she did not stop. Her skirt dragged in the deepening snow, spruce branches raked at her face, and more than once she nearly fell, but she felt neither cold nor pain. All she knew was the rush of blood in her ears and a hot rage that with each step began to cool to a sort of grieving stupor.

She slowed as the land dipped into a ravine and the trees gave way to overgrown bushes, their thick branches lying across the earth like something set to snare her. She climbed under and over them, the lantern swaying in one hand. None of them grew to the size of a tree, but neither were they like the blackberry brambles back home. Some limbs were as thick as her leg and dry brown leaves clung to many of the branches. Mabel grabbed at one and brought her hand away with a cluster of tiny cones. Scattered amid these bushes were devil's clubs, bare of their broad green leaves but not of their spines. In places the limbs and shrubs were so entangled that her chest tightened in panic — what if she couldn't find her way out?

At last the ground climbed slightly and Mabel again found herself among spruce, birch, and scattered cottonwood. She stopped and looked back the way she had come. There was no sign of the cabin and, beyond the lantern's small circle of flickering light, blackness closed in from all sides. Her hair was damp against her neck and her clothes hung heavy and cold. But she would not go back. He could stay in the cabin waiting, not knowing, just as she had spent so many hours. She would find the girl and make this right.

She held the lantern high and peered into the snow-filled darkness. Where the light spilled ahead of her, Mabel saw that the snow was disturbed. She ran to the tracks. She looked up and down the trail, trying to see where they went and where they came from. Could these be the girl's? But which way? Having run so blindly, she no longer had any sense of home, the river, the mountains. Something seemed wrong about the tracks, the snow too deep for her to make out footprints. Just the same she followed them.

The tracks led over a fallen birch tree, and she wrestled with her long skirt as she climbed over it. By the time she cleared the log, she was drenched with sweat and snow and her legs trembled with exhaustion. She followed the trail to her left, half running. When her throat burned and her lungs felt as if they would burst, she paused only long enough to take in a few gulps of air. She pictured herself finding the girl huddled against the storm. Mabel would grab hold of her and never let go. She wondered how far she had come. Could she be getting close to the foothills? The land was flat, but it seemed as if she'd been running for hours.

It was only when Mabel came again to the fallen birch and saw where she had already climbed over it that she realized her mistake. She was a mad old woman, running in circles, chasing herself through the woods at night. She was aware that any living thing in the forest with eyes would be able to see her as clear as day in the lantern light, while she would be blind to it. Then it was as if she were hovering in the treetops, looking down on her own madness. Mabel saw herself, disheveled and desperate, swiveling her head this way and that, twigs clinging to her wet hair, and it was an awful unraveling, as if in this act she had finally come loose and was falling. She thought of Jack in the cabin somewhere behind her, saw him as a steady light in the midst of the wilderness. She could turn now and follow her tracks back home. She hadn't gone that far yet. But the rage had not burned itself out.

When she began to run again, she no longer searched for trails or the outlines of mountains in the black sky. Everything was strange and unknown and she could see only a few steps in front of her. Sometimes clumps of frozen cranberries on bare branches or spindly spruce trees or the mottled trunks of paper birch were caught in an instant of light before passing back into blackness. At one point she realized that something was crashing through the trees beside

271

her and she stopped, her heart pounding, her breath ragged.

'Faina? Is that you?' she whispered loudly. But she knew it wasn't the child. It was something much bigger. There was no answer except the snapping of branches. She strained to see farther than she knew she could, past the steam that rose from her own body. She wasn't sure at first, but the noise in the forest seemed to move away from her. She wanted to go home, if only she knew the way.

She had no more strength to run, and at first she wasn't sure if she could even walk. Hot and thirsty, she scooped up snow in her gloved hand and brought it to her mouth, letting it melt down her throat. She was tempted to take off her hat, even her coat, but she knew she could freeze to death like that. She touched a clump of snow to her forehead, then continued walking. She hoped to find a trail again, any trail, and let it take her where it would, perhaps to the mountains, perhaps to the river, maybe back home. In her fatigue she shuffled and her boots caught on bushes and roots.

When she fell, it was so hard, so sudden, it was almost as if something had shoved her from behind. She wasn't even able to bring her arms up in defense as she plummeted to the ground, and the blow forced the air from her lungs. At the same moment, the lantern dropped to the snow in a clatter and hiss, and when she was able to pull her face from the snow she had the fleeting thought that she had been knocked blind. She had dropped the lantern. Mabel blinked again and again, quickly and then more slowly. The blackness was so complete that, except for the touch of cool air, she could not tell whether her eyes were open or closed. She got to her hands and knees and pawed the ground until she found where the lantern had sunk into the fluffy snow. The glass was still hot to the touch, but the flame had been extinguished. Mabel stood and was so disoriented, the same black when she looked up to the sky as down to the earth, that she nearly fell again. She stood swaying.

God help me, what have I done? Tripped on my own clumsy feet. Thrown away my only light. No matches. Not a stitch of dry clothing. No shelter. No sense of direction. Perhaps, she found herself thinking, no sense at all.

She wondered if she could find her own tracks. She crouched and patted the snow around her, and thought she found some indication of footprints. She followed, bent over, walking and feeling, until something snagged at her hair. She tried to stand and hit her head on a branch. When she reached out, her hands brushed something hard. She took off her gloves and felt, the way a blind person might feel a face. It was a tree trunk. She hadn't found her own trail but had stumbled beneath the branches of a great spruce tree. She felt the ground at her feet and was surprised to find not snow but a bed of dry needles. Perhaps this was all she could ask for, but still, with no source of warmth or dry clothes, she couldn't possibly survive until daybreak. She sat at the base of the tree and leaned against it.

The chill approached along her hairline, damp

with sweat and melted snow. It crept down the nape of her neck and up the backs of her wet legs. As it made its way beneath her clothes, along the skin of her ribs, down the curve of her spine, she knew it for what it was — a death chill, a chill that if allowed to take hold would freeze the life from her. As if to confirm her suspicions, her teeth began to chatter. It started as a small shiver along her jaw as she sucked air between her clenched teeth, but soon her whole body shook and her very bones seemed to clatter.

'Jack.' The name came as a whisper from her cold lips. 'Jack?' Only a bit louder. He would never hear her. Who knew how far she was from the cabin? 'Jack!' She crawled away from the tree and, when she felt herself free from its branches, stood and yelled as loud as she could.

'Jack! Jack! I'm here! Can you hear me? Jack! Help me! Help! Jack! I'm here! Please. Please.' She stopped yelling and strained to hear, holding her breath for a moment or two, but the only sound was something she didn't believe she could possibly be hearing — the relentless tiny taps of individual snowflakes landing on her coat, on her hair and lashes, on the branches of the tree. 'Oh, Jack! Please! I need you. Please.'

She yelled and cried until she was hoarse and her voice a noiseless screech. Please, Jack. Please. She crawled back beneath the spruce tree, feeling for its branches, its wide trunk, its bed of needles. There she curled up, her clothes clinging wet and cold, her body racked with tremors, the snow settling on the branches over her head.

274

She woke to the breaking of twigs and the flash of fire in the darkness, and for a moment she thought she was home and had nodded off in front of the woodstove. That wasn't right, though. It was too dark, too cold. Her body ached and she couldn't move. Something bound her. It was heavy and smelled familiar. Like home. Out of the corner of her eye, she saw movement in front of the fire. A figure bending over, putting something to the flames. Then breaking something over a knee, then more flames. The figure turned toward her, blocking the light.

'Mabel? Are you awake?'

She couldn't speak. Her jaw seemed sealed, the muscles stiff. She tried to nod, but it hurt. Everything hurt.

'Mabel? It's me — Jack. Can you hear me?' And he was beside her, kneeling, brushing her hair back from her face.

'Are you warmer? I've got the fire going good now. You feel it?'

Jack. She could smell him, the scent of cut wood and wool. He reached around her, pressing at her sides like he was tucking a child into bed, and she knew why she felt bound. She was wrapped in blankets. She was confused again. Was she home, in her own bed? But the air was so cold and stirring slightly, and overhead there were branches and beyond them a sky so black and full of stars. Stars? Where had they all come from, like bits of ice?

'Jack?' It was only a whisper, but he heard. He had turned his back to go to the fire, but he returned to her side.

'Jack? Where are we?'

She heard him clear his throat, maybe the beginning of a cough, and then, 'It's all right. This is going to be all right. Let me get that fire bigger, and you'll warm.'

When he stood, hunched beneath the branches, and moved away from her, his body blocked the light and heat of the fire. Mabel closed her eyes. She'd done something wrong. He was angry with her. It came back to her the way grief does, slowly. She remembered the child, the snow, the night.

'How did you find me?'

He was feeding the fire, building it higher and higher until she could see his face and feel its heat. 'I don't know.'

'Where are we? Are we far from home?'

'I don't precisely know that either.' He must have expected this to frighten her, because then he said, 'It's going to be fine, Mabel. We're just going to have to rough it here for a few more hours. Then light'll come, and we'll find our way.'

His voice faded. Mabel drifted, sank into the warmth, and it was like a childhood fever, dreamlike and nearly comforting.

'Can you sit up?' Jack held a canteen. She wondered how long she had slept. Beyond the fire it was still dark.

'I think so.' He grasped her around the shoulders and helped her to sit. When she reached for the canteen, the blanket fell open to reveal her bare arm. She was naked.

'Careful. Don't let that loose,' he said.

'My clothing? Why on earth . . .'

He pointed toward the fire where her dress hung from a branch, along with her undergarments. Closer to the fire, her boots were propped open near the flames.

'There was no other way,' he said, almost as if apologizing.

She tried not to gulp the water, but to take small sips. 'Thank you.'

'Sometimes I could hear you calling my name,' he said. 'I thought I heard you in the brush, but it was just a cow moose and her calf. Then I tripped over the lantern and I knew you had to be nearby.'

Jack went to the fire. He took down her dress and shook it out.

'It stopped snowing,' he said as he crawled under the tree with her. He groaned softly as he leaned against the trunk and put his arm around her. She thought of his barely mended back. 'Cleared off and got cold. You were soaked through.'

Mabel leaned her head against his chest. 'How does she do it?'

He didn't answer at first, and Mabel wondered if he understood her question.

'She's got something different about her,' he said finally. 'She might not be a snow fairy, but she knows this land. Knows it better than anyone I've ever met.'

She cringed at the words 'snow fairy', but knew there was no malice in it.

'I can't imagine, spending every night out here. How could you let her . . . I'm not angry anymore. It's not that. But why didn't you worry about her? She's just a little child.'

He kept his eyes to the campfire. 'When she didn't come back in the spring, I went up to the mountains looking for her. I was sick with worry. I thought I'd made a terrible mistake, and that we'd lost her.'

'I can't bear the thought of something happening to her,' Mabel said. 'She may be lovely and brave and strong, but she's just a little girl. And with her father dead . . . she's out here all alone. If something were to happen to her, we would be to blame, wouldn't we?'

Jack nodded. He put his arms around her again. 'It's true,' he said.

'I just don't think I could stand it. Not again. Not after . . . ' She expected Jack to shush her, to pull away, to go back to the fire, but he didn't.

'I've always regretted that I didn't do more,' she said. 'Not that we could have saved that one. But that I didn't do more. That I didn't have courage enough to hold our baby and see it for what it was.'

She turned to look up into his face.

'Jack. I know it's been so long. My God, ten years now. But tell me that you said a proper goodbye. Tell me you said a prayer over its grave. Please tell me that.'

278

'His.'

'What?'

'His grave. It was a little boy. And before I laid him in the ground, I named him Joseph Maurice.'

Mabel laughed out loud.

'Joseph Maurice,' she whispered. It was a name of contention, the two names that would have shocked both their families — two great-grandfathers, one on each side, each a black sheep in his own right. 'Joseph Maurice.'

'Is that all right?'

She nodded.

'Did you say a prayer?'

'Of course,' and he sounded hurt that she had asked.

'What did you say? Do you remember?'

'I prayed for God to take our tiny babe into his arms and cradle him as we would have, to rock him and love him and keep him safe.'

Mabel let out a sob and hugged Jack with her bare arms. He tucked the blanket around her and they held each other.

'A boy? Are you certain?'

'I'm pretty sure, Mabel.'

'Curious, isn't it? All that time the baby was inside me, tossing and turning, sharing my blood, and I thought it was a girl. But it wasn't. It was a little boy. Where did you bury him?'

'In the orchard, down by the creek.'

She knew exactly where. It was the place they had first kissed, had first held each other as lovers.

'I should have known. I looked for it because I

realized I hadn't said goodbye.'

'I would have told you.'

'I know. We are fools sometimes, aren't we?'

Jack got up to feed the fire and when it was burning well he sat again with Mabel under the tree.

'Are you warm enough?'

'Yes,' she said. 'But won't you come in with me?'

'I'll only make you cold.'

She insisted, helping him strip out of his damp clothes and opening her blankets to him. He did bring in cold air, at first, and the coarse wool of his long underwear rubbed against her bare skin, but she burrowed more tightly against him. Up and down her body, she felt his leanness, how age had pared back his muscles and left loosening skin and smooth bone, but his hold was still firm. She rested her head on his chest and watched the fire flare and send sparks up into the cold night sky.

30

Mabel would reduce the child to the shabby clothes and slight frame of a flesh-and-blood orphan, and it pained Jack to watch. Gone was Mabel's wonder and awe. In her eyes Faina was no longer a snow fairy, but an abandoned little girl with a dead mother and father. A feral child who needed a bath.

'We should inquire about schooling in town,' she said just days after Jack had told her the truth. 'I understand the territorial government has assigned a new teacher to the area. Students meet in the basement of the boarding house. We'd have to take her by wagon each morning, or she could stay there for several days at a time.'

'Mabel?'

'Don't look at me like that. She'll survive. If she can spend months alone in the wilderness, she can certainly stay a few nights in town.'

'I just don't know if . . . '

'And those clothes. I'll get some fabric and sew her some new dresses. And some real shoes. She won't need those moccasins anymore.'

But the child was not so easily tamed.

I don't want to, she said when Mabel showed

her to the tub of hot water.

Look at yourself, child. Your hair is a mess. You're filthy.

Mabel pulled at the ragged sleeve of the child's cotton dress.

This needs to be washed, maybe just thrown out. I'm making several new dresses for you.

The child backed toward the door. Mabel grabbed her by the wrist, but Faina yanked it free.

'Mabel,' Jack said, 'let the child go.'

The girl was gone for days, and when she returned she was skittish, but Mabel took no heed. She pinched at the girl's clothing and hair, and asked if she had ever gone to school, ever looked at a book. With each prying question, the child took another step back. We're going to lose her, he wanted to tell Mabel.

Jack wasn't one to believe in fairy-tale maidens made of snow. Yet Faina was extraordinary. Vast mountain ranges and unending wilderness, sky and ice. You couldn't hold her too close or know her mind. Perhaps it was so with all children. Certainly he and Mabel hadn't formed into the molds their parents had set for them.

It was something more, though. Nothing tethered Faina to them. She could vanish, never return, and who was to say she had ever been loved by them?

No, the child said.

Faina's eyes darted from Mabel to Jack and in

the quick blue he saw that she was afraid.

I will no longer allow you to live like an animal, Mabel said. Her movements were sharp around the kitchen table as she stacked dishes, gathered leftovers. The girl watched, a wild bird with its heart jumping in its chest.

Starting right now, you will stay here with us. No more running off into the trees, gone for days on end. This will be your home. With us.

No, the child said again, more forcefully.

Jack waited for her to fly away.

'Please, Mabel. Can we talk about this later?'

'Look at her. Will you just look at her? We've neglected her. She needs a clean home, an education.'

'Not in front of the child.'

'So we let her go back into the wilderness tonight? And the next, and the next? How will she find her way in this world if all she knows is the woods?'

As far as Jack could see, the girl found her way fine, but it was senseless to argue.

'Why?' Mabel pleaded to him. 'Why would she want to stay out there, alone and cold? Doesn't she know we would treat her kindly?'

So that was it. Beneath her irritation and desire to control was love and hurt.

'It's not that,' Jack said. 'She belongs out there. Can't you see that? It's her home.'

He reached up to Mabel, kept her from picking up a bowl. He took her hands in his. Her fingers were slender and lovely, and he rubbed his thumbs along them. How well he knew those hands.

'I'm trying, Jack. I am. But it is simply unfathomable to me. She chooses to live in dirt and blood and freezing cold, tearing apart wild animals to eat. With us she would be warm and safe and loved.'

'I know,' he said. Didn't he want the child as a daughter, to brag about and shower with gifts? Didn't he want to hold her and call her their own? But this longing did not blind him. Like a rainbow trout in a stream, the girl sometimes flashed her true self to him. A wild thing glittering in dark water.

Mabel let go of his hands and turned to the child.

You will stay here tonight, she said.

She took hold of the child's shoulders, and for a moment Jack thought she would shake her. But then Mabel smoothed her hands down the girl's arms and spoke more gently.

Do you understand? And tomorrow we will go to town to ask about school classes.

The girl's cheeks flushed and she shook her head no, no.

Faina, this is not your decision. It is in your best interest. You must stop running around like a wild sprite. You will grow up some day, and then what?

No, she said.

Quickly, quietly, the child was nearly away, already wearing her hat and coat. Mabel stepped toward her.

It's for you, don't you understand?

But the child was gone.

Mabel lowered herself into a chair, hands clasped in her lap.

'Doesn't she understand that we love her?'

Jack went to the open door. It was a clear, calm night, the moon shining through the branches. He saw the child at the edge of the forest. She had stopped and was looking back at the cabin. Then she turned away and, as she began to run, she shook her hands out from her sides in a gesture of frustration. Snow began to swirl.

Snow devils. That's what they had called them as children. Wind-churned funnels of snow, almost like white tornados, but these had sprung from the child's hands.

The girl vanished into the forest, but the snow devils circled and circled and grew. Jack watched in wonder, fear even. The snow churned toward the cabin, growing and circling, until it consumed everything. The yard darkened. The moonlight disappeared. The wind howled and the snow whipped at Jack's pant legs.

Into the night, the snowstorm beat itself against the cabin and sleep would not come to Jack. He lay staring at the log ceiling of their bedroom and felt Mabel's warm body against his. He could wake her, slide his hands beneath her nightgown and kiss the back of her neck, but he was too distracted even for that. He forced his eyes closed and tried to stop his brain from spinning. He rolled from one side to the other, then climbed out of bed. He fumbled until he was in the kitchen. He lit a lantern, dimmed it as far as he could, and took the book down from the shelf. At the table, he turned the pages of illustrations and foreign letters.

He did not notice Mabel until she sat down in the chair opposite him. Her hair was loose and untidy and her face creased from where it had pressed into the pillowcase.

'What are you doing awake?' she asked.

He looked down at the book. 'It is strange, isn't it?'

'What?' she asked, her voice hushed as if there were others to wake.

'The child we made out of snow. That night. The mittens and scarf. Then Faina. Her blond hair. And that way about her.'

'What are you saying?'

Jack caught himself.

'I must still be half asleep,' he said. He closed the book and gave her a small smile. 'My brain's muddled.' He hadn't convinced her, but she stood, straightened her nightgown, and returned to the bedroom.

Jack waited until he heard her crawl into bed, pull the covers up, and then, after some time, breathe the deep, slow breaths of sleep. He opened the book again, this time to a picture of the snow maiden among forest animals, snowflakes falling through the blue-black sky above them.

He had said too much, but not as much as he could have. He hadn't told Mabel about the snow devils, or about how Faina had scattered a snowfall like ashes on her father's grave. He didn't tell her how, as she stood over the grave, snow fluttered against the child's skin as if she were made of cold glass. The flakes did not melt on her cheeks. They did not dampen her eyelashes. They rested there like snow on ice until they were stirred away by a breeze.

31

'The boy's brought you something, Mabel.'

Jack opened the cabin door wider so Garrett could follow with his bundle, wrapped in leather and tied with a string of rawhide. It tucked easily under the boy's arm, and it didn't look to have the stiffness or bulk of a dead animal. All the same, maybe he should have asked before letting Garrett bring it inside.

'Well, good morning. Come in. Come in.' Mabel wiped her hands on her apron and tucked a few strands of hair behind her ear. 'Would you like something hot to drink?'

'Yes, thank you.'

'So how's trapping?' Jack asked.

'I'm just getting the sets out now. But Old Man Boyd said I could have his marten line. He's retiring down to San Francisco.'

'Is that so?'

'I guess he found a small run of gold in a creek up north, and now he's set. Says he wants some warm sun for his old bones.'

'Are you running his line, then?'

'Not yet. But it won't be long. He's got all the poles in place. And he's selling me his number one long-springs. Says he won't be trapping anything but good-looking women in California.'

Mabel was taking coffee mugs out of the cupboard and didn't seem to be listening, but the boy flushed a sudden red. 'I mean . . . that's just what he . . . '

'Is it a long trail, his trapline?' Jack asked.

'It'll take me two days to check it. I've got a wall tent I'll put up so I can stay overnight when the weather's bad.'

'Are you frightened?' Mabel asked from where she stood at the window.

The question seemed to confuse the boy.

'When you're out there, alone in the woods,' she said, 'aren't you frightened?'

'No. I can't say that I am.'

Mabel was quiet.

'I mean, I suppose I've been scared a few times,' Garrett said. 'But not for no reason. Fall before last, I had a black bear act like he was hunting me. Followed me all the way home, but I couldn't ever get a clear shot at him. I never saw anything like it. I'd holler at him, try to chase him off, and I'd think he was gone. But then I'd see the top of his head through the shrubs. All the way home it was like that.'

'But bears don't usually go after people,' Jack said with a glance toward Mabel.

'Oh, sometimes. You hear about that miner down toward Anchorage? Grizzly bear took his face right off.'

Jack frowned at the boy. Mabel was stiff and silent at the window.

'Oh, sure. I mean, that's not real common, though,' the boy fumbled. 'Most often a bear will hightail it in another direction.'

'But are you lonely?' Still Mabel did not face them as she spoke.

'Ma'am?'

'Lonely. When you are all alone in the wilderness, there must be something terrible about it.'

'Well, I don't spend all that much time in the woods by myself. I'd like to. Longest I've been gone is a week, when I went salmon fishing downriver last summer. And I liked it just fine. I fished all day and sometimes all night 'cause the sun never went down. I dried and smoked the fish on alder poles. That was the first time I saw a mink. It came down a creek and tried to steal a whole salmon right from under my nose. I was laughing too hard to take a shot at it. It was tugging and dragging that salmon away as fast as it could go.'

'But if you have a safe, warm home with a family, why would you want to be out there?'

The boy hesitated and looked at Jack.

'I don't know,' he said with a shrug. 'I guess maybe I don't want to be warm and safe. I want to live.'

'Live? Isn't this living?' She let out a long sigh.

No one spoke again until she came to the table with the pot of coffee, and it was as if the boy had just arrived. 'So now you're here. And what's this you've brought?' she asked.

Garrett's face brightened, and he turned bashful.

'Well, I uh, well . . . ' and he pushed it across the table toward her. 'It's for you.'

'Shall I open it then?'

The boy nodded, and Mabel untied the string and folded back the leather. Inside, Jack saw fox fur. Silver and black.

Mabel was expressionless as she touched it with the tips of her fingers.

'It's a hat. See?' And the boy took it from her and lightly punched it from beneath, so the crown stood up.

'Betty sewed it for you. It's got ear flaps you can tie on top, like this, or you can pull them down and tie it under your chin.'

He gave it back to Mabel, who turned it slowly in her hands.

'I hope it fits. We used my mom's head to measure.'

'I can't . . . I can't accept this.'

The boy's face fell.

'It's all right,' he mumbled. 'If you don't like it.'

'Mabel.' Jack put a hand on her arm.

'It's not that,' she said. 'It's too much.'

'It didn't cost me a dime. I traded her out in furs.'

'It's too fine. I have no place to wear it.'

'But it's nothing fancy,' the boy said. 'Trappers wear them. You don't have to save it for trips to town or anything. It's warm.'

'Try it on, Mabel,' Jack said quietly.

He wasn't ready for the effect. As Mabel pulled it down and tied the strings beneath her chin, the dense black fur, tipped brilliantly in silver, framed her face, and her eyes shone gray-soft and her skin looked like warm cream. She was stunning. Neither he nor the boy said a

292

word but only stared.

'Well! The way you two gawk, I guess it must not suit me,' she said and tugged off the hat in an angry fluster.

'It suits you fine,' Jack said.

'You could be in one of those fashion magazines from Back East,' the boy jumped in. 'And I'm not just saying it either.'

'He's right. It suits you better than fine.'

'You're not just flattering me?' She touched her hair with one hand.

'Put it back on, so we can see again,' Jack said.

'It does fit well,' she said, 'as if it were tailored for me. And it is warm.'

Jack stood and showed her how to tie the flaps up so that it fit like a Russian fur hat.

'I guess I'll be the finest-dressed farmer's wife you ever saw,' she said.

Mabel sent the boy home with several books from her trunks. When he had gone, she sat by the woodstove reading. Jack came up behind her and softly touched the nape of her neck.

'You're tickling me,' she said and brushed distractedly at his hand.

'I think the boy was smitten with you in that hat.'

'Don't be silly,' she said. 'I'm an old woman.'

'You're still beautiful. And you don't seem to mind it being made of fox. I'd thought you'd object.'

'It is practical. I'll be warmer with it.'

32

Where were you, child?

Just now? I was at the river. That's where I found this.

In her hand, Faina held a wind-dried salmon skull. Mabel was trying to draw it, first this way, then that.

No. Not just now. Always. This past summer. Where did you go then?

To the mountains.

Why? What is there for you?

Everything. The snow and the wind. The caribou come. And little flowers and berries. They grow even on the rocks, near the snow, up by the sky.

You're going to leave us again, aren't you? This spring, you will go back to the mountains.

The girl nodded.

And tonight, when you leave, where will you go? Home.

What kind of home can you have out there?

I'll show you.

The next bright day, the child came for Mabel and led her away into the forest. Jack sent them with a knapsack of food but told Mabel not to worry. Faina knows her way. She'll bring you back safely.

She followed the girl away from the homestead and along trails Mabel alone never could have seen or known — snowshoe hare runs beneath willow boughs, wolf tracks along hard-packed drifts. The day was cold and peaceful. Mabel's breath rose around her face and turned to frost on her eyelashes and along the edges of the fox-fur hat. She stumbled in Jack's wool pants and the snowshoes he had strapped to her feet; ahead of her Faina strode in ease and grace, her feet light on the snow.

They climbed out of the river valley and up toward the blue sky until they were on the side of a mountain.

There, the girl said.

She pointed to the fanned impression of a bird's small wings on the surface of the snow, each feather print perfect, exquisite symmetry.

What is it?

A ptarmigan flew.

And there?

Mabel pointed to a series of small dashes in the snow.

An ermine ran.

Everything was sparkled and sharp as if the world were new, hatched that very morning from an icy egg. Willow branches were cloaked in hoar frost, waterfalls encased in ice, and the snowy land speckled with the tracks of a hundred wild animals: red-backed voles, coyotes and fox, fat-footed lynx, moose and dancing magpies.

Then they came to a frightening place, a stand

of tall spruce where the air was dead and the shadows cold. A bird wing was nailed to the trunk of a broad tree, a patch of white rabbit fur to another, and they were like a witch's totems where dead animals ensnare passing spirits.

The child approached a third tree, and a stretch of brown fur squirmed. It was alive.

Mabel took in a breath.

Marten, the girl said.

The animal swiveled from a front paw, suspended by a steel trap on a pole. Its small black eyes were wet and shining like onyx. Unblinking. Watching.

What will you do with it?

Bemused or dissatisfied — Mabel couldn't read Faina's expression.

Kill it, the child said.

She took the writhing thing in her bare hands and pressed its thin chest into the tree trunk until the animal went limp.

How do you do it?

I squeezed its heart until it couldn't beat any more.

It wasn't the answer Mabel sought, but she didn't know how else to ask the question. Faina released the paw from the trap.

May I?

Mabel removed her mittens and took the dead marten. It was warm and light, its fur softer than a woman's hair. She put her nose to the top of its head and it smelled like a kitten in a barn. She studied its narrow eye slits and ferocious little teeth.

Faina reset the trap and put the marten in her pack.

Later they found a dead hare strangled by a loop of wire and later still a white ermine in a trap, frozen open-eyed and stiff as if bewitched. All went in Faina's pack.

The trail led across a frozen swamp where black spruce stood half dead and leaning, and then up a steep bank and back into a forest of broad white spruce and twisted, knotted birch. They came to another pole with a trap, but it held only an animal's foot, ragged edge of bone and ripped tendon, brown fur frozen to steel. Faina put the trap to her knee, released its hold, and tossed the paw into the woods.

What was it?

A marten's foot.

Where is the rest?

A wolverine stole it, the child said.

I don't understand.

Faina pointed to tracks in the snow. Mabel wondered that she hadn't seen them before, each clawed print as large as the palm of her hand. The wolverine tracks circled the tree in larger and larger gallops until they disappeared into the forest.

It ate the marten out of my trap, she said.

Faina seemed unburdened by this knowledge. She walked on, her steps as quick and easy as they had ever been. Mabel followed without speaking, eyes newly alert for tracks and her chest filled with the rhythm of her own heart and lungs. And then she realized they had come back around to the river and were traveling toward their homestead.

But wait — we can't go back yet. You haven't

showed me your home.

It's here. I've showed you.

Here? Mabel wouldn't argue. Maybe the child was ashamed of her dwelling. Maybe the place where she slept and ate wasn't worth seeing.

But she knew the truth. The snowy hillsides, the open sky, the dark place in the trees where a wolverine gnawed on the leg of some small, dead animal — this was the child's home.

Can we stop here, just for a moment? Mabel asked.

It had been a long time since she had felt the urge to draw so strongly. They sat on a rise looking over the valley. She took her sketchbook and pencil from her pack and ignored her numb, cold fingers as she began to draw. Faina held the marten before her so she could again study its whiskered snout and angled eyes. Then she quickly drew the fur and claw of its brown, padded feet. She flipped the page and did a rough sketch of the snow-heavy spruce branches above them, and then the mountains looming up from the river. As the light dwindled, she tried to recall the bird wing nailed to the tree and the ermine tracks across the snow. She tried to remember it all and to think of it as home. Maybe here on the page she could reduce it to line and curve and at last understand it.

She could see, now that she had been shown. The sun had disappeared behind them, and the girl pointed across the valley to the mountain slopes aglow in a cool purple-pink. Silhouetted against the sky, tendrils of snow unfurled from the peaks, whipped by what must have been a brutal wind. Here on the rise, though, the air was still. The colors were distant, impossible, untouchable.

That's what my name means, Faina said, still pointing.

Mountain?

No. That light. Papa named me for the color on the snow when the sun turns.

Alpenglow, Mabel whispered.

She felt the awe of walking into a cathedral, the sense that she was being shown something powerful and intimate and in its presence must speak softly, if at all. She stared into that color, trying to imagine a father who could name his child for such beauty and then abandon her.

We should go, Faina said. It will be night soon.

The child led Mabel back to the homestead, to the warm cabin where Jack waited with hot tea and bread he had baked in a Dutch oven.

So, he said. What did you see?

33

Dear Mabel,

Your letters and sketches have become quite an attraction at our home. Whenever one arrives, we host a dinner party and invite many of our closest friends and relatives. With your permission, I have read the letters aloud and your sketches have been passed from one hand to the next, along with exclamations of 'Remarkable!' 'Such beauty!' More than once I've been told that you are the frontier equivalent of an Italian master studying human anatomy. Your sketches of the sable's snarling teeth and clawed feet were among the favorites this last night, as were your studies of the alder cones and winterkilled grasses. Your letters, too, catch glimpses of this wild place that has become your home. You always did have a talent for expressing yourself, and perhaps no other time in your life have you had such wondrous sights to express. Our only wish is that you would write more often. I do believe I will hold on to everything you send and someday you should publish a book of your drawings and observations. There is something fanciful and yet feral about them.

Along with your interest in the tale of the snow maiden, I am reminded of the time you spent as a child chasing fairies in the woods near our home. As I recall, you slept more than one night in those great oak trees, and when Mother found you the next morning you would swear you had seen fairies that flew like butterflies and lit up the night like lightning bugs. I remember with some shame that the rest of us teased you about seeing such spirits, but now my own grandchildren chase similar fancies and I do not discourage them. In my old age, I see that life itself is often more fantastic and terrible than the stories we believed as children, and that perhaps there is no harm in finding magic among the trees.

Your loving sister,
Ada

34

Esther burst into the cabin like a friendly hen, flapping and chattering and nearly knocking Mabel over as she tried to open the door for her. In one hand she held a towel-covered cast-iron pot and with the other she hugged Mabel and kissed her on the cheek.

'So is this what it takes to have dinner with you two?' she said and pushed past Mabel to set the pot on the woodstove. 'George's got the dessert. That is if he doesn't eat it on the way in here. Should be enough chicken and dumplings for all of us. Lynx and dumplings, I should say, but it just doesn't have the same ring to it. Guess we could call it 'kitten and dumplings'.' Esther laughed and flung her coat across the back of a chair.

'Lynx? You've cooked a lynx?'

'Oh, don't make that face. Have you ever had it? Absolutely, positively the best meat you'll ever taste. Garrett had it live in a snare, so he killed it clean and brought home the meat. Guess we raised him right after all.'

'Has he come, too?'

'Nope. That's the only reason we might have enough food. That boy could eat a side of beef and then ask for seconds. But he's out these next few nights, siwashing it on his long trapline.'

'Siwashing?'

'Like an Indian. No tent. No creature comforts. He packs light and travels hard.'

'Oh.'

'You got a spoon I can stir this with?'

Before she could help, Esther had found one, and Mabel watched with fond amusement as Esther once again took over her home. Within minutes she had tied one of Mabel's aprons around her waist, taste-tested the lynx, set the table and added another log to the fire, though Mabel had just stocked it.

'I want to hear all about what you've been up to. But first, you've got to take a nip of this.' Esther pulled a small glass bottle from the back pocket of her men's work pants and set it on the table. 'Cranberry cordial. Positively heavenly. Quick. Get us some glasses so we can finish it off before the men come.'

Mabel didn't move from her seat, as Esther was already on her way to the cupboard. She came back with two of Mabel's jelly jars and filled each half full with the deep red liquid. It was sweet and tart and thick on Mabel's tongue, and it warmed her throat.

'It's delicious.'

'Told you. Here, have a bit more. This is my last bottle and I'll be damned if I'll let George have any of it. He polished off the last of my blueberry cordial without even asking!'

Mabel drank it in a gulp, then took another after Esther emptied the bottle into their glasses.

'There now. That'll do.'

Just then George and Jack came in, kicking

snow off their boots.

'Well, where's the cake? You didn't leave it in the wagon, did you?'

George smiled sheepishly, one hand behind his back.

'Sorry, dear. Couldn't help myself.' He smacked his lips. 'It was mighty good though.'

'You'd better be joking or I'll — ' George grinned and pulled the cake out from behind his back. 'Not one piece missing. Jack'll vouch for me.'

Jack gave a nod with exaggerated gravity. Then he looked at Mabel. 'Are you feeling well?'

'What makes you ask?'

'Your cheeks are flushed.'

Mabel saw Esther out of the corner of her eye, tipping a thumb up to her lips as if her hand were a bottle. 'Tried to slow her down, but you know how she can be.'

'Esther!' Mabel protested.

'Oh, I'm just teasing. That cordial does have a kick, though, doesn't it?'

'A kick? You mean it has alcohol in it?'

'Does it have alcohol in it? Are you pulling my leg? Don't know what the point would be otherwise.'

'Oh, Jack. I had no idea. I thought it was just a sweet dessert drink. But it did seem hot in my throat.'

Jack grinned and kissed Mabel on the cheek. 'You got any more of that, Esther?'

'Nope. Your wife polished it off.'

The room was warm and soft-edged as Mabel tried to keep up with the flow of conversation and the passing of food around the table. For a moment she seemed to slip out of her body, and it was a pleasant sensation to see four friends sharing food, laughing and talking in the small cabin in the wilderness.

'Well? Cat ain't so bad, eh?'

'No, George.' Jack leaned back in his chair and patted his belly. 'I've got to say, I had my doubts, but that was tasty. Thanks, Esther. And give our thanks to Garrett, too.'

After they cleared the table, Esther insisting the men help as well, Jack and George went to the barn to look at the plow they had been trying to patch together for another season. As the men left the cabin, the fresh night air rushed against Mabel's face and she stood in the open door and breathed deeply. Behind her she heard Esther fussing with the dishes.

'Oh, please don't wash those. I'll take care of them tomorrow.'

'Splendid idea.' Esther sat down heavily at the table and propped her feet on the chair across from her. 'Wish we had a spot more cordial.'

Mabel laughed. 'I think I've had enough, thank you very much. But I'll get us some tea.'

'Good, and then sit down. We've got some catching up to do. I'm a little worried about you.'

'Worried? What makes you say such a thing?'

'I'm hearing things again. About you and that little girl. Now don't think I don't see your lips sealing up tight. You think you're not going to say a word, but we've got to talk this out. Why is this all coming up again?'

The cabin became so quiet Mabel could hear the fire crackling and the clock ticking. She didn't speak or move for some time, while Esther waited patiently. Then Mabel went to the shelf and handed the book to Esther.

'What's this?'

'A children's book. It's one my father used to read to me. Not read, actually. See, it's in Russian.' She opened the pages to one of the first color plates.

'And?'

'It's the story of an old couple who desperately want a child and they make one out of snow. And . . . she comes to life. The snow child does.'

'I don't think I'm following you here.'

'My sister always said I was a scatterbrain, my mind too full of fancies. A wild imagination, she called it.'

'And?'

So Mabel told her everything, about the winter they had shaped a child out of snow and how Faina had come wearing the red mittens and scarf and looking so much like the little girl they had made. She described how Jack had buried the father in the mountains and learned he had died, leaving Faina an orphan, just hours before they built the snow figure. It was that night the child had come to them for the first time.

'We have tried to convince her to stay with us, but she refuses. She says the wilderness is her home, and I've gone with her there, and it's true.

It is her home. She walks on top of the snow. And I know it seems unbelievable, Esther, but she can hold a snowflake in the palm of her hand without it melting. Don't you see? She was reborn that night . . . reborn out of snow and suffering and love.'

'Not to be quarrelsome, but nobody else has seen any sign of her. Me and Garrett, here working the farm with you those months. Nary a glimpse of the child.'

'She left. She was gone the entire summer. Just as I told you.'

'And now?'

'She came back. With the snow.'

Esther silently flipped through the pages of the book and looked at each illustration.

'You think I'm crazy, don't you? It's like you said — the winters and the small cabin. A fever, didn't you call it? Cabin fever?'

Esther let out a long sigh, then turned back to the first illustration of the old couple and the child, half snow and half human.

'Is that what you think?' Esther asked.

'No,' Mabel said. 'As fantastic as it all sounds, I know the child is real and that she has become a daughter to us. But I can't offer a single bit of evidence. You have no reason to believe me. I know that.'

Esther closed the book and with her hands folded on top of it looked directly at Mabel. 'I got to tell you, I had you wrong.'

'What do you mean?' Mabel asked.

'There at the beginning, I took you for soft. A woman whose thoughts could be twisted around by a lonely winter. Someone better suited to a different place, a different kind of life.'

Mabel's temper started to rise in her chest.

'Don't go getting all riled up,' Esther went on. 'Hear me out because I've thought this through. I was wrong. I've gotten to know you pretty well, I'd say. Count you one of my dearest friends. And you're no weakling. A bit standoffish at first. Too tenderhearted, I suspect. And God knows you think too much. But you're no feeble-minded simpleton. If you say this child of yours is real, then by God she must be real.'

'Thank you, Esther, but I know you are humoring me. As a friend, I'm pleased to hear. But humoring all the same.'

'Have you ever known me to change my mind just to humor someone?' Esther said.

Mabel gave a small smile, slowly turning the teacup around in her hands.

'Why aren't you jumping up and down? This might be a first. I'm owning up that I just might be wrong about something. But don't tell George. The shock would probably kill him dead.'

'It's almost spring, you know,' Mabel said. 'Have you seen how the snow is melting? The river will soon break up.'

'Yep. Seen that. What's that to do with . . . '

'Soon she will leave again. It's just like in the fairy tale. Faina will leave us in the spring, and I just can't bear the thought of it. What if we lose her? What if she never comes back to us?'

'Hmmm.' Esther sipped her tea thoughtfully. Then she set her cup down and looked at Mabel as if carefully measuring her words.

'Dear, sweet Mabel,' she said. 'We never know what is going to happen, do we? Life is always throwing us this way and that. That's where the adventure is. Not knowing where you'll end up or how you'll fare. It's all a mystery, and when we say any different we're just lying to ourselves. Tell me, when have you felt most alive?'

35

The March days began to lengthen. Jack watched the sun climb higher above the mountains each day. The snow was heavy and wet and melted from the eaves. Water ran along the surface of the river ice. And then one night the skies cleared and cold fell like a fog over the valley. Jack awoke to find the fire burned to black coals and the windows frosted inside and out. After kindling the fire and pulling another quilt over Mabel as she slept, he set off for town. It was the coldest it had been all winter, and by the time he arrived at the general store, he wondered if his nose was frostbitten. He stood just inside the door and rubbed it gingerly. 'Don't worry,' George teased from where he stood at the potbellied stove. 'Mabel probably won't leave you when it falls off.'

Jack joined him at the stove and rubbed his hands at the heat, trying to work some sensation back into them.

'I've been meaning to tell you, Mabel still wears that hat most every day. It was a generous gift your son gave her.'

'You know that's the only silver fox he's ever caught? The boy could barely contain himself. Weeks on end he kept asking me if Betty was done with it yet.'

'Well, she puts it on even if she's just dashing out to the outhouse. Especially with this weather.'

George laughed and slapped his own backside, as if his pants had gotten too hot. 'Esther'll get a kick out of that — Mabel in the outhouse with a fine fox-fur hat.'

'Now don't you say a word, or you'll get me in trouble for sure.'

George laughed again.

'That boy of mine is going gangbusters this winter — running traps up and down the river, gone days at a time. Boyd's old marten line, and now he's going after the wolves Esther saw out at our place.'

'Wolves?'

'A pack brought down a cow moose by the river. Not much shakes up my wife, but that did. She watched the whole bloody mess. The cow struggled hard, with the snow so deep, and the wolves nipped at her and ripped out her guts even while she was trying to run. Me and Garrett walked down to the kill site a few days later and there was nothing left but bones. You could see their teeth marks along the rib cage. Plucked clean, not even a speck of gristle left. Never seen anything like it.'

'We've heard them howl a few times over our way. That sound stays with you.'

'That it does. That it does.'

Jack decided he wouldn't mention the wolves to Mabel. He had made that mistake once before, after George told him about a lynx. One of the Bensons' neighbors had a small flock of domestic ducks. One night the farmer was marching his flock into the shed when a lynx ran in and snatched a duck right out from under his nose. The wildcat returned again and again over the next several weeks, slowly picking off birds and destroying the farmer's investment. The lynx would come in at night, kill a few, feed off them for several days, then return to take more. One morning as the man opened the duck shed, the lynx dashed out at him. Nearly gave the farmer a heart attack. Both George and Jack got a few chuckles out of the thought of the poor farmer stumbling backward as the overgrown housecat charged past him.

Mabel, however, had not been amused. She refused to go to the outhouse after sunset, said she was afraid some wild animal would be lurking there. Jack tried to reassure her, but found himself standing guard by the outhouse door more than one night.

Jack was preparing to leave the general store with a crate of supplies when he caught sight of the ice skates, their blades gleaming in the sunlit front window. He had not thought of them since he was a boy skating on the cow pond. It was a crazy whim, but he went home with three pairs.

The next evening Faina came and they settled into their familiar habits of preparing dinner and gathering at the table. When Faina yawned, Jack stood and announced, Get your coats. We're going out.

What? Going out where? Mabel asked.

Down to the river.

The child jumped to her feet, her eyes alive. Will we all go? she asked.

Jack nodded.

But it's freezing out there, Mabel said. And why on earth would we go to the river?

No time for questions. Get dressed.

He rarely gave orders so bluntly, and Mabel seemed surprised into submission. They got their coats and boots, and Jack insisted Mabel put on long underwear and wool pants. He wrapped a scarf around her neck.

There now. Mabel, you take the lantern.

He grabbed a canvas bag from beside the door.

What's that you're bringing? Mabel asked.

He merely raised an eyebrow comically and grinned.

And why are we going out in the middle of the night?

Again, just a flick of the brow.

I don't think I trust you. Not one little bit.

It was cold outside, clear and still, with a nearly full moon shining just above the mountains. With the fresh snow and moonlight, they didn't need the lantern, but it gave a comforting glow. They followed the trail down to the Wolverine River.

This way, Jack said, and he led them through a stand of willows and out toward a small side channel of the river. The wind had blown the ice clean of snow and it glistened black beneath the moon. Jack found a driftwood log and had Faina and Mabel sit side by side. He knelt by their feet.

For heaven's sake, Jack. What are you doing?

Jack pulled the skates out of the bag. Mabel started to stand.

Oh no you don't, she said. Have you lost your mind? You are not getting those on my feet. I'll fall flat on my back, or I'll break through the ice and drown.

Jack laughed, grabbed her feet, and buckled the blades onto her boots. Mabel sputtered indignantly.

Quick, Faina, Jack said. Do you know what these are?

The girl shook her head, her lips pinched tight in fear and excitement.

They're ice skates. You put them on your feet and slide on the ice.

He showed her how to put them on and buckle the straps. Then he returned to Mabel and put his mouth to her ear.

I'd never let anything happen to you. You know that, don't you?

Mabel's eyes glittered in the moonlight.

Yes. I do know, and she wobbled as she stood up.

The river's still frozen thick, he said. All this last thaw did was smooth the ice to a perfect shine. And even if we did fall through, this isn't the main channel. The water's only a foot deep. We'd just get cold and wet, but even that won't happen. I promise.

Jack put on his own skates and led them onto the ice.

Mabel was hesitant, but soon her childhood

came flying back to her and she slid confidently across the ice. The child, on the other hand, seemed to have left her braver self, the one who slayed wild animals and slept alone in the wilderness, back on solid ground, and she surprised Jack by clinging to his arm like a toddler.

It's all right, he told her. Even if you fall, it only smacks your bottom a bit. No harm done.

As if on cue, Mabel slipped and fell.

Dash it all! she said.

Before Jack could shake free of Faina and rush to her side, Mabel had eased onto her knees and stood again.

I should have strapped a pillow to my back side.

She laughed and dusted herself off.

Jack skated faster, while Faina merely held on and let herself be pulled. Mabel joined them and the three held hands and slowly skated in a circle. The riverbed echoed with the sound of their whoops and laughter and their blades carving into the ice.

Mabel let go and skated farther up the channel.

How far is it safe? she called back.

All the way to that corner, and he watched as Mabel gained speed.

Will she be all right? Faina whispered, still holding on to his arm.

Yes. Yes she will.

Eventually Faina grew comfortable on the skates, and Jack set the light in the center of the ice. Mabel returned to skate slowly but gracefully around and around the lantern, while Faina followed like a long-legged fawn learning to walk. Jack skated in the opposite direction and caught Mabel by a hand.

We used to skate like this together when we were young, he said as they passed Faina. Do you remember?

How could I forget? You were always trying to kiss me, but I could outskate you, so you never got the chance.

She laughed, pulled her hand free and skated upriver. Jack pursued her across the ice, the night-blackened trees and sky flying past him.

Faster! Go faster! Faina called out, and Jack didn't know who she was cheering on, but he skated as fast as he dared and prayed his blades would not catch in a crack or rough spot. Mabel stayed just out of reach, until she slowed and swung around to face him. Hand in hand they skated back to where Faina stood in her small circle of lantern light. Without a word, Jack and Mabel each took one of the child's hands and skated up the river, following the curves of the bank. Faina squealed in delight. Even through the cushion of their thick coats, Jack could feel her small arm folded in his, and it was as if his very heart were cradled in those joined elbows. The ice was like wet glass and they glided fast enough to create a breeze against their faces. He looked at Mabel and saw tears running down her cheeks and wondered if it was the cold that made her eyes water.

As they neared the corner, where the small channel rejoined the main river, they slowed to a stop and the three of them stood arm in arm, Jack and Mabel gasping for breath. The moon lit up the entire valley, gleaming off the river ice and glowing on the white mountains.

Let's keep going, Faina whispered, and Jack, too, wanted to skate on, up the Wolverine River, around the bend, through the gorge, and into the mountains, where spring never comes and the snow never melts.

Part 3

As she gazed upon him, love . . . filled every fiber of her being, and she knew that this was the emotion that she had been warned against by the Spirit of the Wood. Great tears welled up in her eyes and suddenly she began to melt.

'Snegurochka' translated by
Lucy Maxym

36

He wasn't always there. Some days Mabel crept through the snow and down to the creek behind the cabin, and the creature wouldn't show himself. There'd be only the trickle of water through snow and ice. But if she sat, patient and silent, at the base of the spruce tree, eventually he might appear. His small brown head would peek up from a pool of open water in the creek, or his tail would disappear over a snowy hummock.

This November day, the river otter did not keep her waiting. She heard ice splinter, a splash, and then he was just the other side of the small creek. She expected him to dash across a log or run humpbacked down the bank as he always did. Instead he paused at the water's edge, turned toward her, and stood up on his hind legs. He was remarkably still, supported by his thick tail, his front paws dangling at his chest. For longer than Mabel could hold her breath, the otter stared at her with his eyes like deep eddies. And then he dropped to all fours and scampered down the creek.

Farewell, old man, until we meet again.

She had no way to know its age or gender, but there was something in the light-colored chin and long, coarse whiskers that reminded her of an old man's beard. From a distance the otter gave a comical, mischievous impression, but when it slithered close Mabel could smell fish blood and a wet chill.

She told no one of the otter. Garrett would want to trap it; Faina would ask her to draw it. She refused to confine it by any means because, in some strange way, she knew it was her heart. Living, twisting muscle beneath bristly damp fur. Breaking through thin ice, splashing in cold creek water, sliding belly-down across snow. Joyful, though it should have known better.

It wasn't just the river otter. She once spied a gray-brown coyote slinking across a field with his mouth half open as if in laughter. She watched Bohemian waxwings like twilight shadows flock from tree to tree as if some greater force orchestrated their flight. She saw a white ermine sprint past the barn with a fat vole in its mouth. And each time, Mabel felt something leap in her chest. Something hard and pure.

She was in love. Eight years she'd lived here, and at last the land had taken hold of her and she could comprehend some small part of Faina's wildness.

The seasons of the past six years had been like an ocean tide, giving and taking, pulling the girl away and then bringing her back. Each spring Faina left for the alpine high country where the caribou migrated and the mountains cupped eternal snow, and Mabel no longer wept, though she knew she would miss her.

Homesteaders called that bittersweet season when the river ice gives way and the fields turn to mud 'breakup', but Mabel found something tender and gentle in it. She said goodbye to the girl just as the bog violets bloomed purple and white along the creeks and cow moose nuzzled their newborns, just as the sun began to push winter out of the valley.

And then, when the days stretched long, the land softened and warmed and the farm thrived. Beyond the barn, beneath a cottonwood tree, there was the picnic table Jack and Garrett had built, and often on top of it during the summer there would be a moonshine jar filled with wildflowers. Most Sundays, they shared a meal with the Bensons, sometimes here, sometimes at their homestead. When the weather was fine and the bugs miraculously scarce, they ate outdoors. Jack and George would build an alder fire in a pit early in the morning and then roast a hunk of meat from a black bear Garrett had shot in the spring. Esther would bring potato and beet salad; Mabel would bake a fresh rhubarb pie and spread a white tablecloth. Then the two women would walk together arm in arm and pick fireweed and bluebells. In the background they would hear the men talking and laughing as the flames in the pit sputtered and flared with the bear-fat drippings. When Mabel went into the cabin to get plates and silverware, Jack would sometimes come up behind her, softly pull back the wisps of her hair, and kiss her neck. 'You've never been more beautiful,' he would say.

Harvest would come and sometimes during those long, exhausting days, it would be as Mabel once imagined — she and Jack together in the field as they gathered potatoes into burlap sacks or cut cabbages from their stalks, and even as she wiped sweat from her face and tasted grit between her teeth, she tried to breathe in the sweetness of the moment. At night they would rub each other's sore muscles and jokingly complain of their aches, Mabel always more than Jack, though she knew his pain was so much worse.

Then, when the days shortened and the first frost came, they whispered their blessings and prayed for snow. Mabel would try to guess how much Faina had grown since they had last seen her, and she would sew wool stockings and long underwear and sometimes a new coat, always blue wool with white fur trim and snowflakes embroidered down the front.

Each time the girl arrived, she was taller and more beautiful than they had remembered, and she would bring gifts from the mountains. One year it was a sack of dried fish, another it was a caribou hide, tanned supple and scented with wild herbs. She would hug them and kiss them and say she had missed them, and then she would run off into the snowy trees she called home.

Mabel no longer shouted Faina's name into the wilderness or tried to think of ways to make her stay. Instead, she sat at the table and by candlelight sketched her face — impish chin, clever eyes. Then she tucked these sketches into the leather-covered children's book that told the story of the snow maiden.

Winter after winter, Faina returned to their cabin in the woods, and in all that time, no one else ever saw her. It suited Mabel fine. Just as with the otter, she came to guard the girl as a secret.

37

Garrett watched the fox through his iron sights. It was still a few hundred yards away, but its gait did not falter as it traveled up the river toward him. It wouldn't be long before it closed the distance. Garrett leaned back into the cottonwood log, wedged his elbow against his knee, steadied his rifle. His finger rested lightly at the trigger.

He knew it could be the one. For years, Jack forbade him from killing the red fox that hunted the fields and riverbed near their farm. He said it belonged to a girl who lived alone in the forest, hunted in the mountains, survived winters that killed grown men. A girl no one ever saw.

Garrett's rifle gently rose and fell with his breaths, but his eyes remained fixed on the animal. He couldn't be sure. In the fading November light, it could almost be a cross fox, a mix of silver-black and red. It stopped and raised its nose to the air, as if it had scented something, then resumed its path up the snowy river. The sun sank a degree and the last golden rays disappeared down the valley.

He let the fox come. When it was less than 150 yards away, Garrett sat forward, put his cheek to the rifle stock, shut his left eye, and lined the iron sights on the fox's spine. But the fox veered, abruptly turned its tail toward Garrett and passed behind a willow shrub, headed for the nearby poplars. It moved quickly. Garrett lowered the rifle. He'd hesitated a moment too long. It would soon be too dark to shoot, and the fox would be lost to the trees.

Then he saw that the animal had stopped and sat watching him from the forest's edge. Garrett leaned again into his rifle, squinted down the barrel and pulled the trigger.

It took only the one shot. The impact was enough to flip the small animal onto its side, and it did not move again. Garrett ejected the shell, then got up from his position against the log. With his rifle at his side, he walked until he stood over the dead fox.

The animal had thinned to a scruffy frame, and the fur along its muzzle and hackles had whitened with age so that perhaps, in poor light and at a distance, it could be mistaken for a cross. But there was no doubt. It was the one.

All these years, Garrett had obeyed Jack's command. The fox would dart across a field or cross his path in the forest, and Garrett would let it pass. Each time was an irritation. Nothing indicated that this fox was anything more than a ranging wild animal.

But now that he had killed it, he regretted it. He was honor bound. He should take it to Jack and Mabel's door. He should confess, apologize. Jack's reproach would be stern. Mabel would be silent. She would smooth her apron with her hands, gently shake her head.

He had to get rid of it. He could skin it out

and try to sell the pelt, but it was shabby and practically worthless. His mom would ask where he got it. His dad would want to see the fur. Garrett would end up telling lies, and lies had a way of getting complicated.

He shouldered his rifle, picked up the fox, and carried it into the trees. He was surprised at how thin and bony it felt in his arms, like an old barn cat.

Beyond the poplars, in a dense stand of spruce, Garrett arranged the animal in the snow at the base of a tree. He broke off evergreen boughs and laid them over it. He hoped it would snow again soon.

As he turned to walk home in the dusk, he no longer felt like a nineteen-year-old man, but instead a shameful little boy.

❄

'Garrett. Glad you could come over.'

Jack greeted him at the cabin door and shook his hand. 'We were hoping you'd make it this evening.'

At the kitchen table, Mabel smiled up at him.

'Mom said you all wanted me to come over.'

'Yes, it's about time,' Mabel said.

'What's it about?' Garrett's stomach turned.

'Have a seat,' Jack said. He held out a chair.

'All right.'

Garrett sat and looked from Jack to Mabel and back to Jack again.

'So this is how it is,' Jack began. 'We've been wanting to talk to you about the farm . . .'

'But maybe we should eat dinner first?' Mabel asked.

'Nope. Business first. This is something we've been meaning to do for a long time.' He looked at Garrett. 'You know we couldn't have made a go of this place without you.'

'I don't know about that. Just been a hired hand. Could have been another one.'

'That's where you're wrong. These past years, we haven't been able to pay you near what you're worth.'

'And you were never just a hired hand. You've been so much more, to both of us,' Mabel said. 'What would I have done without you to discuss Mark Twain and Charles Dickens with?'

Garrett's shoulders relaxed some and he let out a slow breath.

'You know what this is?' Jack gestured toward some papers spread on the table in front of them.

'No. Can't say that I do.'

'These are legal papers that make you a partner in this farm. And they also lay out that when we are both gone, this place will become yours. Now, hear us out before you start shaking your head. You know we don't have a son of our own to leave this place to. And the truth is, you made it what it is today.'

'I don't know . . . '

'Now we understand farming hasn't always been your aim,' Jack went on, 'but it seems to us that you take pride in what you've helped us do here. And maybe you'd be able to run this place along with your trapping and such in the winters.'

'Or,' Mabel added, 'you would be free to sell the place. After we're gone.'

'I wouldn't . . . I don't know.'

'Well, think it over if you'd like,' Jack said. 'We aren't rushing off to the grave yet, are we, love?'

'No. I hope not any time soon. But Garrett, whatever you decide, we want you to understand how much you've meant to us. We are proud of the man you've become.'

'Mabel, you're embarrassing the boy.'

'Please let me finish. It is true, what Jack said. We wouldn't be here, this farm wouldn't be here, if it weren't for you and all your hard work. We don't have much in this world, but we want to offer you what little we do have.'

'Are you sure? I mean, isn't there anybody else, somebody from your family?' Garrett slid the papers back toward Jack.

'Nope. You're the closest we've got,' Jack said.

'I was never expecting anything like this.'

'We know. But it's the right thing to do.'

'I should talk it over, with my folks,' Garrett said. 'But I guess it's mostly up to you two.'

'We've never been more sure,' Jack said, and he reached across the table and shook his hand again.

38

It was only the middle of November, but the snow lay heavy and deep across the land. Garrett went on foot to search for tracks. Wolf, marten, mink, coyote, fox — but it was wolverine he had his heart set on. He was a trapper of experience, and yet every winter this one animal eluded him. He couldn't have put it into words, but he hungered after its bold will, its ferocious and solitary manner. To enter the wolverine's territory, he would have to travel farther into the mountains than he ever had before.

He hiked up from the riverbed into the foothills and, as the land steepened, he wished he had worn snowshoes. He carried a light pack with enough supplies to get him through the night if necessary, but in this weather he would be wet and cold. As the morning wore on, it began to snow again, and he considered turning back. But always the next ridge, the draw beyond, lured him on. Maybe just ahead he would find a rocky, narrow valley and wolverine tracks. When he crested a foothill dotted with spruce and saw spread before him a marsh, its hummocks of grass covered in snow, he turned to go back. There would be no wolverine here, and the fresh snow was burying any tracks.

He was stopped by a sound like a woodstove

bellows, air forced hard. He spun around and saw something at the other end of the marsh. He crouched low behind a birch log and squinted against the falling snow.

At first it appeared to be a mound of snow like the others in the marsh, but larger and strangely formed, and then great white wings, broader than Garrett's own arm span, beat against the air. Again he heard the sound of bellows and knew it came from those wings. He crawled on his hands and knees around the fallen birch, the snow up to his chest. He crept closer, hiding behind one hummock and then another. When he again focused on the white creature, he saw something else. Blond hair, a human face. Snowflakes pelted his eyes, and he blinked hard, but the face remained among the beating wings and the awful hissing sound. His skin prickled along his neck and sweat ran down his back, but still he crept closer, so close that the next time the creature beat its wings, he thought the air moved against his face.

A white swan, its long neck serpentine, turned its head to the side and looked at him with one of its gleaming black eyes. Then it lowered its head, hunched its wings, and hissed. Behind the wings the face appeared again. A girl crouched in the snow just beyond the swan. She stood and at first Garrett thought she had spotted him, but she was looking only at the swan. Her blue coat was embroidered with snowflakes and on her head she wore a marten-fur hat.

It was her, the one they had whispered about all these years. The child no one but Jack and

Mabel had ever seen. The girl who made a pet of a wild fox. Winter after winter, not even a passing glimpse, not a single footprint in the snow, and now here she was before him. And she wasn't the little girl he had always pictured. She was tall and slender, only a few years younger than he.

The swan's head nearly reached the girl's shoulders and its wings enveloped her as it flapped them in warning and hopped toward her. Garrett saw then that one of its feet was bound in a snare loop. It was not the thin-boned hare or downy ptarmigan she had probably intended to catch. The swan was a beautiful giant, muscle and sinew pounding beneath white feather, black eyes set deep and fierce to the black beak. He wondered if the girl would set it free. Perhaps she could slip behind it and snap the snare, but he doubted she could get close enough without the swan attacking her.

Then he wondered — would she kill it? The possibility sickened him and he didn't know why. Because the girl was willowy, with delicate features and small hands? Because the swan had wings like an angel and flew through fairy tales with a maiden upon its back? Garrett knew the truth — the swan meat could feed the girl for weeks.

She began to unbutton her coat. Spellbound, Garrett watched even as he felt he should look away. She set the coat on a bush behind her, then her hat as well. She wore a flowered cotton dress with what looked like long underwear beneath it. She bent and removed a knife from a sheath on her leg.

The swan strained at the willow bush that anchored the snare. The girl held the knife and crept slowly around a hummock to the other side of the swan, trying to position herself behind it. But it followed her, turned its head and hopped around to face her. She would never be able to take it head on. The bird's beak would cut through her skin, break her small bones. It hissed again and swept its wings at her, not to fly but to attack. Garrett lowered himself to the ground, not wanting to be seen.

As the girl stepped toward the swan, the beating of its wings became more powerful, swirling the snow and air, and its hisses turned into a terrible, cracking growl. She circled quickly around its back and jumped onto the swan. Its free leg gave way and it crumpled, but its massive wings still beat beneath her. The girl held tightly, her face turned to the side, and grabbed the swan's sinewy neck. She slid one hand up until it clenched just below the bird's head and she held it at arm's length. It seemed fatigued from the struggle and for a moment both were still. Garrett could hear the girl breathing.

But then the swan's neck writhed in her hand and it lunged toward her face. The beak glanced across her cheek. She shoved the swan's head down into the wet snow and spread herself on top of the bird. Garrett could imagine the heat of the swan's body beneath her, could hear the bird hissing and sputtering and that growl from somewhere in its strange round body. The swan fought, then calmed, and the girl reached with her knife toward its head, slid it under the neck, and cut sharply upward.

She wiped her face with the back of her bloody hand and then, beneath her, the swan's wings flapped weakly, spasmed, were still again. The girl collapsed beside the bird, its dead wings stretched broad. The blood spread brightly beneath them and the snow fell.

She didn't move for some time. Garrett's legs were stiff from the cold and he felt the need to stand but, mesmerized, could not.

For the next hour, he watched as she gutted the swan and cut off the head and black webbed feet. Steam rose from the body cavity and strewn entrails. She set aside the liver, the plum-sized heart, the sinewy neck. She steadily skinned the swan until she held a sagging pelt of white wings, white feathers, and bloody skin. Garrett expected her to throw it aside, but instead she laid it out in the snow and carefully rolled it up, the wings folded within the skin. She put the pelt inside a sack. Then she dragged the cleaned carcass away from the kill site, where the scraps and blood would attract ravens, magpies and other scavengers. Garrett watched her climb a small spruce at the edge of the clearing and begin to tie the carcass and sack to a limb.

She was facing away from him, so Garrett crawled as quickly as he could back the way he had come. When he reached the spruce trees, he hid behind one and watched her kneel in the marsh and scrub her hands and the knife blade in the snow. Then she put on her coat and hat. Garrett turned down the hill and ran.

The snow had stopped and it was beginning to clear. Twilight hinted at winter to come. Twisting swaths of fog rose up from the river and, as he ran down the mountainside, it was as if he were descending into clouds. Overhead he heard a V of migrating snow geese cry their goodbyes into the purpling sky and, for the first time in his life, the sound frightened him.

39

Mabel and Faina were cutting out paper snowflakes to decorate the little spruce tree in the corner of the cabin when the Bensons showed up unannounced with Christmas gifts. Esther shoved the door open without knocking, and Faina bolted to the opposite side of the room, her eyes wide with fear, her muscles taut as if ready to spring. For a moment, Mabel feared the girl would try to break out the glass window. She went to her and gently took hold of her wrist, hoping to calm her with her touch.

Esther stood stock-still, her mouth gaping. Mabel would have found it amusing had it not been for Faina's terror.

Mabel straightened, still holding on to the girl's arm, and took a slow breath.

Esther, she said. I would like you to meet Faina. Faina, this is my dear friend Esther.

Just then George and Garrett bumped noisily through the door behind her and Esther waved a hand and shushed them as if they were about to startle away a woodland creature.

It's the girl, George, she whispered without taking her eyes off Faina. She's here. She's right here, in front of me.

George laughed out loud, but behind him Garrett was silent. The boy's eyes were dark and wide, until he caught Mabel looking at him, and then he stepped back behind his father.

Mabel nudged the girl.

Hello, Faina said quietly.

My God, Esther said. She is real. Your girl is flesh and blood.

The next few hours were awkward. Esther tried to include Faina in the barrage of gifts and treats, as if she'd known all along she would be there.

Oh, here. This one is for you, Esther said, handing her a wrapped package.

Faina was silent and at first did not even put out her hands to accept it. Mabel and Jack both moved to intercede, but stopped themselves. The girl took the package and, with a somber expression, held it in her lap.

Well, go on then. Aren't you going to open it? Esther said.

Faina looked so frightened and confused, her cheeks flushed an unhealthy crimson, that Mabel longed to open the door to let her escape into the cold.

Do you need help, Faina?

The cabin was stiflingly hot. No one spoke. All eyes were on the girl. Finally, Faina began to pull away the paper. When at last she held up a flower-embroidered handkerchief and smiled as if in polite recognition, Mabel thought she would faint with relief.

Thank you, Faina said, and Esther's eyes glistened.

340

As the two families gathered for dinner, the tension eased. Faina remained quiet, but she was well mannered, carefully passing dishes when prompted and giving a small smile here and there. Garrett, however, seemed incapable of speaking or looking at anyone, particularly the girl. Her very presence seemed an affront to him, and Mabel did not know what to make of it.

'You know the boy is catching a pile of lynx this year,' George said around a mouthful of fruitcake. 'The hare population is up, so there are a ton of cats all over the valley.'

'Is that so?' Jack asked.

Mabel looked at Garrett, and his face called to mind that first summer he came to work on the farm — irritable, petulant.

'Well? The man asked you a question.' George swung his arm across the back of Garrett's chair. Garrett looked back down at his plate and mumbled incoherently.

'Hmmm,' Jack said agreeably, though Mabel knew he had not heard Garrett's response either.

'What's the matter with you, boy? Speak up. You've got nothing to be ashamed of. You've been doing some good trapping this year.'

'Yeah, I guess I've gotten a few.' And then his head was down again and he poked at his dessert without ever taking a bite.

Was this the honorary son, the one who now cast sullen looks in everyone's direction? Wasn't it at this very table that Garrett had shaken

Jack's hand and said it would be a privilege to be farming partners, to inherit the homestead when that time came?

For the rest of the evening, the boy did not utter a word.

George and Esther went on with their stories. Mabel cleaned up dinner and paced behind Faina. The girl was shrinking in her chair, beads of sweat gathering on the bridge of her nose. Mabel fanned her with a napkin and wiped at her temples.

Too warm, much too warm, Mabel whispered to herself.

At last the Bensons said their goodbyes, and Mabel was relieved to usher them all out the door — George, Esther, and Garrett to their horses and wagon, and Faina to the snowy forest.

40

Garrett cursed and urged his horse up the steep hill to follow the footprints. He ducked to avoid a low spruce branch but still managed to get covered in snow. When he reached the top of the ridge, he reined in the horse, shook the snow from his shoulders, and leaned from the saddle. The tracks were old, shapeless indentations beneath several inches of snow, but they were hers. The horse shifted, antsy to either go back or go on, so Garrett went on, following the tracks as they wove among the spruce trees.

He was tired of the girl. For six years he had listened to Jack talk about her. Faina, Faina, Faina. The angel from the woods. And yet, for all the talk, never once had Garrett seen hide nor hair of the girl. Each winter he watched for her tracks, half hoping he'd spot them, half hoping Jack and Mabel were crazy. Sometimes he would think he saw a flicker in the brush, but it would only be a bird.

So how was it that this winter was different, that everywhere he went the forest snow was riddled with her tracks and he couldn't be free of her?

Everything about the girl filled him with guilt. He had shot her fox and told no one. He had spied on her. Again and again his mind returned to the scene, to the girl's struggle with the swan. The emotions it sparked bothered him, but he could not leave it be.

As he pursued her he told himself he was only going where he wanted — toward the mountains, toward the wolverine. And it was true. Wolverine roamed higher in the alpine country, closer to the glacier. He would never catch one in the lowlands where he trapped coyote, fox, beaver and mink.

He followed the tracks up into a narrow ravine where boulders were hidden by the snow. The horse stumbled occasionally, and finally Garrett dismounted and led the animal. Although getting on in years, the gelding was still steady and sure-footed, and knew the mountains like few other horses.

Garrett's traps and chains clanked in the burlap sacks strapped behind the saddle. Water ran down through the boulders, beneath the snow. At any moment he expected to see the stout, bearlike paw prints of a lone wolverine. Instead he saw small tracks, this time fresher. The girl again. Probably today. Garrett paused, hands on his knees, to look at the trail. Bare traces on top of the snow, like a lynx or snowshoe hare. The girl was nearly as tall as Garrett, so how could she be so insubstantial as to not sink into the snow? Irritated fascination twisted in his gut. He stomped ahead, erasing the delicate tracks with his boots.

She was near. He was certain. Something in the air had changed. It was the same when he stalked a moose — abruptly the woods quieted and his senses sharpened. When he looked ahead, he saw the girl standing just out of the trees, her blue coat decorated in snowflakes, her hair an unearthly blond. He could turn back, but surely she'd seen him, too. She waited for him. He continued up the ravine, trying to walk slower than his heart raced.

She did not move or speak until he was within several feet of her. She eyed the horse nervously, but when Garrett started to tell her to not be afraid, she spoke over him.

You are the one who killed my fox.

For a moment Garrett could not make his mouth work. How could she know?

Yes, he finally choked.

Why did you come here?

He could have asked her the same. He had no reason to feel inferior to her.

Wolverine, he said. I'm scouting for wolverine.

Here?

There's got to be one on this creek. I'm sure of it.

The girl turned her head side to side. Fury slowed Garrett's heart to a dull thud.

What do you know? he asked. You know this whole valley?

She gave a short nod.

Why should I believe you?

Garrett pushed forward, as if to go past her,

345

and caught her scent. Labrador tea, elderberry, nettle, fresh snow. It was so faint that he found himself inhaling deeply, trying to catch more of it.

The girl turned her back and bent to the ground. In the snow was a woven birch-bark pack he hadn't noticed. She stood it up at her feet and began to pull something from it. When she faced him, she held a dead wolverine by its front paws. Its head was like that of a small bear, its body compact, legs short and powerful. It was a large animal, close to forty pounds, Garrett guessed, and she should have struggled under its weight, but she easily tossed it at his feet. Behind him the horse nickered and pulled back.

What's this? he asked.

A wolverine.

I can see that. What are you doing with it?

I'm giving it to you. So you can leave.

Garrett was speechless for a moment.

I don't want it, he said crossly. Not like this.

I'll skin it for you, said the girl, and she turned again to her pack.

What? Hell, that's not what I mean. Why should you give it to me?

I don't want it. You do.

Why'd you kill it, if you didn't want it?

It was stealing marten and bait. Take it.

Garrett had never been so mad in his life. To think of the years he had tried to find a wolverine to trap, and here was this girl throwing one at his feet like a discarded carcass. And ordering him to leave. He turned back to his horse, grabbed the saddle horn, and mounted.

Won't you take it with you? The girl's voice was higher pitched, more childlike than before.

Garrett didn't answer. He shook the reins, and the horse began to work its way slowly down the ravine.

There are no others here, the girl shouted after him. Just this one.

He did not look back.

Take it with you, she called. So you don't have to come back.

I don't want your blasted wolverine, he yelled over his shoulder. And I'll be back if I want to. You don't own this land.

He did not allow himself to look back until he was nearing the ridge. When he did, he saw the girl still standing in the same place, the wolverine at her feet. He couldn't be sure, but he thought there was anger in the tight line of her lips.

Once Garrett believed he was out of the girl's sight, he dismounted again. The ground was too treacherous to ride. Beneath the snow, creek water was frozen in pools and ice coated the boulders. He led the horse to a bit of open water in the creek and let it drink. When the horse was done, he crouched and scooped some of the water in his hand and drank. It was sweet and cold, and left him queasy.

He had no intention of going home yet. He still had most of the day ahead of him and he had not set a single trap.

He had always been respectful of other

347

trappers' territories. A bachelor not much older than Garrett had claimed the land downstream from Jack and Mabel's, and he did not trespass there. He hadn't trapped Boyd's trails, even when he saw that the old man's pole sets went untouched, until Boyd bestowed the line upon him. A man could be shot for stealing a trapper's catch, and even edging in on his territory was considered disrespectful. But this? This was just a girl. A girl snaring a few rabbits. Never mind the wolverine. That had been a fluke, surely.

But he knew it was no such thing — wolverine weren't caught on a fluke, and he had watched her kill the swan. She was capable.

He wiped creek water across his brow and dried his hand on his coat before pulling his leather gloves back on. It was beginning to snow. He hadn't anticipated that. The sky had been cloudless this morning. When he had gone to the outhouse before sunrise, he had seen the northern lights twisting and turning through the blackness the way they do only on clear, cold nights. But here it was, only a few hours later, snowing. He looked toward the mountains, but low-lying clouds had swallowed them.

'Well, Jackson. Time to head home after all, eh?'

He didn't normally talk to his horse, but he was uneasy. The snow was falling steadily now, and a slight wind blew up from the riverbed. He pulled himself into the saddle and was momentarily disoriented. The air was so thick with snowflakes he could see only the outlines of the nearest trees.

'Down the hill, Jackson? Can't go wrong by heading toward the river.'

Soon, though, blowing snow blinded Garrett, and the horse stumbled along the disappearing trail.

'Jesus,' he said under his breath. 'Where did this come from?' Never before had he seen a winter storm come up so quickly, whipped out of nothing.

He turned up the collar of his coat and pulled a wool hat out of his saddlebag. He slid off the saddle and the snow was above his knees. It had come down fast, and it was still falling. He got back on the horse and maneuvered it through the trees, but he had lost his bearings. He thought he had been following the slope down toward the river, but now he seemed to have fallen off into a ravine running the opposite direction. He tried to remember what he had brought with him. No tarp. No bedroll. Only his most basic emergency supplies — some matches, a pocketknife, a spare pair of wool socks. The lunch his mother had packed for him. Not much else. He saw the vague silhouette of a large spruce tree and headed toward it.

He could wait out the storm here, for a while. He broke off some of the tree's lowest branches, and then used the edge of his boot to scrape snow away from the trunk. It was a shelter of some sort. He broke the branches over his knee into smaller pieces, then peeled some bark off a nearby birch. He had his ax. Once he got the fire going, he could chop larger pieces of wood.

Sitting cross-legged beneath the tree, he piled

the bark and spruce branches and lit a match, but it quickly sputtered out in the driving snow. Another. Another. Only a few left. Eventually he got a small piece of the papery bark to light, but only for seconds before the wind snuffed it out. He stood and kicked at the pile. Snow from the branches above toppled onto his head.

'Well, Jackson. Guess we're pushing on.'

As he rode through the trees he thought of stories he had heard of men killing their horses and climbing into their body cavities to stay warm. 'Don't worry, Jackson. We're not that desperate yet.'

But this wasn't good. He could see that. He had slept out many nights, but never so ill-prepared in such bad conditions. Snow was embedded in the creases of his pants and coat. The horse's mane was coated in ice. He had no choice — he rode on, not knowing his direction.

When he found himself on the banks of what appeared to be a frozen lake, a lake he had never seen or heard of before, he was afraid. He dismounted and stood beside the horse at the snowy shore.

Goddamn. Goddamn, and he kicked the ground in front of him. The horse slowly blinked, too fatigued to move away from the commotion.

You're lost.

Garrett jumped at the voice, an eerie whisper in his ear. Over his shoulder he saw the girl like a

350

ghost in the snow. Angry at being startled, he shouted, What do you want?

You have lost your way, she said, and again her voice was hushed and nearer than the girl herself.

No I haven't.

But they both knew he was lying.

You won't find your way home, she said.

No, I damn well won't. But I don't see you can do a thing about it.

The girl turned and began to walk away.

Follow me, she said.

What?

I'll show you the way.

He wanted to yell, to kick his feet, to fight this absurd turn of events, but he took up the reins and led his horse after the girl. Without looking back she walked quickly and easily through the snow. At times he lost sight of her, but then she would reappear, waiting beside a birch or in a stand of spruce.

I didn't mean for this to happen, she said. Even though I was angry. I didn't mean for you to lose your way.

Well, of course not. How could this be your fault?

The girl shrugged and walked again. The snow slowed and patches of blue sky appeared overhead. When the mountains again revealed themselves, they were not where Garrett thought they would be. Where would he have ended up, he wondered, if she hadn't come for him?

The girl's steps laced through naked birch trees and a few times she lightheartedly looped an arm around one of their trunks as she passed by. She didn't seem to take note of where she was going or where she had been. She was like a fearless child playing in the woods, and yet she was tall and almost a woman, her blue coat tapered in at the waist, her hair blond and straight down her back.

You were there, she said, when I killed the swan.

She did not look back at him when she spoke, but ran ahead, her feet light on the snow, and for that, at least, Garrett was grateful. He didn't have to answer. He just had to follow and hope she never, ever spoke to him again. They traveled for some time in silence.

Your horse won't make it up here much longer, she said after a while. The snow will be too deep.

Garrett stopped walking and rubbed the back of his neck. Of all the blasted things she could say.

I know that, he said. Don't you think I know that? I need a team of dogs. But my folks won't let me. Jackson's a good horse, though. I was going to use him a while, then snowshoe in. It would have worked.

If it weren't for you, he wanted to add. But he hated the whiny sound of his own voice, like a spoiled boy who hasn't gotten his way. Why couldn't he just keep quiet? That's what a man would do.

There, the girl said, and pointed down through the trees. It was Jack and Mabel's place. He could see the fields white with snow and smoke curling up from their stovepipe.

He nodded and mounted his horse. When he had ridden down into the clearing, he spun the horse around to search the trees for the girl, for her blue coat and shining blond hair, but she was gone.

41

Faina came with a tall basket made of birch bark that she wore as a pack with moosehide straps. Outside the cabin, she shrugged it from her shoulders, set it in the snow beside her feet, took a fish from it, and held it up to Jack.

It was the most hideous creature he had ever seen. It draped nearly two feet between the girl's hands, skin mottled and slick, long body fat and limp as a slug. It had thick lips and a wide, flat head with a barb jutting from its chin. Like an overgrown, malformed tadpole.

What in God's name is that?

A burbot, she said. I caught it through the ice just now. I brought it for dinner.

I don't think Mabel will allow it in the kitchen, Jack said.

Oh.

No, I'm only teasing you. I've never seen one before. Is it safe to eat?

Yes, she said. They swim in the deepest, coldest water. They are hard to catch, but the very best to eat.

Well, then, I guess we'd better clean it.

He led the girl behind the cabin and down to the creek.

You have a river otter, Faina said, pointing to the opposite bank.

Jack saw the tracks where they veered around a fallen tree.

Otter, you say? I never noticed it.

She crouched beside a pool of open water, took a knife from a sheath at her leg, and opened the fish belly with a slice.

Here, let me do that, Jack said.

She stayed by the creek, pulled the entrails from the fish and tossed them into the flowing water. Then she put a hand inside the body cavity and scraped the kidney from the spine.

Why does Garrett come to the mountains? she asked as she shook the clotted blood from her fingertips.

You've seen him?

Yes. Many times. Why does he come?

Must be putting out traps.

Oh, she said.

You don't have to be frightened of him. He doesn't mean you any harm.

All right, she said.

She set the fish in the snow and washed the blood from her hands.

42

Garrett's nights were haunted by the girl. The day she led him out of the snowstorm, he returned home exhausted but found he could not sleep, and he did not sleep well for weeks. He lay in his bed and thought of her blue eyes and the delicate features of her face, but they were always veiled by falling snow or covered in the fall of her blond hair, and he could not re-create them clearly in his mind. He tried to remember the shape of her lips. He wondered what it would be like to touch them. And more than anything he wanted to remember her scent, vague and so familiar.

He returned again and again to the foothills to find her trails skimming across the snow. He told everyone, perhaps even himself, that he was trapping, and yet for days he did not put out a single set and sometimes even forgot to bring his bait and snares. He no longer thought of wolverine, but only of her, and his eyes grew weary from watching for any flash of a blue coat or white-blond hair. He suspected that she kept herself hidden, but still he went back.

Just as the girl predicted, the snow in the

mountains was soon too deep for his horse, so he snowshoed. Sometimes he siwashed, sleeping beneath a canvas tarp and cooking on an open campfire. Those nights were the worst because sleep never came. He stared into the cold blackness and listened for a whisper of movement. He was sure the girl was just outside, watching him from the trees, and sometimes he found her footprints the next morning. But still she did not reveal herself to him. Not until the day he stood desperate and exhilarated beside her fresh trail and called out her name.

Faina! Faina! I just want to talk with you. Won't you let me?

The trees were silent. The sky was overcast and dense with snow yet to come.

Faina! I know you're there. Won't you come out?

I'm here, she said and she stepped from behind a snow-heavy spruce branch. What do you want with me?

I don't know. Garrett was surprised at his own honesty. He was reckless and emboldened. I don't know, he repeated.

She narrowed her sharp blue eyes but did not retreat.

Have you seen any more wolverine? he asked, only because he could think of nothing better to say. The girl shook her head.

And you? Have you found your wolverine?

No. Never, actually. I've never caught a wolverine.

Oh.

I've always wanted to.

Is that why you're here?

No, it isn't.

Why then?

You. I think.

The girl shifted, wary now, but she stood her ground.

I'm sorry about your fox. I shouldn't have shot it. Wait. Don't leave. Won't you talk with me? I've never met anyone like you before.

She shrugged. A peculiar expression passed over her face, and he thought she smiled.

Do you want to see something? she asked.

All right.

She darted around the spruce tree and was gone. Afraid to lose sight of her, he ran as well as he could in the snowshoes. He followed her through the trees, up through aspens and alpine blueberry bushes. They made their way above the tree line, where the snowy slopes rose over their heads into rocky mountaintops. Although he was damp with sweat and his lungs ached, the girl seemed tireless. She waited on a wind-blown rock until he managed, huffing, to climb to her.

Faina had taken off her mittens and she put a finger to her lips, shushing him. Then she pointed across the slope to one side. Garrett saw nothing but white. It was humiliating. He always had keen eyes for game, but this time he had to shake his head no, he did not see.

She smiled, not unkindly, and knelt beside the rock. From her coat pocket she removed a handful of rounded and smooth stones, all of similar size, as if carefully chosen. She picked one, stood, and threw it. Garrett heard a stifled squawk and saw a white flapping. The girl chose another rock, threw again, and another bird was hit. Without looking back at him, she sprinted across the slope toward her prey. A flock of pure-white ptarmigan burst to life from around her feet in a noisy flutter. Hundreds — more ptarmigan than Garrett had ever seen at once — filled the sky and dispersed in all directions, some landing just a few hundred yards away and disappearing white into the white, others clumsily flying over the next ridge.

The girl ran to him, smiling and holding two dead ptarmigan by their feathered toes. Annoyed he sat with arms crossed. He had tried such a trick before. After hurling dozens of rocks, he had poorly wounded one and had to shoot it with his shotgun after all.

So, is that what you wanted to show me? he asked.

No. You are rested now?

Instead of leading him higher up the mountain, as he expected, she began to traverse the slope. Where her feet touched, tiny snowballs formed and rolled down the hill, leaving dotted trails. Covering the steep ground in snowshoes was difficult, but Garrett knew if he removed them he would sink well past his waist in the snow, so he slogged on. Soon they descended into a steep-sided ravine thick with alder bushes.

At the base of a small knoll, the girl went to one knee and again gestured for him to be quiet. Deep snow covered the hill except for a spot no bigger than a man's head. Come closer, the girl said with her hands.

It was a gloomy hole in the earth, part of a much larger entrance mostly buried in snow. Recognition sank in as a cold shiver up his neck and along his scalp. She had led him to a bear den.

Garrett squatted in his snowshoes beside her and leaned into the hole. He thought he could make out roots and black dirt, but it was so dark he couldn't be sure. He expected it to be cavernous and foul, but all he could smell was snow and earth and maybe damp leaves and fur. He could hear nothing but his own breathing.

He pointed and raised his eyebrows at the girl as if to ask, Is it in there? She nodded, her eyes lively and her mittened hand on his shoulder in warning. Even through his heavy winter coat, he could feel the pressure of her hand on his skin, and it left him light-headed. They slowly backed away from the den and walked in silence until they were down in the creek bed.

Is it in there? he whispered. Now?

Yes. I watched it dig the den from up there, and the girl pointed to the slope on the opposite side of the creek.

Brown bear? Garrett asked. She nodded. A boar?

No. A mama, with two cubs.

No animal in the wilderness more dangerous, Garrett thought. He had watched brown bears on mountainsides, seen their muscles ripple across their humped backs, their fur undulate in waves. Each time he caught even a passing glimpse of one, he was awestruck. But never had he been this close. Snow alone had separated him from a sow grizzly, heavy with sleep and power, her cubs nursing at her side, her long claws trailing from her padded feet.

43

The boy was at Mabel's door, covered with snow and leading a half-grown puppy on a rope leash, and he came asking after Faina.

'Pardon?'

'Faina? Is she here?'

'Why, no, Garrett. She isn't. But come on inside.'

He paused in the doorway and looked down at the black-and-white, floppy-eared pup.

'I suppose you can bring your new friend in as well,' Mabel said, gesturing them through the door and closing it before too much snow blew in.

The puppy wagged its tail furiously and, when Mabel bent beside it, tried to jump into her lap. She laughed and let it lick her face before she stood again and wiped her hands on her apron.

'So you got yourself a new puppy?'

'Naw. You know Mom and Dad won't let me have any sled dogs,' he said. He remained near the door, shifting awkwardly in his boots. 'No, actually, well, I brought it for her.'

'Not for Faina?'

'You don't think she'll like it?'

'Oh. Well, yes. I suppose most any child would adore a puppy, but I'm not sure . . . '

'She's not a child.'

His tone was unexpected — irritable, even a little defensive.

'No, I guess she isn't a child anymore, is she?'

Mabel had noticed a change in Faina. Her cheeks had thinned so that the bone structure was more striking and her limbs had gracefully lengthened. She seemed taller, more confident. Close to sixteen or seventeen years old, Mabel guessed.

'Are you expecting her tonight maybe?'

'I don't know. We can never be sure when she will come.'

The puppy was cavorting around the small cabin and had already managed to leave a puddle of urine in one corner, drag a dish towel to the floor, and begin chewing Jack's slippers beside the woodstove. Mabel grabbed the dish towel and began cleaning up the mess.

'I'm sorry, Garrett. I don't know when we'll see her next, and to be honest, I'm not sure it's such a good idea. She might not be able to care for a puppy on her own.'

'She could.'

'Well, let's see what Jack thinks. He'll be home in a few hours. I'd offer to keep the puppy here until her next visit, but it would be rather inconvenient.'

'Could I stay here, with the puppy? In the barn maybe, until she comes again?'

'Oh. Well. I suppose. If that's what you'd like to do. It will be cold, though.'

'I'll be all right. And she'll probably come soon enough, don't you think?'

Garrett took the puppy outside to romp in the

snow, and Mabel was left to muddle through her thoughts. What an odd turn of events, the boy bringing Faina a puppy. Mabel doubted the girl would even come into the house if she knew Garrett was there. Faina never visited when strangers were around. How long would Garrett stay, waiting to see her?

'Garrett's here?' Jack said when he returned just before nightfall. 'Saw his horse is in the barn.'

'Yes. He's come with a gift for Faina.'

'Faina? What kind of gift?'

'A puppy.'

'A puppy?'

'Yes. Garrett said it's a husky, one that could be trained as a sled dog.'

'A dog? For Faina, you say?'

He seemed puzzled at first. Then he grinned broadly.

'A puppy!'

'You think this is a good idea?'

'Of course. She needs a friend.'

'But can she care for it?'

'Oh, she'll manage fine. It'll be good for her.'

'Are you sure?'

Jack must have noticed her anxious tone because he looked at her more closely.

'She's lonesome, Mabel. You must see that. Pulled between here and there — uneasy in our home, all alone in the woods. I'll bet she's never even been around a happy-go-lucky pup.'

Mabel was tempted to explain her other

reservations about Garrett and his peculiar behavior, but she couldn't find the words to express them and knew she would sound fretful and silly.

❄

When Faina knocked at the door later that evening, Jack, Mabel, and Garrett were on the floor with the puppy, tossing a knotted rag around the room. At the sound of the knock, Garrett stumbled to his feet.

Mabel opened the door, wondering if Faina would sprint away when she saw they had company, but the girl stood just inside the door without removing her hat and coat. When she saw Garrett, her eyes widened.

Here, child, Mabel said. Let me take your coat. Has it started snowing again?

Though Faina did not answer, she removed her hat and coat, her stare never leaving Garrett.

You remember Garrett, don't you? Esther and George's son? He was here earlier in the winter. He . . . well, he has brought you something.

Garrett had been holding the puppy by its leash, but now he slipped the rope from its neck. The puppy charged toward Faina, tail wagging, tongue flapping. The girl backed away, until she was pressed against the door and the puppy was jumping at her.

It's all right, child. It's only a puppy, Mabel said. And I'd say it's already quite fond of you.

He won't bite. I promise, Garrett said.

He knelt at Faina's feet and put his hands on the dog to settle it.

See? He only wants to play. He's young, just a few months old.

Garrett reached up, took Faina's hand and brought it down to the dog's head.

There. You can pet him.

The puppy lapped at the girl's fingers, and Faina giggled.

So, you like him? Garrett asked. Faina nodded, smiling and letting the puppy lick her fingertips.

Because he's for you.

The girl looked at Mabel, then back to Garrett, her brow furrowed.

That's right. He's yours, Garrett said. I know he's not like your fox. I thought about trying to live-trap one for you, but then I thought a pup might be better.

Faina put her palms to the puppy's cheeks, and the puppy leaned into her touch so that it seemed to be grinning.

You'll have to feed it regularly, Jack spoke up for the first time. He stood with an amused expression and his arms folded. Just feed it whatever you're eating, and it will do fine.

And I was thinking maybe you could sleep with him inside your coat, until he gets a little bigger, Garrett added.

Faina was still petting the dog in pure wonderment. Mabel expected her to say thank you or ask a question, but the girl was silent.

You don't have to take the dog if you don't want it.

Even as Mabel said this, she knew it was ridiculous. Faina would not leave without the dog.

You'll have to think of a name, then, if he's going to be yours, she said.

Faina nodded earnestly, like a child prepared to make any promise to keep her pet.

That's a sled dog you've got there, you know, Faina, Jack said. He'll carry a pack or pull a sled. And these dogs love the snow. He'll go everywhere with you. Take him out in the yard, you'll see what I mean.

Jack opened the door then, and the dog bounded out into the snow. Faina and Garrett followed, buttoning their coats as they ran. Jack closed the door after them and went to the window to watch with Mabel. The cabin's lantern light spilled outside and near the trees she could see Garrett and Faina tossing snow at the puppy and running as it chased after them.

'So, you're sure this is a good idea?' Mabel said.

Jack nodded and squeezed her shoulders. She could see, though, that he was thinking of the dog, and she wasn't certain that was what she had meant.

Over the next few weeks, Garrett and Faina and the puppy cavorted through the snow and trees outside their cabin. Often Garrett would come early in the day, usually with some excuse of bringing a jar of his mother's jam or an ax handle he had mended for Jack. Then, inevitably, Faina and the dog would emerge from the forest. The girl's blue eyes were alight with joy, yet Mabel was apprehensive. She tried to enjoy the afternoons when they all came indoors, the young dog sprawled beside the woodstove, Garrett and Faina eating pie at the kitchen table. This, too, had been part of a life she once hoped for herself — children dancing outside her window, children safe at her table. She tried, just as she had during harvest when she and Jack had worked together, to take every bit of pleasure from that moment, knowing it might not last.

Garrett soon hatched a plan to train the dog, and Mabel teased that this had been his motivation all along, to have a hand in raising a sled dog. He laughed but said he knew this pup was born for the snow. The next time he came, he brought a small wooden sled he had built and a harness he had fashioned out of rope and leather. Since the dog was far from full grown, he said, it would pull the sled empty. Mabel watched as the puppy charged toward the river, the sled bumping along behind it, and Garrett and Faina running after. They were gone for some time, long enough that Mabel began to worry. When Jack came in from the barn, she told him as much.

'They're fine, Mabel. Those two children know these woods better than anyone I've ever met. Did you see that pup run? He'll make Faina a fine dog.'

Garrett returned alone just before sunset. 'Tomorrow we're going to take the dog for a long run, up the river. We're meeting here in the morning. Can I sleep in the barn for the night?'

'Sure,' Jack said. 'Looks like you found her a good husky.'

'Yep. He's a fast learner, and there's nothing he wants to do more than work.'

'Tomorrow then? You're going up the river for the day?' Mabel was wringing her hands like a grandmother, old and fussy.

❄

The next morning, as she gave Garrett a lunch she had packed for the two of them, including a chunk of moose roast for the puppy, she could no longer keep her silence.

'Garrett, promise me something,' she spoke in a near whisper. Jack didn't need to hear what she had to say.

'Sure. What?'

'Promise me you won't build a fire?'

'A fire?'

'Yes. When you stop for your lunch or if you catch a chill. Promise me you won't build a fire, even just a little one of twigs.'

'But why would . . . '

'This is important,' Mabel said, and she had to keep herself from reaching up and shaking the young man's shoulders. 'Promise me that you will never let Faina near any kind of fire.'

As her voice climbed, Jack glanced up from the paperwork he was reading at the kitchen table, but then, distracted, went back to it. Mabel quieted herself.

'I know it must sound like a strange request, but will you promise?'

Garrett looked down at her kindly, and for a moment she wanted to tell him the truth. Maybe

370

she and Garrett could laugh at the improbability of it, and then it might never come to pass.

'I don't understand, but I promise,' Garrett said earnestly. 'And I would never let anything happen to Faina. You must know that.'

And in his face, she could see that he believed his own words.

44

The bear den was a gift Faina had given him deliberately and with some understanding of his heart. It took Garrett time to think of a gift of equal significance, and at first he worried the puppy was a mistake. He hadn't foreseen that she would be frightened of it.

Weeks later, he was more confident in his choice. The puppy was thriving under her care, its black coat thick and shiny. It watched Faina closely with its one blue eye and one brown. When it thought she had disappeared, it would sit and wait somberly like a much older dog. When she reappeared, the pup leapt and yipped. She still hadn't named it, but called it easily to her side with a whistle like a chickadee.

And Faina — she was transformed. Where she had been quiet and serious around Garrett, she now laughed and danced. She and the puppy would chase each other in tighter and tighter circles until the girl fell giggling to the snow and the puppy bounded on top of her. When she was on her feet again and had shaken the snow from her long hair, she sometimes took Garrett by an arm and pulled him through the trees as she ran after the puppy, and it was as if he were swimming through a snowy dream. In that dream, he sometimes even kissed her cool, dry lips.

Now, they headed up the Wolverine River, sunlight flashed off the snow and every branch and dead leaf glittered with frost. The air stung Garrett's lungs, and the exposed skin of his face burned in the cold. Until they began walking in earnest, his feet felt half frozen. Faina and the dog ran ahead and then waited for Garrett to catch up. When they stopped for lunch at a pile of driftwood logs, Garrett thought of starting a campfire to warm themselves but then remembered Mabel's plea. They ate cold sandwiches from wax-paper wrapping and fed the puppy the bit of frozen moose roast.

We could head back now, Garrett suggested when they were finished eating.

No, just a little farther. Please?

So they continued north, sometimes crossing the frozen channels, other times weaving through the trees along the shore. The riverbed was blown clear of snow and Garrett could see where the white-blue ice had buckled and frozen into great swells and dips. In places he hesitated to walk the ice, but Faina beckoned him across. He believed in her, trusted she knew where it was rotten and sheared and where it was strong and clear as glass, and he always made it safely to her side.

As they came to a bend, Garrett realized this was the farthest he had ever traveled upriver. Around the curve, the valley opened up and, in the distance, spires of blue ice glowed. It was the river's source — a glacier cradled between white mountains. From so many miles away, the craggy peaks of ice seemed to waver in the sunlight like a mirage, close and distant, real and unreal.

Come on! Faina called, and she and the dog darted across hard-packed snowdrifts and into a stand of willow along the riverbank. Garrett tried to follow but he could not weave so easily between the frost-encrusted willows. Stumbling through the brush, he did not see the girl until suddenly she was in front of him. She had hooked her arm around the trunk of a small willow and it bent gently under her weight. She leaned out from the sparkling branches and gazed at Garrett with a look he did not understand. Then she leaned closer and he felt her breath cool on his skin. Like a startled snowshoe hare, Garrett didn't move, not until her lips touched his.

Her cheeks were so smooth, so cold against his, and she tasted of the fragrance that all winter had haunted him — mountain herbs and wet stone and new snow. He slowly circled his arms around her and pulled her closer still. He shook off a glove and put his bare palm to her hair, something he now knew he had longed to do since he had first laid eyes on her, that day when she killed the swan. Pressed against his, the entire length of her body was delicate but steady, alive and cool, like nothing he had ever felt before.

You are warm, she whispered against his lips.

Garrett let his mouth follow her jawline down to her neck and back to her ear and he knew he could lose himself in the place where her blond hair met her soft skin. He could lose himself in her pale smoothness, in her gentle fingers, in her wide blue eyes.

He wanted to let his knees give way and pull them both down, to lie together in the snow, but he didn't. He stayed on his feet, one arm around her waist, the other at the back of her head, his face against her neck.

It was her — she reached up and began unfastening the silver filigree buttons of her coat.

No, no, Garrett mumbled.

Why?

You'll be too cold.

She didn't speak again, but continued unbuttoning her coat. Garrett shook his other glove to the ground and slid his hands beneath the wool, his rough skin catching on the silk lining. A wave of guilt shuddered through him, that somehow what they were doing was wrong, but it was too late. There, along her delicate rib cage . . . there, against her beating heart . . . there, he was lost.

45

'I'm troubled, Jack.'

He'd seen it coming. The way Mabel had been staring out the window all day, biting her lower lip, sighing as she swept and washed. Why she always waited until mealtime to make her worries known he had never been able to figure.

'Hmmm?' He ladled some beans onto his plate.

'I'm concerned about the children . . . well, that's it, isn't it? They aren't children anymore. A young man and a young woman, I should say.'

'Hmm.'

'Are you listening, Jack?'

He was buttering a slice of bread, but nodded.

'Well, it's just . . . they seem awfully close, don't you agree? They spend so much time together, just the two of them, and I'm not sure it's appropriate. Considering their age.'

'Hmm.'

'Jack, for goodness' sake. Do you even know who I'm talking about? Are you listening to a word I say?'

He set his knife and fork down and looked across his plate at Mabel.

'I'm not eating my dinner, am I?'

'I'm sorry. It's just . . . it's Garrett and Faina. I think they may be, well . . . '

'What?'

'Haven't you noticed? All the time they spend together? The way they walk arm in arm.'

'They're just kids. It's good for her to have a friend.'

'But Jack, they aren't children. Not anymore. Don't you see that? Faina must be sixteen or seventeen now, Garrett nearly nineteen.'

It did surprise him, how time had passed. Faina had been a small child when she first came to their door, and only yesterday Garrett was a thirteen-year-old boy keenly interested in trapping weasels and not much else.

'I suppose you're right, Mabel. The years have slipped by me. But I wouldn't trouble yourself. Garrett isn't one for chasing after girls. And courting is still a long ways off for those two.'

'No, Jack. You're wrong.'

'We were nearly twice their age when we courted.'

'But we were unusual. My youngest sister was married by the time she was as old as Faina.'

Jack stared down at his cold beans and hardening bread. Mabel's knack for conjuring troubles, present or future, wore on him. Sometimes he wished he could just eat his beans warm and his bread fresh and leave worries be.

'I'm sorry, Jack. Maybe it's nothing. It just seems dangerous for them to be spending so much time alone together without chaperoning. And I've seen a change come over Faina, something I can't quite explain. But what can we do? It's not as if we can forbid her. She isn't our daughter, is she?'

This last shot struck its target. How many times had he spoken those precise words? Faina wasn't their daughter. They couldn't determine her life. All they could do was be grateful for any time they had with her. And this other bit, about Faina running off into the woods with the boy, this rubbed like a small pebble in a boot. At first it seems like nothing but a nuisance, but eventually it hobbles you.

For days, Jack thought of little else. When he had been a young man, he had been oblivious to girls. While his friends spiffed themselves up each weekend for dances, he was more interested in spending the evenings whittling on a wood project or caring for a foaling horse. Sure, he had kissed a few girls behind the barn, but only when pressed to, and he often wondered what had been different about Mabel that his attention was caught and firmly held. She was quiet and gentle and preoccupied, and at first showed no interest in him. Over time, though, they had formed an affection that was also quiet and gentle, and at times reserved.

So he had thought it would be for Garrett. Esther had joked that there was no one on God's green earth who would be willing to put up with that headstrong boy. While his older brothers rushed into marriages with pretty, giggly girls, Garrett tended to keep to himself. Jack suspected that eventually, maybe years down the line, a woman with an unlikely temperament would come along and be the perfect match for Garrett.

But Faina? It was impossible. No matter her age, she was childlike, pure and fragile. Garrett had more decency than to defile that.

Then he watched the two of them, the way they stood so their arms touched as they talked, the way they squeezed hands when saying good-bye to one another. One night in bed, Mabel broke the news, and in her voice he could hear vindication and alarm.

'Faina isn't leaving. She says she will stay for the summer.'

'What?'

'You heard me. She's not leaving when the snow melts.'

'Why?'

'Do you have to ask?'

'What did she tell you?'

'She says Garrett wants to take her salmon fishing and to the tundra to hunt caribou. She says she'll stay all summer.'

Jack couldn't put his finger on why it unnerved him. Wasn't this their wish? The girl would be with them all year, and for those long summer months they wouldn't have to wonder about her safety. But it wasn't what he wanted. He missed her when she was gone, but he liked even more to think of her in the mountain snow, far from the hot sun and the mosquito-infested river valley.

'Don't you know what this means, Jack?'

He said nothing.

The sun came and the snow began to drip, first from the eaves and tree branches, then down the mountainsides. Spring came fast and warm, and the river broke up in a great crashing rush. Jack told Mabel he was going to watch the ice flow past, but in truth he was following them. Garrett was already staying in the barn, though planting season was far off, and this morning the boy rose early and met Faina and the dog in the yard. They hadn't even come to the cabin to wish Jack and Mabel a good morning or a goodbye or a how-do-you-do before they walked down the trail toward the river.

'I'll be back in a bit,' Jack said. He avoided Mabel's eyes. All morning she had been subdued, speaking little and moving quietly around the cabin. As he put on his work jacket, she reached out and took one of his hands. She looked up at him as if to say something, but just kissed his cheek.

While the yard and main road were muddy, the trail to the river was more pleasant as it meandered among spruce trees. The ground was dry and mossy and webbed with roots. A squirrel chirped overhead, but Jack couldn't see it in the slanting light. Here and there patches of snow still clung to the earth. Dwarf dogwood leaves and fern heads sprouted from the damp ground. Soon he heard the roar of the river, and when he neared the water, he saw soft, silvery pussy willows budding. He went to pick some from the limbs to bring back for Mabel, then remembered his grim task and kept walking.

He hoped to find them at the shore, throwing rocks at rotten river ice or tugging a stick from the dog's mouth. They weren't there, so he followed the trail along the river and through the willow shrubs until it eventually led him back onto higher ground and into another spruce forest. Here the trees were taller and thicker, and the land had a hushed, shaded quality. He kept his eyes down to avoid tripping over roots, and his glance caught on a cluster of small pink flowers blooming up through moss and fallen spruce needles. Fairy slippers — that's what Mabel had called them. Once he had picked a tiny bouquet of the wild spring orchids for her and she had scolded him, telling him they were rare and every flower he had picked had meant the death of the entire plant.

He stepped around the blooms. The trail dwindled to nothing, but occasionally he heard voices. He could call out, alert them to his presence, but it would be senseless. He was here to spy on them, and he was sick with it.

He found them finally, tucked under one of the largest evergreens, their coats spread beneath them like blankets. It was a beautiful place; the sun shone through the needled branches and dappled the ground, and the air was scented with sharp, clean spruce. He watched through the trees only long enough to understand what he was seeing, and then he looked away and was so overcome by shame and rage that he could barely see to find his way home again.

It seemed such a terribly long time that Jack was gone, and Mabel passed back and forth in front of the window more times than she could count. She had made a mistake, telling him. She should have set aside her own uneasiness and talked frankly to the girl herself. Now it was too late.

When Jack walked back into the yard she was at first relieved. He was alone. Then she noticed how upright he strode toward the barn, how he kicked at the door to enter and then slammed it shut again, turning in place as if he didn't know where to go or what to do with himself. He went to the woodpile and picked up the splitting maul. My God, she thought, he is going to kill him. But he began splitting logs, one after the other, and she was nearly as distressed. Garrett had split and stacked enough wood this past winter to last them years. Jack wasn't doing a chore — he was unleashing his fury. She wanted to go to him, to tell him about the genuine affection she had seen in Garrett's face, or how she had watched the girl pull him by an arm. She now realized that despite everything Jack had said about Faina not being their daughter, he was viewing this all through a father's eyes.

Mabel didn't notice when Garrett came out of the trees, but when she no longer heard the rhythmic crack of wood, she looked out the window and saw the two men standing beside the woodpile. She couldn't hear their words but they were speaking — first Jack, then Garrett. Jack waved his hands and she saw the young man's shoulders slump. Then he stood straight again and spoke more animatedly. Mabel was at the window, one hand against the glass pane. And then, seemingly without warning, Jack punched Garrett in the jaw and sent him sprawling to the ground.

Maybe it was some mistake. She had never seen Jack strike anyone, and she prayed she had misjudged the scene. But when Garrett sat up, he rubbed his jaw with the back of his hand. Jack reached down, perhaps as an offer to help him stand, but the young man refused and stumbled to his feet.

When Jack came into the cabin, neither he nor Mabel spoke. She led him to the washbasin where she soaked his swelling knuckles and wrapped them in a cold wet cloth. Outside she heard Garrett's horse gallop from the yard.

46

This summer we'll go down the river, toward the ocean.

Will we?

That's where we'll catch salmon fresh from the salt water, when they still shine all silver. We'll make a bonfire of driftwood and sleep in the sand. Maybe we'll go all the way to the ocean.

I've never been there.

It's big.

I know. I've seen it from the mountains.

You know what else we'll do?

Faina turned her head against his chest. No, she said. What will we do?

We'll swim in the river. We'll take off all our clothes and swim naked in the river.

Won't you be cold?

Nah. There's these little ponds on the riverbed, where the water just sits and gets warm from the sun. They're clear and blue. You'll see. We'll swim and float on our backs and when we put our heads under the water, I'll kiss you. Just like this.

It was like a terrible thirst. He could drink and drink her in and it was never enough.

When they were together, wandering the riverbed or hiking up a creek, they shared everything they knew. The color of a black wolf's eyes. The way to catch a muskrat through the ice. Where snow geese nest and marmots den. The sound of a herd of caribou running across the tundra. The taste of mountain blueberries and tender spruce tips.

They studied the mud in the trails, pointed to tracks and named them. Garrett tried to teach her how to call like a lovesick bull moose. Faina tried to teach him the songs of wild birds. Then they would laugh and chase each other through the trees until they found one with wide boughs and a bed of spruce needles beneath it. There they would huddle together and taste each other's lips and eyes and hearts.

And when they were apart, he felt as if he were dying of thirst.

47

'So I guess that's that,' Jack said. He smacked the soot from his hands. At his feet was a pail of ashes he had cleaned out of the stove. 'I guess we're through with him. We won't be seeing that boy around here again.'

'You don't know,' Mabel said.

'I know. He won't be back. Planting time, and I'll be out there breaking my back, trying to get the fields done. And where is he?'

'I think you underestimate him.'

'We'll see.' He knocked on the stovepipe and listened to the creosote fall. Then he shoveled it from the stove into the pail.

'He's the same young man we've always known. He's just in love.'

'We'll see.'

The horse was gone. Jack closed and opened the barn door again, thinking he had lost his mind. But no, the horse still wasn't there. He walked through the barn and out into the pasture and saw, on the far side, that the gate was open.

He was late coming out to feed and water the horse. He'd meant to be working the fields just after daybreak. The end of May and the ground was finally starting to dry. Several of the largest fields still needed plowing. But his back had been stiffer than normal this morning, so he had eased his way slowly around the cabin for several hours.

As Jack crossed the pasture, he noticed boot prints in the mud. He shut the gate and followed the trail toward the nearest field, wondering if he should have gone back for his shotgun.

Blinded by the sun, at first Jack couldn't see. He stood at the edge of the field and shielded his eyes with his hand.

Garrett was at the plow, tilling along the outside edge of the field.

He thought the boy nodded at him, but from this distance it was impossible to be sure. Jack started to wave at him, then stuffed his hand in his pocket. He turned on his heels and walked home.

'You're back already?'

'The horse was gone. I went looking for it.'

Mabel raised her eyebrows.

'And? Did you find it?'

'Yep. I did.'

'Well?'

'Garrett has it. He's plowing a field.'

'Oh, is he?' Mabel pressed her lips together. Maybe she was trying not to smile. Maybe she was keeping herself from saying I told you so.

'I know, I know. You said so.'

'I just had faith in him. He's a young man who

honors his obligations.'

'Well, when he comes in for lunch, tell him I think the north field will have to be redone. It was too much muck when I went after it.'

'You could always tell him yourself,' she said gently.

'No, that's where you're wrong.'

Mabel sighed.

'I won't be your messenger for ever, you know. You two will have to talk to each other someday.'

'We'll see,' he said.

48

A misty chill hung over the spring morning, but they left the cabin because the girl was like a caged animal, tense and fidgety. Mabel knew something was wrong and that Faina might tell her if they went for a brisk walk, just the two of them. They followed the wagon trails around the fields, striding side by side, until the words poured out of her.

Am I dying? the girl asked without looking at Mabel.

Why would you say such thing?

I was bleeding. For months it came and went, and I doubled over in pain.

Why didn't you tell me? No, it's my fault. I should have talked with you. Have you bled again?

I thought I was better, because the bleeding stopped and didn't come back. But now I wake and eat and can keep nothing in my belly. And all day I just want to lie down and sleep.

Mabel understood at last; she led the girl to the picnic table and sat on the bench.

You will have a baby, you and Garrett. You are carrying his child.

❄

391

The fog lay low along the riverbed, and their breath was visible in white clouds from their lips. Rigid and straight-backed, Faina stood and stared toward the distant mountains.

I know you are frightened, child, but you can do this. I believe in you.

How can I? What do I know of babies, or mothers?

The girl turned to Mabel and her eyes strained in a desperate grief.

But you, she said suddenly. You must know something about babies. Please. You must. Take it and be its mother.

Mabel folded her hands in her lap.

For years, her arms had ached with longing. It was a self-indulgence she didn't often permit herself, but sometimes she would sit in a chair, her eyes closed, her arms crossed against her breast, and she would imagine holding a small baby there — its trusting warmth against her body, its tiny head smelling of milk and talcum powder, its skin softer than flower petals. She had watched other women with infants and eventually understood what she craved: the boundless permission — no, the absolute necessity — to hold and kiss and stroke this tiny person. Cradling a swaddled infant in their arms, mothers would distractedly touch their lips to their babies' foreheads. Passing their toddlers in a hall, mothers would tousle their hair or even sweep them up in their arms and kiss them hard along their chins and necks until the children squealed with glee. Where else in life, Mabel wondered, could a woman love so openly and with such abandon?

So now an infant, or at least the potential of an infant, was unexpectedly placed before Mabel, and she was tempted to accept it as a gift. Perhaps it was fate. Everything had led to this moment when at last her wish was granted.

And it was the right thing to do, wasn't it? How could a girl who lived alone in the wilderness, a mere child herself, keep an infant warm and safe and cared for? Whereas she and Jack, as old as they were, were equipped to raise the baby. They had a home, a living. The child would have a clean bed to sleep in and warm food on its plate. When the time came, the child could go to school in town and compete in spelling bees and draw lovely, silly little pictures for them.

Mabel allowed herself this brief daydream, then pushed it away. As much as she had ever wanted a baby, this one wasn't hers to take. It was Faina's, and she at last told her so.

The girl was poised to run, the way she had so many times before. To the forest. To the wild. Away. Mabel reached up and took one of her hands, gently coaxing her to sit beside her.

You can't run, child. Not from this. It is within you.

Faina's thin fingers, like the cool, pale bones of a bird, rested in Mabel's hand. How different from her own crooked hands, warm and heavy and spotted with age.

You will have help, Mabel said gently. From all of us. Me and Jack. And Esther. She's the most generous woman I have ever known, and she will be only too eager to help. And there's Garrett, too.

The girl cast her eyes down.

You must tell him, Faina. Now that you understand what is happening, that you two have created a child and it is growing inside you. Now that you know, you must tell him.

He will be angry.

No. He won't. He'll be scared, like you, but he won't be angry. He loves you. And I believe in him, just as I believe in you.

Faina left her sitting alone at the picnic table, and Mabel shivered inside her coat and crossed her arms tightly. It was a lonely, forlorn act, giving up a child. Faina, a frightened wisp of a thing, disappeared into the forest, and Mabel was angry at the injustice of it — that she should have wanted a baby so dearly and be denied one, and that this young girl should be cursed with one as a burden she might not have the strength to bear.

'Faina is pregnant.'

Mabel knew it was a terrible habit, waiting for dinner to tell Jack bad news, but it was one of the few quiet moments they had together. This time, though, she feared she might have unintentionally killed him. He was choking, coughing until his face was a horrid reddish purple. It went on long enough that she got to her feet, prepared to strike him on the back to dislodge the object, but then he was able to stop and clear his throat. Mabel waited for him to speak, but he didn't.

'She's pregnant, Jack.'

'I heard you.'

'So . . . '

'So?'

'Well, don't you have anything to say?'

'What is there to say? It's entirely our fault. She was more innocent than a child has ever been, and we were the only ones who could protect her. We let this happen.'

'Oh, Jack. Why does it always have to be somebody's fault?'

'Because it always is.'

'No. Sometimes these things happen. Life doesn't go the way we plan or hope, but we don't have to be so angry, do we?'

He continued eating, but without any pleasure as far as Mabel could tell. It was as if he was gagging down each bite. Finally he gave up and pushed his plate away.

'There'll be a wedding, I suppose?' The disgusted expression hadn't left his face.

'Oh. Well. No one has spoken of it.'

'There will be a wedding,' and it was a hard, clear statement that left no room for argument.

'We'll have to share the news with Garrett and Faina, then,' and she gave her husband an ironic smile. 'But I agree. It's the only way.'

❄

It wasn't until that night, as she lay in bed considering wedding plans, that she thought of the fairy tale. She climbed out of bed and in her bare feet lit a candle and went to the bookshelf. She removed her loose sketches from the book as she opened it on the table, and then she flipped through the color plates until she found the one she remembered. It was a forest meadow, lush with green leaves and blooming flowers. The snow maiden, her white gown glittering in jewels and her head crowned with wildflowers, stood beside a handsome young man. Fair Spring was before them, performing the wedding ceremony. Overhead, the sun shone brightly.

Mabel wanted to slam the book closed, throw it into the woodstove, and watch it burn in the flames. Instead she turned the pages until she came to the illustration she dreaded. There was the crown of wildflowers, no longer on the snow maiden's head, but blooming from the earth like a grave marker. She put a hand over her lips, though it was unnecessary. She made no sound.

Jack stirred in bed. Mabel gathered the sketches and slid them back into the book before returning it to the shelf. It would be a long time before she looked at it again, and never would she speak of it.

49

Jack was calm. He could undo nothing, but at least he had a plan of action.

It began when Garrett came to him a few days after Mabel's news about Faina. He assumed the young man had returned to finish the fight or to end all association. Instead he came with his hat in his hands.

'I'm here to ask permission to marry Faina. I know we're young, and I don't have much to offer her, but we're bound together now and I mean to make the best of it.'

It was like a blow to the chest, and Jack had to sit down in a kitchen chair. Garrett stood by, shifting on his feet and clearing his throat.

He hadn't seen this coming. He was sure they would marry; he had assumed Garrett would take responsibility. But the boy came to him — Jack — to ask permission.

It hadn't happened instantly, the way he had always imagined, with a gush of blood and a piercing wail, but instead fatherhood had arrived quietly, gradually, over the course of years, and he had been blind to it. And now, just as he finally understood that a daughter had been flitting in and out of his life, now he was being asked to let her go.

'I'll do good by her. You have my word.'

Jack's focus returned to the boy, and when he looked up at the earnest face, he saw what Mabel had tried to tell him — Garrett did love the girl. But was that enough? The boy had betrayed his trust, lied to him under his own roof, and taken advantage of circumstances. Jack eased himself out of the chair until he stood eye to eye with Garrett.

'You will do good by her,' Jack said, and it wasn't an agreement but a command. He reached out to Garrett, and they shook hands like two men who had only just met and weren't yet certain of each other.

That night Jack's plan came to him, and he woke Mabel.

'We'll build them a home, here on our homestead.'

'What? Jack, what time is it?'

'We'll build them a cabin down by the river. That way Garrett will be close to the farm, but they'll have their own place.'

'Hmmm?' Mabel was still half asleep, but he went on.

'Faina and the baby will be close to you, so you can help. We'll start building right after planting. Maybe we can even have the wedding there.'

'Where? Wedding?'

'Here, Mabel. They're going to live here, near us. It'll be good.'

'Hmmm?' But Jack let her drift back into sleep. He was satisfied.

He noticed the way the clean morning light slanted in through the window and lit up the side of Faina's face, and he wondered if it was always so hard, being a father. They'd finished a pot of tea and a few slices of bread with blueberry jam, and he was left with no other way around the conversation he'd promised Mabel. At the kitchen counter, Mabel tried to wash the dishes silently. She never washed them in the morning, but now each plate, each fork, was wiped and rinsed and dried as if it were made of precious china, for she was straining to hear.

Jack cleared his throat, hoping to sound fatherly.

Faina? Is this what you want?

It's what you do when you love someone, isn't it?

Your life is going to change. You won't be able to disappear into the woods for weeks at a time. You'll be a mother, a wife. Do you understand what that means?

Faina tilted her head to the side in a half shrug, but then she focused her blue eyes on Jack and their clarity seized him. Her face carried the same look he had seen many times before, a startling blend of youth and wisdom, frailty and fierceness. He saw it when she had scattered snow across her father's grave, when she had appeared at their door with her hands smeared with blood. It wasn't sorrow or love, disappointment or knowledge; it was everything at once.

I do love him. And our baby. I know that.

So you want to marry him?

We belong together.

Jack had expected to be happy. Isn't that what a father should feel? Joy? Not this grief-laden heart? They had hidden their love affair and created a child out of wedlock, but something more weighed on him. Faina would never again be the little girl he had seen darting through the winter trees, her feet light on the snow and her eyes like river ice. She had been magic in their lives, coming and going with the seasons, bringing treasures from the wilderness in her small hands. That child was gone, and Jack found himself mourning her.

50

The strawberry plants were just beginning to green and send out their reddish-purple runners. Mabel bent from plant to plant and with a pair of shears snipped off last year's growth and tossed the curled, brown leaves to the side. When she reached the end of the raised bed, she stood, slid the shears into the pocket of her gardening apron, and pushed the wide brim of her straw hat up from her forehead.

It was still there. The very last patch of snow in the yard, banked in the shade against the north side of the cabin where it had drifted the deepest. It had dwindled in the warming days until all that remained was a circle the size of a wagon wheel.

She squinted up at the sun, already white hot in the sky, and pushed up her dress sleeves. It would be a scorcher, as Garrett was fond of saying. He and Jack were working in shirtsleeves as they planted the fields. They would come home sunburned, she was certain.

Mabel pulled her hat brim down to shade her eyes again, took the rake from where it leaned against a fence post, and began scratching and prodding at the strawberry garden, loosening the soil, cleaning up the rows. Out of the corner of her eye, she watched sunlight glisten off the white snow. It would soon be gone.

She had thought often of Ada's words about inventing new endings to stories and choosing joy over sorrow. In recent years she had decided her sister had been in part wrong. Suffering and death and loss were inescapable.

And yet, what Ada had written about joy was entirely true. When she stands before you with her long, naked limbs and her mysterious smile, you must embrace her while you can.

When Faina stepped out of the spruce forest, the sun's rays struck her and set her blond hair alight in a peculiar golden silver, so that even from across the yard Mabel was reminded of starlit fairies and fireflies. Faina's puppy, grown lanky and big footed, panted up at her and followed her across the yard.

The girl's lean arms and legs were bare. She wore only the plain cotton dress with its pattern of blue flowers that Mabel had sewed for her. Her stride was long and sure as she moved through the newly sprouted grass and beneath the leafing cottonwood tree, and as she neared Mabel saw that her skin was tanned. She wore no shoes or moccasins. Tall and lean, she showed no signs of pregnancy yet.

Faina stopped at the edge of the strawberry

patch and crouched beside the dog. She put one hand beneath its chin and ran her other hand back between its ears, and the dog grinned as it had that first day. When she stood and silently gestured, the dog promptly lay in the dirt, still panting, its black fur gleaming.

She walked down the strawberry rows, and her bare feet pressed so firmly to the ground that Mabel could see the soil squish between her toes. She took Mabel's hands and kissed her on the cheek. When she let go, Mabel embraced her and held her for a long time, even as she could feel the heat of the sun on Faina's back.

You look well, Mabel said.

I am, she said. I am.

51

Jack led Garrett down the wagon trail and out into a meadow within sight of the river.

'It's yours,' Jack said. 'Consider it a wedding gift. We'll build the cabin right in here, facing toward the mountains.'

'It's a fine place.'

The very next evening, after they stopped planting for the day and ate dinner, he supposed Garrett had gone to sleep in the barn. He told Mabel he was going out for some fresh air, and he walked to the meadow. There he found Garrett with a shovel and an ax, rough sketching the outline of a cabin into the dirt.

The work had a rhythm and purpose, and Jack and Garrett fell into it with ease, even relief: the back-and-forth pull of the two-man saw and the thunderous crash of trees falling; the slide of the draw knife along the spruce logs, the bark peeling off in long strips; the chop and slice of the sharpened ax, each notch hand-carved. Love and devotion, the devastating hope and fear contained in a woman's swelling womb — these were left unspoken. At midnight, as they hefted another log into place, they could hear the red-breasted robins and dark-eyed juncos chirping in the trees, and that was enough.

By the time planting was done, they had the log walls up waist high and it went faster now that they had all of each day. Jack let Garrett do the heaviest of the work, and at times he would sit on a log to rest his tired back and watch the younger man work. Mabel often came with lunch in a basket and sometimes she would stay long enough to discuss where a window should go or what kind of front porch they should build.

Faina was nowhere to be seen. Jack assumed she and Garrett met alone sometimes, but the girl did not come to Jack and Mabel's for dinner. For once, it was Jack who worried.

'Shouldn't she be resting, eating regular meals?'

'She's fine,' Mabel said.

'Why isn't she here, staying with us until the wedding?'

'She's where she needs to be. She doesn't have much longer.'

'Much longer?'

'Her life is going to change soon. Whatever else happens, she won't be able to run through the woods like a sprite. Everything will be different.'

'I suppose. I just want to make sure she's safe and healthy.'

'I know,' and Mabel's voice had a bittersweet acceptance in it that he had never heard before.

※

Faina came on a warm June day, she and the dog loping out of the trees as if they were halfway through a close race. Garrett was straddling the unfinished wall as Jack used a pulley to raise another log into place. Faina ran to them in bare feet and a short-sleeved dress, her arms and legs bronzed and muscled, her long hair bleached white by the sun.

She and Garrett gave each other shy smiles, and Jack felt like an intruder. Garrett jumped down from the log wall and led her through the rough-cut doorway and into the roofless cabin.

I know it's hard to see, with just the four walls, but over here, this will be the kitchen and the window will look out to the river. Won't that be fine?

Faina nodded, but her gaze was distant, as if this all were a strange dream to her.

The woodstove will go here. And through there, that'll be our bedroom, and the baby's. I know it's not real big, but don't you think it'll do?

Faina nodded once, slowly.

Garrett seemed unnerved by her silence.

It'll be OK, won't it? Once we get some windows and doors in, it'll feel like a real home. Don't you think, Jack? It's coming together?

Jack started to say that yes, he thought it would be a dandy little cabin for a family starting out, but then he saw the girl smile up at Garrett, a tender, reassuring smile. Jack was struck with the notion that perhaps she was the wiser and stronger of the two.

Faina stayed while the two men worked. She

407

threw sticks for the dog. She ran through the tall, green grass around the cabin and picked bluebells and wild yellow asters, but her eyes kept to the trees. The dog ran, barking, to chase a squirrel into the woods, and Faina followed. When she reached the edge of the meadow, she looked over her shoulder and gave a small wave back toward the men.

'She's leaving,' Garrett said.

'She is, but she'll be back.'

'I know. But sometimes I wonder.'

'What's that?'

'If this is the best for her — a baby. Me. If it's the right kind of life for her.'

'Too late to change that now,' Jack said. He regretted his anger.

'Maybe she doesn't have to give up everything,' Garrett said. 'You know. We'll run traps together this winter, after the baby comes. I'll take her out in the woods and she can put out her little snares. It doesn't all have to change.'

'It will. Everything will change. But you'll do the best you can.'

Jack turned back to the cabin, because that was something a man could do — fell trees and scribe-fit logs and build a home.

'Come on, now,' he said. 'We're almost to the ridgepole. We've got to get this thing closed in before the big day.'

52

'There's no way in hell that cabin is going to be done in time for the wedding.' Esther's hands were on her hips as she stood looking up at the honey-colored logs. 'Just a few more days, Mom. That's what he says to me. We've almost got it wrapped up, he says. Why is it men always overestimate their own prowess?'

Mabel smiled in spite of herself. 'They have done a great deal.'

'Sure they have. But I tell you, it won't have a roof on it before Sunday.'

'Perhaps that's all right.' Mabel thought of Faina looking up through the logs into an open sky, and somehow it was comforting.

'It's all good, as long as there's not a drop of rain or a single mosquito . . . in Alaska . . . in July.' Esther made no attempt to hide her sarcasm. Then she hoisted her overall straps like a man and shrugged. 'Ah well. When you're young, everything is romantic, right? Even a cabin without a roof.'

'It is lovely. I've already sewed some curtains for the windows. And George tells me you're making them a quilt.'

'Yep. And it will be done by Sunday.' Esther laughed at herself and added, 'I might not sleep much this week, eh? But how's the dress coming?'

'It is finished, but Faina has secret plans. She's been working on it these past few nights at our house. She waits until we go to bed, and then she stays up at the table doing something, but she won't tell me what.'

'She is an odd duck, isn't she?'

Mabel had never thought of Faina in those terms, but the girl was peculiar, and even unconventional Esther could have misgivings about her son marrying her. A fascinating stranger was one thing, a daughter-in-law quite another.

'It is true — I have never met another person like Faina,' Mabel said, choosing her words carefully. 'But then, I've never met anyone like you before either.'

'All right. All right. I'll give you that one. And I know I should count my blessings that someone is willing and able to put up with that son of mine.'

'She doesn't just put up with him. I think she's quite taken with him.'

'Hmmm.' Esther sounded doubtful.

'They have a great deal in common. They love this place, and each other.'

'But who is she? She's a wild thing from the mountains. More times than not, Garrett doesn't even know where she is. When she's saddled with a screaming brat and a sink full of dirty dishes, what then? Is she going to stick around long enough to be a wife and a mother?'

Mabel's throat was swelling shut. She walked around the corner of the cabin, pretending to inspect the other wall. Esther was instantly at her side.

'Oh, Mabel. I meant no offense. I know she's like a daughter to you, and my son surely loves her. That'll have to do for the rest of us, won't it?'

Mabel smiled and nodded and blinked away tears. The two women hugged and hooked arms to walk back to Jack and Mabel's.

The nightmares had returned. Naked, crying babies melted as she held them, and dripped to the ground even as she tried to close her fingers and cup her hands. Sometimes she clutched the infants to her chest, only to realize that the warmth of her own body was the cause of their demise.

Then there was Faina — her face would appear in the trees like a scene through a rain-streaked windowpane. In her dream, Mabel would run outside and it would be raining the way it did back home in the summer, a blinding, warm downpour. She would call Faina's name, try to run through the forest to find her, but the rain would fill her eyes and mouth and she would wake gasping. In another dream, Mabel stood hip deep in the river and clenched Faina's wet hands as the current pulled her downstream. Mabel would try to hold on, but she was never strong enough and Faina would slip from her grasp and be carried away in the silty water. The girl would flail her arms and cry for Mabel to help, please, please, help, but she would be unable to move. She would stand and watch as her beautiful daughter drowned at her feet.

Never in these dreams could Mabel cry or move or even speak a word.

❄

The day of the wedding came, and Esther was right — the cabin wasn't finished, but it was all the more lovely, like a cathedral sculpted of trees and sky. Mabel walked there in the morning and was grateful to be alone. It had become a holy place, the sound of the river, the fragrance of the freshly peeled spruce logs, the blue sky, the green meadow. The cottonwood trees were blooming, and the downy white seeds floated on the breeze like feathers.

Jack was back at their own place, loading the wagon with tables and chairs to haul to the cabin. George and Esther were coming just before the ceremony so they could bring the food for afterward. Garrett's oldest brother would marry them. He wasn't a pastor, or even one to attend church regularly, but Garrett had wanted him to perform the ceremony and no one objected. Though he was a well-spoken man, Mabel would have preferred an ordained minister but never said so. The brothers, along with their wives and children, would be the only other guests at the wedding. No one else was invited; that much Mabel had insisted upon.

They had curtained off a section of the unfinished cabin with white sheets so that Faina could put on her dress and prepare herself. She had not yet appeared this morning, and she had the wedding gown with her.

Mabel had sewed the dress from raw silk Esther had given her, leftovers from her oldest daughter-in-law's wedding gown.

'She had to have yards and yards of the stuff,' Esther said. 'She wanted ruffles and pleats and layers. It was a miracle we could see her through it all. All I can say is, I'm glad her parents paid for the dress to be made.'

The ivory-hued silk was shipped from a speciality shop in San Francisco and had certainly cost more than Mabel and Jack could have afforded, but Esther insisted that no one else had any use for the remnants. Mabel did not resist too much — the fabric was exquisite, weighted and fine and textured.

She didn't have a pattern, but she could see Faina's wedding gown clearly in her mind, and she sketched and sewed and embroidered for days on end. She had to be creative with the strips and odds and ends of raw silk; fortunately it was a simple dress that didn't require much fabric. The skirt was straight and ankle length, the sleeves long, and the bodice slightly fitted to just below the ribs. The neckline scooped modestly along the collarbone. It was nothing like the flapper style so popular in recent years; nor was it in the style of the high-necked, formal gowns worn in Mabel's youth. This was something different, something that reminded Mabel of European brides in country chapels, of alpine beauties, of Russian maidens.

The dress itself was easy to sew; it was the embroidery that kept Mabel up late each night, bent over the kitchen table and squinting as if her eyes were failing. Along the sleeves, across the narrow bodice and scattered down the skirt, Mabel used white silk thread to embroider tiny, starry flowers and loops of thin vines and pearl-drop leaves. The pure white stitches on the ivory silk were subtle; when the light caught them just so, the flowers could be mistaken for snowflakes, the vines for eddies in snow.

Still, Mabel had yet to see the gown on Faina. It's a surprise, Faina said. Wait and see.

Mabel had sewed it herself, so how could it be a surprise? But all she could do was make the girl promise that if it did not fit perfectly, she would bring it back in time for alterations. She had not seen Faina since.

Garrett wasn't to be found this morning, either, and he had the wedding rings. Again there was secrecy — Esther had wanted one of the grandchildren to carry the rings and another to serve as flower girl. Garrett said he and Faina had other plans. He asked Mabel to weave a wreath of flowers.

'For Faina's head?' Mabel asked, her voice trembling. No, she thought. I won't allow that. Not a crown of flowers.

'Nah. Not for Faina,' Garrett said. 'It needs to be bigger. About this big,' and he held his arms in a circle the size of a large mixing bowl.

Mabel had waited until the day of the wedding, knowing wildflowers would quickly wilt in the summer heat. And it was hot. Barely past eight in the morning, and already the dew was off the leaves and the arctic sun burned over the mountaintops.

Flowers for Faina's veil and flowers for her bouquet, flowers for the Mason jars and flowers for the wreath Garrett had requested, petals and stems, leaves and blossoms — Mabel longed to be consumed by them, as she had been by the embroidery. She wanted to escape the sense that fate was rolling in over the mountains like thunder. She wanted to forget melting clumps of snow, flower crowns and fiery kisses, and fairy-tale endings.

Careful not to rip her newly sewn cotton frock, Mabel took her metal pail and walked the edge of the meadow: fireweed, their tall stalks just beginning to bloom fuchsia; bluebells with their sweet nectar; wild roses, simple with five pink petals and prickly stems; geraniums, their thin petals lavender with deeper purple veins. Farther into the woods, away from the harsh sun, Mabel bent and plucked delicate white star-flowers suspended above the ground on stems as thin and taut as thread; dwarf dogwood with their fat white petals; oak ferns and lady ferns; and at the last minute, a few wild currant branches with their many-pointed leaves and trailing vines of ripe red berries translucent as jewels.

The Bensons came just as she was arranging the fireweed and oak ferns in glass jars filled with cold river water.

'Well, look at us,' Esther said as she jumped down from the wagon.

'My goodness, Esther, I don't think I've ever seen you in a dress before!'

'Don't get used to it. I've brought my overalls for the reception.' The two women laughed and hugged.

'So where's the happy couple? They haven't upped and eloped have they?'

'I haven't the slightest idea. I hope Faina arrives soon, though. I need to help her with her dress and hair. What time is it?'

'Nearly high noon. Time's a wasting.'

Just then they all turned toward a strange rumbling sound coming from the wagon trail.

'What is that?' Mabel asked.

'That'll be Bill,' said George, and from around the corner appeared a shiny, bouncing automobile, a stream of dust kicked up behind it.

Esther made a disgusted face at Mabel. 'It was a present from her family. Must be nice to be rolling in the dough.'

Jack stood motionless, clearly impressed. 'That one of those trucks I've been hearing about?'

'Yep. A Ford Model A pick-up truck,' George boasted, and Esther rolled her eyes in Mabel's direction.

'They had to have it barged up from California, then shipped out on the train. All so they can drive from our house to yours,' Esther told Mabel.

The automobile came to a grinding stop in the grass just short of the picnic table, and the Bensons' oldest son opened the door and stood grinning on the running board.

'Not a bad way to travel, eh?' he called out. He tipped his white fedora in Mabel's direction.

'You could back it up a few feet there,' Esther said. 'No need to park yourself right in the food.'

'All right, Mom. All right.'

Bill and his wife and two small children piled out of the automobile looking as if they had stepped off the streets of Manhattan. The children were dressed in ruffles and bows and shoes that shined in the sun. The wife was wearing a stylish flapper dress in mauve silk and a brimless hat pulled low over her bobbed hair.

'They don't even look like they're part of the family, do they?' Esther whispered in Mabel's ear. 'But I guess you can't kick them out just for that.' And in fact, Mabel was surprised to find them all warm and charming. Bill's wife, Lydia, quickly offered to help with food and flowers and anything else that needed doing, while the children ran happily around the meadow.

The Bensons' other son, Michael, arrived next with his wife and three daughters, the youngest still in her mother's arms.

'Is she here yet? I can't believe none of us has even met her before,' Mabel heard the two young wives whispering. 'I wonder what she'll wear? Have you heard anything about the gown?'

As she helped Esther spread white tablecloths over the picnic and kitchen tables, Mabel tried to concentrate on the billow of fabric and the feel of the linen over rough, splintery wood as she smoothed out the wrinkles.

I'm here.

The voice was a whisper over Mabel's shoulder, but when she turned, no one was there.

Here. Inside the cabin. Will you help me?

It was Faina. Her voice came through the empty window frame of the cabin. How had she gotten past without anyone noticing? Mabel excused herself and stepped through the cabin door. The log frame overhead broke the sunlight into sections and dazzled Mabel's eyes.

I'm here.

Have you put on the dress?

No. You can't see it yet. But will you help me with my hair?

Faina stood in bare feet, wearing the cotton slip Mabel had sewed for her. There was the slightest rounding in her belly, just enough to pull the slip tight, and across her breasts as well. Faina was no longer a child, but a tall, beautiful young woman, and she had never seemed so substantial, so full of life. Mabel quickly let the curtain fall closed behind her. This morning she had hung the bridal cloche and veil on a hook on the log wall and laid out the boar-bristle brush and hand mirror with their mother-of-pearl shining in the sun. Faina swept her hair across one bare shoulder.

Will you plait it for me?

That would be perfect, child, with the veil I've made for you.

So Mabel brushed Faina's long hair, so blond

it was white. She brushed out the tiny bits of lichen and torn ribbons of birch bark, the knots of yellow grass. Once it was as smooth as silk, Mabel braided it into two plaits, one on each side, that laid neatly down the front of her chest. Just as Faina looked away, out the empty window frame, Mabel pulled a tiny pair of sewing scissors from a pocket in her dress and snipped some hair from one of the plaits. Silently she slid the scissors and section of hair into her pocket.

There. There, now. You look lovely.

For my head, a veil you called it?

You can't put it on until your dress is on.

I can do it. Just help me, please. You mustn't see the dress yet.

Mabel took the cloche and veil from its hook and set it on Faina's head, securing it with hairpins. Then she wove the wild pink roses and white starflowers into the lacework above Faina's braids and across her forehead. But it wasn't a crown, not a circle of flowers that could sprout from the earth.

You will leave now, so I can put on the dress.

Are you sure? It will still be a surprise.

Mabel let her eyes dart around the room, but the dress was nowhere to be seen.

Please.

All right. All right, child. We'll all be waiting for you. Your bouquet is there, in the pail.

Faina reached out for Mabel's hand and squeezed it. Her touch was strong and warm, and Mabel squeezed back and then impulsively brought the girl's hand to her lips to kiss it.

I love you, child, she whispered.

Faina's face was quiet and kind.

I wish to be the mother you are to me, she said so softly Mabel doubted her own ears. But those were the words she spoke, and Mabel took them into her heart and held them there for ever.

When Faina stepped across the cabin threshold and onto the green grass, a hush fell across the small gathering. Even the children quieted and stared up at her, and Faina bowed her head down to them and smiled as if she had known them all her life.

At first, Mabel could not see what was different about the dress. It fit her perfectly and moved with a soft rustle against her skin. Faina wore leather moccasins beaded in shimmering white beads and tied with white ribbons up her calves. The veil flowed down her back and the flowers were sprinkled across her forehead. She held the bouquet of wildflowers, ferns, and currant vines.

Then, as Faina stepped closer, Mabel saw the feathers — white feathers, stitched along the neckline of the dress. They lay flat against the fabric so that they seemed part of the raw silk, a mere variation in the texture. Mabel could see the pattern now, how the feathers went from smaller to larger at the center of her chest. Other feathers were sewed along the hemline, and not one covered her embroidery of snow flowers, but each seemed part of the design.

Mabel heard someone take in a breath,

perhaps one of the young women, but then Faina was walking past her to Jack's side and she could see the back of the dress. Pure white feathers fell down the center of the skirt and fanned out into larger and larger sizes until along the hem some were as long as a woman's forearm, all laid flat against the fabric and moving gently with the silk. Like the fabric, the feathers gleamed ever so slightly, a sort of luminosity that came from within the filaments themselves.

Jack, wearing his best and only suit, took Faina's arm and they began to walk slowly toward the river where the jars of wildflowers sat on tree stumps. The smell of cut spruce was strong in the air. Everyone followed without speaking and the rustle of Faina's gown became the gentle roar of the river. They arranged themselves near the shore, the jagged, snowy mountain peaks behind them.

'Where is Garrett?' Mabel heard someone whisper. They shifted awkwardly in their dress shoes, and the baby let out a whimper. The sun was unbearably hot on Mabel's head and shoulders and her eyes ached from the piercing brightness. When she looked up at Jack, he nodded at her and gestured with his chin back toward the wagon trail. She turned and looked over her shoulder, and there was Garrett, riding his horse at a gallop across the meadow. He, too, wore a fine suit, and with one hand he kept a black hat on his head and with the other he held on to the reins. At the horse's feet, Faina's husky sprinted, his tongue flapping at his mouth.

Garrett slowed the horse as he neared the

cabin and dismounted even as the horse was still trotting. He loosely tied a lead rope to a nearby cottonwood, wiped his forehead with the back of his hand, and walked toward the gathering. Mabel was surprised when he came directly to her.

'Do you have the flowers?' he whispered.

Mabel frowned in confusion.

'The wreath?' Then she remembered and pointed to the table where the circle of fireweed and roses and ferns lay.

'Thank you,' Garrett said, and he kissed her on the cheek.

Curious, she watched him pick up the wreath and then tap the side of his leg with one hand. Faina's dog ran to him. Garrett held up a hand, and the dog sat. He slipped the wreath over the animal's head, and then what looked like a loop of ribbon and a small pouch. Again he held up his hand, and the dog stayed sitting while Garrett walked to the wedding gathering.

'Not a bad entrance,' Bill whispered as Garrett joined him.

As the ceremony began, Mabel held to Jack's arm, but it was as if she were floating and spinning. The hot sun blurred her vision. She would faint, or already had. Words swam and dodged, and she could not tell if they were spoken aloud or only in her head . . .

. . . *Hope is the thing with feathers . . . perches in the soul . . . to have and to hold . . . Do you?*

*. . . hurry . . . hurry . . . to the ragged wood . . . no
roses at my head . . . Do you? . . . until death do
you part . . . until death . . .*

I do . . .

I do . . .

I do . . .

I do . . .

There was a whistle, like a chickadee's, and
Faina's dog trotted past as Mabel's eyes focused
again. She clung to Jack's arm. Faina was calling
the husky to her, and Garrett was grinning
proudly. The dog, the wreath of wildflowers
around its neck, sat obediently at the bride's feet,
and Garrett knelt beside it and untied the ribbon
from its neck. He opened the pouch and poured
two gold rings into his hand. Mabel heard a
child clap and Esther laugh.

Then all sound was lost to the river's roar,
and the ground shifted beneath Mabel. She saw
Garrett and Faina, face to face. She saw the
flicker of the gold rings in the sun, and then they
were kissing and suddenly everyone was
cheering.

'Are you all right, Mabel? Mabel?' Jack held her
from behind, his arms firmly beneath her elbows.
'Here, let's sit down at the table. It's this heat.
It's gotten the best of you.'

Someone brought her a glass of water and one
of the young women swept a fan back and forth
in front of her. At last she could breathe and
think.

'Faina? Where's our Faina?'

'She's over there.' Jack pointed to one of the big cotton-woods where the girl stood, white and shimmering, beside Garrett.

'But . . . is it snowing?' and she heard someone laugh beside her.

'Goodness no, dear.' It was Esther. 'Just cottonwood seeds. But it does look like snow, doesn't it?'

The air was filled with the white down. Some floated up and over the trees, while other seeds drifted lazily to the ground. Faina looked at Mabel through the falling white and held up a hand, a little wave, like when she was a child.

'They're married?' Mabel whispered.

'Yes, they are,' Jack said.

53

The night was cool and pale blue, and Faina lay naked atop the wedding quilt. She was on her side, her long legs askew, one arm beneath her head, the other curved below the slight round of her belly. Garrett took off his suit jacket. His white button-up shirt was clammy with sweat and his feet ached from the dress shoes he had worn all day. He undressed and left his clothes on the rough-cut plank floor. As he walked toward the bed, he let his hand skim across the wedding gown where it had been thrown over a chair, as if a giant wild bird had shrugged off its skin and cast it aside. After the ceremony, as they ate fire-grilled salmon, potato salad, and an extravagant white cake with white frosting and candied rose petals, as the voices ebbed and flowed and the sun danced off glasses of homemade elderflower wine, again and again Garrett let his hands touch the small of Faina's back where the feathers lay flat against the silk, and he knew they had come from the swan.

Aren't you cold? Garrett whispered as he lay beside her. She shook her head and slid her arm around his neck to kiss him. Overhead, moths fluttered along the log purlins of the roof frame and a few scattered stars shone even in the gloaming. It could rain, the bugs could be ferocious, he had told her, but she insisted on sleeping in their unfinished cabin.

It's our home, she had said. So he hauled their wedding bed to the cabin, along with the quilt his mother had sewed for them and the feather pillows and soft sheets they had been given as wedding gifts.

Faina's fingertips grazed his bare arm and she laughed.

But you are cold. Your skin is prickly.

Garrett shrugged.

It's OK. I won't freeze.

As they made love beneath the summer night sky, he tried not to think about the child in her womb or their raw gasps and sighs traveling across the land. He wanted only to think of her.

During the next weeks, as Jack and Garrett worked beneath the endless sun to put the roof on the cabin, then add the door and windows and woodstove and cupboards, Faina disappeared into the trees, her dog trotting beside her. She was gone for hours, sometimes the entire day, and Garrett did not know what to make of it. He politely dismissed invitations to Jack and Mabel's for dinner, not wanting them to know how rarely Faina joined him for meals. He prepared his food alone in the cabin, often nothing more than a can of beans heated atop the woodstove. One night Garrett sat up waiting for her to return until it was nearly morning. No longer open to the night sky, the cabin was dim and stifling, but he wouldn't let himself prowl outside like a restless animal. She would come home.

Where do you go?

When?

Every day. Nights, too. I thought you wanted to be here, with me, in our home.

I do.

So?

But she only blinked her white eyelashes at him and patted the dog. Garrett was reminded of that day at the frozen lake when he had wanted to curse and kick the ground and fight back but instead could only dumbly follow her.

We love each other, don't we?

He didn't want his voice to whine.

She came to where he sat, held his face up to her and kissed him hard. That night she stayed.

When harvest came, Garrett spent long days in the field and could no longer keep track of where she was. After weeks of rain the sky finally cleared and Jack and Garrett worked several nights straight through to cut the hay. He sat in a stupor at Jack's table, eating a breakfast of pancakes, bacon, and fried eggs, and wondered if Faina ever slept alone in the cabin as he had.

It was the end of September and cold. He smelled burning wood one evening as he walked the wagon trail. As he got closer, he saw smoke rising from their chimney and then Faina was standing in the doorway, her hands on her swollen belly. Garrett had never seen anything so welcoming.

You're home, he said.

So are you.

Inside, rows of large birch baskets crowded the floor, each filled to overflowing.

What's all this?

I, too, have been working, she said with a small smile at her lips.

She led him through the rows of baskets and paused to put a leaf to his nose, a berry to his lips. Some he knew — Eskimo potato root, blueberries, tender spruce tips. A few of the plants he had seen before but did not know their names; others, like the mushrooms and lichens, he would have been afraid to eat if he came across them in the woods. He trusted her, though, and carried her baskets up into the tall-legged log cache he had built.

Still she returned to the forest with her canvas pack or her birch baskets. She wore a long wool skirt and full-cut blouse Mabel had sewed for her, and she held the small of her back against the weight of her growing belly. She brought home grayling and salmon, grouse and rabbits, which she skinned and cleaned and dried in strips on racks by the shore of the Wolverine River where the wind kept away the flies. Sometimes she smoldered a green alder fire beneath the racks to lightly smoke the meat.

Each night, as the windowpanes turned darker

with the coming winter, she was home. She served Garrett strange-smelling soups and bowls of nameless mush. It took time to get used to her cooking. Fried wild mushrooms and smoked salmon for breakfast. For dinner grouse soup with spruce tips and ribbons of wet green that Garrett could not identify; rendered bear fat and crowberries for dessert. His mother noticed he had lost weight and smelled of smoked meat and wild plants. She wanted to know what Faina was feeding him, but he would pat his stomach and tell her he was faring fine on her meals. Then he would sneak a few of his mother's buttery biscuits or cookies, and when she forced several jars of sweet jam on him, he did not refuse.

Faina? Faina? Where are you?

Garrett held his lantern against the winter night. He had woken and, alarmed, realized she wasn't in bed beside him. It was a blustery snowfall, the first of the year, but it looked like it would stick. He stood shivering in his boots, bare legs, and wool coat.

Faina?

Here, Garrett. And he spotted her, down by the river shore.

What are you doing out here? It's the middle of the night.

It's snowing.

I know. You'll catch cold. Come inside.

He turned the lantern in her direction and saw that she was wearing only her cotton slip, which billowed around her in the wind and snow.

Yes. Yes. I'll come inside for you.

In the cabin, Garrett set the lantern on the table and put another log in the woodstove. Faina remained just outside the doorframe, her head thrown back. Garrett took her by a hand and pulled her inside, closing the door behind them. She grinned at him, her face damp from the snow, and he wiped the wetness from her cheeks with his palm.

Here, she said, and put his hand to her swollen belly. There. Do you feel it?

She pressed his hand more firmly into her and something pushed back.

Was that . . . ?

She grinned again and nodded. He kept his hand there and Faina's belly moved in a swell, as if the unborn baby were turning a somersault.

Garrett wasn't prepared for the screaming. Faina's voice had always been clear and serene, like a glacier pond, but now it was ripped from her throat in a beastly, tortured growl. He went again and again to the curtained-off door, but Jack put a hand on his shoulder.

'It's no place for you.'

'Is she all right? What's happening in there?'

Jack looked tired and old, older than he ever had, but he was calm.

'It's never easy.'

'I want to see her.'

Just then Esther pushed aside the curtain and

Garrett could only stare at the blood covering his mother's hands and arms all the way up to the elbows, like she'd been butchering a moose.

'We need more rags.'

'Is she OK? Is the baby OK?'

'I said more rags,' and she turned back to the room where Faina lay on their bed. Before the curtain fell closed, Garrett caught a glimpse of her legs, her bare feet in the air, and blood, everywhere blood.

'Jesus Christ. Is this how it's supposed to be?' Garrett thought he was going to be sick. Jack pushed by him with a bundle of dish towels in his arms. The warm, humid smell of blood and sweat and something else, something like a salty marsh, overpowered Garrett and he stumbled to the door.

Outside it was dark and cold. How many hours had passed since he first went for help? He gulped the fresh air and walked toward the river. Then he heard Faina cry out again. Could he do nothing while she suffered? He went back indoors and asked Jack if he should fetch more towels or heat more water.

At some point in the night Garrett dozed in a chair and when he woke to the absence of screaming, he jumped to his feet. He went to the curtain and listened. Faina moaned softly and then there was Mabel's voice, cooing and soothing like a mother's.

'Is it here? Has the baby come?' he whispered loudly through the fabric. His mother came to him and put her hands to his shoulders.

'Not yet, Garrett. Not yet,' and her tone,

gentle and kind, was so unlike his mother that it terrified him all the more.

'Jesus, Mom. Is she OK? Is this all right?'

'It's hard. Harder than what I went through with you boys. But she's strong, and she's still fighting.'

'Can I see her?'

'Not now. We're letting her rest up a bit, before she pushes some more. She's asking for snow, of all things. You could bring her a cupful. It can't hurt.'

He packed a pitcher with fresh snow and gave it to his mother.

'Tell her I love her. Will you do that?'

It was hours later, the sun a faded circle in the sky, when the voices rose again.

There you go. Come on, dear. Push with all your might. Come on. Come on.

There was that feral scream again, and again.

The head's crowning. Come on now. Don't give up on us yet, girl. Come on. Come on.

And then there was a cry like the bleating of a calf, and Garrett didn't understand what he heard. He looked at Jack, who stood beside him.

'It's your baby, Garrett. It's here.' Jack guided him toward the curtain. 'He's coming in now, ladies. Coming to see his baby.'

'Give us just a cotton-picking second. Let us get everybody cleaned up.'

'Is she OK? Faina, are you all right? Can you hear me?'

Yes, Garrett, and it was the voice he loved, the one that was like a sweet whisper in his ear. We're all right.

Then there was the child's cry again, racking and tiny.

There we go, little one, Esther said. Time to meet your daddy.

Mabel stood beside the bed, tears streaming down her cheeks. Esther was at the nightstand, dipping rags into a basin. Faina was propped up in the bed with pillows behind her. Her face glistened with sweat and her hair was a ragged mess. She looked up at Garrett and then down into her arms where a blanket was bundled.

Go on. Don't be afraid, Esther said. Go meet your son.

Son?

That's right. As if there weren't enough of you around here.

When he got to the bedside, he put an arm around Faina's shoulder and looked down into the blanket where a small, wrinkled, and red face looked up at him. The newborn slowly blinked his bleary eyes and scrunched up his brow. Garrett bent and put his lips to the baby's cheek, and the skin was so soft he could barely feel it. Then he turned to Faina and kissed her damp forehead.

54

The days became fragile and new to Mabel, as if she had only just recovered from a long illness and stumbled outside to discover summer had passed to winter while she slept. It was like the time she had followed Faina into the mountains, when the world seemed just cracked open and everything sparkled and shone with the inexplicable wonder of snow crystals and an eternity of births and deaths.

And all of this — the entire world — was held in the little clenched fists of the newborn baby. It was in his crying mouth and in Faina's milk-swollen breasts and in the words Mabel knew Garrett could not speak because he was too full of awe. But it was greater than all that. It was even in the way sunlight shattered against the February snow so Mabel had to squint at the brightness.

Each morning she walked the snowy path to Faina and Garrett's cabin. Garrett had suggested she stay at night, but she knew the three of them needed time alone. In a basket, she brought hard-boiled eggs, bread, or slices of bacon left over from her breakfast with Jack, along with a sack of diapers, washcloths, and clothes that she had washed at home and dried by the woodstove.

How are you today, child? she would ask Faina, and Faina would smile and look down at the baby in her arms.

I am well. And so is he. See how he looks at you when you speak. He knows you are here.

The infant did indeed seem to be thriving. The first few days of nursing had been a trial, but Esther had helped guide the baby's mouth to Faina's nipples and showed her how to stuff his mouth full of her breast. Don't give him a chance to chew on that nipple, or you'll be sorry, Esther had advised as the baby howled and turned his face this way and that. It's up to him, she said. He's got to figure it out.

And he had. Now, two weeks later, he slurped noisily as Faina covered herself with a blanket of muskrat furs she had sewed. She cooed to him as he ate, and closed her eyes contentedly while he dozed, and Mabel took out her drawing pad and pencils and made little sketches.

When he woke, Mabel changed the baby's diaper, his legs bending and straightening as he screamed a protest.

He doesn't get any more used to that, does he? Mabel said, as she pinned the clean diaper.

But Faina wasn't listening. She had gone to the window and was looking out over the bright snow.

You can go outdoors for a bit. I'll stay here with him.

Faina did not speak as she put on her blue wool coat and her knee-high moccasins, but when she opened the door, she glanced back at Mabel and her son. She did not smile, and

Mabel could not read her expression. Did she feel guilty for wanting some time without the baby? Was she frightened to leave him, even for a moment?

Whether because of the gust of cold air or the sudden absence of his mother, the baby fussed in Mabel's arms, so she stood and held him against her shoulder, bouncing slightly as she walked from one end of the cabin to the other. Garrett had gone to help Jack take care of the animals back at their barn and then he was going to haul some more firewood. It had been a cold winter, cold and calm and snowy, and the woodpiles were dwindling already.

Mabel went to the window, still patting the newborn and swaying from side to side. The baby quieted and stared wide-eyed over her shoulder. She turned her face into him, into his smell and warmth, and she was filled with the wonder she had seen all around her. She had just begun to hum into his small ear when out of the corner of her eye she saw the blue coat against the white snow.

Faina was walking across the meadow and toward the trees, but she struggled in the snow and stopped frequently to rest. It was some time before she reached the edge of the forest, and all the while Mabel watched and was troubled by what she saw. It was too soon. She shouldn't have let her go out. The labor and delivery had taken a terrible toll on her body, and she needed more rest. She considered going to the door and calling out for her to come back home, to come inside and lie down, but then Faina was no longer walking. She didn't sprint into the spruce trees like she had so many times before. She simply stood, a single, forlorn figure in the snow, the wilderness stretched out before her, her arms at her sides, her long blond hair shining in the winter sun. And then she turned back toward the cabin, toward her son and home, and followed her own deep trail back through the snow.

Have you named him yet?

Faina did not answer. She rocked the baby in a wooden cradle beside the woodstove.

Night was coming on, and Mabel knew she should begin the walk home soon.

You must give him a name, child. It can't be like with the dog. He can't just come to a birdsong. We all have to be able to call him something.

Still Faina did not answer, but only rocked the sleeping baby side to side.

It was dark when Mabel left. Garrett offered to walk with her, or to send her with a lantern, but she refused both. It was a moonless night and well below zero, but she would find her way. As the glow of the cabin windows turned to flickers through the trees and then to black, her eyes adjusted and the starlight alone on the pure white snow was enough to light her way. The cold scorched her cheeks and her lungs, but she was warm in her fox hat and wool. An owl swooped through the spruce boughs, a slow-flying shadow, but she was not frightened. She felt old and strong, like the mountains and the river. She would find her way home.

✻

Mabel woke with her pulse racing, sat bolt upright in bed, and waited to understand what had startled her.

'Mabel? Are you awake? It's me, Garrett.' A hoarse whisper from the bedroom door.

Mabel scrambled over Jack and pulled a sweater over her nightgown as she walked into the main room of the cabin. She would have been startled by anyone waking her from her bed in the middle of the night, but Garrett's presence was enough to make her trembling old heart sink into the pit of her stomach.

'I'm sorry to wake you . . . '

Mabel held up a hand to Garrett. She was weak and nauseous.

'Let me sit.'

Garrett pulled a chair out from the table and put a hand on her shoulder to steady her.

'There. Let me catch my breath.' She sat and did not speak, and she was tempted to go on like that for some time, keeping the truth at arm's length. But finally she inhaled deeply and said, 'Yes? Faina?'

'She's not well,' Garrett said, and just then Jack came from the bedroom.

'What is it? What's going on?'

'Shh. He's telling us. Go on, Garrett.'

'All day she was restless and not herself. She kept going outside, as cold as it is, and I tried to

439

stop her. But I couldn't. I should have . . . '

'And now?' Mabel asked, trying to help the young man focus.

'She got worse. She said she hurt and when I asked where she said all over, and her cheeks were red. She didn't want to get out of bed, and she wouldn't eat a thing. But she nursed the baby and they both went to sleep, so I thought I'd wait until morning and see how she was. But then, just now, I rolled over and my arm touched hers and she's burning up hot.'

'She should have had the baby at the hospital. We should have taken her to Anchorage,' Jack said.

'She didn't want to go,' Mabel reminded him. She went to the bedroom and got dressed by candlelight. When she returned, Garrett was sitting in a kitchen chair with his head in his hands. The clock said it was just after midnight.

'Where's the baby?'

'I left him at home, sleeping in his cradle. I didn't know what to do. It seemed too cold to bring him.'

'You did fine.'

'In the morning, we're taking her straight to Anchorage,' Jack said as he laced his boots.

'If the train's running. If the tracks are clear,' Mabel said, but then she saw Garrett's frightened face. 'We'll do everything we can. If we can't get her to Anchorage tomorrow, at least we can send a telegram to the hospital and get some advice from a doctor. It's going to be all right, Garrett. Now, let's go take care of her and that baby of yours.'

On the way, Mabel tried to prepare herself for what she would find, and the same kind of calm determination settled over her as when Jack had injured his back. When they arrived, the baby was still asleep in his cradle, and Faina was in bed. Garrett was right to be concerned. She was curled up on her side, arms wrapped around her middle as she moaned softly, and then she rolled over onto her back and Mabel could see her face. Droplets of perspiration ran down her temples and dampened her hair, and her skin was flushed and blotchy. Mabel went to her bedside and put a hand to her forehead. It was hot to the touch. She closed her eyes, her hand still on Faina's forehead, when she felt burning fingers around her wrist and heard a dry-throated whisper.

Mabel? You are here?

She opened her eyes and Faina was holding onto her. At first she thought rivulets of sweat were gliding down her cheeks, but then she saw that they were tears. Faina was crying.

What is happening to me?

Shhh. Don't be frightened, child. We will get you well again.

What sickness is this?

An infection in your blood. That is what causes the fever. But there is a medicine you can take that will make you better.

I won't go to the hospital. I won't leave my baby.

Mabel was relieved to see that defiant jut of

441

the chin, the flash in the blue eyes.

Let's not fret about that now. Here, I brought you water. You must drink it. It will cool you, and it will help you make milk for the baby.

Mabel held the glass to Faina's chapped lips and she drank and drank until it was empty. Then Mabel dabbed a washcloth at her forehead, wiping away the sweat. When Garrett came to the bedroom door, she asked for a basin of snow. She dipped the wet cloth into the cold snow and wrapped a clump inside it. When she pressed this to Faina's skin, the girl gasped and then sighed in relief. Again and again, until her cheeks began to cool and lose their ruddy coloring. With her bare hands, Mabel picked up a handful of snow and slid it across Faina's brow, then put another clump to her lips. Faina opened her mouth, and Mabel broke off a small piece for her to eat. It melted as it touched her tongue.

There. There. Is that better?

Faina nodded and took Mabel's cold, damp hand and held it to her cheek.

Thank you.

She closed her eyes and rested her head against Mabel's arm. Only after Mabel was certain she was asleep did she slide her hand out from under her cheek. She smoothed back Faina's hair, gently pulled it away from her sweat-dampened neck, and brought the bed sheet up over her shoulders.

It was three in the morning when she heard Jack putting more wood into the stove. The two men had alternated sleeping in chairs and busying themselves with contrived chores. The baby woke for his feeding then, and Mabel carried him in to Faina.

Your little one is hungry, dear.

Faina rolled to her side but never seemed completely awake, even as she slid her breast from her nightgown and held the baby against her. Once again her skin was hot and blotchy, and she brought her knees up in pain as the baby nursed.

Not until the baby was back in his cradle, fed and changed and fast asleep, did Faina awake and begin to plead with Mabel.

Please, she whispered. Take me outside.

No, child. You must stay in bed and rest.

Mabel spoke without conviction. Perhaps there was hope there, in the winter night. But what would Garrett and Jack say?

I am so hot, and I feel as if I can't catch my breath. Please?

'She wants to go outside.'

'What? Now? In the middle of the night?' Jack said.

'She's so warm, and it's so stuffy in here. I think she feels as if she's suffocating. She just wants to take in some of the cold night air.'

'We could prop the door open,' Garrett suggested.

'She wants to be outside, under the night sky,' Mabel said, and Garrett nodded, understanding.

'OK,' he said finally. 'We'll take her outside.'

'Are you two mad?' Jack said. 'It's twenty

below zero out there. She'll freeze to death.'

'No she won't,' Garrett said. Then he turned to Mabel. 'Will you help her dress?'

Mabel eased Faina into a sitting position on the edge of the bed. She laced the girl's moccasin boots and pulled her blue wool coat on over her nightgown. Then she took the red scarf and mittens Garrett had handed her, and as she wrapped the scarf around Faina's neck she recognized her sister's dewdrop-lace stitch.

I've always meant to ask you . . .

But she stopped herself and slipped the mittens over Faina's hands.

You must promise me, child, you won't go wandering off into the night. We'll bring a chair outside, and you can sit in it for a few minutes.

It hurts too much.

Sitting?

The girl nodded.

Mabel helped her lie back on the bed. When she explained to Garrett about the pain, he said he knew what to do. A short while later he returned to the bedside and he and Mabel helped Faina to her feet. Garrett put her marten hat on her head and tied the straps beneath her chin.

Come and see the bed I've made for you under the stars.

Faina smiled up at her husband as he helped her walk outside. Not far from the cabin, he had laid several logs side by side, and on top of these

444

he had piled caribou hides and beaver pelts until they formed a thick mattress.

The night was calm and cold, perhaps the coldest Mabel had ever known. The snow squeaked beneath her boots, and the air was sharp. It was the kind of deep freeze that penetrates the thickest wool and strangles the lungs, and Mabel hesitated. Perhaps this was a mistake. But then she heard Faina's long, easy breaths and imagined the cold air against her feverish brow. With each of them holding one of her arms, Mabel and Garrett led her the short way from the cabin to the makeshift bed, where Garrett helped her lie down. She let out a long sigh as he spread a beaver-pelt blanket over her. Mabel had brought the wedding quilt from their bed, and she laid this on top, too.

Look at the stars, Garrett whispered. Do you see them all?

Yes. They're beautiful.

He stayed with her, sitting in a kitchen chair at her side, while Mabel went in to the cabin. A short time later, when the baby awoke wanting to be held, Mabel asked Garrett if he would like to come indoors for a while. She could sit with Faina.

Do you want me to stay? he asked Faina. Maybe you should come in now, anyways?

No, she said gently. Go inside. Hold our son.

Mabel leaned over Faina and tucked the wedding quilt around her sides and pressed the fur flaps of her hat against her cheeks. Then she wrapped herself in a blanket she had brought from the cabin and sat in the chair.

445

Are you well, child?

Oh, yes. Out here, with the trees and the snow, I can breathe again.

It was like an extraordinary dream: Faina's quiet sighs and the occasional pop and crack of river ice and tree branches snapping in the cold; the stars everywhere in the broad, deep night, broken only by the jagged horizon of the mountain range. Illumination behind the peaks shot up into shards of light, blue-green like a dying fire, rippled and twisted, then spun circles into ribbons of purple that stretched up and over Mabel's head until she heard an electric crackle like the sparks from a wool blanket in a dry cabin at night. She looked directly up into the northern lights and she wondered if those cold-burning specters might not draw her breath, her very soul, out of her chest and into the stars.

'Jesus, Mabel, you're buried in snow. Where's Faina?'

She did not remember falling asleep. Who could doze in such cold? But she was warm in her cocoon of wool and blanket, her nose nuzzled down into her coat, and she did not wake until she heard the men's voices.

Faina. Aren't you here, at my side?

But she wasn't.

446

'She must be in the cabin, tending the baby.'

'No. She isn't there.'

Stiff and sore, Mabel stood and wondered at all the snow covering her blanket. The night had clouded over, the stars were gone, and it had snowed several inches. How much time had passed? She went after the men, could hear Garrett calling in the cabin.

'Faina? Faina?'

'Where is she, Mabel?' Jack turned to her, nearly accusing.

'She was just there, beside me. She must be near. Isn't she in the cabin?'

'No. I already said she's not there.' Jack called into the trees, 'Faina! Faina!'

Garrett came from the cabin with a lantern.

'Where is she?' There was no anger in his voice, only desperation, and he ran toward the river. 'Faina! Faina!'

Among the caribou hides, Mabel saw the wedding quilt buried in snow. How could she be so negligent? She picked it up to shake the snow off, and caught sight of blue wool.

'Jack?'

He came to her side, looked down where she pointed, then knelt and with his bare hands swept away the snow. Faina's blue coat, embroidered with snowflakes. Her scarf. Her mittens. Her moccasins. He picked them up one by one, shaking off the snow.

'Oh, Jack.' There, still buttoned inside the coat, was Faina's white nightgown. 'What does this mean?'

Silent, Jack draped the clothes over his arm

447

and carried them inside. Mabel followed with the snow-dampened quilt, and they set them all on the table.

'I'll go after Garrett. Care for the baby,' he said.

'But Jack . . . I don't understand.'

'Don't you?'

'She's gone?'

He nodded.

'But where?'

Without answering he left the cabin.

When the baby woke, crying for his mother's milk, Mabel was at a loss. She dipped the end of a clean cloth into warm, sweet tea and put it to his mouth. He sucked frantically, then turned his head and cried. She walked him back and forth in front of the window until he cried himself to sleep, and all this time she saw no lantern light, no sign of either Garrett or Jack. She sat in the chair and swayed side to side with the sleeping baby and prayed this night was not real, that indeed it was a nightmare. But then Jack came through the door and didn't speak. Behind him, winter dawn was breaking pale. She raised her eyebrows at him, and he shook his head.

'Nothing?' she asked.

'Not even a set of tracks.'

'Where's Garrett?'

'He won't come in. He says he'll find her. He's gone to saddle his horse.'

'Oh, God, Jack. What have we done?'

He didn't speak for some time, but sat to unlace his boots and pull the snow and ice from his beard. He stoked the woodstove and then reached to Mabel, to take the baby. Surprised, she stood and gently slid the bundle into his arms. Jack swaddled the blanket more firmly and ran a finger along the baby's cheek, his head bent so low to the newborn that at first Mabel could not see the tears streaming from his eyes.

'Jack?' Mabel reached up and held his face in her hands. 'Oh, Jack.' She took the baby from his arms and set him in the cradle, rocking it slowly until she was certain he was still asleep. When she stood, Jack was behind her. Mabel went to him and pressed her face into his chest, and they held each other like that for some time.

'She is gone, isn't she?'

Jack clenched his teeth and nodded as if his entire body pained him.

Grief swept over Mabel with such force that her sobs had no sound or words. It was a shuddering, quaking anguish, and she only knew that she would survive because she had once before. She wept until there was nothing left in her, and she wiped her face with the tips of her fingers and sat in the chair, expecting Jack to go out the door and leave her alone. But he knelt at her feet, put his head in her lap, and they held each other and shared the sorrow of an old man and an old woman who have lost their only child.

❄

449

Maybe it was only the wind, or her own terrible grief, but Mabel was certain she could hear Garrett's voice. Sometimes it was like a shout, down by the river. Other times it was a deep, mournful cry that seemed to come from the mountains themselves.

She and Jack stayed with the baby that night, waiting for Garrett to come home to his cabin. Mabel dozed beside the cradle, where the infant slept quietly, but again and again she was jolted awake.

'Did you hear that?' she asked.

Jack stood beside the woodstove, his face drawn.

'What was that?' she asked.

'Wolves, I think.'

But she knew differently. She knew it was Garrett, riding and searching and crying into the starless night sky. Faina. Faina. Faina.

Epilogue

'Hello. Anyone home?' Jack rapped on the cabin door, and then slowly opened it. 'Hello?' Using his cane, he stepped up into the cabin. He stood for a moment in the doorway and listened to the silence. He had come looking for Garrett this autumn day but instead stumbled on memories. There, on a shelf near the woodstove, was Faina's porcelain doll, its blond hair still in neat braids, its red and blue dress as bright as the day Jack had set it on a stump and called out, 'This is for you. I don't know if you're out there or if you can hear me, but we want you to have it.'

Jack did not leave the doorway, but his eyes wandered. Folded neatly on the arm of a chair was the wool blanket Mabel had sewed from Faina's childhood coat. When Jack saw a collection of photographs hanging on the far wall, he did not close the door behind himself or even notice he was crossing the threshold as he walked to them. Most were of Garrett with his brothers, and of Esther and George on their wedding day. But the one that caught his eye was of a woman holding a tiny infant swaddled in a blanket. The only other time he had seen that photograph was nearly fifteen years ago when he discovered it in a hut dug into the side of a mountain. It was Faina as a baby.

Somewhere in the cabin, perhaps folded in a trunk or hanging in a closet, were a feathered wedding dress and a blue wool coat embroidered with snowflakes. Garrett would have kept them, even as he kept these other tokens of her life. But how little there was. This struck Jack as he looked around the cabin. These were the few earthly belongings Faina had left behind.

It happened like this, the grief. Years wore away the cutting edges, but sometimes it still took him by surprise. Like the night just a few weeks ago, when he had spotted the blue leather-bound book on their shelf. It was always there, yet his eyes had passed over it daily without catching. He was fairly sure that for years it had gone unopened. All the books Mabel lent Garrett to read, but never that one. He was certain Garrett didn't know it existed, and neither Jack nor Mabel ever talked of it.

Mabel was in the bedroom brushing her hair when he pulled the book out from the others and, standing at the shelf, flipped through the pages. He touched the colored illustration of the fairy-tale girl, half snow and half child, with the old man and woman kneeling beside her. When pages cascaded to the floor he thought he had broken the binding. Glancing over his shoulder toward the bedroom, he quickly gathered them. They weren't pages from the book; they were Mabel's sketches, and he looked through each of them and marveled at the skill and detail.

Faina's delicate, childhood face, framed by her marten-fur hat. Faina at their kitchen table, chin resting in her hands. Then there were the drawings of Faina as a young woman, a newborn baby at her breast. They were studies, each from a different perspective, some closer and others farther away. Faina's hand on the sleeping infant. The baby's tiny fist. Closed eyes. Open eyes. Mother. Child.

In the soft pencil marks something was captured that he had sensed but never could have expressed. It was a fullness, a kind of warm, weighted life that had settled into Faina during her last days, and a generous tenderness that poured down upon her infant son like golden sunlight.

When Mabel called out to him, asking when he was coming to bed, he had carefully folded the drawings back among the pages of the book and returned it to the shelf, where it remained, unmentioned.

Jack became aware that he was standing, uninvited, in the middle of Garrett's cabin.

'Garrett?' he called out again, knowing there would be no answer. He left and closed the door.

He wasn't far down the trail, walking at his slow, awkward gait, leaning on his cane, when he heard the boy calling through the trees.

'Papa! Papa!'

Jay ran down the trail toward him and not far behind him lumbered the old dog. With no name to come to, Faina's husky roamed freely between the two cabins, but whenever her son was outdoors, the dog was at his side.

'Papa! Look what I caught.' The boy held up a willow branch with one small, dusty grayling hanging from it.

'You caught it?'

'Well, Maime helped. But I set the hook all by myself.'

'Well done. Well done.'

'And Maime said we could eat it for dinner.'

Jack took the stringer from the boy and inspected the fish.

'As I recall, Grandpa George and Grandma Esther are coming for dinner, too.'

'And Daddy?'

'And your father.'

'Did you find him?'

'No. He's still out riding. But he'll be home soon.'

'He likes the mountains, doesn't he? He goes riding there a lot. He says this year I can come on his long trapline, and maybe we'll catch a wolverine.'

'That would be fine, wouldn't it?'

But the boy was already dashing ahead.

'Jay?' Jack called to him. 'Do you think we might catch a few more fish, to make sure there's enough for everyone?'

'Sure, Papa. We can catch some more.'

The boy disappeared around the next bend in the trail, sprinting back toward Jack and Mabel's cabin.

'Just me and you, old man,' Jack said and patted the dog's graying muzzle. 'Think you'll find my pace suits you better.'

The autumn day was chilly, and the trail was

454

littered with yellow birch leaves. Along the mountains, clouds gathered.

'Smells like snow,' Jack said, and the dog held its nose to the air as if in agreement.

Jack made his way past their cabin, through the brush and down to the stream in time to see Mabel reel in a grayling as it splashed through the shallows. The boy pranced excitedly on a nearby boulder.

'Maime caught the biggest one ever! Look, Papa. Look.' The boy jumped to the shore, unhooked the fish from the line, and held it up.

Mabel smiled at Jack, the fishing rod still in her hand. Her hair had gone completely white now, and wrinkles folded softly around her eyes and mouth, but there was a youthfulness in her gaze.

She spent many an afternoon out of doors with the boy, teaching him to catch fish and listen for birds and watch for moose. How easily she talked with the boy. Some days she would tell Jay about his mother, how he had her blue eyes and how she had come from the mountains and snow and knew the animals and plants as well as she knew her own hands. And sometimes she would open the locket at her throat to show the boy the twist of blond hair and tell him about the lovely swan-feather wedding gown his mother wore that day.

'Little Jack could have had that big fish,' Mabel said and kissed the top of the child's head. 'He just let it get away.'

Little Jack. That's what she always called him. Garrett had asked permission, nearly a month after Faina was gone and the baby was still unnamed. Would it be all right if I named the boy after you? He's your grandson, after all.

'Jack? Did you hear me? I think you're losing your hearing in your old age,' Mabel teased as she handed him the stringer. 'Or were you just ignoring me because you don't want to clean the fish?'

'Doesn't seem right,' Jack said, and winked down at the boy. 'A man doesn't get to catch the fish, but he has to clean them.'

'Can I help, Papa? Please?'

Mabel left the two of them at the creek to go back to the cabin and stoke the fire. Jack leaned heavily on his cane as he shuffled to the water's edge. The boy lined up the fish in the yellowing grass. Jack took his fold-up knife from his pants pocket. With a hand on his cane, Jack was lowering himself to a crouch when he felt the boy's small hand on his arm.

'Here, Papa,' the boy said, and though he was too small to be of help, somehow the child's touch made the pain in Jack's old bones seem like not much at all.

The boy gave him a grayling, and Jack held it in the palm of his hand as he slid the knife blade beneath the silver skin and sliced open the belly. He showed the boy how to hook a finger in the lower jaw and pull free the glistening entrails. When they tossed them into the clear running water, young salmon darted and nibbled at the strings of intestines. Jack reached into the fish and slid his thumbnail along the spine to break free the line of kidney like a slender blood clot,

456

and he rinsed the blood into the creek water, until his hands ached in the cold.

The boy waited, crouched beside him.

'Last, the scales,' he told the boy, and he showed him how to run the knife blade against the grain. When Jack rinsed the fish in the creek, the small, iridescent scales shimmered and scattered in the water, drifted on the current, and washed up against the rocks like transparent sequins.

'They're kind of pretty, aren't they, Papa?' the boy said, a single scale pasted to his fingertip.

'I suppose they are,' Jack said.

George and Esther arrived before nightfall, and as always Esther was talking even as she came in the door and her arms were loaded with jars and towel-wrapped goodies. As they were flouring the grayling and frying them in a buttered cast-iron pan, Jay ran to the window.

'It's Daddy! Daddy's here!'

Jay was in his arms before Garrett could take off his coat and hat.

'What did you see, Daddy? What did you see?'

'Well, let me think. Oh, yes. I saw . . . a wolverine.'

'Don't tease the boy,' Esther admonished as she flipped the sizzling grayling.

'No teasing. I was way up high, above the tree line, in this little valley I once visited a long time ago. There used to be a wolverine there, but there hasn't been for years.'

'But you saw one?' the boy asked.

'I did. I'd tied the horse off to a tree and was hiking up over these rocks when, on this ridge, a wolverine was looking down at me. I thought it might jump on my head. He had claws this long.' Garrett held up his index finger and thumb to indicate several inches.

'Were you scared?'

'No. No. And he didn't jump on my head. He just looked at me with his yellow eyes. Then he turned, real slow, and sort of loped away and over the ridge.'

'What else did you see, Daddy? What else?'

'I guess a wolverine's not enough,' Esther said and chuckled.

'Well, not much else. Except for those clouds over the mountains. Looks like snow.'

The boy looked out the window, then back to his father with a disappointed expression. 'It's not snowing.'

'Don't worry. Bet you anything it'll come tonight,' Garrett said.

All through dinner, the boy could hardly stay in his seat, even as they commended him on the good-tasting fish he had helped catch.

'Settle down, Jay,' Esther said. 'You know a watched sky never snows. Go sit with Grandpa George. Maybe he'll share his piece of cake with you.'

George playfully scowled at the boy, then grabbed him in a bear hug and tickled him.

'Good God! Watch out for the dishes,' Esther said. 'You're going to knock the whole table over.'

After dessert, George and Esther began to gather

458

their belongings and talk of going home, and the boy looked crestfallen. He always protested when these gatherings ended, and he once said they should all live together in Jack and Mabel's cabin so that no one would ever have to leave.

Mabel helped Esther put on her coat, Jack shook hands with George, and Garrett said he and Jay would come out to get the horses and hitch the wagon.

'Put your hat on, Little Jack,' Mabel called after him, but the boy had already run out the door.

Jack was stacking dishes on the table when he heard the wagon begin to creak down the dirt road, and then he heard another sound — yips and laughter. Mabel was at the kitchen window.

Jack peered over her shoulder. At first he could see only their reflections in the windowpane, but then he began to see past their two old faces to make out the figures in the night.

Garrett stood near the barn with a lantern in his hand and nearby the boy was leaping and throwing his arms up to the sky. Even from inside the log cabin, Jack could hear the boy's whoops and cheers. The dog bowed playfully beside the boy, barked, then jumped and ran in circles, too.

As Jack's eyes grew accustomed to the darkness, he saw the ground covered in white and, in the light of Garrett's lantern, snowflakes spinning and falling.

He took hold of Mabel's hand, and when she turned to him, he saw in her eyes the joy and sorrow of a lifetime.

'It's snowing,' she said.

Acknowledgements

First and foremost, thank you to Sam, who always believed. To my daughter, Grace, whose incredible imagination fed my own. To my mother, Julie LeMay, a poet who taught me the magic of words and the power of empathy. To my father, John LeMay, who taught me to love wild places, wild creatures and, always, books. And to my baby brother, Forrest LeMay, who first taught me a child's love.

Immense gratitude to my editors, Mary-Anne Harrington, Claire Baldwin, Andrea Walker, and Reagan Arthur, and my agent, Jeff Kleinman of Folio Literary Management. Thank you to everyone at Headline Review, including Samantha Eades, Jemima Forrester, Vicky Cowell and Patrick Insole, and the team at *We Love This Book* magazine. And thank you to the publishers, booksellers, and readers around the world who have welcomed Faina.

To my first, kind readers — John Straley, Victoria Curey Naegele, Rindi White, and Melissa Behnke — your encouragement and advice were invaluable.

Several books influenced my writing — *The Snow Child* as retold by Freya Littledale and illustrated by Barbara Lavallee; *Russian Lacquer, Legends and Fairy Tales* by Lucy Maxym, in particular the story of 'Snegurochka'; and 'Little Daughter of the Snow' from Arthur Ransome's *Old Peter's Russian Tales*.

Many people throughout my life have taught, inspired, and supported me as a writer as I worked toward this first novel: James and Michele Hungiville, Jacqueline LeMay, Michael Hungiville, Kachemak Bay Writers' Conference, David Cheezem and my friends and customers at Fireside Books, 49 Writers, and the Baers. To the Betties — the first six out of the box are yours.

And the parting glass I raise in memory of our dear friend Laura Mitchell McDonald (Nov. 26, 1973 — Jan. 1, 2007).

'Little Daughter of the Snow'

From *Old Peter's Russian Tales*
by
Arthur Ransome

A Note from Eowyn Ivey

One night at the bookstore where I work, I discovered a simple children's picture book that lit up my curiosity and imagination — a retelling of Snegurochka, the snow maiden. It was the first step down a winding, delightful path that ultimately led me to Arthur Ransome's 'Little Daughter of the Snow'. Here, beside little Vanya and Maroosia, I watched Jack and Mabel build a child out of snow in the Alaska wilderness. Here, in the pages of a hundred-year-old fairy tale, a girl I would come to know as Faina began to live and breathe. 'Her eyes shone, and her hair flew round her, and she sang, while the old people watched and wondered, and thanked God.' And it was here that I caught my first glimpse of a fox, darting through a dark forest with Faina at its side.

Without Mr Ransome, I never would have created my own snow child.

The Little Daughter
of the Snow

Spring in the Forest

Warmer the sun shone, and warmer yet. The pines were green now. All the snow had melted off them, drip, drip, the falling drops of water making tiny wells in the snow under the trees. And the snow under the trees was melting too. Much had gone, and now there were only patches of snow in the forest — like scraps of a big white blanket, shrinking every day.

'Isn't it lucky our blankets don't shrink like that?' said Maroosia.

Old Peter laughed.

'What do you do when the warm weather comes?' he asked. 'Do you still wear sheepskin coats? Do you still roll up at night under the rugs?'

'No,' said Maroosia; 'I throw the rugs off, and put my fluffy coat away till next winter.'

'Well,' said old Peter, 'and God, the Father of us all, He does for the earth just what you do for yourself; but He does it better. For the blankets He gives the earth in winter get smaller and smaller as the warm weather comes, little by little, day by day.'

469

'And then a hard frost comes, grandfather,' said Ivan.

'God knows all about that, little one,' said old Peter, 'and it's for the best. It's good to have a nip or two in the spring, to make you feel alive. Perhaps it's His way of telling the earth to wake up. For the whole earth is only His little one after all.'

That night, when it was story-time, Ivan and Maroosia consulted together; and when old Peter asked what the story was to be, they were ready with an answer.

'The snow is all melting away,' said Ivan.

'The summer is coming,' said Maroosia.

'We'd like the tale of the little snow girl,' said Ivan.

'"The Little Daughter of the Snow,"' said Maroosia.

Old Peter shook out his pipe, and closed his eyes under his bushy eyebrows, thinking for a minute. Then he began.

There were once an old man, as old as I am, perhaps, and an old woman, his wife, and they lived together in a hut, in a village on the edge of the forest. There were many people in the village; quite a town it was — eight huts at least, thirty or forty souls, good company to be had for crossing the road. But the old man and the old woman were unhappy, in spite of living like that in the very middle of the world. And why do you think they were unhappy? They were unhappy because they had no little Vanya and no little Maroosia. Think of that. Some would say they were better off without them.

'Would you say that, grandfather?' asked Maroosia.

'You are a stupid little pigeon,' said old Peter, and he went on.

Well, these two were very unhappy. All the other huts had babies in them — yes, and little ones playing about in the road outside, and having to be shouted at when anyone came driving by. But there were no babies in their hut, and the old woman never had to go to the door to see where her little one had strayed to, because she had no little one.

And these two, the old man and the old woman, used to stand whole hours, just peeping through their window to watch the children playing outside. They had dogs and a cat, and cocks and hens, but none of these made up for having no children. These two would just stand and watch the children of the other huts. The dogs would bark, but they took no notice; and the cat would curl up against them, but they never felt her; and as for the cocks and hens, well, they were fed, but that was all. The old people did not care for them, and spent all their time in watching the Vanyas and Maroosias who belonged to the other huts.

In the winter the children in their little sheepskin coats . . .

'Like ours?' said Vanya and Maroosia together.

'Like yours,' said old Peter.

In their little sheepskin coats, he went on,

471

played in the crisp snow. They pelted each other with snowballs, and shouted and laughed, and then they rolled the snow together and made a snow woman — a regular snow Baba Yaga, a snow witch; such an old fright!

And the old man, watching from the window, saw this, and he says to the old woman, 'Wife, let us go into the yard behind and make a little snow girl; and perhaps she will come alive, and be a little daughter to us.'

'Husband,' says the old woman, 'there's no knowing what may be. Let us go into the yard and make a little snow girl.'

So the two old people put on their big coats and their fur hats, and went out into the yard, where nobody could see them.

And they rolled up the snow, and began to make a little snow girl. Very, very tenderly they rolled up the snow to make her little arms and legs. The good God helped the old people, and their little snow girl was more beautiful than ever you could imagine. She was lovelier than a birch tree in spring.

Well, towards evening she was finished — a little girl, all snow, with blind white eyes, and a little mouth, with snow lips tightly closed.

'Oh, speak to us,' says the old man.

'Won't you run about like the others, little white pigeon?' says the old woman.

And she did, you know, she really did.

Suddenly, in the twilight, they saw her eyes shining blue like the sky on a clear day. And her lips flushed and opened, and she smiled. And there were her little white teeth. And look, she

472

had black hair, and it stirred in the wind.

She began dancing in the snow, like a little white spirit, tossing her long hair, and laughing softly to herself.

Wildly she danced, like snowflakes whirled in the wind. Her eyes shone, and her hair flew round her, and she sang, while the old people watched and wondered, and thanked God.

This is what she sang:

'No warm blood in me doth glow,
Water in my veins doth flow;
Yet I'll laugh and sing and play
By frosty night and frosty day —
Little daughter of the Snow.

'But whenever I do know
That you love me little, then
I shall melt away again.
Back into the sky I'll go —
Little daughter of the Snow.'

'God of mine, isn't she beautiful!' said the old man. 'Run, wife, and fetch a blanket to wrap her in while you make clothes for her.'

The old woman fetched a blanket, and put it round the shoulders of the little snow girl. And the old man picked her up, and she put her little cold arms round his neck.

'You must not keep me too warm,' she said.

Well, they took her into the hut, and she lay on a bench in the corner farthest from the stove, while the old woman made her a little coat.

The old man went out to buy a fur hat and

boots from a neighbour for the little girl. The neighbour laughed at the old man; but a rouble is a rouble everywhere, and no one turns it from the door, and so he sold the old man a little fur hat, and a pair of little red boots with fur round the tops.

Then they dressed the little snow girl.

'Too hot, too hot,' said the little snow girl. 'I must go out into the cool night.'

'But you must go to sleep now,' said the old woman.

'By frosty night and frosty day,' sang the little girl. 'No; I will play by myself in the yard all night, and in the morning I'll play in the road with the children.'

Nothing the old people said could change her mind.

'I am the little daughter of the Snow,' she replied to everything, and she ran out into the yard into the snow.

How she danced and ran about in the moonlight on the white frozen snow!

The old people watched her and watched her. At last they went to bed; but more than once the old man got up in the night to make sure she was still there. And there she was, running about in the yard, chasing her shadow in the moonlight and throwing snowballs at the stars.

In the morning she came in, laughing, to have breakfast with the old people. She showed them how to make porridge for her, and that was very simple. They had only to take a piece of ice and crush it up in a little wooden bowl.

Then after breakfast she ran out in the road,

to join the other children. And the old people watched her. Oh, proud they were, I can tell you, to see a little girl of their own out there playing in the road! They fairly longed for a sledge to come driving by, so that they could run out into the road and call to the little snow girl to be careful.

And the little snow girl played in the snow with the other children. How she played! She could run faster than any of them. Her little red boots flashed as she ran about. Not one of the other children was a match for her at snowballing. And when the children began making a snow woman, a Baba Yaga, you would have thought the little daughter of the Snow would have died of laughing. She laughed and laughed, like ringing peals on little glass bells. But she helped in the making of the snow woman, only laughing all the time.

When it was done, all the children threw snowballs at it, till it fell to pieces. And the little snow girl laughed and laughed, and was so quick she threw more snowballs than any of them.

The old man and the old woman watched her, and were very proud.

'She is all our own,' said the old woman.

'Our little white pigeon,' said the old man.

In the evening she had another bowl of ice-porridge, and then she went off again to play by herself in the yard.

'You'll be tired, my dear,' says the old man.

'You'll sleep in the hut tonight, won't you, my love,' says the old woman, 'after running about all day long?'

But the little daughter of the Snow only laughed. 'By frosty night and frosty day,' she sang, and ran out of the door, laughing back at them with shining eyes.

And so it went on all through the winter. The little daughter of the Snow was singing and laughing and dancing all the time. She always ran out into the night and played by herself till dawn. Then she'd come in and have her ice-porridge. Then she'd play with the children. Then she'd have ice-porridge again, and off she would go, out into the night.

She was very good. She did everything the old woman told her. Only she would never sleep indoors. All the children of the village loved her. They did not know how they had ever played without her.

It went on so till just about this time of year. Perhaps it was a little earlier. Anyhow the snow was melting, and you could get about the paths. Often the children went together a little way into the forest in the sunny part of the day. The little snow girl went with them. It would have been no fun without her.

And then one day they went too far into the wood, and when they said they were going to turn back, little snow girl tossed her head under her little fur hat, and ran on laughing among the trees. The other children were afraid to follow her. It was getting dark. They waited as long as they dared, and then they ran home, holding each other's hands.

And there was the little daughter of the Snow out in the forest alone.

She looked back for the others, and could not see them. She climbed up into a tree; but the other trees were thick round her, and she could not see farther than when she was on the ground.

She called out from the tree, 'Ai, ai, little friends, have pity on the little snow girl.'

An old brown bear heard her, and came shambling up on his heavy paws.

'What are you crying about, little daughter of the Snow?'

'O big bear,' says the little snow girl, 'how can I help crying? I have lost my way, and dusk is falling, and all my little friends are gone.'

'I will take you home,' says the old brown bear.

'O big bear,' says the little snow girl, 'I am afraid of you. I think you would eat me. I would rather go home with some one else.'

So the bear shambled away and left her.

An old gray wolf heard her, and came galloping up on his swift feet. He stood under the tree and asked, 'What are you crying about, little daughter of the Snow?'

'O gray wolf,' says the little snow girl, 'how can I help crying? I have lost my way, and it is getting dark, and all my little friends are gone.'

'I will take you home,' says the old gray wolf.

'O gray wolf,' says the little snow girl, 'I am afraid of you. I think you would eat me. I would rather go home with someone else.'

So the wolf galloped away and left her.

An old red fox heard her, and came running up to the tree on his little pads. He called out cheerfully, 'What are you crying about, little daughter of the Snow?'

'O red fox,' says the little snow girl, 'how can I help crying? I have lost my way, and it is quite dark, and all my little friends are gone.'

'I will take you home,' says the old red fox.

'O red fox,' says the little snow girl, 'I am not afraid of you. I do not think you will eat me. I will go home with you, if you will take me.'

So she scrambled down from the tree, and she held the fox by the hair of his back, and they ran together through the dark forest. Presently they saw the lights in the windows of the huts, and in a few minutes they were at the door of the hut that belonged to the old man and the old woman.

And there were the old man and the old woman, crying and lamenting.

'Oh, what has become of our little snow girl?'

'Oh, where is our little white pigeon?'

'Here I am,' says the little snow girl. 'The kind red fox has brought me home. You must shut up the dogs.'

The old man shut up the dogs.

'We are very grateful to you,' says he to the fox.

'Are you really?' says the old red fox; 'for I am very hungry.'

'Here is a nice crust for you,' says the old woman.

'Oh,' says the fox, 'but what I would like would be a nice plump hen. After all, your little snow girl is worth a nice plump hen.'

'Very well,' says the old woman, but she

478

grumbles to her husband.

'Husband,' says she, 'we have our little girl again.'

'We have,' says he; 'thanks be for that.'

'It seems a waste to give away a good plump hen.'

'It does,' says he.

'Well, I was thinking,' says the old woman, and then she tells him what she meant to do. And he went off and got two sacks.

In one sack they put a fine plump hen, and in the other they put the fiercest of the dogs. They took the bags outside and called to the fox. The old red fox came up to them, licking his lips, because he was so hungry.

They opened one sack, and out the hen fluttered. The old red fox was just going to seize her, when they opened the other sack, and out jumped the fierce dog. The poor fox saw his eyes flashing in the dark, and was so frightened that he ran all the way back into the deep forest, and never had the hen at all.

'That was well done,' said the old man and the old woman. 'We have got our little snow girl, and not had to give away our plump hen.'

Then they heard the little snow girl singing in the hut. This is what she sang:

'Old ones, old ones, now I know
Less you love me than a hen,
I shall go away again.
Good-bye, ancient ones, good-bye,
Back I go across the sky;
To my motherkin I go —
Little daughter of the Snow.'

They ran into the house. There was a little pool of water in front of the stove, and a fur hat, a little coat, and little red boots were lying in it. And yet it seemed to the old man and the old woman that they saw the little snow girl, with her bright eyes and her long hair, dancing in the room.

'Do not go! do not go!' they begged, and already they could hardly see the little dancing girl.

But they heard her laughing, and they heard her song:

'Old ones, old ones, now I know
Less you love me than a hen,
I shall melt away again.
To my motherkin I go —
Little daughter of the Snow.'

And just then the door blew open from the yard, and a cold wind filled the room, and the little daughter of the Snow was gone.

'You always used to say something else, grandfather,' said Maroosia.

Old Peter patted her head, and went on.

'I haven't forgotten. The little snow girl leapt into the arms of Frost her father and Snow her mother, and they carried her away over the stars to the far north, and there she plays all through the summer on the frozen seas. In winter she comes back to Russia, and some day, you know, when you are making a snow woman, you may find the little daughter of the Snow standing there instead.'

'Wouldn't that be lovely!' said Maroosia.

Vanya thought for a minute, and then he said, 'I'd love her much more than a hen.'

Other titles published by
The House of Ulverscroft:

THE UNCOUPLING

Meg Wolitzer

A strange, formidable wind blows into Stellar Plains, New Jersey, where Dory and Robby Lang teach at Eleanor Roosevelt High School. Dory is suddenly and inexplicably repelled by her husband's touch, whilst back at school, life imitates art. The new drama teacher's end-of-term play is Arisotophanes', *Lysistrata*, in which women withhold sexual privileges from their menfolk in order to end the Peloponnesian War. And all across town, there's a quiet battle between the sexes: relationships end abruptly and marital issues erupt. Women continue to be claimed by the spell — from Bev Cutler, the overweight guidance counsellor to Leanne Bannerjee, the sexy school psychologist — even the Langs' teenage daughter, Willa, is affected — until everything comes to a climax on the first night of *Lysistrata* . . .

THE MIDWIFE OF VENICE

Roberta Rich

Hannah Levi is famed throughout Venice for her skills as a midwife, but as a Jew, the law forbids her from attending a Christian woman. However, when the Conte di Padovani appears at her door in the dead of night to demand her services, Hannah's compassion is sorely tested. And with a handsome reward for her services, she could ransom back her imprisoned husband. But if she fails in her endeavours to save mother and child, will she be able to save herself, let alone her husband?

HEART OF THE MATTER

Emily Giffin

Tessa seems to have the perfect life. Married to a world-renowned pediatric surgeon, she has chosen stay-at-home motherhood over her career. But Tessa is beginning to question her decision, concerned that it is affecting her marriage . . . Valerie, a single mother and attorney, has given up on romance. Things never turn out the way she plans, so she believes it is best not to risk more disappointment. Although both women live in the same Boston suburb, the two have relatively little in common aside from a fierce love for their children. But one night, a tragic accident causes their lives to converge in ways no one could have imagined . . .

THE STORY SISTERS

Alice Hoffman

The three Story sisters — Elv, Meg and Claire — live with their mother on Long Island. Beautiful and mysterious, they are the object of envy and intrigue. But their happy existence is brought abruptly to an end when Elv and Claire share an encounter with a man that will change them forever. As the girls grow into young women, their secret begins to destroy their close bond. And as their choices haunt and change them, each realises that they have a fate that they must meet alone . . .

WORTH

Jon Canter

In London, Richard and Sarah meet, fall in love, and marry. When they decide to escape the rat race and buy a cottage in the Suffolk village of Worth, they're hard-pressed to find friends. But a friendship develops between them and their new neighbour. Catherine, a single woman, admires their love for each other, whilst they admire her uncompromising nature. And on sleepy weekday nights, the trio's pastime IS each other. A delightful friendship ensues — yet Catherine's evasive manner begins to make them feel uneasy. The rural idyll fades, Richard struggles to find work, and when Sarah takes a job with a woman she meets at a conference, the couple are drawn deeper into the life of their neighbour — deeper than they could ever imagine.